RAGABONES

Kay!
J hope you enjoy
a lifetime of adventures

RAGABONES

DANIEL TWEDDELL

Books & Buildings

Book Cover by Hannah Linder

Map by Cass Merry

Chapter Artwork by TheImageNerd

Illustrations by Paulotarmac (Mantor, Inquisitor), Karin Wittig (god of the dead), Catarina Gonçalves (Holy Fire), Hephaestus (Beach Fight), Phuong Bui (Ice)

First Edition June 2023

Identifiers: 978-1-961379-00-8 (paperback) | 978-1-961379-01-5 (ebook)

To Sheree,
my angel looking down from heaven. You once joked that if you died before me, you'd chase somebody wonderful my way.

To Megan,
my "somebody wonderful;" my friend, lover, and literary genius; my angel that brings heaven down here.

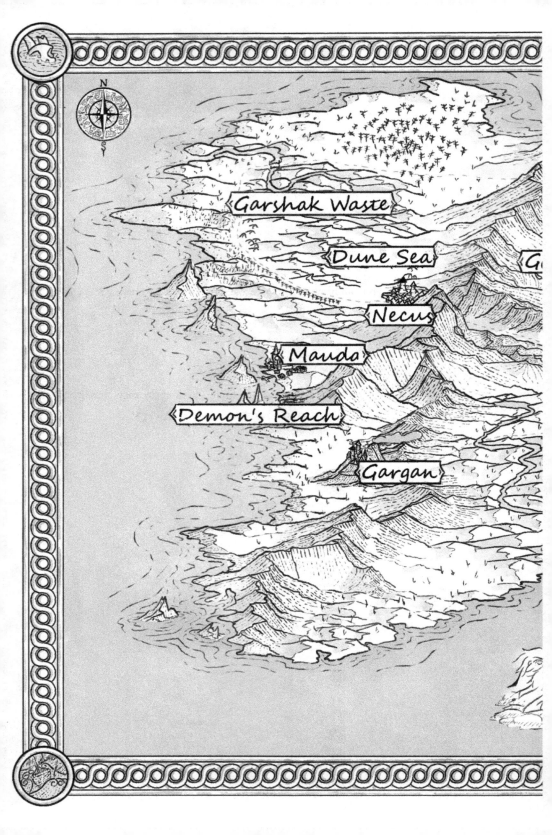

TABLE OF CONTENTS

CHAPTER ONE

SMOKE AND ROT

T he weathered gargoyle clock thunked 3:00 AM, sending goosebumps skittering down Josh's arms. Moonlight sifted through dark curtains and played across an ancient oval desk. Mom had never let Josh or his older brother, Pete, in her office before. They weren't even allowed to look inside. But that was before Josh started to remember.

Papers and picture frames littered the dusty desktop. Josh picked up a small tintype photograph of Mom and Dad. Dad! Josh swallowed a couple times, but the knot wouldn't go down.

The roar of a truck past the window made Josh jump. He opened the curtain a crack. Just across the street, Mrs. Holcombe swayed in her porch swing, cradling a book and coffee mug. A TV flickered blue and white through the window behind her. Did she ever sleep? Cozy suburbia out there felt like another planet. Here, dark walnut bookcases stretched from floor to ceiling on every wall. Leather-bound tomes crowded exotic objects: a fanged human skull, antique pistols, pitted cannonballs.

Josh's eyes went back to the picture of Dad. He memorized every angle and shadow of that face, then closed his eyes. Dad's face disappeared. Sagging, Josh set the picture down. Couldn't he hold on to it for even a second? Then how did he know Dad's voice or remember things he'd said? How did he even know who Dad was?

Josh looked around Mom's office. This place could have been a wizard's lair from Dungeons and Dragons. All it needed was a suit of armor and a couple of swords, maybe a fireplace. He shook his head. Did he even know who Mom was either?

Josh pulled out his phone. Before he could touch the screen, his fingers involuntarily clenched. Pins and needles spilled over his head, washing down his arms and legs. He gasped, his heart instantly racing. Panic rose in his throat. That firefly thing was happening again. Tiny specks of light glimmered on his wrists. They raced in flickering, swirling patterns up his arms. Other glowing pinpoints joined the race in bright reds, golds, and greens.

Images flooded Josh's mind. He and Pete were being carried away, bound and gasping for air. Iron hands clutched and pinched. Josh struggled to make out their captors' faces in the dark. Moonlight glinted on pointed teeth as the creatures barked to each other in manic chatter.

It's not real! Josh fought to bring Mom's office back into focus, but the reek of the creatures' bodies and musty dampness of the midnight forest were more vivid than the present. He gagged on grit and sweat from the cloth stuffed in his mouth.

Staggering, Josh gripped the desk and gritted his teeth until the images and swirling lights on his arms faded. He wiped the sweat from his forehead and picked up his phone. Swiping through his apps, he stopped on the one that put military encryption on his video chat. There was only one contact, a haunting woman with alabaster skin and dark red lips. He shook his head. Why did she like that old picture so much? It didn't even look like her. He tapped it and held the phone in front of his face.

"Hi Mom," his voice was tight.

"Hi Honey. How are you feeling? Are you still seeing the lights?" Worry tightened Mom's smile.

Sunlight shone through an airplane window, illuminating Mom's hair. Dad had called it ember red — black at first glance but fire in the sunlight. They had been a family then. And they'd been happy. But that was two years ago before Dad disappeared, and before Josh's memory got fuzzy.

Josh opened and closed his hand. "It's getting worse."

Mom's eyebrows scrunched. "I'm so sorry. It's what — 3 AM there?" She checked her watch. "I'll be home by dinner. Hold on until then and we'll ..."

"What's happening to me?" Josh blurted. The phone shook in his hands. "I'm seeing monsters. They're so real I can smell them. Am I going insane?"

"Oh honey. No! You're not insane. They're just your memories trying to resurface. Very soon this will all ..."

"What about the lights?" Josh pleaded. "Jordan said I'm having visual migraines. Her mom's a nurse."

"Those?" Mom searched for words. "Those are because you're ... you're ..."

"'Special'? I wish you'd stop saying that." Josh couldn't keep the bitterness out of his voice. "Unless you mean I get my own special hell. Everyone else knows who they are. I don't even know if I like the jokes I laugh at. I don't even know my own body, like how I got this scar." Josh pointed to the jagged white marks on his neck; tooth marks, like some giant beast had tried to rip his throat out.

Mom bit her lip. "I'm so sorry."

Josh deflated. "It isn't your fault."

"Well ..." Mom stammered and looked at the floor, talking half to herself. "I knew this would happen. I should have been home for you."

With nervous fingers, she shifted her dark red hair over the black tattoo on the side of her neck. Barbed characters began under her blouse and twisted their way up to her chin. The glistening ink looked as if it had dripped before burning into her skin.

She sighed again and looked up. "When I get back, I'll explain everything. And I'll help you remember everything."

"Everything?" Josh brightened. Remembering their life before they moved here was like trying to remember social studies homework.

Fear flitted across Mom's face. "I give you my word. For now, just promise me you won't try to remember. It's very important. You mustn't break the blinder before I get there."

"The what?" Josh's throat was suddenly tight.

Mom glanced out the tiny window. "Never mind. And when I get home, we're cutting your hair."

"No, tell me what you said." Josh brushed his bangs out of his eyes.

She gnawed her lip. "Please honey, don't ask me anymore. She took a deep breath. "Before I tell you anything, you need to prepare. There's a very important book you need to read: The History of the Ersha."

"A history book?" Josh's heart sank. "Can't I just watch the video?"

"Video?" Mom grinned, eyes suddenly alight. "You've never seen a book like *this*." She leaned in, her voice low and mysterious. "Before the vast deserts of the Sahara were sand. Before Gytria and Shyntu, Stonehenge and the great pyramid of Egypt, were built. Before civilization even began to write, the two great houses of Alaetia were at war. Necrus and Ersha. Your father's family and mine."

Tiny dust devils swirled in Josh's stomach. Somewhere just out of reach, his mind knew those names. He gripped the desk with shaking fingers and forced his breath into a measured rhythm. His mind churned with questions, but one overshadowed them all; the one that punched the air from his gut. "Dad? Dad's in the book?"

Mom nodded.

Josh's dust devils erupted into tornadoes.

Mom's demeanor hardened, but her voice was tense and breathless. "There's one more thing. Don't touch ANYTHING but the book."

Josh glanced around the room. So many books. A giant one with a wooden cover lay on the floor by the chair. The pages were thick with green edges, as if made of leaves. Maybe it was *that* one.

"Josh!" Mom's tone snapped his attention back to her. "Listen to me. This is very important. You're awakening, which means some very dangerous things will be looking for you. The room is a shield, so stay home from school. Stay in the room. Read the book."

Josh's stomach lurched. "Dangerous?" He touched the scars on his throat.

"It's giving me a heart attack just thinking about you being in there. I'll call Pete when we're done. He can join you."

Josh forced a grin. The last thing he needed was his brother in here ordering him around. "I'm fine. Let him sleep."

"Promise me you won't touch anything. I want to hear you say it."

Don't touch anything? Josh's gaze flicked around the shelves. Smoke-filled flasks, daggers, helmets, and half-melted candles beckoned. There was even a worn bullwhip hanging by the window. Where did she get all this stuff? He sighed. "OK, Indiana Joan."

"Very funny." Mom gave him a flat look. "Now, turn the phone toward the shelves so I can see them."

Josh switched the camera, slowly sweeping the shelves.

"There!" Mom's voice rose a notch.

Josh froze. Gleaming in the phone's light, beside a stack of moldering leather volumes, a pewter globe perched on a stand. Contoured seas and continents were dotted by a dozen tiny gems.

"The globe? I thought we were looking for a book."

Mom swallowed. "Turn the globe until you see a continent that looks sort of like Africa. It's split by a huge mountain range."

Josh slowly rotated the globe, studying the continents and islands. Everything was shaped wrong and in the wrong place. What planet was this, Mars?

"I found it." Josh stopped over a triangular continent with a giant mountain range cutting across the center.

"Each gem is a city. Press the orange one on the peaks. It's Gargan, of the giants."

Josh swallowed. Giants? "This is the world from that book you wrote."

For a moment, Mom's image dissolved into rainbow colors then reformed. She glanced at the window behind her. Thick clouds enveloped the plane. Lightning flashed by the wingtip.

"We're flying into a storm. Quickly, Josh, before I lose you." Her voice crackled. "Find a group of islands in the northern hemisphere that look like broken glass. Press the purple gem. It's Urak, home of the mists."

He barely found it before she was off to the next: Shemek, Reykjavo, and Mustrel. Josh spun the globe, pressing city after city.

Mom's image splintered. Her mouth moved in fits and starts. "The Dune Sea ... Slavering Mountains ... cliffs above a great desert ... black gem is Necrus City."

The hair on the back of Josh's neck stood. Images of stone towers and golden minarets clawed at the edge of his consciousness.

"Necrus City?" he whispered.

"Press it." Mom's voice chattered with digital static.

Josh reached for the button and pushed.

With a soft click, a large section of the bookcase swung open.

Josh sucked in a sharp breath. "Oh, wow."

Before him was a round, windowless room. Light from a bronze chandelier sprinkled gold on walls of obsidian block. A bear skin the size of an elephant covered most of the floor. In the far wall gaped a gilded fireplace.

Josh stepped into the entry. Medieval weapons hung on iron hooks. Stacks of ancient books and a few pieces of jewelry lay on wrought silver shelves.

"What the ..." He couldn't get his mouth to close. Mom wrote fantasy books. She worked for a museum. A locked office with a secret room filled with pirate treasure made sense, right? He stepped toward an ornate sword encrusted with gems.

"DON'T" — a pixelated Mom looked as if she'd climb through the phone — "touch anything but the book."

Josh grinned and looked around the space. "Where is it?"

Mom's lips were tight, her face a swirling snowstorm of colors. She talked fast. "See ... like I taught you ... to see." And with a bleep, she was gone.

"Mom?" Josh tapped the screen. "Mom?" He sighed and set the phone on the desk beside the black-and-white of Mom and Dad. Pete looked more like Dad every day with his square jaw and dark, wavy hair. Josh was skinny and didn't look like anyone, except that messy reddish mop that Mom always wanted to cut.

On a shelf just inside the secret door leaned a set of volumes. Each book was made of a different metal. Rust flaked from the iron book. A green and white patina covered the copper one. See like I taught you to see? What was that supposed to mean? Why couldn't Mom have just said, "Read the silver one."?

Beside the fireplace, Josh spotted a small reading table. A lamp with a gaudy stained-glass shade flickered to life. On the edge of the reading table rested one of the books Mom had written, a leather-bound collector's edition with the title etched in gold foil: Trumpet's Call.

Josh rolled his eyes. Of course! Mom had made him read it so many times. "See like I taught you to see." That was a line from the book — but it was about magic. And magic wasn't real. Feeling silly, Josh half closed his eyes and unfocused on the empty spaces of the shelves. It was like looking at those 3D pictures; they look like nonsense until a shape pops out of the patterns.

He un-stared until his eyes ached. Nothing happened. Why would it? He was an idiot for even trying. Josh was just about to give up when, one by one, books, jewelry, and other strange items filled the empty places.

Magic! Josh yelped. He tripped on the rug and sat with a thump.

It took a minute to catch his breath. It wasn't magic. Parabolic mirrors along with appropriately placed lights could easily create that effect.

Nice prank, Mom. Josh stood and looked around the room. None of the books stood out.

"This is lame," he grumbled under his breath. How soon would Mom be out of the storm so they could talk?

He gave the room one last sweep. When his gaze reached the reading desk, his heart nearly stopped. A book lay open in the center, shimmering gold and gray, the way heat rises from a desert road. Thick pages of aged parchment with torn edges and bent corners heaped on either side of the tome's granite hinge.

Josh took two steps forward and froze. The wall next to the fireplace wasn't empty either. A gray-skinned warrior woman in gleaming medieval armor towered over the desk. She was at least seven feet tall. One giant gauntleted hand rested on a sword pummel. The other was closed in a fist at her waist. She stared down at Josh, gray eyes boring into his.

Josh caught his breath — and then let it out. The grim face under the helm wasn't skin, it was stone. It was just a statue with armor on it.

Josh clenched his teeth and strode across the room. He wiped a finger across the gleaming armor. Dust. "I knew it."

He glanced up at her face. "The stories you could tell. Why don't you show me what's in that fist?" He gestured toward her hand and froze. It was open. Josh's lungs suddenly didn't work. That hand had been closed ... right? Josh gaped up at the stone face. Cold eyes glowered down at him, still as death.

Josh couldn't tear his eyes away. His heartbeat thundered in his ears. Seconds clinked from the gargoyle clock in the office. Minutes. The statue didn't move. He forced his eyes closed and reopened them. Still nothing.

He shook his head. Of course nothing moved, it's a statue. The hand had only seemed closed from back there. The eyes were carved to look as if they followed him. All the great sculptors did that.

Magic, Josh reminded himself, is just science unexplained. Look closely enough and you'll see the truth. When Mom got home, he'd ask her if he could put the statue in his bedroom.

He leaned toward the warrior. Nestled in her palm was a tiny obsidian box, a rounded coffin the size of a glasses case. Strange blocky letters covered the outside. Each rune was inlaid with something yellow — the same yellow as the bony claws in the office. Josh shuddered.

He looked around the room. The same letters were carved into the walls.

Mom's voice rang in his ears, "DON'T touch anything but the book." But there was something about the box that dragged at his fingertips and sent butterflies all through his stomach.

Josh glanced over his shoulder at his phone and picked up the box. He gasped, fumbling and almost dropping it. It was like ice. Turning it over in his hands, he traced the engravings, pausing now and then to rub chilly fingers on his jeans.

There were no seams or hinges. How do you open this thing? "Open," he thought.

And with a sigh, it did.

A red glow filled the room. Josh sucked in a sharp breath. Nestled inside the polished black obsidian was a glowing, finger-length shard of crystal. The gem moved like liquid within a cobweb of gold wire.

"Woah." Josh reached for the gem and paused. Rainbow lights danced across his hands and arms. He clenched his jaws, waiting for the memories. None came. Weird. Mom did say the room was a shield. He glanced up at the statue. For expressionless stone, those gray eyes were sure full of disapproval.

"Whatever," Josh snorted and picked up the gem.

——————◄◊►——————

Thunder shook the room. The shelves and fireplace disappeared in an explosion of dust and rock. Walls collapsed inward, driving Josh to his knees. Boulders pinned him to the floor, crushing the air from his lungs. He tried to scream, but he couldn't even breathe.

Help! Bile rose in Josh's throat. His heartbeat thundered in his ears. He couldn't feel his legs. How long until he ran out of air?

STOP IT! Josh forced his mind to still. What did Mom always say? "Fear is a fairytale. Focus on what's real." I CAN'T BREATHE, that's what's real.

Josh squeezed his eyes closed. Kaleidoscope colors swam across his vision. He counted his heartbeats, 1-2; 1-2. You're still alive, that's real. He strained for the sounds of firemen lifting away the rubble.

Behind him, something that sounded like claws scraped on the stone.

Josh's eyes snapped open. He struggled to turn and see, but not even a finger moved. That was when he noticed the room. Trembling started in his hands, racing up his arms and down his torso until his whole body shook.

Mom's office was gone.

He knelt in a large cave. The rough stone floor dug into his knees. He could feel the weight of the boulders and rubble against his back and shoulders, but when he looked, nothing was there.

"A boy." A voice rasped like bone on bone. Its echoes filled the cavern with whispers.

Sweat trickled down Josh's back.

A cloaked figure shuffled in front of Josh, face hidden in the shadows. Its glowing eyes looked him over, pausing for a moment on Josh's neck. The eyes narrowed.

The figure leaned down, its gaze dropping to the gem in Josh's hands. From the under the robe, a gnarled claw slowly reached out. The skin was mottled and lifeless gray, stretched taut over bone. "Give it to me."

Vapor drooled through Josh's fingers, pooling around his feet in a faint dusky red. Hammers battered the inside of his head. This can't be real. It's a memory. It's a memory.

"Now." Bulbous jaws and long yellow fangs gnashed in Josh's face.

Josh gaged on the stench of smoke and rot. He tried to drop the gem, but he couldn't move.

Mom had said dangerous things would be looking for him. Why didn't he listen? Why did he open the box? Why couldn't he just dump the gem and run?

"No?" The creature's claws closed into fists.

Josh felt its rage billow toward him. Terror washed over him in icy waves. "Let go, let go!" his mind screamed at his hands.

The beast lunged, snatching at the crystal shard, but its claw swept through as if Josh wasn't there. "What!?" The beast's voice rose to a howl. It leapt on Josh, tearing and clawing.

Josh's body rippled like smoke. He screamed and tried to turn his face from the talons, but he couldn't move or make a sound.

The cave lurched, knocking Josh backward. Light blazed around him, and the walls rang with the sound of breaking glass. The crushing weight was gone, and he sprawled on the floor, blinking in the glare.

Josh lay on the bearskin rug in Mom's secret room. Books and medieval items still cluttered the shelves. The statue still glowered at him from the corner. His older brother

Pete stood over him, jewel in one hand, obsidian box in the other. Pete held the gem as if diseased. Vapor drifted through his fingers. "What *is* this?"

Sweat soaked Josh's t-shirt. He groped across his chest with shaking hands, but there were no gashes or blood, not even a mark.

Pete shook his head, face hard. "You don't have the slightest idea what this is, do you? Mom told you not to touch anything." He dropped the gem in its box and snapped the lid shut.

Josh couldn't get enough air. All the artifacts that were so exciting before, now seemed like doorways to hell. The walls closed in. Gasping, he wobbled to his feet and pushed past Pete through the doorway.

Stepping in his way, Pete spun Josh around and shoved him back into the room. Pete was almost three years older and a foot taller. "You're staying in there. You're too dangerous. Mom's already having an aneurysm because you didn't answer your phone for four hours. I'm in charge now."

Four hours? Josh's eyes flicked up to the clock behind Pete. 7:00! The memory couldn't have been longer than a few minutes. He glanced down at his aching knees and almost threw up. Dirt marked his jeans where he'd knelt.

"Hey. Hey!" Pete snapped his fingers to get Josh's attention. "Touch anything else, I'll break your fingers." He pointed at an invisible line on the floor between the office and the secret room. "Step across, and I'll break your scrawny little legs."

Josh's face hardened. "You have to go to school."

"Nope." Pete grinned. "School's closed. Tornado warning." Doorbell chimes echoed down the hall. Pete glanced at the clock. "Don't even think about stepping out. Zach and I will be right out there."

"You're friends aren't allowed over when Mom's not home." Josh crossed his arms. "Besides, I have to go to the bathroom."

Pete shrugged. "Pee your pants." He glanced at his brother's jeans. "Again."

Josh glanced down at his pants.

Pete guffawed and pointed. "You really thought you did? Must have been a pretty good daymare." Pete leaned in. "They're not real."

Josh slowly closed his mouth, settling into a scowl. Lamplight cast weird shadows on Pete's face. They made him look evil. Pete was evil.

"Call Mom." Pete picked up Josh's phone and tossed it to him.

Josh glanced at the screen. "It's dead. Can I use yours?"

"I got the Half-Life mod." Zach's voice rang up the hall.

Stepping quickly across the office and into the hall, Pete caught Zach by the arm and turned him back toward the living room. Pete looked over his shoulder. "No, you can't use mine. Plug yours in."

Josh slumped. That's just great. Mom had to be furious. He'd be doing Pete's chores for the rest of his life.

Thunder rumbled outside. Josh glanced toward the window. White feathers of frost spread across the pane. Ice crept around the edges of the window and hung over the sill.

His eyebrows scrunched. Ice? Inside the house? He looked at Pete's invisible line across the doorway, stepped over it, and walked to the office door. Everything was fine. He just needed to turn up the heat.

◆○◆

"What? Nooo!" Kharaq screamed at empty shadows where the boy had been moments before.

He waved a claw. Fire leapt from a chiseled stone bowl at the edge of the cave. Flickering shadows played over a pile of straw heaped with dirty blankets. Vials and bottles of colored liquids littered a rough wood table.

"Impossible." He stared aghast around the cave. The gem was gone. The trap hadn't worked. He imagined Alaelle's pale, condescending sneer. She'd love it, wouldn't she, to see him stuck here, in this demon corpse, in this hole in hell while she took the throne.

He looked at his hands. Not hands, claws! He screamed and tore at the air. He should have killed the red-headed witch when he had the chance. Air rippled around his fingertips. A lopsided bookshelf ripped itself from the wall. Books and glassware flew across the room. Chairs and the small wooden table exploded. Papers and wood fragments whirled in a tornado around him.

He howled and swept his claws in an arc. The bowl's fire roared in the wind of his spell. Everything in the room smashed against the walls and ceiling.

"Im ... poss ... ible."

Gradually, his fury ebbed. His arms moved less violently. The storm slowly subsided, and shattered fragments floated to the floor. He stooped in the middle of the chaos and wheezed.

It couldn't have been his trap that had failed. A failed spell would do nothing, and this one had brought the boy, just not all the way. Why not?

He swayed and fingered a lumpy medallion hanging around his neck, running fingertips along the shattered shield with snakes winding through the broken pieces.

The portal should have opened when the gem was touched. Had she discovered the trap and countered? No, it had to be something else; the spell lacked power. It was as if ... the boy was in a place with no magic.

"Cavaris!" Of course. He spun toward the place the boy had knelt and murmured shadowy words. Wisps of smoke glowed faint red where the gem had been. Bending down, the creature dug claws into the smoke. Black holes festered around each talon.

He grunted and pulled. Cracks appeared in the air between his fingers and spider-webbed outward across the room. The tearing made soft gooey sounds like rotten fruit. Thick black vapor bled over Kharaq's gnarled hands.

When the fissures reached from floor to ceiling, the beast backed away. With sweeping hand gestures, he spat a series of guttural commands. The rip bulged and swelled. Smoke billowed across the roof, reeking of burning metal.

The gash exploded. Sloppy blackness spattered the cave. Covered in dark vapor, an angular block pushed halfway into the cavern, towering over Kharaq.

Smoke gradually drifted away from the object: the portico and gables of a two-story home. Lights from the windows gleamed through the mist in large rectangles.

"There you are." He stepped back with a low chuckle. Soon the gem would be his, as would the throne. This time Alaelle would grovel at *his* feet. He smirked at the thought.

His eyes moved to the pale dawn sky behind the house. Dying moonlight was about to mix with a rising sun. Kharaq smiled, fangs gleaming.

As the first droplet of sunlight splashed on the front of the house, Kharaq sank a twisted talon into the wall where light met shadow. His pale lips muttered dark words. As he spoke, ice spread from his claw. Overhead, storm clouds clotted the dawn sky.

The hooded face leaned in and whispered, eyes blazing. "Run, little thief. Run fast. I *love* a good hunt."

Josh shuffled into the rec room. Pete and his friend Zach sat in front of the TV, shooting their way through an abandoned building.

Zach groaned and dropped his controller.

Pete leapt to his feet, and Karate punched the air. He bowed, then raised his hands, imitating the sound of a roaring crowd. "Once again, you cannot hurt a god of war!"

Zach stood and stuffed an empty, plastic water bottle and burrito wrapper into Josh's hands. "How about you get me something besides water?" He pushed past Josh toward the bathroom.

Pete's eyes narrowed toward his brother. "You're dead."

"Whatever." Josh looked around the room. Trophies and awards cluttered shelves and wall spaces. All Pete's. Kung fu this, national champion that. Pete just passed his fifth degree: swordplay. He was jubilant. That made him even more of a jerk than usual, if that was even possible.

Josh scowled. Nothing was his. Well, there was a big chess piece for winning the last championship, but nobody gave trophies for etiquette, strategy, and concentration games. Pete got all the cool lessons.

"I'll play you." Josh dropped the wrappers and water bottle on the table and reached for the remote.

Pete stepped in his way. "I thought I told you to stay in there."

"I'm hungry, and my phone is ..." Josh stopped. Zach had moved quietly behind him. And Pete had *that* look.

Josh lunged toward the hallway, but not fast enough. Pete twisted Josh's wrist behind him. Zach grabbed his feet, and the bigger boys dragged Josh, squirming and shouting, down the hall. They shoved him into the closet and slammed it shut.

"PETE!" Josh smashed his shoulder against the door.

"It's for your own good," Pete shouted through the door. "Next time, do what I tell you."

Josh heard them drag something against the door and walk away. Their laughter faded into the rec room. Soon the only sounds were muffled gunfire and explosions.

Josh threw himself against the closet door again and again until the table pushed against it tipped, and Josh sprawled into the hall in a pile of magazines and family pictures.

Slipping on magazine covers, Josh scrambled to his feet and stormed to the rec room. Fists clenched, face on fire, he stood in the doorway. Pete was a brainless, pigheaded Nazi. He wanted to scream at his brother, rush in and punch and kick him into submission. But Dad's voice rumbled in his ears, "Winners are not ruled by their emotions." Josh swallowed the words. They went down like a fist full of gravel.

"What's your problem?" He shouted so hard the veins in his temples felt like they'd burst.

"You are," — Pete glanced up from the game — "Mr. *Special*. Do you think I like it here any more than you? Why don't you just man up for once and take your lumps like the rest of us? Go read your book until Mom gets home."

"At least you can remember," Josh raged back.

"Look at him shaking," Zach laughed and made a punching motion to his own chin. "C'mon hero, show us what you got."

"Gentlemen! What's all this about?" A stern elderly man stood in the doorway, shocks of snow-white hair trimmed in stylish waves. He frowned at the boys, undoing the top button of his custom, pinstriped Brioni.

"Grandpa!" Josh scowled at his brother, then ran to the old man and hugged him.

Pete dropped his controller and snapped to 'attention.'

Breaking into a smile, Grandpa hugged Josh and turned to Pete. "How is your training, son?"

"I just graduated blade-work. Hammers and cudgels start next week," Pete beamed.

"Well done. Your father will be very proud." Grandpa's eyes shone. He beckoned to Pete, standing the boys in front of him. "I have bad news. We have a bit of an emergency—"

"It's Mom?" Josh's words caught in his throat.

"No, no," Grandpa squeezed Josh's shoulder. "She's fine—aside from a nervous breakdown over not being able to get hold of you two. There is"—he glanced at Pete, pausing for a moment—"an *electrical* storm around this neighborhood that seems to be interfering with the phones. We need to leave right away. We'll call your mom when we are outside the storm."

While he spoke, a slender man with a messy mop of light brown hair and round glasses stepped through the front door.

"ET," Grandpa turned to the man. "Would you be so kind as to help the boys pack their necessities?"

"ET?" Zach whispered to Pete, brows crinkled. "As in Extra Terrestr ..."

Pete rolled his eyes. "It's short for Etienne, genius. He works for my mom at the museum."

"We'd better hurry, boss, it's getting worse." ET gestured to the sky outside.

The boys followed Grandpa to the door. Dark, storm clouds gathered overhead. In the center, directly above the house, lightning lashed across a crater of black and purple thunderheads.

"That doesn't look good." Josh's voice sounded squeaky.

"No, it doesn't." Grandpa's eyes dropped from the sky to the planter beside the door. His face paled.

"What?" Josh tried to follow his gaze.

"Perhaps you could pick one of those for me." Brows jutting, Grandpa gestured to the planter.

Josh knelt and picked a flower. The stem snapped with a tiny cracking sound. He frowned and looked up. "They're frozen." With widening eyes, he looked out over the lawn. Grass faded from a healthy green at the road to a ghostly winter pale around the house.

"Frozen?" Pete's words came out as a croak.

"We'd best forget about your things, and leave *now*." Grandpa took both boys by the arms and started toward the car.

"What is it?" Josh swallowed hard.

"I'll explain on the way." Grandpa stopped, turning Josh toward him. "Did you close the door?"

Josh looked toward the front door.

"No." Grandpa's eyes flicked to Zach for a moment. "The *other* door, in your mother's office."

Josh swallowed and shook his head.

"You need to close it. Quickly. Others will see the storm."

The color left Pete's face. "Nadris?"

Grandpa nodded, the creases in his face suddenly deep and ominous.

Josh turned to go inside, but he couldn't pull his gaze away from the ice crawling up the walls. Visions of red eyes and tearing claws from the cave glued his feet to the walk.

Grandpa put a hand on Josh's shoulder. "We'll go together."

He turned to ET. "Would you please fetch the stone case from the car?"

———◆◇◆———

Frost covered the office door handle. Josh pulled a shirt sleeve over his hand to open it. Each breath drifted in clouds of vapor.

"Quickly," Grandpa stiffened and nodded toward the secret door.

Just as Josh pushed it closed. Zach walked in.

"Bruuuuh." Zach took in the office with wide eyes.

"Uh, my Mom's pretty private about this room." Pete turned him around and pushed him back toward the door.

"Very good. Let's go." Grandpa guided Josh out of the office. As he reached the door, several books thumped to the floor behind him.

Everyone spun. The bookcase on the opposite side of the room groaned and drooped. Books and artifacts crashed to the floor as the wall collapsed in a soggy pile.

In the opening stood a figure in a black hooded cloak. Icy wind whipped his robes, gusting into the room with threads of dark vapor. Gleaming red eyes fastened on Josh.

Zach screamed and leapt for the doorway, running into Grandpa.

The cowled head snapped toward him. A gnarled talon reached out. The voice was ice water down Josh's back.

"Stone!"

Zach arched backward. His cry cut off with a hideous cracking sound. He and Grandpa were gone, and in their place stood two neat stacks of lichen-covered stones. Dark vapor drifted from the human-sized cairns.

"Grandpa!" Josh leapt toward the pile.

Red eyes snapped to Josh. The creature's claws stretched out. Pete was already moving, thin-lipped and pale. As Josh felt his brother yank him toward the doorway, the chilling voice rang again.

"Stone!"

CHAPTER TWO

I'VE BEEN WAITING

"S tone!"

Josh sprinted after Pete. Behind them, the office door dulled from deep walnut to coarse granite.

"Gah! Haesitio," the dark voice rasped from inside.

The wall and office doorway exploded into a cloud of splinters and stone. The force knocked both boys to the floor. Dust rolled down the hall. Pages from Mom's books fluttered in the chaos.

Pete was first to his feet, grabbing Josh just as the hooded figure emerged. Pulling his brother behind him, Pete raced across the living room.

Over his shoulder, Josh saw mottled claws point his way.

"Inferneus!" the creature grunted and thrust its hands forward. Rivers of flame roared after the brothers.

Pete pulled Josh sideways into the kitchen. Fiery waves smashed into the wall just behind them, splattering burning rain across the room. Smoldering fragments skittered across the floor.

Pete reached for the back door and froze. Black vapor from outside drifted around the frame.

Josh's eyes darted around the room. There was no other escape. No matter what was on the other side, this was a Zugzwang; any other move lost the game.

Smoke alarms screamed. Josh leapt for the door with Pete on his heels.

"Inferneus." The creature thrust his hands forward again. Instead of blazing torrents, tiny flames guttered around his fingertips and sputtered out.

He clenched his claws. "Cavaris! I hate this impotent world." He strode after the boys and muttered curses in his dark tongue.

As he passed the fireplace, he stopped and slowly turned, staring at the collection of pictures and knickknacks on the mantle. "Of all the houses on Cavaris." He leaned toward a picture of Mom and the boys and laughed under his breath. "I should have known. And who says fate has no favorites?"

From beneath his robe, the creature lifted his misshapen medallion and pressed it against the wood mantle. Woodsmoke curled across his mottled claws.

He stood back and admired the insignia burned into the wood: snakes winding through the cracks in a shattered shield. He leaned toward the photograph of Mom. "You'll want to know how they died." With a dark chuckle, he strode through the smoldering debris toward the back door.

Josh missed the back step and landed in the dirt on his hands and knees. Pete stumbled a few steps and caught his balance. Both boys froze.

There *was* no back step. No backyard. No cold rainy morning.

Josh swiped the hair out of his eyes. Afternoon sun swam on the forest floor in dappled droplets. The breeze smelled of pine and rich, dark soil mixed with the faintest hint of the sea. It was ... so familiar.

They were in the middle of a clearing lined with strange squat trees. Each trunk was fat enough to be a delivery van on end. Rather than branches rising toward the sky, they spread sideways, mingling with the next in a massive, twisting, leafy circle.

A few feet away in midair, hung their back door. Wisps of dark vapor drifted at the edges. Josh staggered to his feet and rubbed dirty hands on his jeans. He walked around the door. It just hung there on nothing.

This can't be. It just can't. Josh squeezed his eyes shut. "I'm dreaming. None of this is real. Even Pete is part of my delusion."

"Ow!" Something thunked against Josh's forehead. His eyes snapped open. He rubbed the stinging spot and looked around. It felt like someone just hit him with a rock.

Someone had!

"And here's another delusion." Pete tossed a small stone in the air and caught it again.

Josh glared at his brother. "What did you do that for?"

Pete rolled his eyes. "You know, being the smart one, you can be pretty stupid. Just because you don't understand something doesn't mean it's not true."

"Then why don't you fill me in? For once." Josh crossed his arms and scowled.

"Mom said I shouldn't ..." Pete closed his mouth. His eyes flicked to the scars on Josh's neck.

Chills crashed over Josh in waves. The lights on his arms exploded like fireworks. Memories ripped reality from Josh's grip. Blue sky faded to night. Bloodthirsty howls poured from every direction. His heart battered at his ribs.

Mom and Pete stood with Josh in the center of the clearing. Around them, soldiers in bright armor faced the trees in a protective wall. The woods rang as they drew their swords. Shadows between the trees erupted with coal-black wolves. Hundreds of them, charging. Soldiers disappeared in a flood of fur and snarling teeth.

Between the trees stood the pack's leader, a wolf the size of a small horse. Its yellow eyes searched the fray until they found Josh. Then it sprang.

Josh thrust both hands in front of him, staggering backward. Wolves and soldiers faded into a tranquil afternoon. He spun left and right, swiping at the battle, but there were only trees. The forest, which had seemed so warm and welcoming, now beckoned with crooked arms with claw-like branches. The air smelled of blood and oiled steel.

Pete spun Josh toward him. "I saw your runes flickering. What did you remember?" He studied Josh's face.

Josh sucked lung-fulls of air in heave after heave. Sweat beaded on his forehead. "What"—he choked out between breaths—"happened to me?"

The door handle rattled.

Pete spun toward the woods. Several paths gaped like hungry jaws, ready to swallow them down into the dark bowels of the forest.

"That one!" Pete pointed and ran.

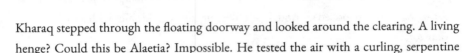

Kharaq stepped through the floating doorway and looked around the clearing. A living henge? Could this be Alaetia? Impossible. He tested the air with a curling, serpentine tongue. Could the boy have had a key?

He stepped down and looked around the door. If this was Alaetia, the trees on this side would be ... ah yes, burned. But they had leaves again. So, they survived his last visit. They wouldn't be so fortunate this time.

Kharaq shuffled to the oldest of the trees in the circle. Burls jutted at odd angles from a twisting trunk. Roots as thick as his waist sank into dark soil.

He leaned close to the blackened bark. "No 'welcome home' from my old *friends,* the trees?"

Shudders ran up the trunk. Whispers sighed through its canopy. A name rustled leaf to leaf, spreading to the next tree and then the next. Whispers grew until the forest roared with the sound. "Khaaaraaaq."

The dark mage raised hands to the sky. His laugh echoed through the trees. "WEL-COME HOME!"

Kharaq spun back toward the tree. "Do you know what you trees did to me?" His voice rose to a howl. "Well, I survived." Flecks of saliva formed on snarling lips. He plunged a single claw into the quivering trunk. "Now it's my turn. Welcome to your own private hell." He twisted the talon.

Rot spread around the puncture, bark peeling and falling away. Black sap drooled from the hole. The tree moaned and swayed. Its leaves yellowed and curled.

Kharaq watched the decay spread. Leaves fell around him in drifting rain. Cruel satisfaction spread across his face. "Enjoy that for a while, before I chop you down and set this whole place on fire."

The Wizard's eyes flicked around the clearing, searching the gnarled roots that tangled across the forest floor. Aha. Scuff marks. "So it's the Sanctulum, is it?" He glanced toward the afternoon sun. "Run then," he laughed. "Try and outrun the night."

"Obscurim tenebrae caecitoch." The wizard raised his hands.

Shadows boiled on the forest floor, giving off a black fog that slowly floated into the branches above Kharaq. Clouds of it spread from tree to tree, hanging in the canopies until nothing but trunks were visible.

Kharaq looked up and laughed, "Oh all-seeing forest, why don't you tell them what you see now?"

His eyes searched the trunks and roots, stopping at a nearby stump. Black pools of night gathered at the stump's base. "Resuro."

Shadows ran in rivulets from the stump to other shadows. They writhed along the forest floor, bunched and collected, swelled, forming legs and eyes and teeth.

Wolves, black as night detached from the gloom. Drool hung from yellow fangs. Eyes shone brightly.

Talons flexing, Kharaq muttered and growled. Wolves flowed from every direction. Hundreds gathered around the wizard until the ground seethed in a flood of black fur. The forest rumbled with growls and the shifting of clawed feet.

Josh's lungs were on fire. He raced after Pete through the blur of trunks. They leapt over logs and ducked under limbs. Every step put his brother farther ahead.

Josh looked behind. The path was gone? It was as if branches and bushes moved across the opening. The skin on his scalp tingled. He poured everything into catching up with Pete.

Their path abruptly ended. The brothers jogged into a clearing. Birds chirped in the canopy overhead. Leaves covered the ground in a brown and gold mosaic. Everything was sweet with the scent of pine and wildflowers.

In the center of the clearing towered a Stonehenge almost as tall as the trees. Each upright was a massive granite angel or demon. Their giant wings touched in great arches. Stone faces twisted in rage or grim determination as motionless swords and spears clashed.

"At last." A dark-cloaked figure stooped beside an oval stone altar in the center of the statues. His whisper carried across the clearing.

Josh couldn't breathe. His eyes snapped from the cloaked figure to stacks of lichen-covered stones dotting the clearing; stacks just like the ones Grandpa and Zach had been turned into. No wonder they hadn't seen the creature behind them on the trail, he'd been here the whole time.

The figure half turned. "I've been waiting for you."

Chapter Three

God of the Dead

"R un!" Pete grabbed his brother by the arm. Just as the brothers lunged for the trees, a figure stepped from between the trunks. The three collided and landed in a tangled heap.

There was a knee in Josh's ribs. A torso pressed against his face. Frantic, Josh shoved at the tangle of bodies, getting an elbow in the side of his head and a boot in his stomach.

The boot was fitted, well-worn, and made of soft leather. His hand tangled in hair. Long hair.

The slender teenage girl was first to her feet. As tall as Pete, she glared at the two boys, her ears red. She shook the leaves and dirt from her hair; her long ringlets of autumn golds and browns gleamed in the sunlight.

Pete staggered to his feet and then just stood there with his mouth open. Josh wiped dirty hands on his pants and brushed his bangs away from his eyes, and just stared.

She was so pretty. Her skin was the color of woodland shadows, rich and dark. Under a hooded forest cloak, her weather-stained leather jerkin gleamed with a dozen buckles and straps and as many daggers. Scowling, she adjusted her well-worn bow and brace of arrows over one shoulder.

Josh gulped. Other people were in the woods? She was in danger. Run! Just as he opened his mouth to warn her, she pulled a long knife from a knee-high boot. Josh stepped back, eyes flicking across the clearing to the dark-cloaked figure. So, she worked for *it*.

She looked the brothers up and down, leaf-green eyes shining with wild light. Breathing a long, exasperated sigh, she called to the cloaked figure. "Well, here they are. I hope you're happy."

She brushed past the stunned boys and picked up a soggy bundle dropped in the collision. With her knife, she gestured toward the cloaked figure. "His *Tree* isn't very good. Otherwise he wouldn't have wanted to talk to you."

Josh's eyes flicked from her knife to the trees. Branches moved across the path, trapping them in the clearing. At any second the hooded creature would turn to blast them.

She strode to one of the trees and opened the bundle with her knife. "Hello Auntie. Here is some of your favorite muck from the riverbank. This should help with the yellow leaves." The girl emptied her soggy bundle at the base of the tree, then turned back to the boys. "My name's Dandelion."

Behind her the tree sighed in ecstasy, its leaves shivering. A squirrel scampered down the trunk and chattered at her.

Dandelion glanced at it and rolled her eyes. "If they are, where's the Weaver?" She turned toward the boys. "Do you have another brother?"

Both boys gaped back at her. Pete stood with his feet apart, hands loose as if he'd just stepped into a Kung fu ring. Josh kept looking back and forth between her and the shadowy figure across the clearing.

Her lips slowly pressed together, eyebrows sinking to an exasperated flat. She slowly repeated her question, over-enunciating. "Another ... brother?"

Josh shook his head.

Whispers washed through the canopy.

"See?" She snorted and glanced up at the trees. "How can they be the Wizard and the Warrior, they can't even talk." She stuffed the knife back into her boot and mumbled half to herself. "Every time someone new shows up in the forest, you knot-heads think *The Dreams* are coming to pass."

"The Cambium Dreams?" Pete choked out.

"So you *do* talk." Dandelion turned and walked toward the cloaked figure. She gestured to the boys to follow. "Save your questions for him."

Neither boy moved. Josh bit his lip.

She followed their eyes to the hooded creature. "What."

Leaves whispered overhead.

Dandelion glanced up and chuckled. "Oh. Right. The wizard cloak. He's the great Oracle of Yevilia. Much greater than that rotworm chasing *you*."

Across the clearing, the cloaked figure reached up and pulled back his hood. Without moving his feet, he twisted around to look at them. A kindly, wrinkled old face beamed out from a messy bush of white hair.

"The Oracle of Yevilia?" With hesitant steps, Pete walked toward the man. "You work for my dad, right?"

The old man hunched over a knobby staff, his bony frame poking up at odd angles beneath a tattered dark brown cloak. He waved them toward him with a gnarled hand. "Perhaps, perhaps. Come around here where I can see you."

A few steps behind Pete, Josh's mind spun. Dandelion could talk to trees and squirrels? The old man could fight the creature hunting them? He whispered to Pete, "You know him?"

Pete's brows stayed furrowed. "I'm not sure."

As they reached the oracle, Dandelion unwrapped a block of something yellow and handed it to him.

"Cheese?" The oracle gasped. "Is this cheese? Oh you are truly an angel. Where did you get this?"

"You know better than to ask," Dandelion grinned. "I got some flying ivy too."

She pulled a scraggly length of vine from her pack. It had a faint, musty smell of dirt and cobwebs. As she pulled it free, the vine lengthened and thickened, weaving into a tangle the size of a tablecloth. Sunlight glinted from a thousand tiny leaves. The whole thing floated about waist-high.

"That's quite a find." The old man chuckled and shook his head.

"Yeah, but I can't make it stay open." While Dandelion spoke the vine unwound and shrank until it was just a foot-long shrub with wiggling roots.

"You'll figure it out." The oracle smiled at her and turned to the boys. "Come, Come." He beckoned them closer. Eyebrows bristled like wild clumps of weeds.

There was something wonderful about this strange old man. His eyes twinkled with kindness. The lines in that face were full of stories. Everything about that face said Josh and Pete were safe here.

"I'm Josh." Josh couldn't wait to be introduced.

Pete kept his distance. "I don't recognize you."

"But I recognize you, Petri." The old man's blue eyes twinkled.

Pete's eyebrows shot up.

Josh turned toward Pete. "Petri?"

The oracle's smile widened. "And you Jhosa."

Pete's expression sank into a scowl again. "How do you know our names? How do we know this isn't a trap?"

Dandelion spun. "A trap? Are you serious?" She glared at them, hands on her hips. "I could have had you going in circles the minute you walked in the woods. How do you think you got away from Kharaq? The trees block him. The only reason you're still alive is because the trees think you're the ones in their dumb Cambium Dreams."

Dandelion picked up a pine cone and tossed it into the woods. "Anyway, you can't be. You're too young. And you need another brother." She smirked at Pete. "He'd be the smart one?"

Sweat beaded on Pete's forehead. "Did you say Kharaq?"

The old man nodded, his face sagging. "How is it he followed you here? What does he seek?"

His mind reeling, Josh burst out, "Who's Kharaq? Who are Petri and Jhosa? What are the Cambium Dreams?" The names clamored in the back of his mind, just out of sight. Grabbing at his memories was like holding a fistful of water. It made him want to scream. He turned to Pete, breathless. "Do we have another brother?"

The oracle rubbed his beard, eyes narrow. "You do not remember?"

"He doesn't remember anything from here." Pete stuffed hands in his pockets and locked the oracle in an intense stare. "But I do, and I don't remember you."

The oracle stared at the brothers, lips pursed. Clouds drifted across the sun casting the clearing in shadow. The autumn breeze shifted his wild hair.

He sighed. "Much has changed since you two walked these woods. None of it is good. I will answer your questions, and tell you what has happened since you left. But the trees cannot delay Kharaq long, so first, I must know how it is he has come."

Wind whispered through the trees. Dandelion's face darkened. "Better make it quick. Kharaq is conjuring something and the trees can't see what it is. This isn't good."

Fear flickered across the oracle's face. He turned to Josh. "Why don't you tell me how you two came to be in the woods today?"

Josh glanced toward Dandelion and looked at the ground, shoving his hands in his pockets. How much should he tell? It sounded like Kharaq being here was a really bad thing ... and it was his fault. "It's kinda hard to describe."

Smile lines around the oracle's eyes crinkled. "Would you like to try showing me?"

Josh's brows bunched. "Huh?"

The old wizard put his hand on the side of Josh's face.

Peace flowed from the wrinkled palm. All at once the sun was deliciously warm; happy birds twittered all around him. He was ... completely safe. Without meaning to, he sighed and closed his eyes.

This is the way wizards talk.

Josh's eyes flew open. He yelped and jumped back. "Did you ... was that you?"

The old man nodded and smiled.

Josh's head swam. The old man's voice had just spoken in his mind. Well, not really spoken. It was so much more than words. It was an understanding. This is how wizards talk? Josh's heart began to pound. He stepped back toward the oracle. "Can anyone do that or does that mean I'm a ..."

The oracle's smile grew. "Yes. Congratulations." He glanced at Pete and Dandelion. "Our minds can speak."

"I know," Dandelion scowled.

Pete snorted and wandered toward a lichen-covered stack of rocks.

Josh turned back toward the oracle. Something in Josh's chest was doing somersaults. A wizard? Breathless, Josh placed the leathery hand back on his face.

The oracle's voice echoed in Josh's mind. *To talk to me, think toward me.*

LIKE THIS?

Not quite so loud, but yes, just like that. You are doing very well! Now, just think back on your day. If it's scary, I am right here.

"DON'T touch that!" Dandelion shrieked and leapt toward Pete. She grabbed his wrist and spun him around.

"Sheeze." Pete tugged his arm out of her hand. "What's your problem?"

"They're people, you idiot. If you knock them down, they can't ever be brought back." Eyes on fire, Dandelion stepped between Pete and the pile.

"I know what they are," Pete huffed. "If you knew who I was, you wouldn't be so quick to tell me what to do."

"I don't care if you're the Son of the Eventide. Touch it, and you'll have one less hand."

Pete stood straight. "I'd like to see you—"

"Please," the oracle interrupted, his eyes hollow. "We have little time." He turned his attention to Pete. "Like you, she once had a younger brother named Slate. He is now one of those piles. I'm sure you can imagine if your brother—"

Dandelion breathed out loudly. "Can we just get on with whatever it was you two were doing?"

Pete watched the oracle reach for Josh and smirked. "Good luck finding anything in there."

"You don't deserve a brother." Dandelion pushed past Pete.

Pete opened his mouth to retort, but the oracle shushed him, turning to Josh. *Tell your story.*

Josh remembered his whole day starting from packing his lunch for school. When he got to Kharaq's cave, his knees wobbled so badly he gripped the oracles hand with both of his just to stay upright.

As Josh finished the oracle's hand fell limp at his side. His eyes sank to the forest floor. "Oh no. Oh no. This cannot be."

Josh's mouth suddenly felt like he hadn't had anything to drink for days. What just happened? He reached for the oracle's hand to put it back on his face. "Was I telling it wrong?"

Head still hung, the old man shook his head. "No, child. It was I that failed." He wrung his hands and muttered, looking up at the trees. "The gem you took from the box. That's why he hunts. We are lost. We are lost."

"What. What happened?" Josh tried to read the aged face.

The oracle turned to Pete, his voice quaking. "The box. It's still in your pocket?"

"The box?" Pete reached for his back pocket and froze, suspicion twisting his face. "How did you know it was there?"

"He saw the whole day in my head, remember?" Josh hunched his shoulders.

"Child." The old man gripped Dandelion's arm with shaking fingers. "You must get them back to the door. The gem must be returned to Cavaris and their mother. It cannot stay in this world."

Dandelion's brows arched upward in alarm. "What are you talking about? What gem? And who's their mother?" She swallowed. "And it's too late to take them back to the door. While you were mind-talking to him, the trees said it disappeared."

"No." The oracle's voice was thick. "The gem has great power. Kharaq must not claim it. He will plunge this world into a hell worse than you can imagine. You need to help them escape. Who can lead them through the woods better than a dryad?"

Dandelion glared at the oracle. "What does being a dryad have to do with it? Where am I supposed to take them? The Chazrack village? They're as likely to eat these two as help them."

"Where do you live? What about your parents?" Pete chuffed.

Dandelion gave Pete a black look. "My dad died in the war. My mom got chopped down for firewood. OK?" Her lips trembled for a moment before she pinched them tight. "I don't need them. I take care of myself and so should you."

"What's a dryad?" Josh looked her up and down. She didn't look any different than a normal girl.

The oracle put a hand on Josh's arm. "She's part tree. Dryads are the soul of the forest. Many of the trees you see used to have human forms like—"

"Ugh," Dandelion interrupted, waving her hand. "Do we have time for this? How about, dryads are: mind your own business." She turned to the boys. "I'll take you to the city gate, but after that you're on your own."

"Ugh," Pete mimicked Dandelion, waving his hand. "We don't need your help. I know these woods *and* the city better than—"

Eyes blazing, Dandelion pointed a finger at Pete, froze for a moment, then spun toward the oracle, grabbing his arm. "I know what to do. If you're worried about a gem, why don't *you* just claim it? Only one person can claim a magic item at a time, right?"

The grizzled jaw dropped. The oracle's eyes lit up. "You are the smartest girl I have ever met." He turned to Pete. "Son, give it to me. Quickly."

Pete stepped back, feet apart, hands loose. "I don't think so."

Dandelion blew out an exasperated breath and turned to the oracle. "Do we have time for this? Can you just freeze him or something?"

The oracle studied Pete's face and pulled on his beard. "If I were thrust into a similar situation, I would be wary too. I will explain and perhaps it will help you trust me."

Dandelion snorted and rolled her eyes.

The old man glanced at the tree line where the boys had come through and slowly let out a breath. "Two years ago, Kharaq's dark creatures swarmed from the mountains. No place was safe from his spies. So your mother took the two of you to Cavaris to stay with your grandfather until the war was over. But Kharaq burned the tree-henge and she was unable to return."

"Everyone knows that." Pete's voice was quiet.

"I don't." Josh's eyes were big.

The oracle swallowed a couple times. "Kharaq conjured his shadow wolves and sent them to dismember cities and villages. Your father gathered armies from every nation. Battle raged across the lands. The dead from both sides clogged our roads, filled our fields, and littered our forests. We should have won. But, no matter what we did, he would not die. We discovered that Kharaq had a gem that made him invincible, a gem he'd stolen from your mother.

"The gem could not be taken by force, so we concocted a plot to trick him into relinquishing it. Once he'd taken it off, we needed a spell powerful enough to break his claim to the gem, banish him to the underworld, and shatter his soul to dust.

"It was our desperate last stand. To create that much magical power, the entire eastern forest sacrificed itself. Those trees poured their life force into one man for one mighty spell."

"Into *you*." Dandelion put her hand on the oracle's arm.

The oracle's face drooped. "Yet, in our moment of victory, we were defeated. Defeated." He leaned heavily on his staff, breath rasping.

Josh's eyes flicked to the other teenagers. Pete's face was white. Dandelion fidgeted with one of the buckles on her jerkin.

The oracle cleared his throat. "Our wizard council had a spy in Kharaq's court, a young servant woman. She agreed to spill hot reeking tar on Kharaq and the necklace holding the gem. We hoped this would make him take it off.

"The ruse worked. He screamed. He tore the chain from around his neck and I spoke the shattering spell. Yet as I cast, Kharaq banished the poor servant girl to stone."

"His favorite curse," Dandelion muttered.

The oracle dabbed his forehead. "The magic of the trees collided with Kharaq's spell and the power of the gem. My spell wiped out Kharaq and much of his army,"—his voice wobbled and cracked—"but everyone for miles was banished to stone. Millions of people. This city. Our entire army."

Dandelion reached for the oracle's hand and squeezed.

The oracle slowly looked up at Pete. "You don't recognize me because the force of the collision burned away my youth and my magic, and left me like this. Wrinkled fingers lifted the hem of his robe. Instead of legs and feet, the boys stared at roots and a tree trunk.

Both brothers gasped.

The old man took a deep breath. "I am an empty shell. My connection with the trees is all that keeps me alive. But it was worth it to have defeated Kharaq."

"Until I brought him back." The words slipped out of Josh's mouth before he could stop them.

Josh shrank backward. Dandelion's eyes followed him. Her gaze burned. Condemnation blazed from every tree and creature in the forest. Mountains of smoldering shame crushed him into the dirt. His eyes sank under its weight. Why did he have to open the box? This was all his fault.

The oracle's voice was quiet. "The Cambium Dreams are our only hope."

When Josh spoke, only a croak came out. He cleared his throat several times. "What are *they*?"

The old man raised his eyes to the trees. "The Cambium Dreams are the story of our world. They are sung by the trees and ring beneath the earth among their roots. It tells past, present, and future. Those who hear it say it's beyond the mind and the page. In the Dreams, the Eventide Wizard, Warrior, and Weaver are bringers of dawn to this age of most grievous darkness."

"What's the weaver? Maybe we have another brother? Somewhere?" Josh's flicked a hopeful look toward Pete.

With sad eyes, the oracle turned to Josh. "The Weaver is the other member; the binding thread that keeps the journey from unraveling the trio. Without the Weaver, there is no hope for the three. Yet despite the Weaver, one will die. In the dreams ..."

"We don't have another brother," Pete interrupted the old man.

"I knew it." Dandelion scowled and crossed her arms.

"Pete." Josh gnawed on his lip. "I think you should give him the box."

Still frowning, Pete handed over the gleaming obsidian box.

The oracle's wrinkled hands turned the box over and over. His watery blue eyes followed its twisted runes. Sunlight danced in fiery flecks across its surface. Finally, he looked up at Josh. "*You* must open it. Your mother locked it and only your line holds the key."

Josh didn't take the box, he just touched it. Hairs rose on his neck. A mixture of terror and excitement raced down his spine. His mouth filled with the taste of rust. *Open*, he thought. And it did. Just like last time.

Trails of vapor followed the crimson gem.

Dandelion gasped, "Drompa, that's a—"

"Shard of the Zothoran. One of the five." The oracle beamed.

Dandelion's voice was breathless. "Nine the stars that rule the light. Five the lords of endless night."

She fidgeted with excitement, "Why didn't you tell me this was *that* gem? Drompa. That's what gives the rulers of the underworld their power. You won't just be able to kill Kharaq, it will make you a god! My book on necrotic gems says—"

The oracle gently shushed her. "Not me child. A hundred times zero is still zero." Fire in his blue eyes burned toward Josh. "Him!"

Josh gulped and stepped back. He shook his head.

Pete glanced at Josh and grinned. "God of the dead? Sick! *I'll* wear it."

The old wizard smiled at Pete. "You have a different sort of magic. The magic of feet and hands and steel. The magic of battle."

Pete's grin faded. "I know what I have." He rolled his eyes sideways toward Josh, "He's *special*."

The Oracle gripped Josh's arm. "Claim the gem and no one can take it from you, not even Kharaq. If he does not have the gem, we have the chance to defeat him."

A shudder swept over Josh. The last time he'd touched that thing, he'd come face to face with Kharaq. Even now Josh's soul felt attached by only a thread. No thanks.

The oracle held the box toward him. "I understand how you feel. The trap Kharaq set the first time is gone. Claim the gem. It is your only escape from Kharaq — and your only way home."

Josh didn't move.

"Sheeze," Pete snorted. "You sure it wasn't the Weiner and the Warrior?"

Josh clenched his teeth. This wasn't fear, this was strategy. 'Live to fight another day'. He stared at the glowing gem. Liar. He was terrified.

Wind whistled through the treetops.

Blood drained from Dandelion's face. "Shadow wolves! That's what Kharaq was doing. We need to get to the city. To a stone house. Now!"

As if to punctuate her words, the distant, haunting cry of a wolf floated through the forest.

Pete's eyes bulged. "*Take it*, Josh!"

Josh couldn't move.

"Josh!" Pete stepped toward Josh like he was going to slap him, but instead, he gripped Josh's arm. "Shadows and Heroes, Josh. Remember, Shadows and Heroes."

A thousand tiny sparks burst from the backs of Josh's hands and shot up his arms. The forest spun around him. Light faded from the sky, The leaves softened to blankets and pillows. "No." Josh grabbed at Pete for balance. "What did you do?"

Icy winds wailed and hammered angry fists against the house. Mom sat on the bed beside Josh stroking his hair. She reached down and picked up a wooden toy dragon.

"Once, this dragon only existed as an idea. It took creativity and determination to make it real. Both fear and bravery are like that. They are ideas that cannot become real until you act on them. Nothing outside can create anything inside. It only works the other way."

"But 'real' bad things happen to people. Like this." Josh jabbed a finger at the scar on his neck. "And that makes me scared."

Mom fastened the top buttons on her gown and pulled her long red hair over the tattoo on her neck. Josh had never really thought about it until then, what was that?

Her whisper barely rose above the wind. "There are things no one but your dad knows about me. When I was a little older than you, I lost *my* dad. I was ... taken away. They did awful things to me ... left me to die."

Josh's mouth fell open.

"For years I woke up screaming. But I learned something about fear. Fear is like a shadow. Inside each shadow is a hero. When you face what you fear, you kill the shadow and become the hero."

"Hero?" Josh's throat was dry. His question came out as a croak. He leaned in.

Mom's eyes were far away. "There were years I wasn't sure I even wanted to live. When I was afraid, I would reach my mind out for my dad. We would face the shadow together, even though he wasn't there."

"And then it was OK?"

Mom shook her head. Her eyes glistened. "No ..."

Josh's throat was suddenly tight.

"And yes. A hundred times my dreams were crushed and my life destroyed. A hundred times I cried for help. A hundred times I saw nothing, felt nothing, knew I had been abandoned ..."

Josh held his breath.

"And yet"—her smile trembled—"a hundred times it worked out OK. And now when I look back, I am a hundred times stronger and a hundred times wiser."

Josh's mind churned. What had Mom gone through that was so bad she couldn't tell anyone? Josh leaned over and hugged her. "I'm sorry about what happened to you. I'll listen if you ever want to tell me."

Mom smiled softly. "Do you understand what I'm telling you about fear?"

"I ... I think so." Josh squeezed her hand and slipped under the blankets.

Slowly, he closed his eyes and imagined Dad standing next to Mom. Dad's big hands slid gently through her hair. He smiled down at Josh. Josh smiled back. Was Dad real? As real as anything Josh feared.

Dad, Mom, and the bedroom faded into Pete, Dandelion, and the Oracle. All three stared at Josh, faces tight.

Josh let go of Pete and stepped back. "How did you make me remember?"

Pete deflated. "I didn't. It was just a guess. There was a long time after Kharaq took us where we couldn't sleep. Mom walked us both into our 'shadows.' It's the only magic I know, and you needed it right now."

Looking at Pete was like seeing a ghost. Josh swallowed hard. Was this how Pete used to be — nice?

Dandelion crossed her arms. "Whenever you're done with family time ... I'd rather not get eaten."

The oracle gave her a chiding glance and held the gem toward Josh.

Josh's mind snapped back to the forest and the wolves. He took a deep breath and imagined Dad standing beside him. What would Dad have said? *Feeling* afraid is normal; Courage is what you do, not what you feel. Josh took tentative steps forward. The oracle put a hand on Josh's shoulder.

I am here. Do not be afraid. We will step into this shadow together. Close your eyes. You're thinking of your father. Very good. Never go into a shadow alone.

An image flashed across the oracle's mind. Josh sensed him hide it. Too late. Josh saw a stack of rocks molding in a deserted stone courtyard. The same kind of piles that used to be ET and Zach. The same ones all over the clearing.

"Dad?" Josh choked.

The oracle winced. *I'm so sorry. He was a great man. I wanted to tell you earlier, but along with everything else, I feared it would be too much.*

Kharaq? Josh felt his face flush. He clenched shaking fists. Kharaq had killed his dad. Kharaq was the reason Mom never slept and their family was in shambles. Kharaq was probably the reason Josh had no past. A scream of rage welled from deep within Josh's chest.

Oh no, child. You need to focus. Think of this instead.

In an explosion of flames, a burning dragon swooped from the oracle's mind into Josh's. For a moment, revenge dissolved in dragon fire. The creature's scales were coal black with glowing red centers. Flames licked at their edges. On the dragon's back rode the most magnificent warrior Josh had ever seen.

Scars crisscrossed every inch of the warrior's face. There was a fury in it that caught Josh's breath. But the fury wasn't against Josh, it was against anything that might *hurt* Josh. It was protective, like ... Dad.

Prickles raced up Josh's arms and down his back. Lights danced on his skin. *Oh no. It's happening again.*

Greens and browns of the woods faded to frescoes on the walls of a collapsing cathedral. Overhead a hundred stained glass windows spanned the ceiling to form a single giant image. Sunlight lit a warrior on a flaming dragon. He scooped a child from a sea of monsters and snapping teeth. Tears ran down the warrior's face.

Don't fight what you see. The oracle's mind was like a steadying hand. *Let your memories come.*

Josh tried to go with it. His nostrils filled with the dry smell of wet soil. Despite the ferocity of the image, Josh loved it. *The way he scoops up that kid makes me feel safe, as if it were me. Who is he?*

He's the best person you can bring into any darkness. His name is Vastroh, lord of the seraphs.

Seraphs?

Flying, burning, serpents. Vastroh is the heart of the Nine living stars. Open your eyes and look at the sky.

Josh opened his eyes and searched the sky. There was only one star. *The red one?*

The oracle nodded. *There are nine, so close they look as one. They burn day and night. Some say they are not stars at all, but holes in the sky. They say magic and light pour through them into our world. Vastroh is the star in the center.*

Josh imagined himself in the stained glass window being scooped up from the jaws of wolves. It was as if gentle fingers pried his fists open and the anger leaked out.

Yes, son. Like that. Good.

Why is he crying?

I don't know. Perhaps compassion is the purest strength. Hold your breath and count to twenty.

The Oracle's grip tightened. "Pete put it around his neck." *Now, son, claim it. Think, 'it is mine.'*

It is mine.

Every shred of air was ripped from Josh's lungs. A thousand icy knives plunged him to the bottom of a frozen lake and held him there. Josh fought for freedom, but they were too strong, too sharp. Minutes ticked by. His lungs were on fire. Terror thundered in his chest. He was drowning.

Open your eyes. The voice was calm.

Josh floundered and struggled.

Open your eyes. Breathe. The oracle's voice thawed through Josh's icy panic.

Slowly Josh opened his eyes. Pete had just let go of the gem's chain. No time had passed at all.

The oracle beamed. "You did very well! A joining is intense for magic users. I think I wet myself during mine. Well ... I was a little younger than you." He laughed. "Give it some time and you'll crave it. There is nothing like a good joining."

Josh looked at him, confused.

"You must claim a magical gem to have access to its power. Wait until you try the fiery ones," the Oracle's eyes crinkled in a smile.

A blood-hungry howl echoed through the woods. Before the first cry ended, another joined, and another. In a moment the forest rang with their wails.

"The hunt," Dandelion gasped.

The oracle's smile disappeared. "Listen carefully. What you are wearing is very danger-ous. To control it, you must know magic. Even a little."

"What for?" Josh looked around at the neatly stacked stone piles scattered across the clearing. "I'm no match for Kharaq."

The oracle squeezed Josh's shoulder, his voice electric. "You do not need to be. I have a plan.

Pete's eyes darted to the trees. "We don't have time for a plan. We need to get to the city, and I need a sword."

"We don't have time *not* to plan," The oracle scowled. "Now listen. The creature you saw as Kharaq is not his true body. After we destroyed him, his three generals stole his bones and hid them. We were fools for not thinking of such a ploy and destroying them when we had the chance."

Realization dawned on Dandelion's face. "He's a ragabones. They want to bring him back ... because wizards can be restored using their bones."

Eyes alight, the oracle nodded, "Yes. So all we have to do is get his bones, burn them on this altar, and he will be destroyed forever."

"How?" The teenagers stared at the old man.

The oracle grinned and spoke quickly. "From the port at Ersha, it's only two days sailing to the dungeon where the bones are hidden. Dandelion will fly you in and out on her flying vine. You will sail back here and we'll destroy the bones. In a week Kharaq will be nothing but a bad memory, and you will all be heroes.

"There are a few challenges, but we can overcome them. The first is the location. My men traced the bones to ... The Throat."

"The throat?" Dandelion paled.

"Just listen," The oracle shushed her.

Red-faced, Dandelion exploded. "The throat and back? In a week? You make it sound like a walk through the palace gardens. What about the moon storms? What about Throat squalls and the gargoyles, not to mention insanity from breathing soul dust? What about reaver threads, devourers, and voids? What about—"

"Child, child." The oracle patted her on the arm. "I've thought about that already. You'll go with a team of warriors and beasts. You don't have to go all the way in. My sources say the bones are in the cathedral in the Western Spire. Fly in, grab the bones, fly out."

"What's The Throat?" Josh didn't like the look on Dandelion's face.

Dandelion practically frothed at the mouth. "Hell's Throat is a dungeon whose prison cells hang into the world of the dead. Prisoners can be held there for lifetimes without dying. Oh, and the few that have been brought back look like chewed cow cud. They scream and swipe at invisible creatures." She spun on the oracle "And what about armor? We can't use ordinary steel against underworld creatures."

"My Dad has a room with enchanted armor, and better warriors than yours." Pete stepped forward, chest out. "He'll help us."

"Dad's dead." The words burst out of Josh, almost a sob.

"Wha ...?" Pete stumbled backward, eyes flicking between his brother and the old man.

"Not dead," The oracle's voice was low. "Trapped. He was turned to stone with the rest of the city. Defeating Kharaq is the best chance to save your father."

Pete stood frozen, arms tight to his sides, fists clenched.

Josh's breath was quick and shallow. He imagined sneaking into the dungeon. They'd brush cobwebs aside and collect Kharaq's dried white bones from a stone crypt and burn them. All the stone piles in the city would be turned back to people. He could hear the crowds cheer. Dad and Pete shouted the loudest.

"Son," the oracle tried to get Pete's attention. "Son."

Pete stood stiff, vacant eyes locked somewhere in the past.

"Pete." Josh elbowed his brother.

"What." Pete didn't move, his voice as empty as his eyes.

Sadness filled the old man's face. "I'm so very sorry about your father ..."

"I can still get us into the armory," Pete spoke through gritted teeth. "There's enough enchanted armor and weapons to outfit us and your team. But it's my sword that takes the head off that rotten carcass of a wizard."

The oracle glanced at the other two and nodded. "Very well."

Wolf howls made the four of them jump.

"Quickly." The old man gestured them close. "You must flee the wolves. Go to the river where they cannot follow your scent. Return tomorrow when the sun is high." He gripped Josh's arm. "Before you go I must teach you a little magic. We'll use the most basic of spells: ice."

Thoughts poured into Josh's mind.

Magic is the deepest science. All matter is built of blocks, that are built of smaller blocks, that are built of even smaller blocks, and so on.

The Oracle's ideas came across clearly. Josh fumbled to form his own thoughts coherently enough to pass them back. *My mom wrote a story about that. She said the blocks are things like atoms, neutrons, and quarks. They keep getting smaller and smaller. Human will and emotion make up the smallest of blocks. Matter is built from things like love, faith, and fear — emotions that require action to become real. I didn't know it was true.*

Josh could feel the Oracle's approval.

Open your hands. You must change an element from one of its natural forms to another. See the sweat? Now, see it as ice. Will it to change.

Josh willed as hard as he could. Nothing happened.

Howls rang through the trees.

Dandelion paced and fidgeted. "Hurry it up or you'll be learning magic inside a wolf stomach."

Memories of the beast lunging for his throat filled Josh's mind. He tried to focus on magic, but his mouth was dry and his heart thundered in his ears.

The oracle's calm drifted in. *"You must control your fear. The gem will amplify whatever you give it. Fear can build powerful magic, but it will seize control.*

I'm trying. It's not working.

I'll do it with you. Do you feel what I'm feeling?

Yeah. I think I get it. Oh. Tingles and swirling lights raced up Josh's arms. "Ow!" Josh brushed hands on his pants. Tiny bits of ice fell away from his palms.

The oracle beamed. "Well done! Tonight, you must practice it a thousand times until you can do the spell by yourself."

"OK." Josh looked up at the wizard with his best attempt at a brave smile. "Is this going to help us?"

Pete threw his hands up. "Sure. Now we can make Kharaq catch a cold. Can't you teach him fire or lightning or something not so wimpy?" He looked toward the trees and muttered to himself. "Sissy magic. Give me a sword."

The old wizard winked at Josh. "Learning Ice is just the foundation. Tomorrow we will make your brother speechless. Now go!"

CHAPTER FOUR

ICE

Wide and fast-moving, the river stretched forever in either direction. Shrouded in mist, the far bank seemed miles away.

"Ice," Josh muttered over and over, staring at his hands.

"We're swimming to that." Dandelion pointed out to the middle of the river.

Jumbled sticks and logs jutted out of the water in a tangled mishmash. The huge messy pile split the current. Eddy lines trailed out behind in a great V.

"It's a Nadu nest. When the mist is gone, you can see a lot of them out there."

Howls grew louder.

Pete swallowed. "Swim to that? The current will wash us a half mile downstream."

The wolves were so close, Josh could hear barks and yips between the howls. When Dandelion said "swim," his stomach lurched. His breath drifted in a cloud of white vapor.

"Maybe you'd rather try your luck with the Shadow Pack." Dandelion tied her boots around her waist.

"Dandi!" A nasally voice squawked from the water's edge.

Five furry faces popped up between the reeds. They looked like giant sea otters, mocha brown with tawny faces, and great tufts of whiskers that stuck out in all directions.

"Who'r they?" One of them waddled toward Dandelion. It shook itself from head to tail and grinned at Josh and Pete with large fangs.

Was it a grin or a snarl? Both boys backed slowly away.

The creatures stood as tall as Dandelion, and had huge beaver tails and webs between clawed toes. The one closest had a white teardrop on its chest.

"Jraena? Oh, is it good to see you." Dandelion enveloped the creature in a bear hug, then shrieked as it spun and pulled her into the water.

Before either boy could react, the others leapt from the reeds and dragged them into the river.

They were a dozen yards out before the Nadu let Josh come to the surface. Josh gagged and coughed. Claws dug into his shoulder as the creature dragged him further from shore. The great tail beat against the water, leaving a glistening wake.

Josh's head spun. He was being dragged to some underwater lair to be eaten. Josh tore at its grip. He spun toward the Nadu, put his feet against the furry torso, and kicked with everything he had.

The creature let go, and with a quick flip, smashed its tail into the side of Josh's head.

The edges of Josh's vision blurred. Josh tried to keep the Nadu in view, but his arms were putty. That tail felt like a 2x4.

The Nadu was behind him again, gripping and pulling. "Kick me again and I'll knock your eyeballs out. By the way, you're welcome."

"For what?" Josh mumbled.

The Nadu pointed to the bank. The shoreline boiled with black fur, gleaming eyes, and yellow teeth. Hundreds of wolves swarmed the bank. They howled and barked. Some splashed partway into the water.

"If you have to kick something, how about helping swim?" the Nadu spoke between breaths.

"Oh. Sorry, uh, thanks," Josh spluttered and began to kick his feet.

Josh was the last one to arrive at the nest. What had looked like sticks from the shore were actually logs. Nadu nests were a lot bigger than he'd thought.

Huffing and blowing, the Nadu dragged themselves out of the river and draped over the timber.

"You guys are worse than the logs Dad makes us haul!" One of them laid back and laughed.

"And their heads are just as hard." Josh's Nadu pointed at him and told about how he'd tried to get away.

They giggled and chattered about who was fastest.

"What's going on here?" A deep voice growled above them.

Standing on the top of the pile was a Nadu twice the size of the others. He had a scar across one eye, a broken fang, and fur streaked with gray.

"We just saved Dandi and her friends from the Shadow Pack." Jraena flopped over on her stomach and pointed at the writhing riverbank.

Without a pause in her speech, she propped herself on one elbow and batted her eyelashes at Josh. "What's your name?"

"Uh." Josh glanced between her and the large Nadu.

"Uh," Jraena sighed and leaned back. "At least your name's easy to say. I'm Jraena. Those are my sisters, Omaeli, Rendea, Sreshelle, and Dyanina. Oh, and that's my dad. He's the Chief. Uh, are you married? I always wanted to marry a wizard." She sighed and flopped onto her back. "But, I don't know if I could be with anyone who doesn't swim well."

"Shush child. Do you ever stop talking?" The large Nadu walked on all fours down to the boys. "What do you know about all this?"

"Kharaq sent them after us." Pete stood and smoothed the water from his clothes. "We just need shelter until morn—"

"Kharaq?" The Chief hissed, turning his attention toward the bank.

Dandelion wrapped arms around herself. "He's back. And the trees think those two are the Wizard and the Warrior."

"I knew it! I knew you were a wizard." Jraena leaned over toward Josh. "I could tell by that thing around your neck. No one but a wizard has cool stuff like that. Right, Dandi?

She's an expert. Can I touch it? I tried wearing a necklace once, but it always tangled in my fur. What's it like having no fur?"

"Jraena!" The father clamped a paw around her muzzle. "Let them speak."

Jraena pushed his paw away and scowled at him. She shook herself from head to tail and sat down with a huff.

Josh glanced at Jraena and stuffed the gem inside his shirt. The cloth was freezing and stuck to his skin, but it wasn't half as cold as the gem.

Behind the chief, warm yellow light spilled from the entrance of the nest. Inside, there was probably a hot fire and warm food.

"Uh, what spells do you know?" The large Nadu turned back toward Josh. "Can you throw fire?"

Josh twisted his fingers. "My name is Josh, not 'Uh,' and no, I can't throw fire. I can't even make ice. I can't really do anything."

"Josh." Jraena sighed wistfully.

"Are you going to invite them in for dinner?" A large female Nadu appeared above the Chief with three fluffy baby Nadu clinging to its fur.

Before anyone could answer, her babies squealed with delight. "Dandi!" They swarmed down logs and jumped on Dandelion, almost knocking her into the water. Once she caught her balance, she hugged, scratched, and cooed.

"I get to sit by Josh! Mom, we dragged them across the whole river." Jraena stood and gestured animatedly toward the bank.

"Yeah Mom, you should have seen it," the other sisters chimed in. Soon the whole group talked at once.

"Girls." The Chief gestured for silence.

No one noticed.

"Girls. Please." He raised his voice.

The chatter just got louder.

The Chief opened his mouth and closed it. He put his face in his paws and shook his head. "Gods, how did I end up with *nine* of them?"

He turned to Pete. "Son, *are* you two the Wizard and the Warrior?"

"Dad." Jraena tapped on the Chief's elbow. He ignored her.

Pete stood tall, shoulders square. "It doesn't matter. The land is imperiled by a grievous evil, and I'm ready to fight."

Josh gave Pete a baffled look. Imperiled? What was wrong with him?

"Dad." Jraena tugged on her father's elbow.

The Chief ignored her, giving his full attention to Pete. "Tell me what happened."

"DAD!" Jraena practically shouted.

"Jraena, I'm talking!" Fangs bared, he spun toward her. "You need to wait your turn."

Jraena raised a smug eyebrow and pointed at the riverbank.

Wolves leapt into the water in clumps. They swam toward the nest but didn't make it halfway before washing past.

"They can't swim well enough to reach us. They'll wash downstream, over the Great Falls. And good riddance." Mom smiled from the top of the pile. Her tone didn't sound as confident as her words.

She made a grunting noise toward her babies. They climbed down from Dandelion and scrambled back up to her.

Jraena pointed upriver. Wolves ran upstream along the bank and then charged headlong into the water. Each group made it closer and closer to the nest before sweeping past.

"If they keep that up, they'll reach us before sundown." Pete's eyes were big. "Is there any way to get to the other bank?"

The Chief's gaze flicked upstream. "The current is too strong since the rain. *We* can swim that far, but not pulling you."

Brows furrowed, he climbed to the top of the nest. Glistening eyes stared into the mist. He finally shook his head and growled softly. "We must stand and fight!" He glanced toward Pete. "I have a knife for you. The rest will use long sticks to push them past."

He looked toward his daughters. "Omaeli, Jraena, each of you take a baby and swim with your mother to Xheja's nest. The rest of you each swim to one of the war captains. Tell them we need an army back here."

"Dad." One of the daughters, her voice squeaky, climbed toward him and grabbed him around the waist. "It's too far. There isn't enough time to make it there and back."

He kissed her on the top of the head. "We cannot leave the humans here to die. So you *must*."

With surprising speed, he grabbed his daughters and pulled them toward him until they were all bundled around in a giant bear hug. "You girls need to know"—his growly voice faltered—"that I'm the luckiest, proudest dad in the world. You are all the smartest and bravest and most beautiful creatures this river has ever seen. Now go!"

"No!" Eyes on fire, Josh stared at palms that glistened with ice. He looked up at the large Nadu. "We can't let you risk your family. *We* have to leave."

Pete gaped at his brother.

Josh gestured toward the nest. "Are there any extra sticks to make a raft? Pete and I can paddle for the other side."

The Chief shook his head. "You'll get washed over the falls before you even get close."

"*What* if we push them?" Jraena bounced up and down, eyes alight. "We could do it. They'd be safe on the other bank. Chazrack hate the wolves."

"Found your magic, have you, boy?" The Chief nodded toward Josh.

The Chief turned to the girls. "The dry ones we've gathered for the babies' room. We'll build it in the eddy behind the nest. Jraena you ..."

Halfway through the sentence, he spun with a snarl and leapt over the boys

At the nest's edge, yellow eyes bobbed just above the river's surface. Black fur matched the dark water. The wolf was huge.

Snatching a large stick, the Chief jabbed at the beast's head.

Josh could not believe the ferocity of the wolf. Snarling, it tore at the end of the stick. Even with its head pushed underwater, it wrenched this way and that, savaging as it drowned. Josh was afraid the Chief would get pulled in. At last, the wolf floated past. The end of the stick was shredded.

"You two keep them away while we build the raft." He handed his stick to Pete and grabbed another for Josh.

Josh swallowed loudly and glanced at Pete. They were smaller than the Chief. Even a little wolf might pull them in.

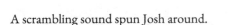

A scrambling sound spun Josh around.

"Come, quickly." The Chief's face peered over the top of the nest.

The brothers scrambled after him. Josh paused at the top of the pile and looked back.

Seeing that some of their number had made it to the nest, wolves poured into the river. Great lines swept toward them. The water churned white.

"Go, go." The Chief ushered them toward the raft.

Simply made, the raft was six or seven small logs and two crosspieces lashed together with twisted grass rope. With all three teenagers on board, water sloshed over the top, but the raft floated well enough to be pushed.

The Chief climbed back to the top of the nest and called to his kids. "*My* girls are the best swimmers on the river. You can do this!" The large Nadu's eyes flicked to the wolves. His voice faltered to a whisper. "They can do this."

Dandelion and both boys were barely on the raft before the sisters beat their broad tails against the water, and the raft lurched forward. All swimmers and passengers were silent. Each hardly dared to hope.

First a yip, then barks, and then the night erupted in howls of rage from a thousand throats. It rang up and down the river and off the faraway mountain cliffs.

The stream of black fur and yellow eyes stretched out a half mile. With a mixture of relief and terror, Josh saw that it now bent toward them and away from the nest.

Despite the power and speed of the Nadu, the wolves closed in. It was a race. If the girls could get the raft upstream, across the wolves' path, the wolves would never catch up. Yet, the wolves had the current in their favor.

All three teenagers held their breath. The Nadu sisters pounded relentlessly at the water. Wake churned behind them. Josh could hear them gasp for air and grunt with effort.

They reached the crossing point, directly downriver from the pack. Wolves were yards away.

"I think we're going to make it," Pete muttered.

Then a rope snapped.

Two branches rolled and one cross piece flailed outward. Dandelion lost her balance and splashed into the water. In an instant, she was a yard behind.

Two sisters swam back to get Dandelion. The others pushed the raft back together. Logs rolled and bobbed. Pete lost his balance and dropped the knife. Josh fell to all fours. No one could find the end of the rope.

Heart thudding against his ribs, Josh watched the boiling tide of savagery bear down on them. He glanced at the gem. It was powerful, right? But how could he use it? Josh could still see the fear on the oracle's face when he warned Josh about it. But what other choice did he have?

Josh's hands shook so badly, he could hardly grip the logs. He forced his mind on the shard, away from the wolf howls and the screams of his friends.

"Ice!"

Frozen knives shot through his chest. Blue lights danced across his skin, exploding outward from his hands. Vapor rolled out across the river. Water between the branches froze. Popping and cracking like dry twigs. And the raft became solid.

For a moment the girls gaped at Josh, and the raft spun lazily in the current. Then the first wolf reached them.

In an instant, their world was a biting, snarling, foaming frenzy. Yellow fangs sunk into the long stick Pete used to push at the wolf. Before he could react, the stick had broken and the wolf's front feet were on the raft. It lunged and snapped. Pete swung the stick like a baseball bat. Nothing phased the wolf.

Jraena was on the wolf's back, her fangs sunk into its neck. With a howl, the wolf spun on her and the two sank beneath the surface. Two sisters plunged after her. Red tinted the surface of the river.

Josh stood, but couldn't move his feet. The ice holding the raft together had not stopped growing. It covered his feet and ankles. "My fear," he gasped, clenching his fists. "Fear feeds the magic. Control the fear or the magic controls you."

"Josh, stop!" Ice had covered Pete's feet.

With pops and snaps, the ice grew faster and faster. Past their knees. Past their waists.

"Look, look. Nadu warriors are coming," Dandelion shouted from the water, pointing behind them.

Josh's lungs were heaving. "Faith." He clenched his teeth. "I have faith it will be OK. There is nothing to fear." The hammering in his chest disagreed. He squeezed his eyes shut and tried to ignore the snarls and cries. "Breathe."

That was when he heard the roar. *The waterfall!* The raft moved faster. It dipped and rose in the swells. He could taste the spray. His focus shattered.

"JOSH STOP!" Pete lifted hands above the growing ice. It had climbed over his chest. "It's making us top-heavy. We're tipping over!"

Dandelion screamed and pointed.

With each swell, the raft sagged further. Two sisters appeared out of the water and tried to level it out. They swam and pushed. It only leaned further. Wolves scrambled at the other side and howled in triumph.

Then they were upside down.

The cold water was a jolt of electric terror. Josh hadn't had time to catch a breath. Time stood still. A slow-motion world moved to the driving booms of his heartbeat. He watched with a strange clarity and detached calm. Above him, hundreds of black paws churned the water white.

With frightened faces, Dandelion and the Nadu swam underwater around him and Pete. They still tried to tip the raft back up.

Pete was already white as death. His hair swayed in the current. Bubbles dribbled from his nose and mouth. One hand was free from the ice. Josh grabbed it. His eyes locked with his brother's. *I'm sorry.* Did Pete understand?

Still, the ice grew. It climbed up over his nose and mouth. The shard burned deep blue and bathed the world around them in an eerie light.

More Nadu appeared. Through the ice, each seemed the size of a house. Giant tails and webbed claws pounded the water. They swam under the wolves. Were they going to fight? Would they be able to stop the raft?

Instead, they caught the sisters and pulled them away. The girls and Dandelion fought to stay, but they were dragged off, faces wrenched in horror.

Slowly, the raft turned in the current. Paws above them changed direction, churning wildly away. They had reached the falls.

Something squeezed Josh's hand. Pete stared at him. Was that forgiveness? As Josh slipped into the deepest, darkest, most terrifying night, one thing made it somehow bearable: he didn't have to go alone.

———◄◇►———

"It's a viewport spell." Kharaq stood near the Oracle, hands tracing a ragged circular window. It looked like glass with edges that dissolved into air. It stood half as tall as he was. Through it, the scene at the river unfolded.

"I *know* what a viewport spell is," the oracle spat. "Mine were clearer."

"Ah, but mine allows me to see through the eyes of my creatures. Even at your best, you never mastered that."

The oracle looked up at Kharaq. "Now, *there's* something I don't see every day, a man in a rotting demon suit. Your new look fits you."

Kharaq looked at the oracle's wooden arm. "Is it solid? I see your limbs are catching up to your head."

"Maybe. But I can still smell. Perhaps you could move downwind."

Kharaq snorted. "You'll burn nicely along with your tree friends."

The oracle barked a sarcastic laugh. "Like last time?"

"You were unusually lucky." Kharaq's fangs snapped at the old man. His lips slowly twisting in a condescending smile, he gestured toward the window. "It seems your little heroes aren't fairing so well."

The Oracle's eyes narrowed at Kharaq. "The trees say they are the Wizard and the Warrior."

Kharaq spat. "The trees? That Dream changes with the wind."

The oracle's spindly finger jabbed at Kharaq. "*That Dream* says your doom is upon you."

"It seems my doom is not the one you should be concerned with."

Only its tip above the horizon, the sun turned the river the color of rust. Bathed in an eerie red, they watched the huge block of ice reach the falls, stop, then slowly heave over, two motionless boys caught in its center. The falls seemed to stretch down forever. Twisting lazily as it fell, the block of ice shrank in the distance and finally disappeared into the thundering mist.

"Noooo!" Dandelion's scream rang through the window.

"Oh no, no." The Oracle's voice was thick. His eyes sank slowly to the forest floor. The woods were still as death.

"Yes," the dark voice rasped. "My wolves will gather the gem from their little corpses. And my goblins already march here. This forest needs a good burn, don't you think?"

CHAPTER FIVE

DEATH STONE

"Y ou're fired, you ... you eggplant nosed witch," a high-pitched man's voice shouted nearby.

Josh didn't open his eyes. He was awake at last. He breathed a sigh of relief. That was the worst, most realistic nightmare in his entire life — red-eyed wizards and wolves and ice and waterfalls. For the first time ever, being bored on a Saturday morning sounded amazing.

"Here? Here? Really? Out in the middle of nowhere?" The whiny voice drifted as if there was nothing around but wide-open space.

Josh squeezed his eyes tightly. He was in his bed. He visualized his electric guitar in the corner, his Bluetooth-retro-record player on the side table. There were still some waffles in the fridge for breakfast. Bright morning sunlight probably billowed in the chessboard curtains over his window — his open window — because the annoying man was going on and on right outside.

A croaky woman's voice whined back. It sounded something like, "I told you so."

"You're still fired," the man spat the words. "When we get there."

They stopped talking. Finally. It was so quiet. Josh listened as hard as he could. Mom's voice in the kitchen? Pete watching TV in the rec room? Even birds outside?

There was nothing.

And it was hot — really hot. And it stunk like farm animals. Wind muttered around his ears. Sweat trickled down his neck. Something poked in his back. Footsteps crunched nearby.

Josh's heart started that awful thudding.

"Are you awake?" A tiny voice floated to his ear.

Josh jolted up, eyes wide open. He wasn't in his bed; he was in a pile of straw on the floor of a small wooden cage. Dozens of other cages floated around and behind, roped together in a long messy train.

A girl half Josh's age walked beside Josh's cage, one hand on the bars, the other gliding through golden knee-high grass that stretched on three sides as far as he could see. In the other direction, sand dunes flowed to distant blue mountain peaks.

"I'm Jili. I brought you some food." She pulled a piece of stale bread from her ragged dress and grinned up at him.

"Huh?" Josh's head was spinning.

A squawk snapped Josh's gaze upward. With a whoosh, a magnificent bird Josh landed on Jili's shoulder. Feathers of silver, gold, and red foil shone in the desert sun, so bright Josh had to squint. Sunlight reflected from the bird, dancing in shining flecks on the grass and cages.

"This is Aura. He's a firebrand." Jili tilted her head toward the bird.

Aura twisted his head and fixed an eye on Josh. "You going to eat that?"

"Wha ... huh?" Josh followed the bird's gaze. A large beetle walked along one of the bars.

"Ugh." Josh flicked it away.

With a squawk, the bird swooped and caught the bug. "Thanks." It landed back on Jili's shoulder and crunched noisily on the beetle.

"Aura! Do you have to do that right by my ear?" She screwed her face in disgust.

"Why am I in here?" Josh rubbed his eyes. His head was full of cotton.

"We found you at the waterfall. You've been asleep a long time. I thought you might be hungry." Jili pushed the bread through the bars.

"Yes, yes. You were quite broken." Aura bobbed up and down.

Memories flooded back. Josh's breath caught in his throat. Freezing. Falling. Smashing. Pete laying beside him surrounded by broken pieces of ice. Their hands still gripped each other.

Josh ran hands over his chest and arms. His clothes were tattered, but he was unmarked. Where was Pete?

"Your brother is over there. He's fine." Aura lifted a foot over one wing and scratched his neck.

"My, uh." Josh looked behind him in the cage. Pete slept, covered in straw in one corner. Josh was sitting on Pete's hand. Pete had no bruises or cuts either.

"It was the death-stone around your neck. A bridge between death and life." Aura jumped in the air, flapped once, and landed again. "Quite a stone. Quite a stone. Looks delicious."

Josh's gaze hardened. "Why do you have us in a cage?"

"Oh. You're a slave now." Jili's smile disappeared. She pointed to the front of the cage-train. "To him!"

Josh followed her eyes. A fat man with a goatee led an iridescent snail on a short, frayed rope. The snail was the size of a small car, and pulled a gaudy gypsy wagon with no wheels. Ropes ran from the wagon to the cage-train. All of it floated three feet above the ground on a trail of acrid, yellowish smoke.

"I'm a slave too." Jili's lower lip trembled. She reached around the side of Josh's cage and pulled the door open. "But you don't have to stay in there. He leaves them unlocked so us kids can work for him. See?" She tossed a brown clod under the next cage.

Until just that moment, Josh hadn't really thought about the surrounding cages. Exotic creatures slept or paced in each. The one beside him housed a gelatinous orange blob. It sagged between the floorboards, dragging a tentacle on the ground. With a snort, the creature snatched the brown clod up to a globular mouth.

Jili wiped her eyes. "Wanna come say hi to the others? You're gonna help us all escape, right?"

Josh glanced at the wide open plain. "Why haven't you just walked away? At night or something? Why do you need me?"

"There's a pinfold." Jili sighed. "It's a spell like a giant bag."

"A what?" Josh looked at the grass and sky but couldn't see anything.

"It's right here." She took a few steps away from the cage and swiped her hand in the air. Oily streaks followed her fingertips. "We can't get out."

Aura wiped his beak back and forth on Jili's arm. "You must use the stone to escape."

Use the stone? Icy fingers gripped Josh's chest. His voice quaked. "Last time, I nearly killed everyone."

Aura's eyes bored holes into Josh. "Die if you do. Die if you don't. How many others will die if you do not try?"

***

"Your wolves were too slow to reach the bottom of the falls." Kharaq stooped on a dais at the end of a towering throne hall that could have held a thousand people. Pillars swept down either side of a wide center aisle, stretching up to vaulted, black veined crystal.

A dragon skull towered over Kharaq, dominating the dais. The fangs and lower jaw had been carved to form a throne.

With a snort, a midnight black wolf as tall as Kharaq's chest stepped from the shadows of the skull. Burn scars covered half the wolf's face and body. One eye gleamed completely white. "Allowing slavery was unwise. Now the slavers fill my woods like fleas hopping wherever they want."

Kharaq slumped into the throne. "How long until you find the gem?"

The wolf bit at something on its foreleg. "We have wings over every caravan and noses in every slave market. Wherever that slaver goes, we'll be waiting. In the meantime, your lords and governors have been summoned to Necrus City."

"Here?" The cloaked wizard flexed his claws, staring at the putrid skin on his hands. "I don't want them to see me like this. Where is Maggoth and the rest of those bumbling fools?"

The wolf pointed down the hall with his nose.

"Your Majesty." A skinny, slump-shouldered wizard with a long face and droopy eyes shuffled toward them. A clump of black-robed sorcerers scuttled behind him.

"Bring my bones. I want my own flesh and form again." Kharaq gave them a dismissing wave.

The droopy eyed sorcerer paused and bowed low. "The Three, uh, your wizard generals, were the only ones who knew the hiding place of your bones, uh, to keep the secret from your enemies."

Kharaq leaned forward. "And?"

The man rubbed hands together. "They never returned."

Kharaq squeezed a giant fang that served as his armrest. His knuckles creaked and popped. He hissed at the cowering group, "How long have the generals been gone? You did not think to search for them?"

An overweight sorcerer palmed a gold medallion hanging around his neck and, with a mollifying smile, slid it under his robe. "Well, Mighty Emperor, due to the nature of your, uh, condition, we decided ..."

"The nature of my condition?" Kharaq jerked upward, and with a loud crack, disappeared in an explosion of oily smoke. Tendrils of night streaked across the dais and down the cavernous hall. In the time it took the sorcerer to gasp, Kharaq stood before him.

With a snarl, Kharaq grabbed the gold medallion and tore it from the sorcerer's his neck. He stared at the medallion for a moment, and raised his eyes slowly to meet the sorcerer's. "It appears *your* condition has markedly improved since I've been gone."

The man swallowed several times and stepped backward.

Kharaq closed the distance between them, his voice rising. "While I rotted in the underworld, you loot my palace?"

The man looked around at the other sorcerers, his eyes bulging.

"Loot hell." Kharaq held an open palm in front of the man's chest.

Up and down the hall, shadows leapt from corners and recesses, sharp as arrows, shooting into the man. Mouth wide in a soundless scream, he fell slowly backward, his skin fading to char, and then black, and then ashes, until the sorcerer disappeared in a plume of smoke.

An acrid smell filled the hall as his tattered robes floated to the floor. The other sorcerers lurched away from the pile. One covered his mouth and retched. The man with the droopy eyes frantically wiped the soot from his face.

"Now find my bones!" Kharaq roared. "You have FIVE DAYS ... before I feed you to the mantor!"

The wizards bowed and backed down the hall, tripping on their robes and stumbling over each other. One turned, and hitching up his cloak, fled for the door.

"Maggoth," Kharaq growled after them.

The droopy eyed sorcerer stopped and stiffly turned.

"Have someone clean that up." Kharaq waved at the smoking pile.

Maggoth nodded and disappeared out the door after the others.

Kharaq turned and strode back to the dais. He glanced up at the wolf and exhaled. "You didn't tell me The Three never returned ... So it's just you and me again."

The wolf wandered to the throne. "I had spies on their ship out of Mauda. It was chartered for the Boiling Seas—"

"The Throat?" Kharaq froze.

The wolf nodded.

"You told this to the sorcerers?"

"I have cockroaches more trustworthy. But if there is news, I'll know. I have albatrosses over the seas and rats under the docks." The wolf stretched and yawned. "Five days? Save yourself the time and give your wizards to the mantor now. It's expensive to feed. We're running out of convicts and dissenters."

"I hear we have plenty of wolves," Kharaq looked the wolf over and snorted. "That's a lot of gray. Should I call for a bowl of warm milk?"

The wolf laughed. "That demon cadaver you're wearing smells like it's been dead a while." It trotted down the dais stair and stopped to look over its shoulder. "It's an improvement."

"Gah," Kharaq spat after him. "Send in my goblin generals. I have a forest fire to start and an old score to settle."

***

Josh, Pete, and Jili walked together beside their cages. Josh ran fingers through the long golden grass.

"Where is Zheek taking us?" Josh gestured at the fat slaver with his chin.

"There." Jili pointed across sand dunes to the distant mountains. "Necrus City has the biggest slave market in Alaetia."

Muscles around Pete's jaw clenched. "Slavery is outlawed."

Jili's face darkened. "Not anymore. You forget that the Necrus are in charge now. Anyway, we were late last season, and no one bought us. I got lucky."

Josh swallowed the lump in his throat. "Zheek is selling us as slaves? I thought we just took care of his animals."

Jili shook her head. Her voice dropped to a whisper. "You can't imagine what they'll do to us."

She plucked a long piece of grass and stripped off the spikelets. "That's why Josh has to learn from Aura."

"I know," Josh mumbled. He looked around for the glittering bird. Aura had been trying to teach him fire magic, but Josh couldn't do it. Memories of ice and wolves made his hands shake and his voice crack. Josh couldn't even make warmth.

They had an escape plan. Pete had pulled bars from an unused cage at the back and sharpened the ends, one for each of the other five kids. Jili collected dried meat and vegetables for food. A couple of the older kids stole extra water. Josh hoped they had enough for the trip back to the oracle. All they needed was for Josh to learn fire.

"Poof," Jili waved her hands toward the gypsy wagon at the front of the train. "You set the storm bees on fire, we open the animal cages, and in the chaos we all escape."

Josh watched what looked like a tiny rainstorm swirl around the gaudy wagon. But they weren't raindrops, they were actually a million glassy hornet-things.

Pete kicked at a rock beneath the grass. "Why can't we just get out the way Zheek does?"

"Oh no." Jili's eyes got big. "Zheek is the only one who can get past — except maybe Aura. Last year, a kid tried to sneak through. He didn't get three steps before the bees got him. Just a couple stings, and he screamed and thrashed nonstop for a week. We had to tie him into a cage. A couple more stings would have killed him."

"Aura can get past. Can he set them on fire?" Hope flickered in Josh's chest.

Jili scratched at something in her hair. "Aura eats the bees if they get too close. But he won't kill things just to kill them."

Josh looked around at the fifty or so exotic caged creatures in the slave train. "Why isn't he in a cage, and why doesn't he just leave?"

Jili shrugged again. "Aura flew in one day and threatened to burn Zheek up if he hit us anymore. It's a lot better with Aura here. It was his idea to leave the cages open so we can take care of the animals."

"I wish Aura would fly out and chase that away." She gestured overhead. A crow floated against the blue. "They serve Viscero, a giant burned wolf who leads Kharaq's spy network and—"

"Everyone knows who Viscero is, especially Josh," Pete interrupted, glancing at the scars on Josh's neck.

Jili scowled at Pete. "Anyway, you'll see a lot more crows as we get closer to the city."

"Can't they see us?" Josh tried to pull his collar up over the scars.

"The pinfold spell, remember? Anyone who looks will only see Zheek."

"Then why are the crows following us?"

"I've been trying to figure that out."

The sick feeling in Josh's stomach seeped down into his knees, making them want to fold. His eyes drifted out across the desert. Smoke-like mountains wafted on the horizon. Josh thought about the mountains on the globe in Mom's office. Gargan, city of the giants, was at the top. Necrus City, the source of his nightmares, was nestled somewhere at the base.

Was there enough time to learn fire before they arrived? Josh twisted his fingers. There had to be. He imagined finding Kharaq's bones and blasting them with flames from his fingertips. Pete would gape in amazement. Dad and Mom would cheer. It was almost enough to make him smile. Almost. "Why are we going this way? Wouldn't it be shorter to just go straight across the desert?"

"Short, yes." Aura landed on Jili's shoulder with a squawk.

"Hi Aura," she scratched his neck and giggled while he crooned.

"Your journey would be very short." Without moving his body away from the scratching, Aura rolled his eyes toward Josh.

Jili's face darkened. "Sand Wraiths. They live in the desert between us and the mountains. We wouldn't make it a hundred feet."

Pete picked up a stone and threw it toward the sand. "Dad fought them once. They make sand into giant monsters and soldiers and ..."

"And feed on human souls," Jili's voice was shrill

Glaring at her, Pete continued. "Every nation has been conquered at one time or other — even the giants, but never the Sand Wraiths. Entire armies have been swallowed by the desert. No one dares cross the dunes."

"There are legends of treasure. Caves of it they've collected from their conquests." Jili's eyes gleamed.

"Yes, very dangerous unless you can fly." The bird shifted so that Jili could scratch the other side.

Pete narrowed his eyes toward Aura. "Why are you in here?"

"Yeah, why do you stay with Zheek?" Josh scratched Aura. The bird croaked with pleasure.

"He won't talk about it. I've asked him a million times." Jili itched under his wing.

Aura shook himself from head to tail, fluffing his feathers up twice his normal size. A cloud of embers floated from the bird.

"Ow. Aura, those are hot." Jili brushed them off her neck and arm.

"Awk, sorry." Aura nibbled at her ear and then turned to Josh. "Time it is for another lesson."

"OK." Josh rubbed his temples. His head still hurt from the last one.

Aura hopped to Josh's shoulder and turned to Jili. "No, not this time. Josh needs to concentrate. You can watch another time."

Jili gasped. "Wow, can you read my mind? How did you know I was going to ask that?"

"Because you ask that every time," Josh sighed and turned toward the back of the caravan.

***

The scenery never changed. On one side, a hot breeze rippled the long grass. On the other, dunes crouched and watched the travelers, a cat stalking a bird. Minutes dragged like days. Days dragged like years. Slavery was beginning to sound preferable to dying of heat and boredom.

Every couple of hours, Aura insisted on teaching Josh fire magic. "Imagine a flame burning in your head. Picture it spreading until all your feathers are on fire. Feel the heat soak in until you are fire." Of course, Aura would choose fire. Everything was about fire for that bird.

Late afternoons were Josh's only saving grace. The sky over the mountains exploded with color, an Aurora Borealis of gold and scarlet. Aura said it only happened every few decades. Ever since it began, something was wrong with the bird.

"We firebrands mate for life."

Josh turned toward Aura. His feathers seemed tarnished and dull.

"That's my home." Aura looked toward the burning sky. His wings drooped. "The Ember World. You can reach it when its edges touch ours."

Josh had never seen Aura like this. He didn't know what to say, so he just listened.

"I said some terrible things to my Shaska, my mate. She flew down here. To get away from me. Somehow, they caught her. " Aura made a choking sound. "Hags use firebrand feathers for charms. They use our bones for their potions."

Aura wheezed with each breath. Pain poured from the croaky voice. Josh knew the sound of a shattered heart all too well — every time he thought about Dad. He looked away from his struggling friend.

They watched the sky churn and seethe. A gentle breeze ghosted across Josh's skin and ruffled his hair. It smelled like dust and hay.

Aura fluttered to Josh's shoulder, his voice almost a whisper. "I found the hags and their village. I found what was left of ... her."

A boulder sat in the middle of Josh's chest. He glanced at Aura. Ash gray feathers quivered.

"I screamed until my throat would make no more sound. I blazed through that village with every ounce of fire in me." Aura's chest heaved. "I burned them, and their houses, and markets, and even their fields."

"Well, uh, they won't kill any other innocent creatures." Josh cleared his throat.

"I went too far. I caught the hags and burned them slowly for days. I wanted them to suffer the way they made my Shaska suffer. But bitterness is a pit that mountains of revenge or even justice cannot fill." Aura closed his eyes and rested his beak on Josh's shoulder. "I found out that she had an egg inside her."

"You have a kid — uh, kid bird?"

Aura shook his head. "They had already sold it. That person sold it again. Firebrand eggs are very beautiful."

"Did you — were you able to get it back?"

Aura slumped. "I followed it for centuries. Through many hands. In and out of collections. Even a museum."

Aura lifted his head. His eyes glowed red. "But I did finally find it"—his voice grew louder and more piercing—"almost three hundred years later!"

"HIM!" Aura's beak pointed at Zheek; the bird screeched so loudly half the caged animals jolted awake.

Josh winced and covered his ear. The slave train echoed with yelps and howls. Above it all rang Aura's shriek. "That fat, filth panderer wears it around his neck."

Aura shone like the center of a furnace. Smoke poured from his feathers.

"Ow." Josh pried at Aura's feet. "Your feet are really hot."

Aura ignored him. "He wears my child as jewelry!"

"Can't you take it?" Josh tried to blow on Aura's feet.

"He has a spell on the egg and necklace. It cannot be removed by anyone but him." The bird turned toward Josh. His eyes narrowed.

Josh's hand went to the necklace. Hadn't the oracle said the same thing about his gem?

"Yes," the bird fluttered to the top of a nearby cage. "Your necklace has the same spell. It's called a god spell."

"A god spell?" Josh rubbed his shoulder where Aura's feet had been.

"The child wants to learn?" Aura chuckled and bobbed. "In what place are you a god?"

Josh shrugged. As usual, he had no idea what the bird was talking about. His head still swam with images of Aura as a ball of fire exploding through a bunch of filthy huts. He wished he could do that to Zheek and this floating prison.

"Here." Aura fluttered back to Josh's shoulder and pecked at the side of his head.

"OW!" Josh rubbed his temple.

"Here, you are god. Here you make the rules, make your own facts. Whether or not they are true."

Josh kept his hand on the side of his head in case Aura pecked again. He still didn't know what Aura was talking about, but he'd learned if he kept quiet long enough, Aura would explain.

"Your fear? Your bitterness? I tell you it is not real. But you are god, so you make it real. It becomes your cage. It prevents you from using your magic. Only you can choose to be free and live as you were born to."

Josh swallowed. Mom said the same kinds of things about fear. How you act is always, always your choice. No matter what anyone says or does to you. But that's a lot easier said than done.

Josh watched Zheek waddle at the front of the train. The egg glittered on his chest. "Why don't you just burn this whole thing down?"

Aura's shimmering wings drooped. "Maybe I'm an old fool," He sighed. "After burning the witches, I made a promise to kill no more. I used to watch the slaver from the sky. But the way he treated the children ... In here, I can protect them from him."

Aura flapped to a nearby cage and fluffed his feathers. "One day, something will make him take his necklace off, and I will rescue my child. Until then, I watch and wait. Now, human, back to your lesson. Hold your hands a few inches apart. Feel the energy between them? Concentrate."

***

That night, they reached the road. Camp was set at the edge where golden grass dissolved to hard packed dirt.

For the first time in their journey, Josh saw other people. Travelers bunched in groups and clumps at the roadside.

Darkness fell and tiny campfires popped up, lines of flickering yellow stars stretching down the road.

Josh climbed into the cage beside Pete. "It's nice to have other people."

Pete nodded and rolled to face the other direction. Gradually, his breathing slipped into the quiet, measured melody of sleep.

Around them, indistinct murmurs of conversations floated in the warm night air. Some groups even laughed and sang. It felt safer having them nearby. Still, it took a long time for Josh to fall asleep. When he finally did, his dreams were full of shouts and screams as giant winged beasts descended on the travelers.

***

Aura woke Josh at first light. Josh slept with an arm over his head to avoid Aura's wake-up pecks. That bird was so annoying.

"Not good. Not good. Look what came last night," Aura's whisper was tense.

Josh rubbed his eyes and squinted. His heart stopped. In the stubble behind them was a new camp. Around its fading fire sat three huge demon-like creatures.

Each beast must have been eight feet tall and was muscled like a thunderhead. Charcoal gray skin overlapped in thick plates. Dual corkscrew Kudu horns jutted from their foreheads.

One of the beasts focused savage eyes on Josh and lazily stretched. Huge bat wings unfurled from its back that could have covered the wagon. The creature yawned, flashing large white fangs.

Those creatures were obviously killing machines. Had Kharaq found them? Chills ran up Josh's spine. "Are ... are you sure they can't see us?"

"No, they can't, but keep talking and they will hear you."

Josh's voice dropped to a whisper. "Do they know we're here? They've come to kill us, haven't they?"

Pete jolted upright, his voice an anxious whisper. "What?"

Josh pointed to the creatures.

Pete let out a long, slow breath.

"Do you know what they are?" Josh stared at his brother.

Pete shook his head. "But I've seen them in battle. Those claws will rip through steel plate like wet cardboard. If it wasn't for our wizards ..." Pete glanced at Aura.

The bird's feathers had lost their luster. He turned to Josh. "Time to practice, child. Perhaps today is the day you grasp the magic. Perhaps before it's too late."

The back of the caravan felt exposed. Concentration was impossible. Josh kept glancing at the winged beasts. When the caravan began to move, the beasts lumbered behind them. When were they going to attack? What were they waiting for? "Are you sure they can't see us?"

"Shut them out of your mind." Aura fluffed. "Feel the burn. Open your beak — uh — mouth. Imagine breathing fire."

Aura was merciless. He had Josh hop on one foot, hang half out of a cage with his head upside down, and even try to catch a little fire-breathing dragon creature in one of the cages.

By the time Zheek hollered for lunch, Josh was dirty, sweaty, and a little seasick. He rubbed scalded fingers. "Can we take a break ..."

Before Josh could finish, dirt exploded around him. A dark shape burst from the road and grabbed him.

The force of the attack knocked Josh sideways against a cage. Rough wooden bars scraped his skin. Aura's screech rang in his ears, but there was no escaping those beasts. Kharaq had won.

CHAPTER SIX

SLAVE MARKET

A ura was in the air. Exploding in a ball of fire, he streaked toward the fight.

Josh's attacker squeezed so tightly he couldn't breathe. The mess of autumn-gold hair and leather buried its face in Josh's neck. "You're alive!"

"Dandelion?" Josh sputtered.

Aura banked at the last minute and landed on a cage. Flames licked where his feet touched the wood. Smoke billowed around him.

"Dandelion? Is that really you?" Josh's voice was muffled in her hair. He thought he would laugh and cry at the same time. He didn't think he'd ever been so glad to see anyone. She smelled like life, like trees and cool fresh earth.

Dandelion didn't say anything, just squeezed.

"Your knives are poking me." Josh squirmed. "Why did you come? I mean, I'm really glad."

She stepped back and held his gaze for a moment. "When my brother needed help, I wasn't ..." she swallowed, looking away and straightening her hair. "I want Kharaq dead as much as you. And you need help getting those bones."

Josh glanced at his brother. Why couldn't he have had a sister instead of Pete? "How did you *find* us?"

Before she could answer, Aura squawked. "And just *who* are you?"

Dandelion turned toward Aura. "The firebrand! Wow, I've always wanted to see one." She turned toward Josh. "Can I touch him?" She turned back toward Aura. "I mean, can I touch you? I mean, my name is Dandelion, and it's nice to meet you. You are the most beautiful thing I have ever seen."

"Well ..." Aura puffed his feathers to twice his normal size. Flecks of mirrored sunlight danced around the friends. Embers drifted in the breeze.

Josh rolled his eyes and scratched behind Aura's ear. "He likes it here."

"And probably here." Dandelion itched under a wing.

Aura lifted the wing and crooned.

"Sorry about the scare. Hiding in the dirt got me into the pinfold — under the snail. Ugh." She wrinkled her nose.

"Dandelion helped us escape the shadow pack. She was with us when we ... we ..." Josh shuddered, remembering the ice.

"Dandelion?" Pete's gasp rang from several cages away. He ran a couple steps, then quickly switched into a nonchalant walk. By the time he reached the group, he had hands in his pockets and looked as if he was heading into math class. "Nice of you to stop by." He grinned.

Dandelion grinned back, then with a furtive glance toward Zheek at the front of the train, lowered her voice, "We have to get you guys out of here. Kharaq's wolves saw you get taken by that slaver. Kharaq's been exterminating caravans all over the plain. It's only a matter of time until he finds you."

Josh swallowed loudly and gestured behind them. "I think it's too late."

She looked behind them at the demon creatures and smiled. "What, the Chazrack? They hate Kharaq more than you do."

"How *did* you find us?" Aura fixed her with a suspicious eye.

"You! At night *you* shine through this pinfold like a lone star in a midnight sky. I could see you for miles."

Aura gulped. "Me? Kharaq will find us because of *me*?"

"Cheap magic pinfolds like this one are thinner on the top and bottom. But he won't see you unless he can fly."

"Then how did *you* see us?"

Dandelion burst into a big grin and pointed at the winged creatures. "How do you think I got here so fast? You guys were gone by the time I got to the bottom of the falls. The sparrows talked about a shiny bird, and I figured out the rest."

"You speak bird?" Josh gaped at her.

Dandelion beamed. "Sure. Crow, a few finch dialects, and some other songbirds. Birds are the best place to get gossip. They're everywhere and they never stop talking." She glanced at Aura and sucked in her lips. "Except maybe firebrands?"

Josh laughed. "Definitely firebrands."

"Anyway, we've hunted and questioned a lot of crows over the last few days. They saw Aura's glow, but none knew you were with him. There were a few times I thought I'd found you too late." She shuddered. "Kharaq feeds people to this giant insect-thing he rides called a mantor. People don't die, they slowly digest. I hope I never have to see anything like that again."

"We have a crow following us too." Josh looked up.

Dandelion smirked. "Three, actually — as well as a few bats at night."

Pete glanced up at an empty sky. "Where are they?"

"Digesting." Dandelion grinned and gestured to the Chazrack.

Pete blew out a long breath. "A missing sentry is a dead giveaway. Kharaq will know *for sure* this is the right caravan."

Dandelion blanched. "I didn't think of that. We need to leave right away!"

"What's your plan?" Aura bobbed his head.

Dandelion paled even further. "I ... I had one, but I didn't know about those." She gestured to the storm bees at the front of the caravan.

"Well." Josh fidgeted. "We have a plan for them, but I need to learn fire."

Terror and frustration rose in his throat. They were running out of time, and he was no closer to fire than on day one. He couldn't even come up with an alternative strategy like he would in chess, because he couldn't remember anything about the land. How could he make a make a strategy if he didn't remember the rules? He gritted his teeth. STOP focusing on the problems. What *did* he know?

Josh squinted at Dandelion and gestured to the Chazrack behind the caravan. "That was really smart thinking to bring three of them. One for each of us, right?"

Dandelion nodded.

"Too bad they don't eat bees." Pete leaned on his sharpened stick and grinned.

A thin trail of smoke drifted from the cage bar beneath Aura's feet. Josh followed it with his eyes. Aura had gotten pretty hot when Dandelion jumped out of the dirt. Smoke ... bees.

"I've got it!" Josh grabbed Dandelion's arm and gestured to the beasts. "Will the bee stingers get through their skin?"

Dandelion shook her head.

Josh couldn't help but grin. "We'd already planned to set the animals loose and escape in the confusion. Bee keepers use smoke to keep from getting stung, right?"

Pete's eyebrows went up.

Josh pointed to the smoke at Aura's feet. "Once the animals are out, Aura sets the cages on fire. When Zheek opens the pinfold to get in, the Chazrack attack him. We get out in the confusion and even if we get stung, your friends can still fly us away."

Dandelion clapped her hands. "It's perfect!"

"Can they carry two people — if they're small?"

Everyone jumped. Jili had walked up to the group unnoticed.

"I don't wanna be a slave." Dirt on Jili's face had dried in streaks from tears. "Please don't leave us."

Dandelion's jaw dropped. "There are other people in here?"

Josh's face fell. "There are five other kids."

"It's too many to fly." Dandelion ran fingers through her hair.

"We could give them to one of the other caravans." Pete pointed over his shoulder with a thumb.

Dandelion turned scathing eyes toward him.

"What." He shrugged. "The family across the road already has, like, eight kids."

Dandelion didn't soften her stare. "And how do we get them out? At their size, even a couple stings could kill them."

The discussion of how to escape began again with the added complication of the kids. Every few minutes, Dandelion pointed out that the mountains were too close. If they didn't do something soon, it would be too late. That only flustered everyone and made it harder.

Josh kept looking up. The sky felt like an open oven. Scorching sunlight melted every shadow. Instead of one crow, there were dozens, with more arriving over every caravan.

He wiped the sweat from his face and glanced behind him. The hair on his neck stood. The Chazrack were gone. Three black shapes shrank into the distant sky.

"They flew away! Why'd they fly away?" Josh's voice trembled. Just when freedom was in their grasp, it was gone. "Is that why?" Josh pointed at the roadside.

It was the smell that first caught his attention — like rotting leaves and old clothes. Blackened and leathery clumps of teeth and hair hung on poles. Dried and cracked in the sun, they stood in regular intervals along the road. Josh had no idea what kind of creatures they had been when alive. Even dead, they gave him chills.

"The Kings' highway," Dandelion's voice sounded squeaky.

Aura shook his head. "Those remains are conquered kings. Every kind of beast and human hangs along this road."

"Sounds like something Kharaq would do." Pete grimaced.

Dandelion nodded, face tight. "He hung them there when he took over last time — reminders to anyone who might rebel. Now he's back, all the Lords come groveling."

Pete's eyes swept the plain, stopping on the jagged black turrets of Necrus City. Above the walls, white tipped spires pierced the sky. "That's why the Chazrack flew away, isn't it? We're too close to the city."

Dandelion wrung her hands. "I didn't find you soon enough."

Doom settled around them like the bitter, reddish black dust from the road. The King's Highway was a gangrenous wound slashed across the grassy plain.

No one spoke while they walked. Carrion colored grit ground its way into their clothes, shoes, and hair. They trudged with chapped lips and throats too parched to swallow.

Desert sand moved in face-like in drifts against the edge of the highway. Josh wasn't sure which side of the road was worse, grotesque kings gaping from one side, or dunes, whispering and shifting on the other.

Voices from the other caravans quieted. With quick steps and nervous glances at the sand, clumps of travelers scurried toward or away from the City.

The pitted, black stone of the city walls loomed overhead. Gate posts carved as gargoyles stood three stories high, their contorted faces snarled down at the passing crowds.

An image made of twisted black-iron covered the gnarled gates, a shattered shield with snakes winding through the cracks and around its edges. The same symbol Kharaq had around his neck in the cave.

Josh clutched at the sick churning in his gut. For the first time, the memories had a name and a place. He pictured the globe in Mom's office, the mountain range with the black gem she'd said was Necrus City. Her words from that night echoed in his ears.

"What's a blinder?" Josh turned to Dandelion.

Pete's eyebrows went up.

"A what?" Dandelion turned toward Josh.

"My mom said something about breaking a blinder."

"Well ..." Dandelion pursed her lips. "A blinder *spell* makes people see only certain things. If the person is told about the hidden things, the spell is usually broken, but—"

"Let's talk about something else—" Pete's voice was louder than it needed to be.

"It can it make people forget as well, can't it?" Josh talked over his brother.

"I don't think—" There was an edge to Pete's tone.

Josh spun toward him. "I didn't ask you. Mom remembers this place. You remember this place. So should I."

Dandelion bit her lip, eyes flicking between the brothers.

Pete's jaw muscles bunched. "The blinder was to keep you alive."

Dandelion's eyes bugged out.

"I can't remember because of something Mom did?" The last two years had been hell. How could she? A thousand thoughts stampeded through Josh's mind, but the only word that came out was, "why?"

Pete let out a long breath. "You're magic. That makes your body a valuable commodity in a world with no magic. Every time you remember, we might as well put a giant neon sign on the house that says, 'Nadris, come and get me.'"

Dandelion scratched her head. "Nadris ..."

"Yep." A grim look shadowed Pete's face. "The Necrus empress who tried to defeat the Modus and was exiled to hell."

"That was thousands of years ..." Dandelion's brows furrowed.

Pete nodded. "She can move her soul into another person's body — if they're the right age."

"That's not possible. How'd she get out of the underworld?"

Pete shrugged. "How should I know? All I know is that she rules the Necrus in Cavaris. Mom's the only reason she hasn't taken over that entire world."

A wide eyed Dandelion looked back and forth between the brothers. "Who *are* you, and who is your mom?"

"Yeah. Who?" Josh squeaked.

"Look, look!" Jili wailed.

Just down the wide cobblestoned boulevard, the buildings opened into a wide plaza. Flags of blue and fiery orange fluttered over rooftops.

"The slave market." Dandelion gripped Pete's arm. "Tell us about your mom later. Right now, we need an escape plan. I have an idea. Zheek has to open our pinfold to sell you guys, right? Aura can distract Zheek, and we make a run for it."

Jili kicked at a stone on the road. "He chains us up when we reach the market square."

Dandelion tousled Jili's hair. "I can pick locks. I'll hide while they lock you up. While Zheek haggles with the slave traders, we'll escape in the crowd. With a little luck, we'll be gone before anyone notices."

Jili's voice was shrill. "It won't work. The bees will find us in the crowd. We don't need luck, we need magic."

Aura bobbed on Josh's shoulder. "Magic. Yes! There is still time to learn."

Jili's eyes brightened a little.

Josh shook his head. "What about Dandelion's idea? My mind is just a big muddle."

The bird shushed him. "Anything worth doing is worth doing badly first. The best nests are made of throw away things. I once found the sleeve of an old sweater ... Never mind." The bird's feet were hot again. "Magic is everywhere around you. Feel it. The pinfold spell hides us and moves people around us. Watch them."

It *was* kind of amazing. People walked right through the caravan. They weaved around cages and didn't seem to notice they hadn't walked in a straight line.

Aura's whisper tickled. "Now, try again. Concentrate."

Sunlight glinted off Aura's feathers, leaving little white dots in Josh's vision. He tried to focus on the light, feel the heat, but his eyes flicked to the crowd. Midnight black wolves drifted between visitors. Hawk eyed archers in chain mail strutted on the rooftops. Kharaq's fingerprints were everywhere.

Murmurs washed through the crowd. Something on the other side of the plaza moved toward the teenagers. People and creatures pressed backward to give it space.

Aura breathed a low hiss. "Don't move."

The disturbance was an enormous black wolf. Burn scars disfigured half its face and body. One sightless eye gleamed white. The gray peppered muzzle stood as tall as Josh. Nose to the air, the wolf sniffed and growled. Each sniff brought it closer.

Jili's chest heaved, a soft whimper escaping with each breath.

The wolf's ears snapped in their direction. In two bounds, it was beside them.

White faced, Dandelion grabbed Jili, wrapping arms around the girl and pressing the little face into her chest. Josh held his breath.

The wolf stepped between Dandelion and Josh, hackles high and ears quivering. The gray peppered muzzle was the same height as Josh's face. It smelled like blood. Breath shifted Josh's hair. Sweat ran down his back.

Josh's eyes darted to the slave train. While they stood still, the last cages floated slowly past. Nausea spasmed Josh's stomach; the end of the pinfold! At any second, he and the others would be pulled forward, right into the wolf.

The crowd around Josh was silent. Every eye followed the hunt. Gray lips lifted above the wolf's yellowed fangs. A growl rumbled in its throat.

Josh's head swam. His lungs were about to explode. Aura's talons dug into Josh's shoulder. The pinfold felt like spiderwebs around Josh's legs and torso, dragging him forward. Josh lifted on his tiptoes, straining backward to keep from losing his balance.

Until he couldn't.

Just as Josh stepped, the wolf wheeled and loped away. Josh stumbled forward, grabbing a cage and clinging to it as he heaved breath after breath.

Aura flapped his wings to keep his balance. "Whew," he whistled. "That was close."

"Who *was* that?" Josh couldn't stop his knees from shaking.

Dandelion wiped sweat from her face with her forearm. "Viscero, head of Kharaq's death squad and lord of the shadow beasts."

Jili hyperventilated. "He'll be back. He'll be back. We have to escape before ... Oh no."

Josh followed her gaze. They had arrived.

◄●►

"Is that where we're getting sold?" Josh's voice was tight.

He knew the answer even before he asked. Dandelion gripped his arm with white knuckles.

Stone buildings towered around an immense cobblestone plaza. It would have taken Josh ten minutes to walk from one end to the other.

Shouts rang from a huge wooden stage that jutted into the square from a sea of brightly colored booths and awnings. Glaring down at the crowd, a bearded man paced the platform. Purple and yellow silk swished around curved toed slippers. "Pure Dryad! Fresh from the northern forest. I haven't seen one like this in ten years. Don't miss your chance."

He dabbed sweat from his forehead and pulled a wispy woman to the front of the stage. Dressed in subtle greens and browns, with dark hair to her waist, she wilted under the crowd's scrutiny.

Smaller stages clustered around the main one. Some of their slaves idly watched the crowds, shoulders square, while others clutched robes around themselves and huddled into the shadows.

A skinny man with long fingernails climbed the main stage toward the dryad. Cruel lips turned slightly upward. He curled her hair around his fingers.

Jili covered her face. "Please, oh please, not someone like that. Send someone nice to buy me."

The lump in Josh's throat wouldn't swallow.

Zheek, their fat slave master, stood near the front of the caravan and haggled with a dull yellow, scaly creature. Six arms waved while the slaver and creature shouted at each other.

Manacles clinked as a huge rhinoceros man chained Dandelion to the other children in the caravan. So much for escaping. All the kids hung their heads. Some cried softly.

Dust from the plaza stung Josh's eyes and clogged his throat. He stared at the pins in the children's chains, the way they caught the sun. "Fire! Melt! Burn! Ugh."

Nothing happened.

"Have faith." Aura's squawky whisper burned in his ear.

Josh watched the rhinoceros man walk away and imagined the manacles unlocking.

Dandelion elbowed Josh and lifted an unlocked manacle.

"My spell worked?" Josh could hardly breathe.

She grinned and shoved a tiny wire into the other manacle. "It's 'a different sort of magic.' Don't feel bad. I'll have us free before Zheek's made the deal. Portals are cheap in places like this. We'll be back at the oracle to pick up where we left off before sunset."

"Really?" Josh's voice cracked.

She nodded. "You can learn fire. I know it." She turned to Aura and slanted her eyes meaningfully toward Josh. "When I'm too nervous to figure out a problem, I think about something else for a while."

"Oh." Aura ruffled his feathers. "Yes. Little wizard, think about something else. Let your mind untangle."

"Look." Dandelion stopping lock-picking and pointed across the plaza.

"Oh no," Jili wailed. "Giants."

Laughter boomed from the far side of the marketplace, drowning the noise of the market. Tall as the surrounding buildings, bulky men and women waded through the crowd.

The shoppers scrambled out of the way. Most heads only reached a giant's knees. People who didn't move fast enough were knocked sprawling. Josh watched a whole group fall like dominoes.

"Giants buy humans as slaves?" Josh's mouth dropped open.

"No, mostly as food," Aura harrumphed.

"Hey, look at that, shimmer folk." Dandelion glared at Aura and swung Josh to the left.

Stumps with branches for arms and legs carried bathtub-sized crystal bowls. People made of water leaned over the edges of their gleaming litters and spoke in splashy, tinkling voices.

"Shimmer folk." Josh muttered, breathless. Glowing spots appeared on his arms and then faded. "They're from the mirror world. I've been there."

"You have?" Dandelion fumbled with her lock-pick.

Josh's eyes flicked from one strange creature to the next. It was as if each passing one wiped away a piece of the fog between him and his memory. His stomach turned somersaults, lights flickered on his arms.

Red gleamed from the cracks of lumpy, shuffling lava creatures. Dad had a battalion of those in his army.

The more Josh looked, the faster his heart beat. Pillars of smoke floated through the crowd. They made great spies. Dog-sized mosquitoes on six-foot legs skittered overhead like giant water bugs.

A whip cracked. Josh jumped. A bulbous, wrinkled man filled a sedan chair. Swathed in silk robes and gold chains, his great belly sagged over the platform's edges.

Eight human slaves carried his litter. The master shouted and lashed with a long whip. A slave cried out and stumbled. The other slaves looked straight ahead with expressionless faces.

Josh's stomach churned. Slaves were everywhere. In chains, under whips or heavy loads, even displayed in finery. They were human, and beast; fur, skin, or stone. A river of desperation and pain ran beneath all their faces. Josh lifted his chains. He knew how they felt.

On a smaller stage. A mother knelt before her slaver, clutching at her baby. The man snatched it from her and gave it to merchants for a handful of coins. She collapsed to the floor, howling.

Josh's face was on fire. His breath came in gasps. The churning in his stomach boiled up into his chest. Suddenly, he didn't care about becoming a wizard. He didn't care about getting free or getting home. He wanted to leap on the cruel masters, pull them from their biers, and trample them into the filth of the plaza.

<hr />

"What have we here?"

An oily voice jarred Josh from his thoughts.

Dandelion gasped.

Around them, the crowd dissolved away from a droopy eyed wizard. Over his black hooded cloak hung a black chasuble with embossed silver snakes twisted in its center.

Several knobby-skinned black-iron guardsmen stood at attention behind him.

"Open the pinfold, Magoth." Viscero, the enormous, burned wolf, stepped up beside the wizard. A tattered crow perched on the wolf's shoulder.

The wizard rolled his eyes and huffed. He waved one hand in a circular motion. The air around Josh turned a waxy sheen and then popped. Little rainbow flecks floated away in the breeze.

The wolf's eyes flicked from Pete to Josh. He swung his giant head toward the crow. "Tell the master we've found them."

With a loud croak, the crow flapped away over the rooftops.

"Ho there, this is my private property." Zheek ran toward the wizard. Red faced, the slave master huffed and sputtered. "I'll not have ..."

Both wolf and wizard turned.

Zheek skidded to a halt, stammering, "Great sires! I beg pardon." He bowed awkwardly and stayed down for an uncomfortably long time.

He finally stood and wrapped his cloak around his great belly with a flourish. "In undying service to his emperor, I offer any of these *very* valuable slaves for only a modest compensation."

The droopy eyed wizard turned to the guardsmen behind him. "Kill the slaver."

Zheek shoved the boys toward the wizard and choked out a tense laugh, voice suddenly high. "No compensation needed. Service of the emperor is my highest goal."

The wizard snorted. "Kill them all. The boys too."

CHAPTER SEVEN

BURN

T he kill order from the wizard echoed over the crowd. Voices from the nearby stages quieted. All eyes turned toward Josh and his friends huddled in front of the guardsmen. Josh's legs were carved in stone as guardsmen drew swords and stepped toward them.

"Wait." The wolf's growl was barely audible.

Guardsmen froze.

The beast turned to the guardsmen. "Throw the boys in the bone cage. The emperor will want the pleasure of killing them himself." The wolf's amber eyes followed Dandelion; black lips curled to show giant fangs. "The Dryad too. There's a flea that's been hopping around in my woods too long. I owe that one a special debt."

Sputtering, the wizard spun toward the wolf. "I give the orders here. You're nothing but a ..."

"Say it, Maggot," the huge animal rumbled between bared fangs.

Droopy eyes flitted from the boys to the wolf. The wizard's sneer faded. He wheezed a laugh and turned toward the guardsmen. "Throw the boys into the cage." His eyes settled on Aura. "I'll take the bird. I'll stuff it."

Aura leapt into the air.

"It's ... ah ... wild." Sweat dripped from Zheek's chins.

"Pah! Shoot it down."

The guardsman's aim was perfect. It caught Aura mid-flight.

"Noooo," Dandelion screamed and covered her face.

It happened so fast Josh could only gape. The wizard's order. The arrow. Aura.

Josh winced, expecting to see Aura twitching on the cobblestones. Instead, the arrow barely reached the bird before dissolving into flame. Smoke streamers streaked away in a dozen directions.

"Try again." With squawky laughter, Aura landed on the slave master's shoulder.

The guardsman notched another arrow.

"Aaah. Get away from me, you turd hen." Zheek swatted around his head and shoulders. He waddled in circles as fast as his stumpy legs would move.

Several of the guardsmen chuckled. Josh couldn't help but smile.

The wolf rolled his eyes and sighed. "Take the little, foul-smelling human instead."

Jili screamed as huge hands unlocked and dragged her from the group. Her eyes were wide with terror. They gripped Josh's, pleading, *you're the wizard, save us.*

"Stop!" Josh untangled himself and leapt at the guardsman. Halfway there, his manacle jerked taut, and he hit the pavement. A large boot pressed him into the dust.

Josh's fingers clawed at the pavers, his feet scrabbing behind him. He shouted until his throat was raw. The boot just pressed harder until he thought his ribs would crack. Dust filled his mouth. Blood oozed from his fingertips.

When he finally stopped moving, guardsmen unlocked his wrist and yanked him from the ground. Half dragged, half shoved, he and the others stumbled towards a contraption that sent shivers from head to foot: the bone cage.

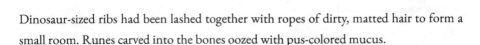

Dinosaur-sized ribs had been lashed together with ropes of dirty, matted hair to form a small room. Runes carved into the bones oozed with pus-colored mucus.

The cage hung just off the ground, swaying gently in the desert wind. Several men and women huddled in its center. One figure lolled on the bottom, mumbling wordlessly. An arm dangled down between the bars, and drool stretched from the corner of his chapped lips.

Josh felt hot feet on his shoulder.

"It's the rib cage of an underworld beast. It's for wizards." Aura's nasally snuffle smelled like smoke. "The runes and underworld bones skew any spells cast within it."

"What about him?" Josh pointed his chin at the drooling man.

Aura shook his beak. "He's been questioned by an inquisitor. See the slime?" A large glob plopped on to the pavement.

"A what?" The hair on Josh's neck rose. He tried to back up. Huge hands forced him forward.

"An inquisitor. Sorcerers and priests use them to get information. But afterward, the mind is destroyed. If you ever see one, fly away. Awk. I mean run."

One of the guards used a hook to open the cage door. The others lifted Dandelion and the brothers to throw them in.

———◆○◆———

The sound began low, quickly growing to a shriek that rang off the buildings and cobblestones. The force of it buffeted Josh in gusts. It wasn't a voice. It was more like the buzzing of a million insect wings.

The Guardsmen froze, then fell to one knee. The crowd drained from the square, people and creatures stampeding toward the edges. Josh could finally see what made the sound.

He should have run when the guard's hands let go of him. All the friends should have. Instead, Josh's legs filled with cement, and he just stood, staring at the thing that lumbered toward them.

Mottled spots covered the shell of a house-sized creature. Maggot yellow and gleaming black, it careened across the square. Half spider and half centipede, the beast was a mass of legs, antennae, and claws. Great jagged pincers scraped on the ground in front of it. Every few steps, it would lift one and snap toward someone at the edge of the crowd.

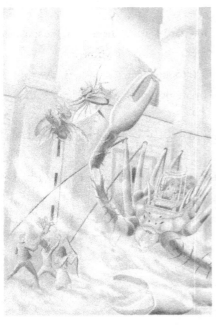

Dandelion gripped Josh's arm. "A mantor!"

High on the mantor's back swayed a giant platform. Shaded under a colorful awning, dignitaries in finery surrounded a hooded figure on a dragon-skull throne.

Squads of guardsmen marched in formation around the mantor. Soldiers in blood red armor rode gleaming black beetles with sharpened, bronze tipped horns.

Occasionally, a beetle would open its wings and buzz into the air. The rider would circle the crowd and land back in the procession.

Screams echoed across the square. The giant creature caught someone from the crowd. Its jaws opened showing a mouth full of pedipalps, frantic, grasping arms. All eyes from the platform watched the struggling figure disappear into the maw. Spectators winced. Shudders ran the mantor's length. Head lifting, it wailed its unearthly cry.

The cloaked figure on the throne laughed and turned toward Josh.

"Kharaq," Josh moaned.

Pete gaped, face white.

The giant armored legs clacked toward the teenagers. Its pincers scraped against the flagstone.

Josh tried to swallow but couldn't. *Run*, his mind screamed. But his feet wouldn't.

The massive head loomed over them. Dozens of gray eyes gleamed between venomous looking spines. Cruel pincers reached for the friends and a collective gasp rose from the crowd. Blood hungry spectators pressed in.

<hr />

Guards stepped back from the boys. Sweat soaked Josh's shirt. His heart hammered so hard it was going to explode. *Do something*, his mind screamed at him. What could he do? Voices flooded his memory. *Face the shadow to find your hero. Don't go alone.*

The Pincers swept overhead, blocking the sun. Josh might as well have been made of stone. *Help.*

"I'm here." A voice whispered in Josh's ear. It wasn't Aura's hoarse, croaky whisper. It was deep and full of power.

Thunderclouds rolled low across the sky, engulfing the rooftops. Lightning and fire flickered through the cloud-bottoms, illuminating the crowd. Everything in the plaza froze in place.

Thunder boomed. The clouds divided, and torrents of fire gushed downward, engulfing the crowds. In the center of the inferno descended a warrior riding a gleaming dragon.

The beast shone like molten steel. Wind from billboard-sized wings whipped Josh's clothes, and drove the flames in gusts across the plaza.

On its back, the warrior in dented plate armor gripped reins of crackling lightning. He directed the beast toward Josh and landed in a flurry of smoke.

The sour bite of scorched steel filled Josh's nostrils. His knees buckled. A gauntleted reached down, lifting Josh on to the dragon's back in front of the warrior. Around them, the slaver's plaza disappeared in a sea of flames.

Josh stared up at a face crisscrossed with scars, and a gaze so fierce it caught his breath. Yet in the creases around the eyes and mouth, there was a deep, gentle kindness.

Josh remembered the oracle's story about the nine living stars who rule the light. Only one rode a burning dragon, Vastroh. They were saved! Josh glanced toward the square for his friends. Nothing was visible but flames. He looked down at himself. Nothing was burning. Was this even real?

Josh found his voice. "You're Vastroh, guardian of those in peril."

The warrior nodded.

Josh's eyes fell to Vastroh's neck. Scars crisscrossed there too, as if some creature had tried to rip his throat out. Josh gasped. "You have scars like mine."

Fierceness softened to a smile. Large dimples creased the scarred cheeks. "They're my favorite ones."

"You're going to save us from Kharaq and that monster." Josh couldn't help but grin.

"No." The smile disappeared.

Josh's heart stopped.

"You are in danger of something much worse."

"Worse?" Iron fingers gripped Josh's chest.

"Will freeing you from the demon and the beast really set you free? Won't you still be a slave?"

"To what?" Josh asked, but instantly knew the answer.

Vastroh watched him. Those eyes saw everything, piercing to his soul.

Josh thought back to Mom's office, where this whole thing started. Why had he picked up the gem? Mom had told him not to, but there was a visceral self-satisfaction in doing it anyway.

Why?

Josh felt Vastroh's presence in his mind. The warrior didn't say anything. He was more like a light, illuminating the jumble of Josh's thoughts and feelings. Picking up the gem was Josh's small way to control a life utterly out of his control. Was that really fear? Yes. Being out of control is terrifying.

That wasn't the only time. He'd cast ice too strongly because he was afraid he wasn't powerful enough. Fire magic wouldn't work because he was afraid of being out of control again. And when he finally *really* wanted to learn magic, he'd obeyed fear too long; it was his master and wouldn't let him.

"But how do I not be afraid?" Even as Josh asked, he knew. It wasn't about how he felt. He must disobey his fear. Go into the shadow to find his hero. Don't go alone. "Will you go into the shadow with me?"

Fire flickered in Vastroh's eyes. Josh saw the answer: *always*.

———◄O►———

Josh blinked. Vastroh was gone. The flames that had stood between him and a horrible death were gone. His peace was gone too.

Had he just imagined the whole thing? The smell of scorched metal still lingered in his nostrils. Josh gritted his teeth. "Vastroh, you left too soon. Weren't we supposed to do this together?"

Spine covered pincers swept downward. Remnants of a skull grinned from one of the barbs. The crowd seethed. Masters lashed their slaves forward. They leaned toward each other across their litters. Money changed hands.

Dandelion screamed. Giant claws closed around her waist, sweeping her up above the mob. She kicked and tore at the spikes. The crowd cheered.

"Stop!" Josh screamed, lunging toward the beast.

A rush of wind filled his ears. The world around him glowed, bathed in gold as if the sun had just dropped below the horizon.

Heat radiated from the gem around his neck. His fingers tingled. Anything metal in the plaza shone, stirrups on horses, strap buckles holding litters, armor, jewelry. It all beckoned.

"Yes, child, yes," Aura croaked and shook his feathers. Smoke poured from the bird.

Josh stared at the great iron pins holding Kharaq's platform. They gleamed in the golden light. "Burn," he muttered.

The iron glowed red. It shifted, sagged, and flowed down the sides of the monster. Smoking pieces plopped on the ground.

Screaming, the mantor reared, pincers flailing. The creature thrashed and trampled the crowd. The platform spun free, crashing to the cobblestones.

Dandelion was flung this way and that, clinging to the pincers.

The crowd stampeded. Masters whipped their slaves. Josh scanned across them, one shackle and chain-link to another. "Burn."

Pins holding manacles burned white; their chains sagged and fell away from wrists and ankles. Slaves snatched whips from their masters. Litters smashed to the pavement.

For a moment Pete stood unmoving, mouth open, staring at Josh. Then he leapt backward, pulling swords from the guards on either side. A blade in each hand, he shouted and strode into the melee.

"Wizard, Warrior, Weaver." Jilli's shrill pierced the crowd's roar.

Cheers exploded from the mob. "The wizard! The warrior! The weaver!"

Guardsmen struggled to quell the crowd. Pete rallied a mass of freed slaves against them.

"Burn, burn, burn," Aura shrieked, racing in circles overhead.

Zheek tugged on his snail's reins, turning his cage-train back toward the gate.

"Oh yeah. Zheek" Josh's eyes settled on the gold necklace holding Aura's egg. "I know what will make you take off that chain. Burn."

The gold chain from his neck glowed white. Zheek screamed and hopped from one foot to the other, pulling it from his neck in globs. Molten gold ran down his front, catching his robes on fire.

He flung the egg free. In an instant Josh realized his mistake: there were too many people in the way.

Between them, slaves pulled a flying guardsman from the air. They crashed sideways a litter where hairy servants pulled their former master from his cushions and luxury.

The egg bounced from the roof of the litter and spun sideways. Josh lunged between the fighting bodies in time to see the egg roll down a bare shouldered slave, only to be flung away as the man swung his shield toward an opponent.

Josh scrambled over litter and dove, landing on the pavement with arms outstretched.

He was too far away. With a sickening crunch, Aura's egg hit the cobblestones inches from Josh's fingers. Somewhere overhead, Aura shrieked.

"No, oh no, please no." Josh crawled to the egg on hands and knees. Light leaked from the shattered shell in a misty pool.

Aura screamed and screamed. Josh had never heard such agony. Lifetimes of the blackest sorrow poured from the bird.

Josh gulped like a suffocating fish. His hot tears dripped on the pavement. The magical golden light faded from the buildings and cobblestones. The world turned lifeless gray. He wished he could sink into the stones and disappear. He could only sob, "Aura, please. I'm so sorry."

Aura's feathers were black and cinder. Beating wings drove swirling gusts of ash around Josh.

Feet trampled Josh. He didn't care. With trembling fingers, he gingerly picked up the glittering pieces of the shell. Something in him died along with that baby firebrand, along with Aura's dreams and his only family. All ruined by Josh trying to be a hero.

<hr />

Josh stared at the broken eggshell with blurry eyes. There was a popping noise. A tiny spark shot from the pieces. It hung in the air, inches from Josh's nose, then buzzed in mad circles around his head, squeaking and chirping.

Aura squawked. The spark squealed and streaked to the firebrand, disappearing in his feathers. Aura exploded into a ball of fire.

"Burn. Burn." Aura streaked over the crowd. Smoke and embers stretched out behind in a flaming trail.

A tiny white hot spark raced beside him. Its tiny voice squeaked, "Buwn, buwn."

Tears ran down Josh's face. The baby was alive? On his knees, Josh watched Aura and his child. Joy exploded in his chest, billowing upward, catching in his throat and filling his eyes. He pressed his forehead on the pavement and wept. "Burn," Josh tried to shout, but only a croak came out.

The crowd thundered. "Wizard, Warrior, Weaver!"

Josh felt hands gripping his arms and legs, hundreds of hands lifting him above the crowd.

From his vantage point, Josh saw the slaver's stages in tatters. Kharaq's platform was a pile of broken rubble, and the mantor was nowhere to be seen. Soldiers were chained by mobs of slaves.

The huge rhinoceros man that had locked them up, lifted Pete next to Josh. He beamed at the brothers. "The Cambium Dreams come true."

Josh glanced from his brother to the man. "I don't think we're *that* Wizard and Warrior."

The man grinned back. "Be it so or nay, we are free." He turned and roared, "Wizard! Warrior!"

The crowd roared back. The brothers floated on cheers and whistles. Everyone wanted to touch them.

Pete turned to Josh, his eyes huge. "You learned fire! That was freakin' amazing. How'd you do that?"

Josh opened his mouth to say something, but nothing came out. How *did* he do that? He looked at his hands. The burn spell had been nothing like making ice. It was effortless.

The slaver's square thundered with shouts of joy. Slaves leapt and hugged and cheered. By the main stage, the slave woman had her child back. Her eyes caught his. Her smile burned brighter than Aura. She waved, and kissed the baby's face.

The rhinoceros man herded Jili and a bunch of other children out of the plaza. Josh's heart flipped somersaults. Tingles raced from his fingertips to his toes. He spread his arms and closed his eyes, turning his face to the sun. He pictured Vastroh's battle-scarred face in his mind. "I know how I did that. It was you. Wherever you are, thank you."

Josh let the cheers from the crowd wash over him, a cool breeze on a summer day. He finally opened his eyes.

Pete stared at him, grinning. "Let's go get those bones."

Josh nodded and looked out toward the plain. "And then we're coming for you, Dad."

———————— ◄O► ————————

Movement in the center of the plaza caught Josh's eye. Kharaq extracted himself from the wreckage of his stage. His wizards stumbled to him from the crowd. Guardsmen formed a protective ring around them.

Kharaq pointed at the crowd and shouted orders. Wizards cast oily back portals. Out of them, hundreds of guardsmen flowed into the crowd. War beetles leapt into the air. With shouts, their red riders stabbed bronze tipped spears toward the sky.

Pete gasped.

"I'm here. Still." The voiceless whisper smoldered in Josh's chest.

The world glowed. Swords and spears gleamed gold.

"Burn," Josh whispered. "Burn."

The soldiers' orderly charge dissolved. Breast plates burst into flames. Swords drooped and folded. Guardsmen writhed and ripped at their weapons and armor. They disappeared under waves of newly freed slaves.

Buckles on beetle saddles burst. Riders fell from the sky into the mob. Some riders clung to the beetle horns. Beetles careened in all directions.

More soldiers poured from nearby buildings. Bowmen appeared on the rooftops.

Josh stared in disbelief. Did nothing affect that black wizard? Gold faded from the world. Help.

"We need to go. Now!" a voice behind Josh spun him around.

"Dandelion!" Josh sobbed with relief. "You're OK."

"Of course." Dandelion floated just above the crowd on a tangle of vines the size of a large tablecloth. Shiny leaves fluttered in the wind. She rolled her eyes at his relief and grabbed at him. "Get on."

"What about them?" Josh gestured down at the freed slaves.

A warrior made of stone, who must have been four feet wide, laughed in a gravelly voice. "Finish your journey. We can take care of ourselves."

He lifted Josh up to the mat and strode into the crowd. "The Wizard. The Warrior."

"The Weaver." The crowd roared back. Around him, slaves formed ranks. Steel rang on steel.

Pete scrambled on to the ivy mat. "You figured out how to get this working?"

"Sort of." Dandelion grabbed the front corners of the weave and spun it toward the city wall.

Josh followed her eyes. Mountains were on one side, deadly desert sands on the other. There was only one direction they could fly to safety — toward the city wall, and over. Dandelion urged the vines forward, and in moments, they raced over the crowd.

A howl behind them turned Josh's head — Kharaq frothed at the mouth, pointing at Josh and his friends. The wizard gestured to his bowmen to the rooftops. Clouds of arrows climbed skyward and arched toward the space between the teenagers and the wall.

"Can this thing go any faster?" Pete gulped, wide eyes calculating their race against black-iron tipped rain.

More arrows whistled upward from archers in the crowd. Dandelion dodged left and right, pulling on the corners of the vine-mat as if they were reins. Josh and Pete flopped with each turn. They clutched at the edges to keep from falling off.

Up ahead, Red guards on beetles burst from behind a building.

Sweat dripped from Dandelion's face. She gasped with effort. "Go, go, you stupid doormat."

The hiss of arrows overhead told Josh they weren't going to make it.

"Are you there?" Josh pictured Vastroh's face. He bit his lip and concentrated as hard as he could. "Burn." But there was no gold hue to the world. Nothing happened.

Wide eyed he watched arrows fall. The sky was black with them. His throat squeezed tight. "You said you'd always be here. Burn."

Nothing.

The first of the arrows clattered on rooftops behind them. Then, whistling like a gale through pines, the air around them sang with deadly hail.

To her credit, Dandelion never looked up, never let go. Her eyes were locked on their escape.

A grim determination settled on Pete as he watched the arrows. Leaping forward, he pulled Josh to the front of the mat. With one arm around his brother and one around Dandelion, he covered them with his body.

Josh squeezed his eyes shut and held his breath. His last breath.

The first arrow hit.

Instead of razor-sharp iron, flaming bits of wood and fletching showered the teenagers. Smoke and glowing embers swirled in the vine-mat's wake.

Josh looked up. Arrows dissolved right above them in a blazing inferno. "Aura?" He had never been so glad to see that bird.

"Burn," squawked the bird.

"Buwn," squeaked the tiny ember behind him.

Not a single arrow made it past Aura, but the leaves and vine branches beneath the friends shrank in the heat. Josh frantically brushed flaming pieces off the plant.

"Watch out." Pete pointed ahead.

Archers poured from the towers onto the wall.

Dandelion gasped. "Climb, climb!" She hauled on the corners.

Pop. An arrow hissed upward between them. The severed end of a branch flapped in the wind. Several feet of vine woven through the mat shriveled and turned brown.

Pop. Pop, pop. Arrows from below peppered the ivy. Large sections of the vine withered. Holes gaped everywhere.

Dandelion wrenched at the threadbare weave, dodging as fast as she could. Josh rubbed where an arrow tip nicked his arm. Pete also bled from several small cuts. The vine mesh sagged and wallowed.

"No, no, no, they're killing my vine." No matter how hard Dandelion pulled, the mat sank toward the wall, and the archers.

Arrows whistled by on every side. They were only alive because of Dandelion's driving. Josh watched her hair flop each time she yanked. Just a few more yards and they'd be free.

Then she grunted and slumped forward, slowly sliding from the mat, an arrow protruding from her chest.

Josh's blood turned to ice. Beside him, Pete snatched at Dandelion's jerkin.

"NOOO!" Josh screamed. He grabbed at Dandelion, pulling her back on the vines, willing life into those sightless eyes and dangling arms. She looked so so small and frail. This couldn't be Dandelion. *She* was a powerhouse, invincible.

The weight of the boys and Dandelion on the front corner of the vine-mat steered it back toward the crowd and the gates.

Vines and teenagers collided with a cloud of flying guardsmen. Beetles careened left and right. Golden spear tips stabbed at Josh and Pete, then they were past the group. The surprised guardsmen shouted and swerved their beetles in pursuit.

"Grab the corner and drive. Turn it back." Pete shouted. He heaved at Dandelion, sinews bulging on his neck.

Josh grabbed branches with both hands. He grunted with effort.

They turned, but not enough, plummeting downward over the rooftops to skim the crowd. Ahead loomed the gates, and the ravenous desert.

Guardsmen swords stabbed up at them. War beetles buzzed just behind. Kharaq roared in the center of it all.

No matter how hard Josh pulled, the vines didn't respond. They dove, past the market, past the fighting slaves, down, until leaves skimmed the cobblestones. Arrows skittered and bounced around them.

"Turn, Josh. Turn," Pete yelled and pointed ahead. Through the gates, yellow dunes stretched to a hazy blue horizon. Evil faces gnashed and whispered in the shifting sand.

Sweat ran down Josh's face. He screamed at Vastroh in his mind. Where are you? How could you let this happen?

Nothing.

They whisked through the gates, across the highway, and out over the hungry dunes.

The teenagers hit the top of a dune in an explosion of sand and tumbled down the steep slope. Pete rolled to his feet. Josh gagged on a mouth full of grit.

As Pete stepped toward Dandelion's body, she crawled to her knees, gasping and wheezing. "I can't breathe." She leaned forward and sucked huge breaths.

"You're OK?" Josh couldn't breathe either. He could still hear the sickening thunk when the arrow had hit. But she was alive? He wanted to whoop. He wanted to grab her and dance — but she'd probably punch him.

The arrow dangled from Dandelion's leather jerkin. "Oh no." She pulled a knife from its sheath by her shoulder. The blade was broken where the arrow had hit.

Josh let a slow breath out. "Wow, good thing you have so many of those."

"That was my favorite one." Dandelion scowled and dug in the pocket for the other half of the knife. She winced and looked down her shirt. "*Dragons,* that hurts."

Pete took the broken blade from her. "You were hit at close range with a long bow. They have a lot of force. Your whole chest is probably black and blue."

"It is." Dandelion looked at Pete with a strange expression. Her voice was soft. "Thanks for covering me up there."

Pete shrugged and studied the broken edge. "You got lucky ..." He gasped and spun. There was nothing but sand and whispers.

Dandelion looked around for the first time. Her eyes followed their descent from the city. The gates. The mangled vine. The *dunes*. Her face turned white. She grabbed at both boys and spun them toward the city. "We have to go. NOW!"

"Not that way." Aura landed on Josh's shoulder.

Soldiers poured from the gates and lined the Kings Highway. War beetles and their riders hovered above. None crossed into the sand.

Through the gates behind them strode the mantor, Kharaq standing balanced on its back. He shouted to his guardsmen, gesturing them into the desert.

Soldiers squirmed and jostled. Finally, they eased off the road toward the teenagers.

"Fly for the mountains." Aura leapt into the air.

"We can't fly."

"Awk. Toward the road. Guardsmen are better than Sand Wraiths."

The last of Aura's words swept away in a roar that shook the ground. The desert at the road's edge swirled downward into a spinning black chasm. Giant tentacles of sand writhed skyward, catching or swatting the flying beetles. Soldiers flipped and spun, crying out as they fell.

"Run for the mountains." Aura squawked.

Too late.

The maelstrom raced toward them. One moment, the teenagers ran facing the sun. The next, they were tumbling, screaming into darkness.

CHAPTER EIGHT

TOMB OF AGES

They fell forever. Sand whipped and tore against Josh's skin. It filled his nose and mouth. He couldn't breathe. Lungs on fire, head over heels, he saw the opening shrink to a speck and disappear.

Dandelion tumbled beside him for a moment, eyes wide with terror. Pete was there too, then was gone. Where was Aura?

Josh's world sharpened to vivid detail. Gleaming dust drifted in clouds. A world of golden snow. The gem around his neck smoldered dull yellow. This was *it* then? That clarity before death.

No! Never give up. Even when there is no hope, choose it and fight. Josh tried to picture the burning dragon and its fierce rider. Where are you? Help.

But there was no answer, no dividing sky and river of fire. Kharaq was still alive while Josh and his friends plunged to their death.

———◆———

They fell.

And fell.

Then they didn't. The roar of wind and sand faded. There was only darkness and deathly silence.

They were dead, right? Where was the shining gate? Were they in hell? At least the stinging sand had stopped, and Josh could breathe again.

"Light."

That voice. Sand drifting over the dunes. A ghost's sigh. A death rattle. Chills ran down Josh's neck and arms.

Nothing changed.

"Light."

The breathy voice was interrupted by another. A man's.

"Oh! Oh! Seriously?" Indignant and effeminate, the new voice rose in pitch until the darkness rang with it. "Years without a word? And then you just show up? No apology. Not even hello. You want light? Well! Make it yourself."

Josh coughed.

The indignant voice gasped. Light pooled around Josh. A pudgy face poked in from the shadow. Perched lopsided on its head was a green silk nightcap embroidered in garish oranges, reds, and purples.

"Guests!" The face shrieked, eyes wide. "Lights, lights, LIGHTS." He clapped his hands with each command, and turned as he shouted.

Lights sputtered on around them, a candelabra, gems in the eye sockets of a skull, the summer sun in a painting. A flood of brilliance swept outward in every direction.

Dandelion and Pete sat near Josh. He breathed a sigh of relief. They'd all survived. They sat in a cave the size of a continent. Fine gray sand stretched in gentle ripples to a gray horizon on all sides.

Josh sucked in a sharp breath. Gold!

Gold items covered the sand. Chests overflowed with it. Heaps spilled from golden tables. Gold swords and spears leaned against golden suits of armor. Gold chariots and carriages sat with wheels half buried.

"Tomb of ages?" Dandelion's eyes were wider than Josh had ever seen.

"Oh. Oh." Until that moment, the pudgy man in silk pajamas had stared at Josh. He turned to Dandelion, hand flying to his mouth. "A dryad?" He rushed over to her in tiny, dainty steps and caught her surprised face between his hands. "Aren't you just the prettiest thing I've ever seen."

Dandelion blushed. The man's face was so happy to see them, it was impossible to be afraid of him.

Josh's mind spun. Who was this guy? He wasn't made of sand. Were they all prisoners? Josh remembered the *other* whispery voice. He shivered. Next-door was probably a cave filled with bones.

"At least half dryad, right?" The little man gushed over Dandelion.

She grinned and nodded.

He puffed his chest and straightened his hat. "I'm Remrald, curator of the Anchialine room, the greatest collection of the Magical since magic itself."

"There are other caves?" Dandelion's eyes bugged further.

"I prefer rooms." Remrald deflated a little. "Although you were probably right the first time, calling it a tomb." He gave a meaningful glance behind them.

"So." He perked up and rubbed his hands together. "Tell me your names. Tell me news of the land above? Last I heard, the Poison Flame rampaged across Alaetia. What a woman." He shook his head. "They say the mountains ran black with troll blood. Is it true she chased a dragon into the Ember World? And that the goblins sealed the mountain gateways out of fear of her?"

Dandelion crinkled her brow. "The rampage of the Poison Flame? Those stories are over a century old."

"A hundred years?" the curator's voice rose.

"Remrald we haven't the time—" the whisper echoed from everywhere.

"You. You ..." The pudgy curator pointed an angry finger at something beyond them. "A hundred years?" He sputtered, face red. "You *hush. A*nd let me enjoy some real company."

Between the treasures walked a woman unlike Josh had ever seen. Josh held his breath without meaning to.

She shone like green diamonds. Long hair floated in waves and curls around a regal face, full lips the color of the deep forest, and eyes like sunlight through water. Her sea-foam-green skin gleamed in stark contrast to robes of rich emeralds and jades.

"The Olivine princess." Remrald bowed low.

Time stood still as she floated toward them. Rainbows reflected from the treasure and shone in a halo around her.

The curator broke the spell. Still bent over, he wiped a finger on a tabletop, and stood, staring with horror at his fingertip.

"Dust! Oh! This place is filthy. Sandwoman, do your dirt thing." He waved around him, face puckered.

"Remrald, there isn't time." She had almost reached them.

The ghostly sand voice had been hers? It wasn't frightening anymore; it was more of a sultry whisper. Josh got chills again.

The curator just blinked at her, hips cocked, hand on his waist, fingers tapping.

She sighed and waved. Angel sleeves swept majestically. Dust rose from the treasure in clouds and settled to the surrounding sand.

"Remrald." She placed a gentle hand on his shoulder. "We swallowed several squads of black guardsmen and their officers. When their belongings are divided among the sand-warriors, they'll notice the death shard is not among them."

At the mention of the death shard, Josh gripped the gem beneath his shirt. So that was it. She *was* a sand wraith. She'd captured them so that *she* could get the gem. And where was Aura? Aura would have seen right through her.

Her eyes never left Remrald. "Word will reach the Ilmenite king. He will trace the gem here."

The curator blanched. "Here? He'll come here? The last time ..."

She nodded

His jowls quivered. "Oh. Oh heavens."

She bent down between Josh and Pete. "Word has reached me of your quest. There are those among us who value peace over power. The world above *and* below has but one hope: *you* must succeed."

Josh couldn't look away. Her eyes shone with the same fierce protectiveness as Mom's. His face must have been bright red. "You're the reason we survived the maelstrom. You're going to help us?"

A thrill raced through Josh. With all this gold, they could hire an army and ships. Josh imagined Dandelion, Pete, and himself in golden armor, saving Dad. Legions of golden warriors cheered. Everyone took turns stamping on Kharaq's bones.

She smiled and touched Josh's cheek. "Your fear is a treasure greater than anything here. Know it and your path becomes clear. Walk into it and your journey becomes legend."

She turned to Pete and gripped his shoulders. Pete looked like he was going to melt. "Warrior, your greatest fight is within yourself. The enemy outside you will show you the enemy within. Seek it to see it. See it to conquer it. Conquer *it*, and you will be undefeatable."

"My beautiful child of all that is green and good." She knelt, her face level with Dandelion's. "The journey to mend a broken heart cannot be charted or hurried. Remember, the darkness outside you is most often darkness inside. Look to the burning star for a dawn of the heart."

In a rustle of skirts and breath of earthy perfume, she stood and looked at Remrald. "Give them weapons and armor from the Fathomless."

Remrald gasped and covered his mouth. "Those are the king's personal collection."

"Then the humans had best be gone before he arrives."

A devious grin crept across the curator's face. The princess winked and smiled back.

"Gabba, get over here." He clapped his hands, then turned to the teenagers. "Quickly, children, get on."

Curator and teenagers flew across the cavern on a carpet the size of a small room. Across its surface, battles were woven in brilliant colors. No one steered, it seemed to know where it was going.

Josh's stomach flip-flopped with excitement. He imagined the oracle's face when they arrived wearing magical armor, with a legion of the princess's sand soldiers. Kharaq didn't stand a chance.

Josh tried to ask about the plan, but Remrald jabbered without taking a breath.

Somehow, Dandelion still peppered him with questions. "Was that Welarch's chariot? Is Xerudia's sarcophagus really here?"

How did she manage it? The more she asked, the brighter the curator beamed. Several times, he told her how impressed he was with her knowledge of magical items.

Dandelion watched the ocean of gold beneath them. "This is every magical item collected since the first of the dune wars?" She practically drooled.

"And before," the curator sighed. "I've been down here too long. I remember when the desert above us had cities and towns. Now there is only Necrus City."

"You saw the battle?" Dandelion's eyes were huge. "I read that the towns were swallowed by giant sand monsters. I read that—"

"Well, I didn't actually *see* it, but yes, I was there." Remrald leaned in. "Sand Wraiths don't just make monsters. I've seen them form cities and mountains. The most powerful can create sandstone."

He waved a hand at the treasure. "Still, everything in their world is sand and even though they despise solid creatures, they love solid things."

"Is it true they want to make the whole world sand? Even the rivers and woods?" Dandelion grimaced.

"Pew." Josh plugged his nose and glared at Pete.

Pete shrugged. "It wasn't me."

Below them, sand had become a sea of thick glistening muck. The surface squirmed.

"Snakes?" Dandelion screwed her face up in disgust.

"Rotworms." The curator covered his nose and mouth with a silk handkerchief.

He pulled a lamp from somewhere in his robes and moaned. "I so hate this part."

"Which part ..."

Their carpet dove toward the writhing goo.

Bulging from the center of the lake was an island carved into a serpent with open jaws. Rotworms and slime fell in great wiggling globs down its throat. That was where the carpet flew.

Dandelion gagged.

They dove and dove until all light from the cavern faded.

Josh's eyes watered. He pulled his shirt over his nose with one hand and gripped the carpet with the other. How far down were they? Miles? Darkness seemed to get thicker every second, squashing the light from the curator's little lamp. Claustrophobic terror squeezed Josh's chest.

Abruptly, the carpet swerved past the dripping worms. Josh almost fell off.

"Gabba! Really." The curator gave the carpet a half-hearted swat. He turned to the teenagers and rolled his eyes. "You'd think dodging the slime was the only fun he had the whole trip."

The carpet racing forward instead of down. The air felt warmer and smelled like dust. Josh lowered his shirt.

Dandelion started to say something, but Remrald raised his hand for silence. The carpet slowed.

"Stop," the curator barely breathed the words. He listened intently. "A little higher. To the left."

Remrald cupped his hands around his mouth and took a deep breath.

Air erupted around them, thunder so loud it knocked the wind from Josh's lungs. Sound pummeled the carpet backward. Everyone flew off.

The curator screamed.

Josh yelled. He was falling. Then he hit.

The carpet? It zagged back and forth, spun, flipped, and twisted. Before Josh could catch his breath, everyone was back on.

The booming roar had changed. Laughter? A grindy, wheezy laughter. A sides aching, gasping for air laughter.

"What was *that*?" Dandelion sat up.

Two enormous eyes opened, twin moons glowing blue. Each the size of the carpet, they illuminated the cavern.

The carpet floated high above a stone giant the size of a skyscraper. He lay on the cavern floor and shook with mirth.

"Remy, I da got you dis time." His dull boom was deafening.

The curator crawled to the edge of the carpet. He sputtered, shook his fist, and pointed at the stone giant.

That made the giant laugh even harder. "No bla bla bla? Da firs time in a tousan years I tink."

Remrald's face looked like it was going to explode. "OH! Oh! Grandak. Not funny. You almost killed us."

The giant sat up and blinked at them, his eyes level with the carpet. He snickered like a naughty child. "You always scare me sleepin'. Dis time, I got you."

They all leaned against the wind of his speech.

"Your breath smells like rotworms." The curator crossed his arms and huffed.

The giant shut his mouth and looked at them with in impish smile.

"Well?" One hand on his hip, Remrald looked down his nose and gestured toward something behind the giant.

"Who are dey?" A finger the size of a school bus poked at the carpet.

"You never mind who they are. Just open—"

"Hi. I'm, uh, Dandi." Dandelion stood took a tentative step forward. She fidgeted with the laces on her jerkin. "You're a Mountain Soul, aren't you? I've always wanted to meet one."

"Dundi?" The colossal face broke into a big smile.

"Look, we don't have time ..." The curator pushed in front of Dandelion.

Dandelion just stepped further forward. "I thought your kind lived in the deep, where rock flows like water."

The big face fell. "Black sand-king magic. I stuck 'ere lonely to watch da door."

Remrald gripped Dandelion by the shoulders and turned her toward him. "You want to be stuck down here *with* him?"

"OK." The enormous, stone smile got even bigger.

"Or spend a few years dissolving in the Rotworm Sea?"

The smile disappeared, and the big, stone head slowly shook. "She don want dat."

"And *that* is the *nicest* thing the Ilmenite king will do. To all of you." Remrald waved toward the teenagers. "Grandak. Please. Open the door. I'll come back later and talk to you."

"Promise?"

"Yes." The curator rolled his eyes.

"OK."

The stone giant turned away from them. With each step, the cavern boomed. His blue eyes lit the towering walls. He waved huge hands over a section. Rock flowed, opening a crack big enough to fit Josh's house.

"Hang on," the curator sighed deeply.

The carpet whisked them through the opening into a winding chasm. Rugged walls blurred past. Up. Down. The carpet dodged through cracks and down tunnels. Everyone clung as tightly as they could.

Remrald harrumphed. "Really Gabba? Is this *always* necessary?"

The chasm widened and straightened. Far ahead loomed a dead end. The carpet sped up.

"Oh dear." Remrald groaned and eased himself to his belly. "Here he goes."

They raced toward the cliff wall.

"Is he going to stop?" Josh tugged on the curator's sleeve.

"Duck."

"Huh?"

"Down." Pete grabbed his brother and pulled him to the carpet.

Then Josh saw it. A hole in the cave wall, hardly bigger than a manhole.

"We're going through that?" Josh sat up, eyes wide. "We can't fit through ..."

"Ohh," Remrald moaned and covered his head.

Just as reached hit the hole, Pete and Dandelion pulled Josh down. Edges of the carpet curled upward around the passengers, squeezing. And they were through. Gabba slowed and flattened.

The pudgy curator leveraged himself to his feet, and shook out a handkerchief to dab his forehead. "Gabba, you're fired." He turned to the teenagers and puffed his chest grandly. "Well, my young friends. Welcome to the Fathomless."

Light from the curator's lamp showed nothing. They simply floated, a tiny bubble of light in an endless darkness.

He took a deep breath and spoke to the black, "awake."

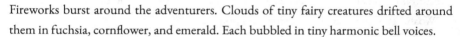

Fireworks burst around the adventurers. Clouds of tiny fairy creatures drifted around them in fuchsia, cornflower, and emerald. Each bubbled in tiny harmonic bell voices.

The group was covered with liquid joy. Dandelion giggled. Pete beamed. Josh laughed out loud.

A peaceful smile flitted across Remrald's lips. "Welcome to the Fathomless."

Their carpet sank through the shimmering mist of fairy creatures. Below, glittered dunes of the whitest sand. Prisms danced in each grain.

"The diamond desert." Remrald smiled at their awe. "And the Beryl forest."

Skyscraper spires of crystal rose from the floor. More hung from the ceiling. Walls of faceted glass split the fairies' light into a thousand colored fragments. The visitors were bathed in rainbows.

All three teenagers' mouths hung open.

"You, are the first of fleshkind to see it." Remrald's smile faded. "So, let's try to be alive when you leave."

As they sank, Josh could see the sand was dotted with shiny objects.

"Are those *all* magic items?" Dandelion's eyes gleamed.

Remrald's face lifted with a sense of pride. "Not just any magic items. The most powerful and deadly collection in existence."

The carpet settled next to an ornate table stacked with books. Nearby, gems shimmered from iron boxes. Swords, suits of armor hung on stands.

Remrald lined all three teenagers in front of him. His double chins squished outward. "Which of you would like to make it out of here alive?"

They shifted their feet.

"Don't touch *anything*. These objects are terribly old and very powerful. Most are war pieces and would kill you just because they're bored."

Pete stared off at a sword.

"Hoh!" The curator snapped his fingers and waved in front of Pete's face. "In fact, don't even look at them. Too much attention, and they'll eat your puny minds for lunch."

He pointed at the kids. "Little fish." He waved at the surrounding objects. "Hungry sharks. Got it?" He glared at each separately until he got a nod or 'yes'.

"The two of you" — he gestured at the boys — "will stand *right* here. Do not step off this carpet." His face softened toward Dandelion. "Your dryad blood should make you safe enough as long as you're with me. Gabba," He glanced toward the carpet. "Entertain the children."

Remrald and Dandelion walked away. Pete and Josh looked at each other and fidgeted.

"Woah." Pete stepped off the carpet and pointed at it.

The battle scenes embroidered into the carpet came alive. Giants riding dinosaurs thundered into battle against humans on horses. Eagles and dragons fought in the air while glowing lava spewed from volcanoes in the background.

The brothers watched the war until Josh was sure he'd seen every possible way a person could die.

"That's the battle of Chrugen." Pete gestured to a tattered flag on a castle wall. Beneath it, a sandwraith ripped the gates off their hinges, as if the oak and iron were paper. "Humans didn't stand a chance until they made a treaty with the dragons."

"This is worse than late night Cinemax." Josh rubbed his eyes.

"Yeah." Pete grinned.

Once the battles were over, there was nothing to do. Pete poked at the giants until one caught his finger and almost pulled him in.

Josh was tired of standing. What was taking Remrald so long?

Pete shifted his feet, putting his hands in and out of his pockets. He kept looking out over the sand. Finally, he burst out, "that's Dad's sword."

Josh glanced up, then quickly looked back at the carpet. "I'm not looking."

Pete stared at the sword.

"Stop it." Josh grabbed Pete's arm. "Remember? Sharks?"

"It's the one he wore the day we left. The one he *died* wearing." Pete was never one for mincing his speech. Years of bitterness saturated that single word.

"He's not dead. We can save him." Josh couldn't help but look at the sword.

Pete snorted and stepped toward the weapon. "I'm going to get that sword and ram it down Kharaq's throat."

Before Pete had taken two steps, the curator and Dandelion walked around a dune carrying a small chest between them.

"Oh! WHAT did I just tell you?" The curator scowled and pointed at the carpet until Pete stepped back on it. He and Dandelion set the chest on the carpet.

In tiny steps the curator swept to the cluster of swords jutting from the sand. He glared from weapon to weapon, hands on his hips. "Stop it. *Now.*"

Dad's sword faded from shining silver to poisonous green. Cruel spikes grew from the guard, jutting toward the blade and handle. Tiny spines covered the grip. It was an incredibly beautiful weapon, but with a toxic sheen.

Triumphant, the curator turned toward Pete. Halfway there, his eyes stopped on a nearby chest. "Oh!" He rummaged in the bottom until he held up a ring. "I forgot about this. Since you're not magic, it will protect your mind by showing you the truth. All you have to do is wear it."

"Can non-magical people claim things too?" Josh watched Pete put it on.

Remrald's eyebrows rose.

Dandelion replaced one of her daggers with one that seemed made of light. "Mostly, the item needs to match the user's abilities. Weapons for warriors, spell books for wizards. A magic fire ring won't do a non-magical person much good."

Josh looked at Pete's finger. The ring was the ugliest he'd ever seen, rotted, black twigs twisted together. As he looked he noticed It wasn't twigs at all. Tiny carvings in fine grained wood linked in a story with wizards, princesses, and cave doorways. Black, brown or tan pieces gleamed with gold and silver wood-grain. Josh couldn't tear his eyes from it.

Remrald turned to Josh, his face softening. "I wish I had one for you, but you're magic. You will be much too sensitive to their voices." With his foot, he nudged the chest. "Sort through this to keep your mind busy until I get back. You'll know what's for you."

Something shuffled behind them. Hung on a wooden stand, a suit of armor slowly melted. Rainbow colors danced and spun across an impossibly polished chrome surface.

The helmet plopped into a gooey pile on the sand. Gauntlets followed shortly.

"Oh." The curator huffed at it. "*You* stay where you are. I don't care if ... Oh!" He stopped mid-sentence, attention caught by an object on a nearby table. He scuttled to it and pulled a golden hourglass from the pile of artifacts.

Two huge diamonds were set point to point in a dainty golden frame. Carved across the frame were gem eyed dragons, flying unicorns, as well as all kinds of strange creatures Josh didn't recognize.

"Window into morrow" — he held up the hourglass — "the Ilmenite king will seek us out. Mark our moments until he comes." He tipped it.

At first the sand trickled slowly, then with a plop, half it fell to the bottom. Remrald gasped, "Oh! Oh my."

He handed the hourglass to Josh and clapped. "Gabba."

The carpet leapt into the air. Boys and treasures were dumped in a pile.

The curator patted the carpet. "Dandelion. Quick, quick."

He scrambled onto the carpet and pointed at the hourglass. "Shout when it gets below that mark." With a whoosh, they disappeared over the dunes.

"What mark?" Josh lifted the hourglass and tipped it sideways to look for the mark.

"Josh." Pete grabbed Josh's hand and straightened out the hourglass.

Etchings showed regular intervals down the glass face. Josh sighed. "*The mark*" could be any one of them.

The boys sorted through the pile of things from the chest. Daggers and glowing arrows were obviously Dandelion's. A belt woven from black iron — for Pete. A short sword with red fire-like veins that curved down the blade, obviously Pete. There were gloves, rings, and a few other weird things. Neither Josh nor Pete could figure out who they were for.

Every couple of seconds, Josh glanced at the hourglass. Sometimes it barely trickled. Sometimes it poured. It was impossible to gauge how much time they had. One thing was for sure, the sand disappeared too quickly.

They sat for a while and watched the hourglass. Pete put on the belt and took it off.

Josh wondered if the mystery items were magic things for him. What did they do? He picked up a gleaming silver feather pendant. Was taking the Ilmenite king's stuff such a good idea? Now they'd have *two* evil creatures hunting them. Maybe they could just borrow Remrald's carpet and fly to the bones. He imagined the pride in Dad's face when they swooped down to pick him up.

"I'm bored." Pete stood. "I'm going to look around."

"What? No. *Pete.*"

Pete was already around the edge of the dune. Josh groaned and sank his chin in his hands. Like he wasn't bored too? Now he had to sit by himself with all this creepy stuff.

A rustle behind Josh made him jump. The silver armor had completely melted. The pool of molten chrome dribbled slowly down the dune's face. Josh swallowed and watched it inch toward him.

Josh dug through the pile again. Where was that sword? At the bottom of the pile lay a gray hooded robe. Made from chain links carved out of stone, it must have been worn by a huge man. Josh could hardly lift it.

Josh spread the robe on the sand. On its chest, the links were carved from gems forming a flaming dragon with open jaws. Josh imagined riding a dragon like that. Like Vastroh. He'd be undefeatable.

Should he try it on? He should wait for Remrald. He stood. He sat back down. He glanced at the chrome armor flowing toward him. It still had a long way to ooze.

Sand trickled through the hourglass. Could be minutes, could be half an hour. Josh looked at the robe. The curator *had* included the robe, after all. It would be safe, right? No, he should wait.

Boredom finally won out. He hefted and struggled. By the time he finally got it on, he was breathing heavily. It was so big his shoulders almost fit through the head-hole. The waist hung down to his knees.

Tingling ran down his arms. The robe must be magic! Josh took a step, walked on the hem, and fell face first into the sand.

Laughter echoed from the dune above him. "In a battle, you'll make a good rug." Pete shook his head and wandered out of sight.

Josh's face burned. He tried to get up, but the armor was too heavy. Both arms tangled in folds of stone. "Pete." Half of Josh's face was smooshed in the sand.

Thoughts poured into Josh's mind. Josh didn't need Pete to fight his battles. Pete was older, but Josh was more powerful? Why call for his brother, *claim the robe.* Images flowed into Josh's head; he led soldiers down the halls of The Throat prison to get Kharaq's bones. Underworld creatures lunged and tore at Josh, but their fangs and claws broke on the robe's stone.

They'll eat your puny minds for lunch. The curator's voice nudged the back of his mind.

Claim the robe. Josh couldn't shake the thought. Should he claim it? Shouldn't he? Suddenly, he didn't care. He'd lost too much already, his memory, his dad, even his simple life at home. Without the robe, he'd lose his chance to be a hero too.

It is mine.

Stone clinked on stone with the sound of breaking glass. The links slithered and twisted, scratching his skin as if he were dragged across gravel. The robe shrank until it fit perfectly.

Josh was on his feet. Fearless. Invincible. Com'on Pete. They'd teach Kharaq a lesson he'd never forget.

In the back of his mind, the curator's voice shouted at Josh to stay where he was. Instead, Josh strode to where he'd last seen his brother. Even though the robe was stone, it weighed nothing, shifting around him like summer cotton.

<hr />

Josh was lost. Pete wasn't at the top of the dune anymore, so Josh kept walking. Magic objects cluttered one dune after another. They all looked the same. The invincible feeling was gone. Josh's heartbeats boomed in his ears. That familiar fist squeezed his heart.

How much sand had flowed through the hourglass by now? Should he yell for help? They'd call him a fool for walking away. Remrald would be furious at him for claiming the robe. He thought about taking it off, but the robe was the only thing between him and all these magic items.

This was the third time he'd walked past that table; an iron demon crouched in the sand with wings unfolded flat to form the tabletop. The table was odd because only one item sat on it: a little black box.

The first time Josh walked by, he wondered why the box sat by itself. The second time, he noticed the box was open and looked inside. It was empty except for a hole the size of a silver dollar in the bottom. This time he realized the hole wasn't just in the box, it went all the way through the table.

Don't look at them. Don't even think about them. How are you supposed to *not* think about something? He knew. Think about something else. He couldn't.

He looked into the open box and slid his foot under the table. Yep, there were his shoes.

With a fingertip, Josh pushed the box over a couple of inches. There was no hole in the table. No, the hole must have moved. He could still see his foot.

Nothing had happened when he touched the box. Maybe his robe protected him. Using two fingers, he gingerly picked up the box. There was no hole in the table. He turned the box upside down; there was no hole there either. Too weird.

Then something landed in his palm. It felt like a silver dollar. Only heavier. And really cold. But there was nothing in his hand.

Except a hole.

A roar boomed through the cavern. Josh's heart stopped. The ground shifted beneath his feet. The smell of burnt earth filled his nostrils.

Overhead, fairy clouds winked out. Ghostly gray light bled from the crystalline towers. The magical objects around him cast eerie shadows in the sand.

Wind whooshed. Before Josh could turn, something hit him and knocked him forward, grabbing and lifting. Dunes shrank beneath him.

"Dragons, you're heavy." Dandelion hooked a hand under his arm.

Pete had his other arm. They pulled Josh aboard the carpet.

Gabba picked up speed until the air whistled around them. Remrald knelt at the front, anxious eyes staring into the dusk. Beads of sweat stood out on his forehead. "He's here."

"He?" Josh swallowed hard.

"The sand king." Pete's eyes were wide.

"Shhh." Dandelion leaned over the edge of the carpet.

Diamond sand boiled beneath them. Midnight stains bled outward from the cavern's center.

"Oh! Fly, Gabba fly." Remrald clenched at the carpet's tassels until it seemed like he'd pull them out.

Everyone crouched. The carpet sped toward the hole in the cave wall.

Below them, sand gathered and swelled, a tsunami in a race with them toward the cave wall.

With a thunderclap, the wave exploded. Tiny black diamonds stung the teenagers' faces. Between them and their escape tunnel towered a three headed beast.

Gray-black with eyes blazing white, it stood at least 80 feet tall. Horns jutted in all directions from its heads. Scaly hide hung loosely in folds from its belly and shoulders.

With a roar, the beast swiped at them. Claws of jagged stone splayed like tree branches from paws the size of a car. The carpet jolted left, but Josh still felt their wind, heard them rip the edge of the carpet.

Dandelion's leg was bleeding, leggings torn down her thigh.

"Your leg ..." Josh's words were swept away as the carpet dropped and shot to the right. More claws whistled past.

Stomach in his throat, knuckles white, Josh clung to the carpet. They all did. Gabba dodged this way and that, climbing, rolling, dropping. The air around them blurred with snapping teeth and slashing claws.

One of the skyscraper stalactites spun toward them, smashed from the ceiling by the beast. The carpet careened right. Josh flew left, into mid-air.

Dandelion screamed. She and Pete grabbed for Josh and missed. Their faces were white. The carpet didn't slow.

Somehow Josh caught a tassel on the back corner. He whipped behind the carpet, arms pulled straight, legs flailing. His grip was giving way.

A giant, snarling face filled Josh's vision. Josh lost his grip. The jaws opened wide, and he was inside. Stale, hungry, angry dusk washed around him. He tumbled, wincing as the teeth crushed down.

Instead, he felt hands. The carpet lurched underneath him and spun sideways between the fangs.

The jaws crashed shut, but they were out. Dandelion and Pete pulled Josh back on.

The two other heads lunged.

The carpet rolled and dove in a free fall. Teenagers and curator mashed into a lump as it curved around them.

Everything went dark.

"Oh." The curator exhaled and pressed his face to the carpet.

They raced down the chasm beyond the hole. The carpet flattened out. Remrald lifted his head. He fished a lamp from his pajamas and looked back.

Behind them, black sand poured through the hole, forming a bridge across the narrow chasm. The Ilmenite king materialized in the center, his long robes shimmering black. Gleaming black hands adjusted a black crown. Burning eyes watched the teenagers. His lips curling, he pointed.

He shrank in the distance behind them, but the breath of his whisper was so close Josh could feel it on his face. Everyone jumped.

"Sand rises fathoms above you; descends fathoms beneath you. To where do you think you'll escape? Every grain is mine. They will fill your lungs, pump through your veins, until the last gasping flicker of your life drains into *my* darkness under the world."

CHAPTER NINE

SCRAWLED IN BLOOD

I t seemed like forever since they'd left The Fathomless. Josh watched the rugged cavern walls drift lazily past in the light from Remrald's lamp.

His heart still raced. The sand king's words still echoed in his ears. "Isn't he going to chase us?"

Remrald didn't look up. "Why would he, there's no sand in here? He just has to wait for us in the cave above."

Josh's relief at their escape changed to a knot in his throat. They'd almost died. And once again, it was his fault; Remrald had given *him* lookout duty. So far no one had said anything, but Josh could feel their silence.

Should he say sorry? He clenched a fist around the hole in his hand; he had a lot more than the hourglass to say sorry for.

What about finding the bones and rescuing Dad? Josh's heart sank even further. His idea of borrowing the carpet crumbled. Gabba wasn't doing well. There were no dodges or swerves this trip. Josh pressed a finger against the weave. It sagged like worn-out elastic.

"Oh." Remrald ran feverish fingers along a gash down one side, then moved to a tattered corner. Threads trailed from a dozen nicks and tears. "Oh Gabba, are you alright? Can you fly?"

"Can he understand *us* too?" Dandelion followed the curator.

Remrald nodded.

"You were amazing. Thank you." Dandelion stroked the carpet.

Tiny ripples sighed across the weave. Embroidered figures turned their eyes toward her.

Remrald snorted. "Oh! Gabba!" He looked down at the carpet, then back up at Dandelion. His pudgy cheeks slowly dimpled into a smile. "He doesn't like anyone but *me*. I'm ... jealous."

Twisting his body away from the others, Josh tried to pick the hole off his hand. He pretended as if he were scratching his leg. The hole wouldn't come off.

Remrald probably knew what to do, but Josh could see the scorn on their faces when they found out.

No. He'd figure it out himself. He'd drop it somewhere in this tunnel. No one would ever know.

"How are we going to get to the surface?" Josh held his fist behind his back.

The curator's face fell. "I hope the princess has a way. I'm going to work on Gabba." He dug around in his pockets, and pulled out a bone needle and a round wooden box the size of a coffee mug. Needle between his teeth, he tugged the box open.

There was a blur from the box. Dandelion shrieked. She leapt to her feet and brushed frantically at her chest. A spider the size of her hand raced up her jerkin toward her face.

Covered with thick black hair, the spider's skin shone purple. Yellow and blue leopard spots peppered its abdomen. As she swiped, the giant arachnid leapt to the carpet.

Even though the carpet was flying, everyone was on their feet, tripping over the other. The teenagers tried to get away from the spider. Remrald tried to catch it.

Finally snatching it in his fist, Remrald sat back down, wiggling spider legs sticking out between his fingers.

The other three huddled at the far end of the carpet.

"Oh heavens." He rolled his eyes and brushed the spider's abdomen with the butt of the needle. Pulling a strand of shimmering web, he began to sew the carpet. Glittering silver dust streamed out behind the stitches, and slowly the rip disappeared.

The teenagers sat in a circle in the middle of the carpet. Dandelion pulled item after item out of her backpack. She sighed and grumbled about the things they'd had to leave behind.

She distributed scrolls, rings, gloves, necklaces, and various pieces of armor among them. Now and then, she'd hold up a strange one for the curator. He'd wave the spider toward one of them and go back to sewing.

She was ecstatic about her "library," a large book made of rough hewn crystal with a clasp and hinges of burnished gold. Its pages flowed like silvery water.

Pete strapped on a sword that would cut through anything. Dandelion donned a quiver full of lightning bolts and a choker that gave her a dozen *more* languages.

Josh's pile was mostly jewelry and scrolls. He had boots that Dandelion said would make him faster than Pete, but Remrald wouldn't let him claim anything until Josh learned what they did.

"How'd you fit all this stuff?" Josh looked at Dandelion's knapsack. Aside from the buckles and ties, it could have been a school backpack.

Dandelion beamed. "It's an echo-pack. It's magic. No matter how much you put in, it never gets heavier. This one could hold a city."

She held up a dull colored pin cushion for Remrald. He was busy sewing and didn't respond. She sniffed it, shrugged, and put it back.

Josh was careful to keep his hand out of sight. He'd already picked up a ring only to have it fall through.

Dandelion glanced at Josh. "What's wrong with your hand?"

"Nothing." Josh quickly changed the subject, grabbing a worn leather-bound book from his pile. "What's this?"

Dandelion scowled at him and handed him a tiny glass bell. "Figure this out first. It's called, Tempest."

The bell looked like something from a Barbie collection. Golden designs scrolled around the edges. When Josh moved the bell, the designs made glowing streaks in the air.

"What does it do?" Josh flicked his wrist.

Dandelion grabbed his hand. "Are you crazy? That's one of the most powerful weapons ever made against the sand wraiths. Its sound blows them to bits."

"I can't fit all this in my pockets?" Josh shoved his pile toward Dandelion.

"Oh. It chose you." The curator glanced up at Josh.

Dandelion beamed at Remrald. "I told you."

"Oh. Such a clever girl." He rolled his eyes and went back to sewing.

"What." Josh looked back and forth.

"The robe, genius." Pete flicked it and pursed his lips. "Stone?"

Dandelion grinned. "From the underworld. Igneous soul dust, cast from the molten sea."

"Aaahh." Josh jerked his hand up. Liquid silver flowed from inside a helmet on Pete's pile. Strands stretched like gum to Josh's hand.

"Oh! No, no, no! How did *you* get on board?" The curator shouted at the silver pool. He stuffed the spider back in the box.

"Here." Eyes still on the pool, he handed the box to Dandelion. The lid was only partially on. Several legs poked out.

"Set me free," a cold voice reverberated in Josh's head. Sharp and crisp, it rang like a sword drawn quickly from its scabbard.

The curator plunged his hand into the pool. Josh could feel Remrald's heavy breathing in his mind. The armor spoke again.

"Set me free."

"Oh! You! Let the boy go or I'll drop you in a barrel of salt water and let you rust for the next thousand years."

"Set me free and I will serve the young warrior."

The curator's mouth opened, but nothing came out. He glanced at Josh, then Pete. "No. You're Necrus. You'll ... you'll twist his mind ..."

"You want to serve me?" Josh's voice squeaked.

"Oh! No. You're a wizard. *He* serves warriors — Necrus warriors." The curator looked like his face would explode.

"What *is* he?" Josh stared at the liquid steel. Josh's reflection was handsome and rugged, and wore shining armor.

"He's Armor. He's been worn by the most black-hearted and brutal warriors in Alaetian history. He's a vicious, aggressive killer."

"It's armor?" Pete knelt next to the pool. "I'm the warrior. He wants to serve me?"

"No. Get back over there."

Pete stared at the armor and pinched his lips. Pete's reflection wore a crown and had bulging muscles.

"Pete. No!" Dandelion grabbed at him.

Pete plunged his hand into the silver pool.

The pitch of the armor's voice changed. Excited. Hungry.

"*I am Campitius. Legends of my name are scrawled in blood across the history of Alaetia. Lord of war, prepare to become a god. You and your sons after you. Allow me to serve you and nothing will stand before us.*"

"NO!" The curator pulled at Pete's arm.

Too late.

"Yes," whispered Pete.

"*Yessss,*" rang the metallic voice.

"Fool of a child." Remrald fell back, eyes bulging.

Silver flowed up Pete's arm and ran along his shoulders. It circled his neck and poured down his chest.

Pete slowly stood and looked down at himself and his gleaming silver breastplate. Pauldrons jutted from his shoulders, and tassets covered his hips and thighs.

"Like his." Pete looked at Josh's chest.

While they watched, the same red and gold dragon flowed onto Pete's chest. Pauldron shoulder pads shrank. Gold designs scrolled around his neck and chest.

Pete beamed. Josh had never seen him look so smug.

"The armor only serves Necrus warriors, why did it choose you?." A wide eyed Dandelion scooted away from Pete, brows arched up at sharp angles. "You're Necrus? Like Kharaq? I thought you were Ershan."

Remrald stared at Pete with the same shocked horror.

"We're both. Mom's Ersha and Dad's Caerdes." Pete radiated menace.

"Caerdes?" Josh mumbled?

"Gods of war. They're an ancient race of killers bred by the Necrus." Dandelion started stuffing things into her pack, her anxious eyes never leaving Pete.

Pete grinned. "He's never lost a fight."

Josh watched his brother's face. "Neither have you."

Thundered rolled around them, "Hi Remy. Hi Dundi."

The cavern widened. The carpet slowed and stopped.

The curator's double chin pushed out. He glared daggers at Pete and snatched the spider box from Dandelion.

"Sandy king mad, uh?" Giant blueish moons blinked at them. "Oh, I 'eard 'im."

"Grandak. Please close that door. And close it tight."

"OK."

"We have to hurry. We can't talk right now."

"Ya. No worms for Dundi." The big face smiled at Dandelion.

Dandelion waved as the carpet shot away into the darkness.

The curator turned toward the brothers. "You"—he scowled at Josh—"were supposed to watch out for us."

"You ..." He glared at Pete. "You ..." His lips tightened.

He spun back toward the front of the carpet. "We'll pay. We'll all pay. Me. The princess. Every unsullied sand soul. Every life in the green world. We have children instead of heroes." He shook his head and spoke into the wind. "The Cambium Dreams say one will die. It's wrong. We'll all die."

There was a hole in Josh's chest where his heart should have been. Every ounce of him wished he was *the* Cambium Dream wizard. But he wasn't. Remrald and the princess had just risked everything for a couple of random kids.

"Don't be afraid," a whisper burned with golden fire in the back of his mind..

Vastroh? Josh perked up and looked around. "Are you here?"

Nothing.

A warrior god on a flaming dragon could really turn things around right now. Josh pleaded silently into the wind. "Even Remrald thinks we're going to fail. Help!"

Nothing.

Josh sagged. Every father figure he'd known was non-existent when he needed them most.

Stop it.

He struggled to force the thought away. "Always" meant "always," and just because he couldn't see Vastroh didn't mean he wasn't there — right?

But miles of rock stretched between Josh and the surface, and as hard as he tried to hold on to the golden whisper, it slowly drowned in the black emptiness.

Dandelion watched Josh's face. Her hand squeezed his. "It's not so bad. The oracle's plan can still work. We have magic armor and I have enough gems in here to hire an army." She patted her backpack.

"Enough to rent a ship as well?" Pete glanced at her pack.

"A fleet of them." Dandelion grinned.

"There's a seaport called Mauda just around the cape from Necrus City." Pete scooted in.

"Mauda's an armpit." Dandelion wrinkled her nose.

Pete beamed. "And full of reckless, bloodthirsty pirates, perfect for a job no sane person would do. Besides, it's closer to The Throat than Braxoni, and we'd avoid the storm giants."

Josh glanced back and forth between the other two. The subterranean blackness felt a little brighter. They just needed to find the princess and get to the surface before the sand king found them.

------◄O►------

They rose through the Rotworm Sea and raced out across over gold-strewn sand. Remrald had finished sewing, so Gabba flew really fast again.

Josh stared at the sand. Any second, a three-headed monster would rise. This time, there was no escape hole.

Dandelion saw it first. By the time she gasped and pointed, it was already too late. A dust devil erupted into a roaring, spinning tornado. The whirling sand spout reached up toward them.

Josh's heart stopped. Or did it all happen between beats? The faces around him froze. Pete's wide eyes. Dandelion's bloodless pale. Remrald's arched brows and fistfuls of carpet.

As fast as it appeared, the tornado was gone. Instead, fragrance; rich, earthy, and wild. The Princess knelt in the middle of the carpet.

"Turn back"—her breathy whisper echoed in their ears—"to the other side of the lake. A tiny crack reaches up to the beach."

The curator recoiled in horror. "You can't! It's treason. He'll kill you."

She laid a tender hand on his. "If I return to the sand palace, I will be killed. My father is dying, so I will return to the sea."

Remrald opened his mouth and closed it again. "You were banished. Your father won't change his mind. They'll kill you there too."

"Death is inevitable. Only Life is a choice." The princess turned to the teenagers, her full lips curved in a sad smile. "It's the same for all of us."

"Your father is the sand king?" Josh gave her a confused look.

The princess shook her head. "The Ilmenite king is my husband."

The curator straightened a little. "She's the first daughter of Calcareous, Emperor of the deep." The way he said it sounded grand.

Dandelion sidled closer to the princess. "You're married to the sand king? Doesn't that make you queen? Why were you banished?"

The princess smiled and touched Dandelion's cheek. "The dry sands have been bitter enemies with the ocean sands since the dawn of time. The beach is a kind of middle ground. It is forbidden for all Sand Souls. Especially for me.

"But I loved the beach. One moonlit night, Sidereus was there too. He was the most beautiful thing I'd ever seen."

Josh tried to imagine the scene. "Sidereus? Is that the sand king? But aren't you guys made of sand? Can't you change shape?" Up ahead was the Rotworm Sea. Josh plugged his nose.

The princess laughed softly. "We are souls that wear a body. Like you, only ours is sand. It's very dangerous for us to be without sand. It is true we can shape sand as we wish, but what you see now is what I look like."

Dandelion glared at Josh, and turned to the princess. "Please finish your story."

The princess gave a shy smile. "Sidereus, that's the Ilmenite sand king's name. He was just a prince back then. Sidereus and I met secretly for months. At night we'd lay on the wet sand and soak in silver pools of starlight. We'd dream of a world without war where our peoples could live in peace.

"We married in secret and found a little place in the sand city. We both had to sneak away from our "other" lives to be there. But we were so happy ... I thought. Then I became pregnant."

The carpet slowed and landed. No magic items lined the sand on the far shores. Brine seeped through a blanket of moss covering the cavern wall. Tiny black roots rippled in the shadows from Remrald's lamp.

Walking along the shore, the princess studied the wall's surface. At each crack, she'd stop, reach out a hand, then move on.

Dandelion followed so closely, she kept bumping into the princess. "Then what happened? After you got pregnant."

The curator looked across the lake. He fidgeted with the buttons on his pajamas. The carpet floated behind him. "Your highness, we need to hurry ..."

The princess nodded to Remrald, then turned to Dandelion, brows knit. "News of the father's identity flooded my kingdom. I'd shamed my family, even my ancestors. I was disowned and banished from the sea.

"*His* family sent him away to war. I was alone. I worked at the marketplace to survive. Our baby was all that kept me from losing my mind. She was so beautiful, emerald stars in a velvet sky. Then ... then ..." The princess covered her mouth and closed her eyes.

Dandelion took the emerald hand. The princess squeezed tightly but didn't move.

"Liuna got sick and ... There was nothing anyone could do." The princess's words were barely loud enough to hear. Anguish washed across her face.

She started to speak several times, but stopped. When she finally spoke, fragments of a shattered soul ground in her voice. "Sidereus came back from the war, vicious and corrupt. His older brothers began to die. Rumors whispered about bargains and black magic from the heart of the mountains."

"Kharaq?" Dandelion's eyes were wide.

The princess nodded. "When there was no one left between him and the throne, his father mysteriously died and my Sidereus became king.

"But he wanted an heir, so he never publicly made me queen. You see, I'd almost died when Liuna was born and couldn't have more children.

"His dilemma is that he cannot remarry while I live. But he cannot find a way to kill me without starting a war."

For the first time in the story, the princess smiled. "Without an heir, his kingdom would go to me if he died. Imagine selling your soul for a kingdom only to give that kingdom to your rival."

She turned to Josh and Pete, taking one of their hands in each of hers. Her skin felt cool and soft. "Do you see why you must not fail? All who are good and desire peace in our world are in mortal danger, both sand and fleshkind."

"But how do we ..." Just as Josh began, the princess stiffened.

She turned sad eyes toward Remrald and gestured to the wall. "It's here."

"Oh! Oh. This is terrible. I hate goodbyes." The curator's face sank into a half-dozen frowns. "Oh. Heaven's sake." He looked up and dabbed his handkerchief below his eyes, then grabbed all the teenagers in a giant bear hug. "Come back and visit old Remy once you've saved the world, OK?"

"You're not coming with us?" Dandelion's eyes were suddenly glossy.

"He cannot. Curator's need treasure like you need air." The princess opened her arms and gestured the teenagers toward her.

Remrald pulled off his cap, and the hair around his bald head sprang in all directions. He waved the cap, shooing them toward the princess. "Go on."

"You're not mad?" Josh looked up at him.

"Oh. No." The curator's puffy eyes blinked at Josh. "Today was more fun than we've had in a thousand years. Right Gabba?"

The teenagers jostled awkwardly against the princess.

"Dear me." The curator held his cap against his chest and dabbed his eyes again.

A dull boom echoed across the lake. Foul wind washed around them.

The princess caught her breath. "Quickly."

Waves rolled on the wriggling sludge.

She gathered the adventurers like a mother covering her children. Josh hugged her back. Everything faded to whirling sand.

———◆O◆———

Sand from the princess's whirlwind melted like smoke. They stood on a small strand of beach. Jagged precipice walls stretched up to an overcast sky behind them.

"This is Demon's Reach. The tide comes in quickly, so you don't have much time." The princess pointed to where the beach ended in a pile of boulders. "You must run there and climb to safety. Get away from the sand. Further down the cliffs is the seaport city Mauda."

"Mauda?" Dandelion stiffened. "That's where we're trying to go."

The princess hugged them. "Things will work out as they should. You are all so brave and strong. If I could have had children, I would want them to be just like you."

Josh closed a fist around the hole in his hand. "I don't think I'm very—"

She put her finger on his lips. "Words hold the power of creation, especially from a wizard. Speak light instead of darkness."

Her face settled into a soft, sad smile, her whisper almost inaudible. "I'm scared too. May Vastroh walk with us into the unknown ..."

She gasped and spun, "RUN!"

Dull booms echoed from the cliffs. A black stain spread across the beach, cutting off their escape. Out the center rose the Ilmenite King. His skin shone with dark luster.

He bowed and snarled a smile. Pointed teeth shone white against black lips. "My queen."

Behind the king, the waves leapt and frothed. Clouds bunched overhead. Chill air bit through Josh's shirt. No one dared move.

The king's smile faded. "See for yourselves," he shouted.

Every inch of the beach boiled around them. Bubbles grew to man-sized mounds, and burst. In moments, thousands of Sand Wraiths crowded the shore from cliff to water.

The sand king's voice roared over the waves. "See how she betrays us — brings human vermin to infest our unsoiled kingdom? What is the penalty?"

The sand crowd murmured and shuffled. Several shouted, "the pit, the pit!"

The princess stood stiff, eyes huge, arms pressed against her sides. "The pit? "

Robes whipping in the wind, the king strode toward her. Around her neck hung a large blue-green gem; strands of gold shot through it like lightning in a storm cloud. He tore it from her and held it aloft. "My people deserve a real queen. Not one polluted by the sea."

She gasped and clutched her chest as if he'd ripped away her robes.

He smirked. "What do we do with the human thieves?"

"Bury them alive!" The crowd backed away from the teenagers.

Josh gasped. Sand gurgled around their feet. In moments, they had sunken to their knees.

"No." The princess put a hand on the king's arm. "They are children. Let them go."

The king looked her up and down. He turned to the crowd and raised his hands in question. Voices murmured.

"Very well." He turned to the princess, fangs flashing. "After we skin them."

The crowd roared.

Sand whirled around the teenagers. Dandelion screamed and pulled her hood up. Josh and Pete covered their faces.

"Sidereus." The princess gripped his arm.

The Ilmenite king laughed and pulled his arm free. His whirling sand picked up speed. The teenagers cried out, huddling together.

"No!" the princess screamed. In a swift motion, she lifted the king over her head and threw him against the cliff.

Chunks of black sand exploded in every direction. A crumbling lump stuck to the wall where he'd hit.

The sand swirling around the teenagers stopped. Red faced, they spat and wiped their eyes.

Black sand lay scattered across the beach. The crowd was silent.

With a whoosh, the dark granules swept to up to the lump on the cliff face. A fully formed sand king leapt down, landing easily. His eyes slowly lifted to the princess. They burned white.

The crowd shouted, fists in the air, "Treason! Death to the traitor."

The princess hadn't moved. She stared at her hands. Closed her eyes tightly. Opened them again. Then covered her mouth.

"Oh no." Dandelion sucked in her breath. "He's going to kill her."

Sand swirled around the king. Robes melted into scales, and fingers stretched to claws. Heads grew from his shoulders, and in moments, the beast from the Fathomless towered over the shore.

Excited shouts rippled through the crowd. They moved back, encircling the king and queen.

The giant heads roared. The king turned to the teenagers, lifted a huge hoof, and stamped it down.

An emerald blur streaked across the beach from the where the princess stood. It slammed into the monster's chest, knocking him backward.

It took Josh a moment to realize the blur was the princess — sort of. She was sea-foam green and sixty feet tall. Her two legs had become four scaly sea serpent tails.

She wrapped her limbs around the sand-king monster. Jagged fins on her tails lashed at his legs and body. Her fangs sunk into his middle neck, tearing the head free.

Her once gentle hands were now webbed and taloned. Webbed wings stretched beneath her arms. Thick hissing eels coiled and writhed instead of hair.

She slashed at his chest with barbed fins jutting from her forearms, almost splitting him in two. Black sand rained down.

The force of her attack slammed him against the cliff. The king howled in pain. He flailed and bit and clawed.

Sand wraiths surged toward the fight. They hooted and punched the air. For the moment, the teenagers were forgotten.

Josh and Pete lifted Dandelion from the quicksand. She, in turn, helped them out. They'd barely pulled Pete from the sand when the colossal frenzy of fangs and claws crashed down where they'd been standing. The ground shook.

As the monsters fought, the princess forced the king into the ocean. As long as she kept him there, she dominated the fight. Waves roared and swirled around him, slowing his movements and washing away the sand that made up his massive bulk.

But he was larger and dragged the fight up on dry sand. Again and again, he would smash her against the cliff walls. The crowd howled each time.

At first, she just reformed, but more and more clumps of green sand stuck on the uneven cliff face or littered on the beach. Bit by bit, she shrank.

Two of the king's heads were missing. His scaly hide was shredded to ribbons. Black sand gushed from huge gashes crisscrossing his belly.

With a roar, he lifted the princess overhead. Her razor-like fins wrapped around his arm, almost cutting it off. But she was too slow, and the king hurled her against the cliff.

Green sand rained down, and her beast was gone. The princess lay face down on the beach, robes piled around her. She didn't get up.

The king's beast lurched over to her. He rolled her over with a hoof. She stared up at him, gasping for breath. With a roar, brought the huge, barbed hoof down.

Josh heard the awful thud and the princess's muffled scream. She tried crawling backward, but the king's monster stamped on her over and over. The crowd roared.

"Stop!" Dandelion screamed, leaping toward the fight. Pete grabbed her and held her back. She fell to her knees in the sand, sobbing. "Stop, please stop."

Josh tried to swallow, but couldn't. It felt like his throat was full of sand. With every thud of those awful hooves, with every muffled cry from the princess, pieces of Josh's heart were ground to dust. What could he do? He wanted to scream.

Where was Vastroh now? Josh's mind reached for the warrior and his flaming dragon. *Help*!

Nothing.

Wasn't Vastroh supposed to be with her too? How was this OK? Where are you? Josh clenched his fists.

"The bell, Josh. Ring the bell." Dandelion grabbed at Josh's pockets.

"What? How?" Josh dug out the bell.

"How should I know? Use your magic."

The king staggered back. As he lifted his remaining head and roared toward the sky, his beast dissolved and he stood over her in his robes and crown.

The crowd closed in, cheering. The king stood with hands raised, soaking it all in.

Chills ran down Josh's spine. Something terrible was about to happen. He shook the bell.

It did nothing.

Josh stared in disbelief. What was wrong with this thing? Faint whimpers bled from where the princess lay in the sand. Tears ran down Josh's face. He gripped the bell and whipped it up and down as hard as he could. Ring, you stupid bell. Ring! Nothing happened. "It won't ring."

Dandelion knelt in the sand and wept. Pete was stone faced. Sand Wraiths flowed to the king.

The king motioned for silence. "She has denied us an heir long enough. Water and air do not mix. What do we do with *salty* sand?" His black eyes blazed.

"Destroy it," the crowd hissed.

The king shrugged. "I've had my fun with her. Your turn."

The crowd surged forward, swarming the place she lay. Her screams rang from the cliffs.

"Stop it," Dandelion screamed. "Stop it! Josh, do something."

Josh slammed the bell against his other hand, then his leg. There was no sound.

"Claim it." Pete's face was white. He grabbed Josh's arm. "You need to claim the bell."

Josh stepped away from the others. "It is mine."

Josh prepared himself for the icy plunge of a magical joining. Instead, tiny black fissures raced from the hole in his hand, up his arm, and across his torso. Before he could even take a breath, his whole body was opaque with cracks.

He gaped at his palm. I meant the bell, not *that* thing. That's *not* mine.

His skin burned white hot, crackling and peeling. Josh screamed. His skin froze, white with frost, and crumbling to pieces. He screamed again.

The shard on his chest blazed black. Oily vapor boiled downward, billowing across the beach.

Then Josh exploded. Whirling shards spun off in every direction. A thunderclap reverberated from the cliffs.

And he was gone.

The air seemed made of cloth, cloth with a hole torn as tall as Josh had been. Wind whipped across the beach, howling through the opening. Ragged edges of the hole flapped in the growing gale. Within it, flowed a river of darkness.

The Ilmenite King's cloak whipped outward. He spun, eyes wide, then dropped to the sand, digging in with his fingers. His boots and hands gouged furrows in the beach as he slid toward the void.

Wind roared through the crowd of sand wraiths. One fell. Then another, and another. In moments, they all tumbled over each other toward the gap.

Just inside the opening, Josh scrambled to his hands and knees. He knelt on a gray beach, sticky-damp with the rotten reek of sulfur. The only light was from the hole.

The muscles in Josh's arms and legs cramped. The cracks were gone, but his body felt like broken glass. Josh heaved breath after ragged breath.

He'd had opened a hole into hell. He didn't know how he knew. He just knew. Josh strained toward the opening, but the wind roaring through shoved him back. He dug fingers and toes into the sand.

A ghost-like sand wraith spun through. All its sand-grains were stripped away, leaving it semi-transparent.

It clutched for him and missed, spinning into the darkness. Shadowy forms whooshed by. Light glinted on massive wingtips. The sand wraith screamed.

More sand wraiths tumbled past Josh, clutching at him. He flattened himself on the sand.

Fanged jaws darted out of the darkness, plucking sand wraiths from the air. Roars echoed around him.

Josh's heart thundered. Remrald's words about them all dying burned in his mind. He had to get out of here.

On the other side of the opening, the wind knocked Dandelion over. She screamed, clawing the sand.

Her cries drove a sword through Josh's heart. It wasn't just Josh who'd pay for his choices. Why hadn't he just told Remrald about the black hole on his palm? Pride. Mom's voice echoed in his mind, *"even the tiniest seed of arrogance to grows into a giant fool."*

Vastroh, help! Josh stared up at a starless sky. Help me make it right.

More sand wraiths tumbled through, bouncing off the edges of the opening. Was it shrinking? It was! Terror and hope surged over Josh in icy chills. What if his friends held on until the hole closed? What if he got out before it shut? If the sand wraiths were all pulled through, he and his friends could escape.

Josh dug in and pulled harder than he'd ever done anything. As he reached the hole, a sand wraith flew through and caught his robe. The force almost jerked Josh free, yanking the robe tight against his throat. He gagged and choked.

Another sand wraith tumbled through and caught hold of the first. Their weight dragged Josh backwards.

"No!" Josh gasped.

More wraiths caught hold until dozens trailed in the wind behind Josh.

Josh grunted, straining against the weight. His fingers cramped. His forearms were on fire.

On the other side, the princess clung to a large boulder, green robes flapping in the wind.

Sand pealed from the Ilmenite king. Other wraiths swept past, reaching for him, begging for help. He shouted and beat away their hands.

Losing his balance, he spun and caught the princess's ankle. She kicked, but he hung on. Slowly, her hands slid over the boulder.

"Let her go." Josh gnashed his teeth.

The princess's grip broke free. She and the king skidded toward the hole.

Dandelion spun into the air. Pete caught her wrist. His feet and other hand gouged deep troughs.

As the princess reached the hole, she caught the lip and hung on. The king streamed out behind her.

The opening continued to shrink.

"Please." Josh begged silently, "Please let it close before Pete and Dandelion are pulled through."

The weight of the sand wraiths was too much for Josh. Beads of sweat broke out on his forehead. He wasn't going to make it, but his friends still might.

He reached for Vastroh with his mind. "At least let my friends survive." Josh could bear the thought of dying if he knew his friends were OK.

Pete cried out. Josh looked up. Pete and Dandelion flew toward the hole.

"Please no," Josh groaned.

Dandelion and Pete hit the princess and the king. All four flew into Josh. Josh lost his grip. Head over heels, they all tumbled into the darkness.

CHAPTER TEN

MADMAN

With a snap, the hole shut and the screaming wind went silent. The Ilmenite King, the princess, and the teenagers landed in a heap with a dozen sand wraiths.

It took a moment for Josh's eyes to adjust. They were on a ghostly version of the beach. Gray waves lapped on twilight sand. Shadows formed a thousand evil faces on the cliffs.

A dim circle of light danced around the teenagers and each of the sand wraiths. The gem burned white at Josh's chest.

The Ilmenite king slowly stood. Falling through the hole had stripped away his sand, and he gleamed with the dull silver of dirty glass. He straightened his robes with opaque hands.

The other Sand Wraiths, in translucent browns and grays, gathered around him. They watched the teenagers with narrowed eyes and snarled lips.

The king took in the scene and laughed. "So, even a Black Doorway fails against the Zotharan?"

He turned to the Sand Wraiths. "I *want* that gem."

Wraiths slowly surrounded the princess and teenagers. Sand drifted up from the beach and gave them form. It smelled like garbage.

The friends and the princess huddled back-to-back. She was sand-less, shimmering in semi-transparent greens.

Pete drew his sword. Fiery lettering danced on the blade. Dandelion held a dagger in each hand; their edges crackled green.

Josh wrung his hands. Everyone knew swords and daggers wouldn't work against Sand Wraiths. He'd lost the bell. What could he do?

He shoved hands in his pockets. There were a couple rings and amulets. After what happened with the hole, he didn't dare claim anything else.

He felt a hand on his arm, smelled the ocean's salty freshness. "Don't be afraid."

"But the last time ..." Josh hissed.

She smiled. "The last time you saved my life. Destiny is created with steps forward. Regret, is stepping back. Have faith."

Josh closed his eyes. Magic could save them. With Vastroh's magic, he'd set a whole city ablaze. *Help*. He reached toward Vastroh in his mind. But nothing was there. Where are you? He felt completely alone.

"You're not alone." The princess's whisper was the soothing hush of waves on a sandy shore.

Josh's hand closed around a ring in his pocket. What did it do? What if it made things worse? *Step into the shadow*. Josh slid his finger into the ring.

Sand exploded around them. A leathery cat-like creature the size of a rhinoceros landed in the middle of the sand wraiths. Its huge bat-wings beat the air. Armored spikes rippled down its back.

"Torgogs," Dandelion hissed, backing the huddle away.

Sand Wraiths scattered. The torgog pounced on one, biting and shaking its head.

More demon-cats swooped from overhead. Two fought over a sand wraith, pulling until, with a flash of light, it ripped in two. One beast flew away with half. The other gobbled hungrily, and turned toward the teenagers, sand bleeding from the great jaws.

Waves of gray sand rolled to the Ilmenite king. His monster form rose above the fray. Roaring, he raised stone claws to the sky.

In an instant, the air filled with torgogs, pouring from the darkness to cover the sand king. They howled as they bit and slashed.

Vertigo swept over Josh. There was no winning against these things. Run! But run where? The creatures were everywhere.

The sand king ripped beast after beast from his body, hurtling them into the night. Each time, great chunks of sand tore free. But for each demon-cat he flung away, two more would land in its place.

The Ilmenite king's roar of triumph thinned to a wail of terror. His beast form flailed at the swarm. The torgogs howled and bit and clawed until there was nothing left of him but thrashing stumps of arms and cratered remains of the giant body.

With a scream, the sand king's monster collapsed. The robed figure leapt free and sprinted down the beach. Torgogs tumbled down the sand pile and streamed after him, yowling and batting at each other.

Josh wiped the grit from his face. His throat was full of cotton. The torgogs were distracted. It was now or never. The ring slid from his finger. "Quick. Before they come back." He pointed to a section of the cliff face full of cracks and hollows.

Dandelion nodded, twin daggers still held out in front. Back-to-back, the group edged toward the cliffs.

On the distant beach, the sand king disappeared in a flood of beasts. A moment later, he spun head over heels above the storm. Torgogs leapt from below. More swooped at him from overhead. Again the king disappeared, and again was flung over the beasts. The swarm lurched left and right across the beach as the creatures batted him back and forth, biting off pieces.

Light flashed from the center of the mob, and with a scream, the king was gone. The torgogs howled with triumph.

"Run ..." Josh's shout smashed into the sand. A torgog stood above him with one claw on him and one on Pete. Josh tried to scream, but it felt like the cliff had fallen on him. The surrounding scene wavered in gray semi-consciousness.

Above Josh, the beast raised its face and roared.

Pete's liquid silver armor flowed, and with a pop, he slid free.

"Josh!" Dandelion screamed at Pete.

Pete scooped up his sword and swung toward the beast. Dandelion plunged both daggers into the torgog's foot. With a roar, the beast swatted them away. The two cartwheeled across the beach. Pete landed at the base of a cliff. Dandelion hit a rock and crumpled like a rag doll.

More torgog's landed on the sand.

The demon's jaws bit down on Josh. Sinews on its neck bulged as it pulled and twisted. Josh's consciousness fled.

Pete staggered to his feet. The gray cliffs spun around him. Fists balled in front, he turned left and right, looking for his attacker.

Out on the beach, torgogs swooped and chased Sand Wraiths in every direction. In the cliff's shadow, the princess limped from boulder to boulder to where Dandelion lay.

One of the beasts gnawed on something between its paws, a giant dog with a bone. Josh! No! Pete grabbed for his sword, but it wasn't there.

It fell by the precipice. The metallic rasp of Pete's armor rang in his head. *The beast knocked it from your grasp. A warrior needs an alternate weapon. We will seize one in the next town.*

Pete's eyes swept the nearby sand until they caught the glint of steel. He sprinted for the sword. *Campitius, will the beasts die?*

My wearers have killed many. The metallic voice rose in expectation.

Pete's mouth was dry. Campitius could melt back together after being torn to pieces. He wouldn't be so lucky. Those torgogs must weigh 2000 pounds.

Another Beast swooped down on Josh. The two tugged on the teenager, growling and twisting. Giant claws dug furrows in the sand.

"Josh!" Pete scooped up his sword and ran toward his brother.

Tonight we will bathe in torgog blood, Pete's armor hissed with excitement.

Campitius poured images of previous battles into Pete's head. *Their first attack is always by claw.* The warrior in Pete's mind rolled under the torgog's swipe and buried his sword in the beast's belly, pushing the point up under the ribs.

Pete's legs were lead. A Kung Fu studio was a lot different than fighting rhinoceros sized demons. Not to mention, those other warriors had been a lot bigger and older than Pete.

Pete ran for the bigger of the two creatures. That's what Dad would have done; win the biggest and the smaller might flee. Just before Pete reached it, the smaller one wrenched Josh free and leapt into the air. The other chased after it. Both beasts disappeared into the dark sky.

"Come back!" Pete screamed after them, jabbing his sword in the air.

The cowards. Pete's armor heaved a disappointed sigh.

The tiniest piece of Pete was relieved — there were no more monsters to fight. Shame washed over him. How could he even think that? What kind of person would be OK with watching his brother die?

"Nooo," Pete shouted at himself as much as at the beasts.

Pete's breaths came in gulps. He turned his attention to his armor. *Will my brother's armor protect him?*

Perhaps. The armor's tone was flat.

How do we hunt them? City lights glimmered on the horizon. Pete stared, hoping to see the torgog's silhouette.

I know of no way. Campitius brooded in Pete's mind. *You must not stand in the open. There are other things floating in the darkness we cannot defeat. You must—"*

I know. Regroup. Make a plan, Pete snapped, turning toward the cliff in a stumbling run. The scene of the beasts ripping at Josh and then flying away played over and over in his head. It was like being kicked in the stomach again and again.

Yesterday is changed tomorrow, Dad would always rumble after Pete had really screwed up. There was no going back, but he could make sure it didn't happen again. Pete imagined himself spinning through the torgogs and hacking them to pieces.

Campitius approved.

Pete found the princess and Dandelion kneeling in a hollow at the base of the cliff. Blood matted Dandelion's hair and trickled down her forehead.

Dandelion looked around, dazed. "Where's Josh?"

"One of those monsters ..." Pete couldn't finish his sentence.

"Oh no." Dandelion gripped Pete's arm

Pete swallowed a few times. There was a volcano of rage and tears swelling in his chest. He forced an I-don't-care look on his face and leaned against the entrance with his hands in his pockets. "We have to ..." His voice cracked like an eleven-year-old. He turned toward the beach so they couldn't see his face. "Campitius said his armor might protect him. We have to find him."

"Where are we?" Dandelion's eyes didn't quite focus.

"I believe this is the Shadowline." The princess pushed herself to her feet with a groan. "When I was young, I had an unhealthy fascination with this place."

"We're dead?" Dandelion bit her lip.

The princess shook her head. "This is the transition between the living and under-worlds. The unlucky dead float here like leaves on water. But all eventually sink."

"Can we get back up, or out, or whatever?" Pete's voice was fragile as glass. He helped Dandelion stand.

"There are those who can travel to this place and beyond." The princess pursed her lips.

"Ferrymen." Dandelion paled. "They're practically ghosts themselves."

The princess pointed at the glow of city lights in the distance. "That glow is living souls. It's the city of Muada. Perhaps we will find a ferryman there."

"What about Josh?" Pete wrung his hands.

The princess gestured to the glow around each of them. "Ferrymen are skilled at finding souls."

Pete stared off at the lights. How many hours would Josh survive out there alone? He looked at the princess. "Can you carry us there in a tornado — like in the treasure cave?"

The princess shook her head and looked down at her sand-less hands. "Sand here is poison, a sea of bitterness. Even the tiniest grain will chain me to this dark place. We will walk." She limped toward the entrance of the hollow. "Slowly."

Dandelion took Pete's hand and squeezed. "Josh is OK."

Pete swallowed and looked at the ground.

The princess enveloped both teenager's in a hug. Dandelion and Pete hugged her back. It was a long time before anyone moved.

Finally, with a nervous eye on the sky, they edged along the beach close to the cliff. Hoarse screams rang in the dark.

— ◆◇◆ —

A newspaper skittered down the dirty cobblestone street. Main street. Docks lined one side, shops and taverns lined the other. Garbage lay in jumbled heaps between buildings.

Pete plugged his nose and glanced at the other two. This place was a dump.

It was a grand city in my day, Campitius snorted with disdain. *The ruler should be executed. Let us do it.*

Pete ignored his armor.

Crowds jostled past store fronts. Giant snails pulled floating carts. Scaly ape-like creatures carried stacks of crates, stooping under the weight as their masters urged them forward.

"How do we find a ferryman if no one can see or hear us?" Pete stepped through a man carrying a large basket of fish.

He'd given up trying to walk around people or stepping aside. It was easier just to walk through. It was as pointless as trying to talk to people. Pete had shouted until his voice hurt. No one heard.

Dandelion sidestepped a pile of trash. "We need to look for a shop that ..."

"The three, the three,

That none can see,

None can see, but me, but me."

A voice grated from the street corner. The minstrel sat cross-legged on a ragged cloak along with several dirty coins. He squinted at the princess and teenagers, his white hair sticking out in every direction.

Hackles stood on Pete's neck. Dandelion grabbed her companions and pulled them to a stop. They stared at the man.

"Sir, can you see us?" The princess stepped toward the minstrel.

Crooked yellow teeth peeked from under an untidy mustache. "Aye." He only had one eye. The other was a sickly green marble that leered crookedly in their direction. Dull colors formed a lopsided iris.

The eye of Demergeris, Campitius growled. *It gave special sight to the Necrus kings. He deserves to die for possessing it.*

Pete sighed, *You think everyone should die.*

And then you and I would rule this world. The armor chuffed.

The princess faced the musician, standing tall and regal. "We carry out a very important quest. Would you render us aid? We seek a ferryman or passage back into the world of the living."

His smile grew. Half his teeth were missing. "A passage back to the living? 'Tis all ye shadows ever want." His lopsided gaze swept over the group. "There is but one way."

Coins tossed from a passing man clinked in the minstrel's lap. The minstrel leaned over his lute and strummed. A broken string bobbed on the neck. Worn gilding peeled from ornate designs across the instrument's belly.

"For a drink, I'll tell the way,

"Naught but beer on summer's day,

"Sunlight clear and golden brown,

"Hell and heaven going down."

The group looked at each other. He sang about every type of beer. Several times, the princess tried to get his attention. He ignored them, strumming and singing extra loudly. If a word didn't rhyme, he'd mispronounce it, and cackle.

Pete shook his head. "He's crazy."

Yes! Pete's armor was triumphant. *One strike of your sword. One less crazy human.*

Scowling, Pete shushed his armor and turned to the princess. "Are you fading?"

The princess bit her lip. "We all are."

Dandelion turned toward the minstrel and stomped her foot. "You want a stupid beer? How are we supposed to get that? We can't even touch anything."

The minstrel clucked. "No? *He* got one."

They looked where he pointed. Pete and the princess gasped.

Dandelion screamed. She was running before the other two even caught their breath. "Josh!"

Josh stumbled down the street, mind churning. His hands throbbed, but the minstrel had been right.

"Josh!" Dandelion almost knocked him over in an enormous bear hug. The beer he carried sloshed everywhere.

"Ho! My beer. Be careful." The minstrel shook his lute at them. "Ye ghosts have naught for sense."

Several people walked past and shook their heads.

"You're OK." Pete and the princess caught up to Josh, joining the hug. More beer spilled on the ground.

Dandelion sobbed and laughed at the same time. "We thought you were dead." She glanced at Pete. "We were coming to find you."

The minstrel sputtered at them, pointing at his beer. He finally settled into a scowl and counted his coins.

Dandelion ran a hand over his arm. "You don't have a mark on you."

Josh was still a little dazed. He hooked the hem of his robe and lifted it toward them. "The robe turned into a rock. They kept fighting over me and dropping me and finally gave up. Then I walked toward the lights and hoped you guys would too."

Josh closed his hand around the hole on his palm and shifted his feet. "We're dead, aren't we?"

The princess pursed her lips and looked meaningfully at Josh. "Yes and no. We float between life and death. We're in the Shadowline. Were it not for the gem you wear, the black doorway would have swallowed us all."

Chills ran down Josh's spine. She knew this was all his fault.

Pete narrowed his eyes at Josh.

Dandelion gaped at the princess. "Black doorway? That hole we fell through? I didn't think they were real. Who opened *that*?"

"It stuck to me." Josh put his hand behind his back.

"Josh?" Dandelion's brows bunched in dismay.

"Oh child," the princess sighed.

"What's a black doorway?" Josh mumbled, eyes to the ground.

Dandelion crossed her arms. "It's a weapon. If a battle was lost, the losing side could invoke it and everyone in the battle zone was killed. Xerudia of Necrus is the only one who knew how to make them. She died using the last one against Sand Wraiths."

She turned to the princess, eyes lighting up. "Legends say her bones are hidden in the Tomb of Ages. She waits in the underworld, in the Black City, for a wizard to bring her back."

The princess raised her eyebrows. "If they are, and if we ever return, I'll have Remrald throw them in with the rotworms."

A tiny thrill spun in Josh's stomach. They weren't dead after all? And there were ships and sailors everywhere. Maybe they could still kill Kharaq and save Dad. He reached out to Vastroh in his mind. *We need a way out.*

The princess turned to Josh. "Is it still attached to you?"

Josh flinched and stuffed his hands in his pockets.

She touched his shoulder. "Every soul alive has made mistakes. You know some of mine."

Josh stuffed his hands deeper and stared at the pavement.

"Until I expose my mistakes, I am doomed to repeat them." She lifted his chin until his eyes met hers. "You cannot free your father or defeat Kharaq without making mistakes. You cannot become the wizard you were meant to be without making those mistakes right."

Josh shuffled his feet. Blood still caked in Dandelion's hair. That was his fault. The princess cradled her arm and walked with a limp. That was his fault. His brother was stuck here in this halfway-hell. That was Josh's fault too.

Why was sorry so hard to say? They all looked at him. It made throat dry and his chest hollow. He tried, but his mouth just wouldn't say it.

Instead, Josh changed the subject. "Every time I do magic, it goes completely wrong."

The princess let out a disappointed sigh. A cold breeze shifted her hair. Her eyes played over his face. "Mistakes are a sword with two edges. It's true we are in this place, but the dark sand army is vanquished and we still survive. You are the first wizard in history to accomplish such. Have faith."

The first in history? Really? Josh stood a little taller.

"The thing around your neck. I can smell it." The minstrel picked at something between his teeth with a dirty fingernail. "It's from death and longs to return."

Dandelion spun toward the minstrel. "You're lying. See, we've already stopped fading since Josh got here with the gem. Besides, who asked you? You weren't going to help us unless you had a ..." She swallowed and looked at Josh.

Her eyes went to the empty beer mug. "How did you get that?"

Josh flashed a shy smile. "I can use the gem to reach into the living world. He says I could step into death too, but ..." Josh shuddered.

Dandelion grabbed Josh's shoulders. "Remember what the oracle said about the gem?"

"God of the underworld." Pete's eyes narrowed.

Dandelion bounced on her toes. "You can bring us all back."

Pete straightened. "We can kill Kharaq and save Dad. Campitius says we'll be heroes, legends in our own time."

"Get me that beer and I'll tell ye how to go about it." The minstrel waved his lute at them.

They looked at the empty mug, then at each other.

The minstrel licked his lips. "Well ... be quick about it then. Do ye want to know or not?"

"In there." Josh gestured toward a group of sailors. One strutted with thumbs under a crimson sash, a huge, jeweled scimitar at his waist. He and his friends shouted to some passing women before disappearing into a pub.

The teenagers followed. The only light in the dingy great room was one filthy window. It took a moment for Josh's eyes to adjust. Sailors crowded dark, rough-hewn tables, laughing and waving giant mugs of ale.

"Over here." Josh led them through a clump of singing deckhands to the bar.

"Oh," Dandelion gasped and pointed. "Is that butter?"

All three of them stared at a steaming platter. Roast chicken and freshly baked bread filled the plate. A slab of butter slowly melted on one side. Pete's stomach growled.

"This is how I push through." Josh reached toward a beer on the counter. Dark cracks webbed in the air around his hands as if a thin sheet of ice were between him and the beer. As he pushed, shards of the barrier tumbled to the floor.

Other cracks zig-zagged up Josh's hands and arms. He winced and gasped. Smoky threads stretched between the hole and his fingers.

Grunting with effort, Josh grabbed the beer and the platter of food, took a couple of deep breaths, and pulled the food back through. The cracks disappeared, and everything looked as it had before, except the beer and food were on their side.

Beads of sweat stood out on Josh's forehead. He handed the items to Dandelion and rubbed his arms. "I've tried to get farther through, but I can't."

They walked back to the minstrel. Shouts and curses rang behind them.

"Hoy, the food!" The cook stared at the empty counter. He yelled at the barmaid, who cuffed the cleaning boy.

The teenagers devoured bread and chicken while they walked. Pete wanted some of the beer.

When they reached the minstrel, Josh pushed the beer through to him and stepped back.

Dandelion stood in front of the minstrel, an impatient hand on a defiant hip. Mouth full, she pointed at him with a piece of bread. "OK. How do we get out of here?"

The minstrel glanced up mid gulp. Froth speckled his beard. "I've fugured ye out. Yer de tree young 'uns who's started the slave riot and disappeared? Town's a buzzin' with talk o' de Dreams comin' real."

Dandelion huffed. "Mind your own business. Tell us the way out."

The minstrel gulped the last of his beer and laughed. More a hack than a laugh. "De beer was warm. I'll be needing a cold one."

He held the upside down glass toward them. "One more, then I'll tell ye."

"What? No. Liar. Tell us now!" Dandelion shouted, red faced.

"You ... you ..." Dark fury exploded within Josh. His fists clenched and unclenched, his breath came in gasps.

He'd been angry before, but this was different. Oceans of the blackest rage poured from the sky above and boiled from the earth beneath. This man deserved to die.

"Ah." The minstrel shook his head and clucked with disapproval. He pointed his chin at Josh. "See 'ow the shadow seeps inta that one? The death shard feeds on anything dark within 'im. Soon not'in will be left of 'im but pure evil. Madness. De story always ends in madness."

A howl grew within Josh's chest.

The minstrel leaned toward the group and whispered, "it were what drove de previous wearer to insanity."

"Kharaq?" Dandelion had stopped chewing.

The minstrel waved off the question as if it were stupid. "He played wid de stone like a child. I speak of its real master. I'll tell ye the story."

"Forget your story. Tell us the way out of here," Josh growled. Black vapor rolled from the gem.

"Yer way out is *in* her story." The minstrel squinted his stony eye at them. He pulled his lute close and lifted his chin with pride. "Twas a time I sang for the Eventide Throne at de Sunset Palace. Herself were dere."

Nimble fingers danced on the strings. A haunting melody drifted around the teenagers.

"Twas one escaped the poison maw,

"Twas turn of age and winter's thaw,

"Curses 'neath her fiery hair,

"Burn-ed black on skin so fair."

"The *what* throne?" Pete stepped toward the minstrel.

"Ah. Hear de story, will ye now? 'Tis a grand one. De Poison Flame. I *am* a bit thirsty for de telling."

"Poison Flame?" Josh sucked in his breath. Lights raced up his arms.

"Fiery hair? A black tattoo on fair skin?" Pete's eyes bulged.

Both boys stared at each other. Josh's heart hammered. Pete swallowed loudly. "Mom!"

They both turned toward the old man. "Tell us the story."

The minstrel smacked his lips. He rolled his eyes meaningfully at the empty mug.

Black veins bloodshot Josh's eyes. He spoke through clenched teeth, "tell me the story."

"Oh ho ho," the minstrel chortled.

"Want to know?

"Before you go?

"No!" He strummed dramatically. "Not until I get—"

The minstrel's words choked off. Josh plunged his hands through and gripped him by the throat. The minstrel writhed on the ground. Black fissures raced up his neck and face from Josh's hands. He ripped frantically at Josh's fingers. Passersby slowed and stared.

"Josh!" Dandelion grabbed his shoulder.

Josh ignored her. His lips peeled in a snarl. "Tell me. Now!" Vapor poured off the gem and drifted along the cobblestones.

The minstrel gargled and choked. His eyes bugged out. He nodded, jerking his head up and down.

Pete stared wide eyed at his brother. "Josh?"

Josh released him and stood, legs wide, towering over the old man. Vapor floated from his head and shoulders.

The minstrel crabbed backwards into his corner, gasping in shallow breaths. He hugged his knees to his chest and, with shaking hands, gathered his things around him. Another string on his lute had broken. He wouldn't look up. "None knew de silver of starlight flowed in her veins, for she were but a child, yung and pretty and pure. Some say de Magick come from her mother, great granddaughter of de last Modus Overload, wild an' fire-haired. Some say de Magick from her father, knight in the royal guard an' second cousin to the king."

"The 'silver starlight' is magic." Dandelion whispered behind Josh.

Pete rolled his eyes at her. "I know."

Josh's stare didn't leave the minstrel.

The wild-haired musician glanced at Josh and then back at the pavement. "De king were no real king. He were but steward to de throne, for though his blood be royal, he had not the blessing of the stars, and those without the magick, be not fit to rule."

Josh gritted his teeth. "The short version."

The minstrel licked dry lips. "Those with de Magick fear for der lives from the de king. 'Twas Kharaq who told her secret, for he loaved her and watched her hungrily from de hidden passages of the castle. When he bared his heart, she despised him. Sayd she rather de Throat.

"So 'twas he who told de king to fear for his throne, he who said she should be made an example, burned with every curse he could conjure. 'Twas he who had her father killed an' then her thrown into de Throat. To eat her words and suffer forever."

"Mom?" Josh whispered. He couldn't swallow. He remembered when she tried to talk about her childhood, the way her brows bunched and her eyes welled up. When he was scared, she'd stroke his hair and say she *understood*.

"The Throat?" The princess covered her mouth.

Dandelion's face was white.

Josh and Pete looked at each other.

Pete pulled his sword free. Crimson lettering glowed and danced on the blade. He strode toward the minstrel, "'Twas one escaped' The Throat? Finish *that* story."

CHAPTER ELEVEN

BRANDED

T he minstrel clutched the lute to his chest. His eyes flicked to Pete's sword, then to Josh.

"How did she escape The Throat?" Josh leaned toward the trembling musician.

Before the minstrel could answer, Josh felt a hand on his shoulder. Dandelion turned him toward the crowd. She covered her mouth and pointed.

A huge galleon rocked against a nearby pier. Tarnished brass curled in dusty green scrollwork down the gunwales and across the stern. The figurehead was a man clawing at the air, his face twisted in horror.

Shouts echoed from the streets. People spilled from the buildings and gathered around the ship.

At the foot of the ramp, a fleshy bald man in sleeveless, blood-red robes towered above the crowd. He scowled at the surrounding people until a large space formed.

Six bare chested slaves shuffled into the opening. Each pair carried a giant bone between them on their shoulders. Huge bells of beaten metal hung from the bones. The slaves formed a triangle near the tall man in red.

From within his robes, the man pulled two large hammers. He walked slowly around the bells and stopped in front of a silver one, tarnished almost black. The crowd hushed.

"What's going on?" Josh couldn't tear his eyes from the man.

"A summoner." Pete's face was hollow. "Campitius says someone's banished to The Throat ..."

BONG.

The summoner spun, arms lifted, robes billowing. His hammers blurred across the bell, moving so quickly their beats rang like a single chord.

Chills washed down Josh's spine. The bell-song was haunting and beautiful. In Josh's mind, snowcapped mountains rose from icy seas; wildflowers filled the ruins of an ancient city.

Instead of slowly fading, the chimes grew louder. Storm clouds filled the sky above the summoner.

BONG.

Hammers struck the second bell. Dark notes mingled with the ones already in the air. The hair on Josh's arms stood. Valleys of shattered volcanic pumice filled his mind. Rivers glowed silver under a troubled moon.

Above them, lightning crackled across the darkening sky. Air in the center of the bell triangle thickened, rising in waves, like heat from a desert road.

The crowd huddled and pointed. Some plugged their ears.

As the summoner stopped in front of the third bell, a man stepped from the crowd. He waited, hunched under a brown rough-spun robe. Black wisps of smoke drifted from a golden censer cupped in his hands.

BONG.

Deep and resonant choir voices joined the chimes. The air between the bells writhed gray and green, a wind whipped ocean in an oncoming storm.

The man with the golden censer stepped forward.

Dandelion drew a sharp breath.

The censer's lid was opened. Smoke snaked around the bells, claw-like. Lightning lashed downward, smashing between them in gleaming arcs.

The minstrel whimpered and covered his head. People shrank behind others in the crowd.

A shape loomed in the bell triangle, polished black, and twenty feet tall. The dock creaked under the weight.

The Bell chords faded and lightning scampered back to the sky. The slaves hefted their bells and followed the summoner into the crowd.

Behind them, the haze cleared. Towering golden pillars stood on either side of black granite gates.

The crowd held their breath. Slowly, the doors opened. Mist poured through the opening.

"The high priest?" Pete swallowed loudly.

The minstrel rubbed the bruises on his neck and glared at Josh. "I hope they bring an inquisitor."

A man strode the gateway, mist swirling in his wake. Spindly eyebrows arched over a gaunt face and long, sharp nose. As he walked, people shrank back. He basked in the gasps from the crowd.

He wore a tight black silk vest and a pleated black cassock. Over it hung a blood red robe lined with white fur. Every piece of clothing swam with gold embroidery.

Two ape-like beasts filled the gateway behind him, each three times the size of a man. Curved boar tusks jutted from thick, flat faces. Black iron chains draped over their mottled blue-gray scales.

"Ogrei." Dandelion shrank back.

One held a pitted iron box jutting with long tool handles. The other carried a crystal cauldron of boiling tar. Smoke poured from the pot. Something writhed in the tar.

As they walked, a droplet splashed on the dock. The tar hissed and bubbled, burning into the plank.

"That black sludge"—Dandelion hissed—"is liquid evil from the River of Souls. It flows through the underworld."

The high priest walked aboard the galleon. Stocks for holding prisoners stood near the mainmast. He leaned on them, and with a flourish of his cloak, faced the crowd. The beasts stood beside him.

"Bring the prisoner." The priest's voice was high and pinched.

Two guardsmen in gleaming red and gold armor dragged a man in tattered finery up to the ship. His messy hair and untrimmed beard were caked with blood and dirt. Straw stuck to his clothes.

Murmurs rippled through the crowd.

The priest raised his hands for silence. "Our emperor, Kharaq, has returned. Yet the Ershan elite wish power only for themselves. The power should be yours."

"Emperor?" Pete snarled. "He's a groveling dog."

"What do we do with traitors?" The priest sneered.

Voices rumbled through the crowd. "The Throat," rang out here and there.

"It's time for a reminder of what happens to those who question the good of the people." The priest gestured to the ogrei holding the box of long-handled tools.

"Stop telling me who deserves to die," Pete muttered under his breath.

"Who are you talking to?" Dandelion raised an eyebrow toward Pete.

"Huh? Oh. Campitius."

"Who?" Dandelion glanced around at the crowd.

"His armor." Josh thought of the ringing steel voice.

The princesses sucked in a breath and turned toward Pete. "I forgot about your armor. He has seen empires rise and fall, and has been privy to war counsels and magic of terrible power. He, more than anyone, may know our path out of this place."

"He doesn't. I asked." Pete frowned.

"Fine." Dandelion crossed her arms. "But he probably doesn't know if what he knows will help. He's *only* armor, after all. You have to tell us everything he says."

"Fine." Pete shrugged. "But you'll regret it. He said, 'only armor? She deserves to die.'"

"Necrus junk," Dandelion snorted and turned back toward the ship.

On board the galleon, the priest held a long iron rod; one end was shaped into a barbed letter.

"That's ... a brand." Josh's voice was hoarse.

Dandelion voice was tense. "The letters are magical runes. Curses."

The priest plunged the brand into the crystal cauldron. When he pulled it free, the metal glowed red.

The prisoner's eyes snapped wide. He kicked at the guards, but their thick hands held him fast. They dragged him to the stocks and locked him in. One Guard grabbed his hair and pulled his head to one side to expose his neck.

The man tried to scream. All that came out was an eerie wheeze.

As the priest plunged the brand toward the man's neck, a large merchant in the crowd stood on his toes, blocking Josh's view. All Josh could see was the prisoner's legs kick out straight and then go limp.

With a pair of tongs, the priest pulled something the size of a golf ball from the pot. The crowd gasped. Dark red and covered with yellow-green veins, the octopus-like creature hissed and spat at the priest.

The priest jabbed the tongs at the prisoner. Moans ran through the crowd.

Josh stepped where he could see. "What just happened?"

Pete looked like he was going to throw up.

The prisoner dangled from the stocks unconscious. Smoke drifted from the brand on his neck. Something squirmed beneath the skin under the mark.

Dandelion's voice was quiet. "Occuts feed on souls. Once the baby pulls itself into the mark, the torment never stops. It's so painful and hopeless, hosts all eventually go mad."

"An occot?" Prickles ran down Josh's arms.

"They're from the Seams." Dandelion watched Josh's face for a moment and continued. "Seams are formed when someone dies. As they slide into the chasm between the worlds, a path is created. Think of the Seams reaching through the world like the veins of iron running through the rock in a mountain. They're everywhere."

Josh's brows crunched. "Is that why sometimes I get chills ..."

Frantic fingers grabbed Josh's arm; Pete's mouth opened and closed, but nothing came out.

"What." Josh glared at his brother.

"That mark." Pete's voice was a rasp. He pointed at the man's neck.

Josh gagged. Suddenly, he was on his knees, coughing and gasping for air.

Dandelion reached for him. "Are you OK?"

Josh choked on the words, "My mom has that mark. It's the same character with the letters that look like they're dripping."

Dandelion gasped.

Pete's face was grim. "That man barely survived one mark. My mom has dozens, all down her neck and body."

Dandelion covered her mouth. She shook her head again and again, but didn't say anything. Her eyes filled with tears.

The princess's face was white. She pulled the teenagers to her, turning their faces from the scene.

"Who would do something like that?" Uncried tears clogged Josh's voice. The minstrel had said she was just a girl.

How many times had Mom hugged him through his night terrors, or said he was amazing when school kids said he was a loser? Who had been there to comfort *her* when *she* was a girl? How many times had Josh touched those marks and seen the hurt behind her eyes? She'd never complained, and he'd never understood.

"Wake him." The priest kicked at the prisoner.

Guards opened the stocks, and the prisoner collapsed onto the deck.

"Acts against the royal house affect more than just the perpetrator," the priest's shrill voice rang above the crowd. "This man's child will not inherit his lands or his title. Instead, she will also receive the mark of a traitor."

A cry snapped Josh's attention back to the massive granite gates on the dock.

Guardsmen shoved a girl out in front of them. She looked about twelve, with long red hair. Smoothing a rumpled dress of pink and white embroidered silk, she stood straight and walked with hesitant steps. Her quivering lips stood bright against alabaster skin.

"Marina," the prisoner croaked at the girl. On his knees, he gripped the hem of the priest's robe. "Please!"

The girl faltered when she saw her father. One hand covered her mouth. The other reached for him.

"Bring her." The priest plunged the brand into the muck.

Josh clenched his fists, breath coming in heaves. The gem around his neck glowed dark red; crimson vapor pooled around the teenagers.

"Josh," Dandelion yelped and snatched her hand away from him. "Your eyes!"

"What." Josh turned, his voice deepened to a coarse growl.

"Dude, they're black." Even Pete looked alarmed.

The minstrel whimpered and clutched his lute to his chest.

Josh stepped forward. That's what Mom must have looked like. So innocent. So helpless before a great bully of a man. How would *he* like a brand on *his* neck?

The girl ran to her father and fell to her knees. She hugged him and wept.

The priest grabbed the girl's hair with one hand, the brand in the other. She screamed, scrambling to get to her feet.

He laughed and jerked her off balance.

Josh roared and lunged forward.

Iron shone crimson as the priest pulled the brand from the muck.

Josh raced through the crowd. The priest twisted the girl's head to expose her neck.

"Josh!" Dandelion shrieked.

The priest stabbed the brand toward the girl's neck.

Bellowing, Josh punched fists through the Shadowline veil. He hit the priest in his chest and snatched at the brand.

The priest staggered backward into the cauldron, sloshing the tar on his robe. He flopped to the deck, screaming and tearing at his clothes.

A splotch of tar landed on an ogrei's foot. With a howl, it jumped sideways, wiping madly at the burn. The crystal cauldron fell and shattered. Wriggling contents spread across the deck, bubbling and hissing. Holes dissolved in the boards.

Josh lost his balance and fell face first into the pool. One of the octopus creatures shrieked and flopped inches from his face. Josh rolled sideways, pulling his hands back into the Shadowline. Even without touching the muck, his skin blistered.

Before Josh could pull his hands through, a silk shoe slammed down on Josh's wrist, pinning it to the deck. Glowing red iron followed, crushed into the back of his hand. His world exploded in white hot pain.

Blackness swallowed everything.

"Here's one on necrotic monster lore. Find anything on prisons?" Dandelion's voice echoed in Josh's darkness.

Josh's shoulders ached. His knees chaffed raw against the deck. Everything was blurry. He tried to wipe his eyes, but couldn't move his hands. He wiped his face on his bicep and blinked. His breath caught in his throat.

Wooden stocks were locked around his wrists. On the back of his left hand was the brand, gleaming, and black as hell. Dark purple-green veins webbed away from the edges of the mark. Something writhed beneath his skin.

Josh looked for the priest. His heartbeat hiccuped. The priest was gone. So was the dock and the entire city. Ocean stretched to the horizon on all sides.

Nearby, Dandelion sat in the middle of a giant pile of books. Pete and the princess helped her look through the volumes.

Thunderheads boiled over the ship. Rain pounded the deck but didn't come into the Shadowline.

"What happened?" Josh's throat was raw.

"Oh. I'm so glad you're awake." Dandelion got up and wrapped Josh in a hug. "Are you OK?" She looked at the tattoo and winced.

Josh shook his head. Moving made it pound even worse. "Where are we?"

"We're on our way to The Throat." Pete's voice was tight.

The Throat? They needed to get to The Throat, but not as ghosts. They were supposed to have warriors. They couldn't get Kharaq's bones like this. How could Josh have screwed this up, especially when they were so close to the quest?

Josh waited for a, "thanks you, idiot," or "way to go loser."

"That was a very brave thing you did." The princess's hand was cool on Josh's forehead.

Pete pinched his lips tightly but didn't say anything.

"Do you think you can pull your hands back into the Shadowline? Maybe that will get you out of the stocks." Dandelion gestured with a book.

"Before nightfall," Pete muttered.

Dandelion shot a nervous glance at Pete.

"Nightfall?" Josh didn't like the look on Pete's face.

Pete pointed with his chin.

In the center of the ship loomed a dumpster-sized crate. Ice formed on the bottom, spreading fingers of frost onto the surrounding deck.

With whispers and nervous looks, the sailors scurried about their duties. Overhead, storm clouds boiled. Lightning crackled across their surface.

"It's an inquisitor," Dandelion mumbled and flipped pages. "The priest wants to know how you did what you did."

Josh's chest was suddenly tight. He remembered the drooling, mindless wizard in the slavers' square. "An inquisitor ... is going to drink my mind?"

Dandelion winced and sat down. "We're looking for a solution. So far, we haven't found anything."

She set a large crystalline book in her lap. She turned pages that flowed like silvery water.

"Here's another one on monster lore." She ran a finger along the gleaming page, then plunged her hand in elbow-deep. She pulled out a worn volume and handed it to the princess. "Underworld Beasts start on page"—she glanced at the silvery page again—"three-eighty-one."

The princes nodded and added it to her pile.

Dandelion followed Josh's eyes to her crystal book. "It's a library, a magic book full of other books." She handed a book to Pete.

Pete opened it, flipped a couple pages, and handed it back. "Everything's blank."

"Another obscurin." Dandelion scowled and put it in a separate pile.

Pete glanced at his brother. "Josh used to have a bunch of them."

Dandelion's eyebrows shot up. She turned to Josh. "Can you read them?"

"I ... I ..." Josh's thoughts jumbled in a fog. He'd been able to see the hidden stuff in Mom's office. Was that the same thing?

Dandelion's excitement faded. "It's OK. The writing is only visible to magic users, so I thought ... Never mind."

Pete gestured toward his book pile. "It doesn't matter anyway, we can't keep up with the ones we *are* able to read. Campitius says the only way to get rid of the inquisitor is to push it into the ocean."

Dandelion glared at Pete's armor. "And how are we supposed to do that? We can't even touch anything."

Josh looked around, eyes grinding in their sockets. "Where is the priest?" His voice rasped.

"That coward saw the Black Doorway on your hand and ran off the ship," Pete huffed. "He made them set sail to get you away from the town."

"Once you fainted, they locked you up and put the occot in your tattoo." Dandelion rubbed the back of her hand. "I'm really sorry about that. Then the priest had the inquisitor placed on board. The ghoul is waiting until nightfall to open the crate."

"The ghoul?" Josh looked back at the crate.

A hunched creature in rough, brown robes hobbled slowly around the wooden container. White and black whiskers bristled from under the creature's hood. Gaunt, clawed fingers with long twisting nails brushed the boards as the ghoul bent or stood on tiptoes to inspect it.

"It's the caretaker." Pete handed a glowing green book to Dandelion. "The crew wants to cut your hands off and throw them overboard. We've been in this storm since they brought that crate aboard and everyone is wet and miserable."

Josh's teeth clattered. Even though the rain didn't touch him, the wind cut to the bone. Maybe he shouldn't have tried to save the girl. But how could he not? Each time he'd screwed up in the past, he'd thought it couldn't get any worse. Each time, he'd been w rong.

Help. Josh tried to picture Vastroh on his flaming dragon, but exhaustion smothered his thoughts like sodden wool. The occot poured images into his mind of everything he'd ever done wrong.

Success is impossible without mistakes. Josh remembered what the princess said on the docks. But he'd never made them right. It gnawed at him that he hadn't said sorry when he had the chance.

"Did the girl get away?" Josh asked and instantly wished he hadn't. He knew he'd failed.

"You scared them off before they branded her." Dandelion gave Josh a hopeful smile. "Maybe they'll let her go."

Josh knew better.

"They threw her dad in *there*." Pete gestured to the forecastle.

A bone cage swung from a giant beam. Several men and women huddled in the center. It looked like the cage in the slaver's square.

The hair on Josh's arms stood. The sky above the ship lit up. Dusk erupted in burning debris as lightning smashed into the crate. Instantly, the deck swarmed with frenzied crew. Some flung burning pieces of crate into the sea. Others sloshed buckets of water over folded sails and coiled ropes.

Josh watched them scurry this way and that, bumping into each other, scrambling up the ropes and ladders. Only the captain seemed unruffled as he strode the deck and shouted orders, grabbing crewmen and pushing them in the direction of a bucket or a burn. Wind whipped rain helped douse the fires as well.

At last, the deck was cleared of debris and the crew gathered where the crate had been. Wreathed in smoke, a dumpster-sized skull sat in a red, smoldering ring. Rusted iron filled all its holes. Stains ran from the eyes and teeth, their brown, black and gold stark against the pale bone.

The lightning had split one of the tiny suture cracks lacing the top of the skull. Mucus colored slime dribbled down into pools on the deck. Wood froze where it touched.

Hammer in one fist and a dozen large rusty nails in the other, the ghoul stood on a wooden box and hammered an iron plate over the crack.

"Will it close?" The captain shouted at the ghoul.

The ghoul didn't look up, his breath drifting in frosty clouds. He bent one of the spikes and cursed.

A short, high-pitched shriek snapped Josh's eyes to the crew. A sailor's mouth froze in twisted horror, his eyes gaping wide. A tendril of inquisitor slime pooled around one of his feet.

Slowly, the man's dead eyes turned toward his crewmates and he stumbled toward them with toneless grunts. Drool dribbled from his chin.

Sailors scattered, yelling and tripping over each other. The captain shouted orders above the chaos.

More tendrils of slime crept outward from the skull. Rain droplets froze and rolled across the deck. Dandelion covered her mouth. The princess gripped Josh's arm.

The inquisitor was out.

Josh watched the mindless sailor stumble back and forth with the roll of the ship. The man lifted his eyes to the rain. Lightning flayed the sky, strobing the man's face in daylight and shadow.

So that's how it was going to end? Josh was being hunted, and he couldn't even run or fight back. They'd lost. Dad had lost. Everything was lost. Kharaq had won, and there was no way out.

"It's not fair!" Josh yanked at the stocks. Where was Vastroh now? "How could you let this happen?" Josh shouted, wrenching at the stocks again and again until his wrists bled.

Dandelion dropped her books, ran over, and wrapped her arms around him. "We'll find a way. I promise. We still have time. The ghoul will control the inquisitor."

Before she finished speaking, lightning lashed across the sky and exploded against the skull. Iron teeth and eyes glowed red. Power crackled around the inquisitor's lair.

With a shriek, the ghoul flew into the air, arcing across the deck. Smoke trailed behind him. Enveloped in electricity, he landed with a thump, bounced, and then lay still. In the lamplight, unblinking, yellow eyes stared at Josh.

Josh gagged on the reek of burning hair. He waited for the ghoul to get up. The creature didn't move.

The first mate ran to the ghoul and put an ear to its mouth.

Wind wailed through the rigging and snapped in the sails. Hackles rose on Josh's neck.

The sailor pulled off his bandanna and wiped his forehead. Face pale, he turned to the captain and shook his head.

Several of the crew stopped their work and stared.

"He's dead?" Dandelion clutched an armload of books to her chest. "We're all dead."

CHAPTER TWELVE

WARD YER SOULS

R oar, Throughout the night, the inquisitor spread. Tendrils of slime crept under
longboats and along the railing.

All but a few crewmen were below deck. Sailors had battened the hatches to keep the
inquisitor out. Josh had no such barrier. He could feel the creature sniffing as it crept ever
closer. Josh's heart hammered as if he was sprinting. He could hardly catch a breath.

Every part of his body hurt. The stocks kept him halfway between standing and
kneeling. He was either bent over, or on his knees with his arms up.

The Occot tore at his mind. There was no hope for this quest. He'd failed everyone and
didn't even have the decency to make it right. Maybe he should just give up. Take that step
into death like the minstrel said he could. That would free him from the stocks. The hurt
in his arms and legs would stop. The torment in his mind would be over. He'd be at peace.

The princess suggested they take turns with Josh during the night. The others slept on
the forecastle. It was as far from the inquisitor as possible.

Pete sat with him last. As the sun rose, he squinted at Josh. "You don't look so good."

Pete seemed to have something else to say. He squirmed. He opened his mouth and
closed it. Finally he sighed. "Dad would have been proud of what you did for that girl."

A giant lump clogged Josh's throat. Those words were liquid sunlight, spreading to every bruise and aching joint. Warmth poured into the loneliest darkness Josh had ever known. He tried to tell Pete, but his voice didn't work. Instead, tears dripped to the deck.

Pete stood and stepped on a knot in the decking as if it were a cigarette butt. "I'm going to wake the others."

Dandelion found a cloak in her magic pack. The princess folded it under Josh's knees.

Josh looked up at the princess. "You said, 'have faith.' It didn't work. I had faith Vastroh would help me, and I stopped the girl from getting branded. But instead of help, I got branded and I have this *thing* in me, tearing my mind to pieces. Kharaq wants me dead. I'm on my way to a prison in hell and that inquisitor will drink my mind. I'll never rescue my dad."

"Look up at the sky." The princess adjusted the cloak. "See that burning star?"

"Yeah, I know. It's holes in the sky or whatever." Josh didn't look up.

The princess put an arm around him. "It's the only star in the underworld sky. They say it is Vastroh watching over all — even the black-hearted dead in the Deep Dark of hell."

"Yeah, but he didn't help me. Won't destroying Kharaq's bones save *his* world? Why wouldn't he help? He said he'd always be there." Josh slumped.

The princess sighed and gently ran her fingers through his hair. "Faith isn't looking forward, it's looking back and *stepping* forward. It's not a feeling, it's noticing. Help doesn't always come in spectacular ways like burn spells. Most often, it shows up in things that look like coincidences."

She wiped a piece of dirt from his cheek with her thumb. "You had faith when you ran on the ship. You had faith when you stopped the branding. When you take a step and fall, Vastroh meets you where you land. Even when everything goes wrong, if he's invited, it still ends up OK."

Josh looked in her eyes, green as a tropical island sea. "That's what Mom always says."

The princess smiled. "His star is always watching. Always burning. In time, you'll learn your journey is not about a what, like whether you succeed or fail. It's about a who."

Josh looked at his hands. The skin was mottled and bruised. The half-moons at the base of his fingernails were dark gray instead of white.

His voice was barely audible. "I'm so scared. This thing inside me sticks to me, like a thousand tentacles, like gum. They stretch but won't come off. It's pulling me down." He looked up at the princess. "I can't hold on much longer."

"Oh child." Her eyes welled. Early morning sunlight glinted green and gold in the droplets on her lashes. She wrapped her arms around Josh, then pulled Pete and Dandelion into the hug. "That's why *we're* here. *We'll* hold on to you too. And pull you back harder than the darkness."

━━━━◆◇◆━━━━

Evening came too soon. As the shadows lengthened, Josh's heart raced. His emotions were in tatters. He'd had no sleep. And there was no way the inquisitor wouldn't reach him tonight. The stocks were the only place it had not explored.

As the sky faded, slime oozed from the skull. Josh trembled. His teeth clacked louder than the other noises on deck. Dandelion and the princess would notice for sure. He bit down, but his teeth wouldn't stop. His knees knocked together and his stomach heaved.

A tendril of slime reached the stocks. It spread and pooled under Josh. Reflections of the sky skittered over its glistening surface.

The princess and Dandelion were beside him, shouting. But what could they do?

In sickening blotches, the creature gradually soaked into the Shadowline, closing in on Josh. Shards of glass exploded in Josh's head. Piercing. Tearing.

Josh screamed, his body rigid. He thrashed against the stocks, the rough wood tearing at his wrists and knees. Flecks of froth spattered his lips.

Then Pete was beside him, sword free. In a flash of gleaming steel and crimson lettering, Pete brought the blade down on the beast.

The ripping in Josh's head stopped. He slumped and hung from his wrists.

Again, Pete stabbed at the gleaming flow. The sword didn't cut, but the inquisitor stopped reaching for Josh and flailed for Pete. Pete danced away, slicing and jabbing.

Quivering with anticipation, the liquid gathered and sprang toward Pete with surprising speed. Pete dodged and jabbed. He ran from one end of the ship to the other, forcing the inquisitor to stretch as far as possible. He laughed and shouted insults. Several times, he ran past the skull and spat on it.

If Pete ran too far ahead, the creature would turn back toward Josh, so Pete danced on the edge of being caught, always barely out of reach.

It wasn't long before Pete began to tire. As he slowed, the inquisitor became more animated. Several times Josh thought the inquisitor had caught Pete.

Eventually, Dandelion took over with Pete's sword. She didn't laugh and spit. Her face was tight, eyebrows knit in concentration.

The Princess took over after Dandelion. They kept the inquisitor busy all night. Eventually Josh fell asleep. When he knelt, he could rest his head on his arms. His wrists throbbed, but he was too tired to care.

His dreams were full of monsters. They caught and ate his friends again and again. When dawn finally came, he ached like the entire crew had beaten him with clubs.

Pete and Dandelion staggered to the forecastle and curled up on the deck. Neither said a word. Both looked haggard. Both were asleep in seconds.

The princess said she didn't sleep much. She talked with Josh and looked through Dandelion's books for answers. She smiled and said everything was going to be OK, but her face was drawn and her lips pinched.

It was afternoon before Dandelion and Pete came down to Josh. They were gaunt and pale, but grinning.

Dandelion stopped between Josh and the princess. "We have an idea. We heard the first mate talking; guess what the ship's hold is full of?"

"Sand!" Pete burst out toward the princess. "You can take over the whole ship."

"We just ... need to get out of the Shadowline." The princess looked confused.

"Exactly." Dandelion grabbed her library. She flipped through a few pages, handing books to Pete and the princess. "Every waking moment needs to be about getting out of the Shadowline. Once you control the sand, you can rip the inquisitor off the deck and throw it in the sea."

Pete slapped his book. "Then we build our reconnaissance team for wizard bone extraction. The crew that helps us gets paid a fortune. The rest get thrown overboard."

Dandelion scowled at Pete.

"It's better than what Campitius wants to do with them."

Dandelion shook her head.

"Fine." Pete shrugged. "We'll throw them in the brig."

While they searched, Josh watched the sun cross the sky. By the time it sank toward the horizon, no one was any closer to getting them out. It'd take days to make it through all those books. Josh didn't think they could last even *one* more night against the inquisitor.

Somehow they'd made it through two nights. Day three had come and gone. The sun sank below distant clouds to touch the horizon. Josh's heart sank with it.

Worry lines furrowed the Princess's eyes. She dug through books with a nervous frenzy, sighing and looking at the sky.

Once again, they kept the inquisitor away from Josh. Dandelion was limping. Pete was quiet and grim. The princess tried to make up the difference with longer shifts, but even she was slowing down. The inquisitor just got hungrier and more animated.

Pete's armor had dulled to a hazy satin. If Pete were caught, the inquisitor would eat the armor's mind too. Pete kept telling Campitius, "no," and to "shut-up." Josh could only guess what the armor said, "sacrifice Josh to save everyone else," probably.

The Occot buffeted Josh's mind. Josh squeezed his eyes shut. Maybe it would be better for everyone if he just died. Josh *knew* Pete and Dandelion resented him, even though neither had said anything. How could they not? He had claimed the black doorway. He had attacked the priest and gotten caught. Because of him, the inquisitor would eat their minds too. And he wasn't even man enough to say sorry.

Why couldn't he step all the way through into the world of the living? He'd tried, but something held him back. At the same time, death beckoned him. He knew he could take *that* step. The pain would be gone.

Something held Pete, Dandelion, and the Princess in the Shadowline with him — it was probably him. Without him, they could go on with their lives and be happy.

Josh closed his eyes and focused on the darkness within. Every time the ship hit a wave, he gasped in pain. His joints felt like they were coming apart. Death was just a step away. Nothing had ever made more sense.

"Escape is a lie." The princess held a book out to Josh. "Pain seems like it will *never* end. As long as you run away, it never will."

Josh stared at her. Could she read his mind? What was she talking about?

"You must take an active role in your freedom. Choose to fight for yourself. That's how magic works. Even if you don't believe it. Do it. Fight." The princess set a book by his feet.

"I can't." Josh looked away.

The princess didn't move, eyes on Josh, lips pressed tightly together.

Josh squirmed under her stare and finally looked at the book. "Is that what you meant by 'faith is what you do'? Do it even when you *don't* believe it?"

Her face softened. "Yes. It never feels like you have enough strength. But when you take that step toward freedom, you'll find you do. Hold on for *one more* night; things always look different in the morning."

She pointed to an earmarked page. "This is the only book we found that mentions that thing in your hand."

Josh wanted to say "I can't," but the princess's face gave no room for it. Instead, he looked up at the burning star. Help.

The princess smoothed the pages of his book. "For me to be free, I used to think that something had to happen *to* me. But true freedom happens *in* me. That's real magic. I can't be free outside until I am free inside."

"OK," Josh mumbled and opened the book. His hands were in the stocks, so he had to use his feet.

It was the hardest thing he'd ever done. The pages might as well have been slabs of stone. The print jumbled in meaningless phrases. Was this really going to help? Mom said the same kinds of things. But he didn't want to read the book. He wanted to give up.

"I *will* not be afraid." Josh gritted his teeth. He closed his eyes and imagined Vastroh was beside him. "But I need help."

The occot dragged at his thoughts. He hated the way his hands looked, like ghoul hands with pasty skin and bulging knuckles. Even his fingernails were black. What did his face look like? It was a useless fight. There was no winning against the beast in his mind.

Mom used to say, your feelings will follow your thoughts. Those dark thoughts were going nowhere good. Would choosing his thoughts set him free inside? Josh turned his mind toward the occot. "Those thoughts are from you, aren't they? I'm not listening. I may lose, but I will die fighting."

He looked to the sky. "You said you were here. I'm going to act like you are. No matter what I feel."

Was the star brighter?

Wind kept turning pages. Stabbing pain shot through his wrists when he shifted his feet to read. He kept asking the princess if this was really going to help. He wanted to give up more than anything. But instead, he gritted his teeth and imagined Dad grabbing him in a giant hug while Kharaq burst into flames.

The sun set. The inquisitor drooled from the skull.

Dandelion pulled a tiny lamp from her pack and set it by Josh's book. Without a word, she and Pete headed toward the skull.

Josh focused on the text. They fought for his life. The least he could do was fight for it too.

Somehow, he read all that night. When dawn came, his eyes were so tired he couldn't focus. But they'd all survived. He'd fought the dark thoughts of the occot and won.

His gaze drifted toward his hands. The icy fist of hopelessness gripped his heart. The princess was wrong; things *didn't* look different in the morning. If anything, it was worse. Pete and Dandelion staggered back to the forecastle to sleep. They didn't even look at him. Dandelion had almost fallen twice. No one said what everyone was thinking. Someone was going to die. Soon.

Josh couldn't believe it was going to end like this. He couldn't even look at the star. "You lied. You didn't help."

That's when he decided. Pete's armor was right. It had to be *him* that died. Relief flooded over him. He'd take the step. Tonight.

⬛◆◆◇◆◆⬛

With evening, the deadly dance began again. Josh was plagued with guilt; he'd promised himself to fight to the death, and yet he was giving up tonight. Maybe he should try one last thing. Dandelion had given him an encyclopedia of magical items along with items to look up — a baseball-sized pin cushion, several rings, and a silver feather pendant. Maybe one could help.

The encyclopedia's pages were blank. *See like I taught you.* Mom's words echoed in his mind. He un-stared until his head hurt. Just as he gave up, words appeared.

Josh searched the book for the dull colored pin cushion. He flipped through page after page of strange bobbles and contraptions. Hours passed and he couldn't find anything even close.

He squinted through the darkness at his friends. They weren't running anymore; at best, it was a fast walk. Often, they took wrong turns and were surrounded by rivulets of slime. Josh gritted his teeth. He had to find an answer. They were losing.

Just before dawn, Pete tripped on the poop deck ladder and fell. Dandelion screamed. The princess was on her feet, but no one could get there fast enough.

The inquisitor lunged.

Josh's knees gave out. Seeing Pete fall was a cannon shot to the chest. He hung in the stocks and gasped for air.

Pete fell and rolled. Instead of swallowing Pete, the slime splashed against the poop deck wall. Pete had fallen *through* the wall into the cabins behind.

"We're ghosts." Dandelion's mouth dropped open. "How could we have forgotten? We've been running around this whole time and could have just stepped through walls."

Pete appeared farther down the deck. His taunting expression was back. He danced in and out of the wall, stabbing at the creature.

Again and again, the inquisitor dashed against the wall. Droplets splattered ice across the deck.

All at once, the inquisitor stopped and pooled around a loose board on the first mate's door. Screams echoed from inside, then a dull, mindless moan. The inquisitor shimmered.

The inquisitor drooled across the wall, testing each door frame, each board joint.

Forgotten by the beast, Pete limped back to the group.

The muscles in Josh's legs and arms trembled uncontrollably. Pete was OK, but Josh still couldn't get to his feet. He just hung there quaking. The realization of what his friends risked for him thundered over him — risks that he had put them into.

"I'm sorry," Josh moaned through chattering teeth.

"What?" Pete turned toward him. "For what?"

Josh couldn't look up at them. "I'm sorry. I'm sorry. I should have said it on the docks. I should have said it in the caves or back at the oracle. You guys should have left me. I should have died ages ago. But instead you're choosing to die with me? I'm like the Shadowline, and you're like the sun in the living world."

Josh barely finished before his voice disintegrated and his eyes welled with tears.

The princess grabbed Josh in a hug. "I'm so proud to be part of this journey with you. I would do it again in a moment."

"Me too." Dandelion wrapped her arms around the other two.

Pete grinned and shrugged. "It's all good."

The cannonball lodged in Josh's chest melted. The shivering subsided. All of a sudden, a huge grin sneaked on to his face.

"Oh, hey!" Eyes alight, Pete pointed toward the Poop deck.

One of the crewmen pounded on the captain's door, shouting that the creature could get through doors. No one was safe. The helmsman secured the helm with a rope and ran below.

"Watch this." Pete grinned and ran to the inquisitor. He stabbed and skipped away, following the man down the open hatch. Streams of slime followed.

Dandelion stared after Pete. "What's he doing?"

Screams and moans echoed up from the hatchway.

Josh tried to turn and see. "I don't know, I ..."

More slime flowed down the hatch. Shouts echoed through the opening, along with more screams.

"Ha." Josh's smile got even bigger. "Now that the inquisitor is below, they'll all die, unless—"

"Unless they throw the skull overboard." Dandelion clapped her hands.

Josh couldn't stop smiling. Pete was a genius.

The first blob of molten sun swelled above the horizon. Golden beams spilled across the deck, chasing the shadows under ladders and behind cleats. *This* morning's sun shone right into his chest; hopelessness and fear just melted.

The princess was *right*. Everything *was* different in the morning. Any minute, the entire crew would be up here with ropes, and that slimy mind-eater would be on the bottom of the ocean.

He and his friends would have time to find a solution. It *had* to be in these books. They'd be in and out of The Throat with the bones in no time. Kharaq would be killed. Dad would be freed.

Josh laughed out loud. It felt like years since he'd laughed. "Give me another book."

Dandelion wasn't smiling. "What if they cut your hands off instead?"

Josh's smile wouldn't fade.

She set a book at his feet. "Here's another magic one on undead creatures and objects. My index says there's a section on inquisitors *and* the Shadowline. I'd open it for you but ..."

"I know. You can't read it." Josh knew she was right. He shouldn't get his hopes up, but they were going to beat Kharaq. He just knew it.

The cover left black marks on the deck as if made from charcoal. The title glowed like dying embers in a barbed, angular script.

Hair stood on Josh's arms. He knew the letters. Dark memories clamored in the recesses of this mind. This was the virulent language of underworld magic. Sparkles raced up his arms. The ship's masts faded to pitted iron bars. The sky darkened to torchlight flickering on the glistening walls of a dungeon cave. Heavyset guards in bulky iron armor loitered in a semi-circle around a single open cell, each with blades drawn. Two leaned against the far walls, arrows notched and pointed at the doorway.

In the center of the guards, sat Josh surrounded by books and scrolls. Inside the doorway skulked a dark, scaly, lizard-like creature with a long barbed tail.

"Think it again. Block the other half of the word from your mind until you learn it right. Equacth, not Eskwach. It's the binding." Using its tail, the creature flipped back a page in Josh's book.

Lamplight brightened back to sunlight. Rough stone floors dissolved to planking. Josh caught his breath. How many languages did he know? How many spells? A thrill churned in his chest. He looked up at the princess. "The book is written in Mordeo."

The princess drew a sharp breath, brows arching upward. "How have you learned such a thing? Read it if you must, but please do not speak it."

Using his toes, Josh opened the cover. Drawings and script were burned into pages of decaying cloth.

Runes were scratched into the title page, a warding spell before reading the book. Josh read the incantation carefully, sounding out every syllable in his mind.

He held his breath after the last word. He didn't blister and die, so he must have pronounced it right. Josh blew out a long breath and turned to the chapter on Inquisitors.

Screams echoed from below deck. Josh did his best to ignore them and focus on the book. Someone had sketched the inquisitors. The skull-house was different, but the creature and the description were the same.

His palm was itchy, so he absently scratched at it while reading. The following page had a hole in it. A hole the size of a silver dollar.

Across the deck, crewmen climbed out of the hatch. The princess gasped, ran to the opening, and disappeared inside.

Dandelion stood frozen in place, eyes wide, mouth wider.

"What." Josh's brow furrowed. Had the inquisitor gotten *her*?

"We're out!" she snatched up a piece of rope and held the prickly fiber to her cheek as if it were the softest silk.

"We're what?" Josh gulped. Something was definitely wrong with her.

"We're out of the Shadowline!" She dropped the rope and leapt for the hasp on his stocks.

"It's locked." Josh muttered.

Dandelion just grinned and dug lock picks out of her vest pocket. "Not for long. You did it!"

"I ... did?" Josh looked around and took a deep breath. The air was wild and salty and alive! No more chill, gray tasting, gray smelling, underworld air.

And the color! The world around him exploded with it: apricot skies splashed across sapphire seas; even the beiges and chestnut browns in the ship's planking were breathtaking.

"How did you do it?" Dandelion selected lock-picks from a little bundle.

Josh thought for a moment. "I don't know. I ... uh ... said sorry?" Sunlight bathed the deck. He was warm for the first time in days. And they were free! Josh closed his eyes before they could tear up.

"And you tried. And you didn't give up."

Josh deflated. "I almost did."

Dandelion beamed back. "But you didn't. I knew you'd find a way out. I knew it."

She dug iron pins into Josh's lock. "Drompa says it might be the thousandth thing you try, but there's *always* a way."

The lock clicked open. Her eyes flicked up toward his face. Her grin was bright as the sunlight. "I think I'm starting to believe in the Cambium Dreams. Maybe your mom *is* the Weaver. Maybe she'll be at the oracle when we get back. She can help us burn the bones."

Josh rubbed his wrists. They were red and raw from the stocks. But they were free. Free from the stocks *and* the Shadowline. His fingertips tingled with life as color flowed back into hands. He beamed at Dandelion.

Suddenly his eyes fill with tears. He grabbed her and hugged as hard as he could. "I thought I was going to die. You saved my life a million times." His voice cracked and all he could manage was a whisper. "Thank you. Thank you."

She squeezed back. "Always."

One of Dandelion's knife handles poked Josh in the chest. He didn't care. Now they could find Kharaq's bones. Now they could save Dad. Everything *was* going to be OK! He searched the sky for the burning star.

Barely visible against the morning's pale blue a speck of fire flickered just over the horizon. He watched it for a while and imagined magic pouring through it into the world. He pictured a smile on the warrior's scarred face. "Thank you."

Thick hands grabbed Josh's arms and neck, jarring him back to the ship. He gulped. He'd gotten so used to being invisible to the living, he'd forgotten to keep an eye on the sailors. A dozen sword points pressed against him and Dandelion.

Sunlight trickled down the sails and across the deck. The inquisitor shrank into its skull.

Pete climbed on deck, sword drawn. Shining plate armor covered him head to toe. It blazed in the sunlight, casting a blood-colored halo on the deck around him.

Crewmen followed at a distance, knives and swords pointing toward Pete. One of the sailors on deck snatched a rope and stepped up behind him.

"Don't ..." A sailor with a map scrawled across his belly grabbed at his crew mate.

Too late.

Silver swam across Pete's back. Needle point stilettos flashed from his armor.

The sailor cried out and fell back, gripping wounds on his arm and shoulder. Two crew mates dragged him away from Pete.

"Come a little closer next time," Pete growled over his shoulder. He turned toward the sailors that held Josh and Dandelion. "Let them go."

The captain's face was dark. He gestured to Dandelion and Josh. "Take another step, and their heads will roll on my deck."

Pete started to speak, but the caption raised a warning finger. "Try me. I dare you."

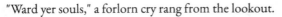

"Ward yer souls," a forlorn cry rang from the lookout.

Sailors muttered prayers to the sky. Several pulled talismans from their jerkins and kissed them. Josh followed their eyes to the horizon. A knot of storm clouds churned around an island-sized stain on the distant waves; gray-green wisps bled toward the sky.

People in the bone cage stumbled over each other to see. The enclosure wobbled and swung. A heavy man wearing gaudy merchant's clothing grabbed the bars and shouted to the crew, "I'll make you rich, every one of you. Mansions and servants. You'll never have to work again. Let me out!"

"What about there?" The sailor holding Dandelion pointed his chin toward the cage.

The captain ran meaty fingers through his beard. "Aye." He turned to Pete. "Into the cage."

Pete tightened his grip on the sword. Runes danced in glowing red down the blade.

Josh caught Pete's eye. "Pete, it's OK. The princess. Remember?"

Put them in the cage? It was laughable. The princess's monster would burst out any second. She'd smash that cage. The crew would obey or get tossed overboard — along with the inquisitor.

Pete slowly lowered his sword. Josh couldn't stop smiling as they all stepped into the cage.

"Shouldn't we take their steel, Cap'n?" The sailor with the map on his belly glared at Pete.

The captain tilted his head toward the distant storm-cluster. "They'll be dead before it does them any good."

Inside the cage, prisoners reeked of sweat. Everything was knees and elbows. Pete kept his sword out as the teenagers huddled to one side.

From the cage, they watched sailors scamper across the deck and up the rigging, trimming the sails and securing the lines. The nearer the ship got to the storm, the wilder the sea became.

Dandelion sat, then stood, then sat again. "Where is she?" Her voice was sharp. Wind flung her autumn curls around her face.

Waves smashed against the hull, washing whitewater across the deck. "Prepare for The Throat squall," the quartermaster shouted above the gale.

The captain buttoned his slicker and nodded toward the giant skull. "We'll dump *that* as soon as we offload the cage."

Lightning split the storm up ahead and, for a moment, the center shone like daylight. Josh saw their destination.

Gray waves exploded white against an island of broken stone. Curving in a crescent half-moon, the old volcanic crater oozed lava like a gaping sore. Masts and the rotted ribs of ships jutted from a gray-green mist where sea met rock.

From the island's center rose a crumbling circular fortress. Rubble from towers and stone walls sloped inward like ruins of a colosseum. In the very middle was a hole larger than the ship. Clouds of sleet and frozen vapor whipped upward in gusts from the dark opening.

"The Throat." A man beside Josh whimpered softly.

"Where *is* she?" Dandelion pried at the lock with a dagger. Her lock picks lay on the other side of the deck. "Josh, help me!" Her voice rose.

"Peace, child." Kind blue eyes smiled at Josh and Dandelion from a sea of wrinkles. "Sit for a moment. Breathe." Light from the foremast lantern glinted off the prisoner's bald head. A thick white beard hung to his waist. Silver embroidery wound in broad patterns along the edges of a blue silk robe that at one time must have been spectacular. His gentle hands reached for Dandelion and Josh. "My name is Vamirrion. What are your names?"

Soft warm fingers took Josh's tattooed hand. Peace and safety soaked through the touch. Josh's aching shoulders and wrists relaxed.

"Josh."

"I'm Dandelion." She sat down beside Josh. Her eyes were still wild, but her breathing slowed.

"Wizard." The shouting merchant turned to the old man. "Portal us out of here."

"I already told you—" the kindly old man began.

"Yah." The merchant brushed away his response. "So portal us when we're between the cage and The Throat. I'll be ready. I'll make you rich."

Thunder rattled the cage.

A woman lounged against the far side of the cage. She wore a dark red cloak with black trim. She rolled her eyes at the merchant and snorted. "Portals fragment near The Throat. Why else would they *sail* us here?"

She turned toward the kindly wizard and threw back the hood of her cloak. Thick black hair curled around her shoulders and hung to the middle of her back. "How about a spell to shut *him* up?" She changed her voice to mimic the merchant. "*I'll make you rich.*"

The merchant glared at her.

Steel will silence him. Campitius's metallic ring echoed in Josh's ears.

Josh glanced at his brother. The space was tight and Pete's armor touched Josh's arm.

The old wizard shifted so his back was to the Merchant. His hands squeezed Josh's again. "That was a very brave thing you did before we sailed, saving that girl."

The dark-haired woman nodded toward Josh. "So the ghost hands were yours, huh, kid? You're more of a man than most men I know." She gave a meaningful glance at the merchant.

He sneered back.

Vamirrion smiled. "Were you able to hold on to the Black Doorway during the scuffle?"

Josh looked at his hand. His breath caught in his chest. The Black Doorway was gone. Of course, that explained the hole in the book. Why hadn't he thought of that? "It's in that book sitting on the deck. I can't believe the doorway's what kept me in the Shadowline."

The old wizard patted Josh's hand. "Gateways into dark places want you to stay there. Ah well, we don't have it. I'm glad you're free. Nothing to worry about."

"Nothing? If we had that, those sea rats would be kissing our feet." The woman looked at Dandelion. "Hey kid, got an extra dagger?"

Dandelion looked blankly at her.

Pockets and loops covered the woman's tight black leather suit. She ran a finger through an empty eyelet on her chest. "They took all of mine. I'm Laevie, by the way. My middle name is Slaughter. Maybe you've heard of me."

Dandelion shook her head.

"Ignore her." The kindly wizard patted Dandelion's hand.

The merchant pushed past him to Josh. "Are you a wizard? *You* portal us out of here."

"Ignore him too?" Josh grinned up at the old wizard.

Vamirrion nodded.

Run him through instead, the armor's silvery voice snorted.

Josh and Pete exchanged glances?

"Is he always like that?" Josh glanced at Campitius.

Like what?

Pete nodded.

"Don't be such a gnat." Laevie waved the merchant away.

Josh watched her face. Her voice was so full of confidence, but her eyes were tight with fear.

"How about those?" The pudgy merchant pointed at Dandelion's lightning arrows. He turned to Pete. "Or you. Use your sword to cut us out of here. Or if you're too *weak,* have your armor do it."

"How about you do us all a favor and stand a little closer to the kid's armor?" Laevie gave the merchant a little push toward Pete. The Merchant squealed and scrambled the other direction.

Yes, closer.

Josh looked around the cage. They needed a leader. The old wizard had a lifetime of experience and probably knew tons of spells. Laevie looked like a smart fighter. The branded man was probably a lord. Any of the others were older and probably wiser than Josh. But no one was taking the job.

Lights twinkled on Josh's wrists. From the shadows of his memories, Dad's voice rumbled, "when you see something that needs doing and don't see anyone doing it, that's likely the call of destiny."

Suddenly, Josh knew who the leader had to be. His mouth was dry and face was on fire. "We're going to take over the ship." He had to swallow between each word.

Everyone in the cage listened.

Pete and Dandelion gaped at him. He knew what they must be thinking. Could they trust everyone in the cage? What if the merchant blew their surprise? Josh shuddered to think what would happen if the sailors got to the princess before she got to the sand.

But controlling the ship and getting the bones required all the help they could get. There was only one way to know who could be trusted. Give a little trust, and see what they did with it.

With a deep breath, Josh stood. "We have another member in our group, a sand wraith. Once she gets to the sand ballast in the hold, the ship will be ours."

"A sand wraith?" Vamirrion's bushy eyebrows rose sharply.

"Impossible." The merchant huffed. He leaned in any way.

Laevie hit his shoulder. "Hush, fool."

"We are on a very important mission and we need your help." Josh choked on the words. What if no one believed him? What if the sailors heard him? "Kharaq's bones are in the throat. We're going to get them and destroy them."

"How do you plan to get out?" The merchant's shrill voice carried over the wind.

"Quiet!" Laevie hissed at him, scowling.

Josh pursed his lips. "Once our sand wraith lets us out of the cage, we fly into The Throat's temple and collect the bones. We need a team to go in with us, as well as people to stay here and make sure the crew behaves. Then we sail back to Ersha—"

"And set this world free from tyranny." Vamirrion nodded in solemn reverence. "I'd heard the Cambium Dreams were unfurling."

"Who's with us?" Josh tried to swallow and couldn't.

Vamirrion smiled. "Most certainly me."

"Roooarrge and Rooaaree fight." Two scaly warriors crossed their arms at the back of the cage. The larger one's voice crackled like wax paper.

Looking at their talons and muscled arms, Josh was glad they joined. There was no human way to pronounce those names. "Can I just call you Royce and ... and Reilly?"

They shrugged and showed large fangs.

Josh hoped it was a smile. He looked around the group for anyone else. His eyes settled on the man whose daughter he'd saved.

The man struggled to his feet. "I am Sir Callan. My daughter owes you her life, and so I pledge you mine."

Laevie opened her arms. "Why bother asking? We're all in. We're not doing anything else."

Before she could finish, lightning tethered the inquisitor's skull to the sky. Smoke wafted across the deck.

"That thing attracts lightning, doesn't it?" Laevie scowled. "Your friend had better get up here soon."

Vamirrion nodded, then turned to Josh. "She's right; we're all with you. Well done."

Dark waves pushed the ship into the tempest surrounding The Throat. Clouds boiled in a bruise colored sky. Spray whirled across the deck. Everyone was soaked.

"Do you think your sand wraith will get to the ballast before we reach *that*?" The wizard pointed.

Ship-sized boulders jutted from the water at one edge of the channel. A rusted iron framework was attached to the top. Cables stretched from the tower to the island.

"What *is* that?" Josh wasn't sure he really wanted to know.

The old wizard sighed, "the cable moves prisoners to the island so ships never have to get too close." His eyes moved to rotted masts and hulls in the channel.

Dandelion's eyes were big. "I read the fortress used to be a secret city that hung down into the world of the dead. Then the volcano broke it open, and the Necrus turned it into a prison. There was a whole book on it."

"The hole in the middle leads to hell?" Josh gestured to the ice storm swirling up from the center of the fortress.

Dandelion nodded. "My book said that gargoyles fly out—"

"Hey Captain. Captain Comerchero. These kids—" The merchant leaned through the bars and shouted.

The captain turned.

Laevie was a blur. Before Josh even realized what happened, she was at the merchant's back, her mouth on his ear. In her hand, one of Dandelion's daggers had its tip pressed into his neck. "You might escape The Throat, but you won't escape hell. Another sound and this gives you a new Adam's apple."

The merchant's eyes bulged. He touched the back of his neck and stared at the blood on his fingertips. He squeaked at Laevie, "I was only ..."

She pressed the dagger. "Not a sound."

His voice quickly faded to a whimper.

"Never mind," Laevie shouted and waved to the captain.

With an annoyed grunt, he turned back to the crew.

Mouth open, Dandelion touched her empty dagger pocket and scowled at the rogue.

Laevie smiled back. "Don't worry, kid. I'll clean it off before I give it back." She turned to Josh. "How much time do you think we—"

"Loose the bowers!" the Capitan shouted.

A collective gasp raced around the cage.

Crewmen arranged themselves around the capstan and lowered the anchor. The helmsman shouted and fought with the tiller.

As the sky darkened, slime oozed from the inquisitor's skull. Lightning struck it again and again until the iron in its eyes and teeth glowed red.

"Where *is* she?" Dandelion gritted her teeth.

The ship bucked and pulled against the anchor. Cables loomed overhead. Sailors clustered around the cage and fastened an iron hook from the cable to a metal contraption on top.

Where *was* the princess? Josh stared at the hatch. She'd burst through any second. Everything was going to be OK. He clenched his fists. It *was* going to be OK.

Crewmen finished attaching the cage. It creaked and shuddered every time the ship moved. The captain smirked at Pete and pulled on a slip knot. The bone cage lurched away from the ship..

"No, stop." Dandelion grabbed at him through the bars.

Too late.

Wave tips slapped the bottom of the cage as it skimmed toward the island. Josh wiped the sea spray from his face. The princess was too late. Even if she showed up now, how would they get back to the ship?

Josh slumped against the bars. An invisible hammer smashed inside his head. Something had gone wrong. He tried to imagine the princess bursting free, or even the flaming warrior showing up to save them, but all he could picture was tumbling down the dark hole into hell. Luck had just run out.

Screams pierced the wind. Bat-winged creatures with dull red skin and bright yellow eyes circled the cage. Each was the size of a large dog. While they flew, muscled arms and clawed feet pulled at the air.

"Gargoyles." Blood drained from the wizard's face.

People in the cage pressed into the center. The merchant wept openly.

"Just when it couldn't get worse." Josh sank to the bottom of the cage.

Shouts rang from the ship. Josh's eyes snapped open. Sand poured from the main hatch, spreading across the deck. Sailors screamed and swarmed up the rigging and ladders. The gargoyles wheeled toward the sound.

The ballast-sand gathered and swelled until the princess's monster towered over the mainmast. Face to the sky, she roared.

"*That's* your friend?" Laevie breathed in a stunned whisper.

Without its ballast, the ship rolled sideways. Waves slapped the tip of the yardarm. Crewmen hung from the rail or slid down the deck.

The princess's monster leapt to the side of the lolling ship. Two of her fin-feet on the keel and two on the cannon ports, she grabbed the main mast, pulling the ship upright. With a splintering crack, the anchor and capstan ripped from the deck.

The galleon wallowed and slowly spun in the current. Without an anchor, the waves pounded it toward the jagged rocks, into the heart of the storm.

Josh's attention snapped back to the island. Their cage swung over a broken-down section in the fortress walls. Sleet spewed up in icy gusts from the bottomless pit in the building's center.

"Swing it back." Josh stepped into the center of the cage, then jumped against the bars. "Like this." He did it again.

For a moment, everyone stared, then followed suit, swaying their weight against the movement of the cage.

The cage slowed.

Josh glanced at the galleon. Lightning crackled toward the inquisitor's skull. For a moment, the skull was a grinning ball of fire. Then it exploded. Spinning pieces of metal and bone rained around the ship.

Inquisitor slime spattered across the deck. Globs landed on ropes and sails. Everything it touched froze. Rigging shattered and sails tore free. Crewmen shrieked and pulled off shirts or leggings. Others fell to their knees, slack faced and drooling.

Frozen chunks of the princess's sand fell to the deck. She howled and tore the remnants of the skull free, ripping a ragged hole in the planks where it had frozen to the deck. With a roar, she threw it at the oncoming gargoyles.

Slime oozed across the deck and ran down the sides. A giant wave thrust the ship skyward. The gunfire splintering of wood rang over the storm as frozen boards shattered like glass.

The galleon teetered on the tip of the swell, lightning crackling around it. Giant cracks raced from one side to the other, and with a boom it split in two.

For a moment, the ship's halves balanced on the crest. The princess roared, straining to pull them together. Then the mountain of angry seawater curled around the hull, and smashed the galleon and princess against the rocks.

Dandelion screamed. Pete wiped his hand over his face, then wiped it again.

Josh gripped the bars. The princess would just re-form. Right? Sand littered the rocks, but she'd be back together in a moment.

Gargoyles howled and swooped, hunting survivors in the wreckage. Josh watched the waves break over the boulders. He held his breath until every piece of sand washed back into the sea.

Dandelion buried her face in her hands and sobbed. Pete was white as death. Every expression in the cage froze in dismay, watching their escape plan disappear in a plume of slime and wood fragments.

The cage swung past the fortress wall and out over the hole. Icy sleet whipped up and around the prisoners. Dandelion pulled her knees up tight. Others huddled near each other for warmth.

Josh couldn't move, couldn't catch his breath. The princess was dead? Just like that? The whole scene was surreal, a black and white movie: colorless, tasteless, lifeless. The only thing he could feel was terror.

Without the princess, he felt naked in a blizzard of evil. Everyone in the cage looked to him for a solution. Maybe everyone in this world did too. Each decision was a cliff's edge. One wrong step and he and millions of innocent people died.

Josh looked toward the sky, where the burning star would have been. Vastroh stood between him and doom, right? But he knew from experience that sometimes Vastroh would let him fail.

Lightning crackled across the cloud bottoms and, for a heartbeat, they shone gold. Beneath the roar of the wind, was the tiniest hint of a whisper. *I am greater than failure.*

Josh tried to feel better, but as quickly as the whisper came, it left, and there was only the storm. Nice thought, but reality was below him, a bottomless pit of eternal torture.

The cage hit the fortress wall with a bang, and the bars sprung open and the prisoners tumbled, screaming, into the endless darkness of The Throat.

CHAPTER THIRTEEN

THE THROAT

I mpact!

Josh landed on his back in an explosion of snow and was instantly tumbling. Spreading his arms and legs, he tried to stop the descent. It didn't help.

The snow reeked with the sharp tang of salt and sulfur, filling his nose and mouth. Roaring filled his ears. He couldn't catch a breath. He spun and spun until the colorless, bitter cold swallowed all sense of motion.

Or had he stopped?

He *had* stopped. But he couldn't feel his arms and legs. Cold blue dusk clamped over his nose and mouth. His lungs screamed for air. Terror exploded in his gut. In a frenzy, of Josh squirmed against the frigid grip.

One arm came free. Then the other. He tore at his face.

Air. Josh gasped and heaved.

By the time Josh dug free, he was soaked. Teeth chattering, he looked around.

He stood on the ruins of a plaza that jutted into the center of what looked like a skyscraper with the center torn out. Only a part of the city square remained, with frozen trees clinging to the lip. Ragged edges of rooms and doorways stretched a hundred feet above and below.

Below!

Josh shuddered and stepped back from the rim. His platform hung above another world. Below was the sky — not a blue sky, a twilight sky of swirling rust, rot, and black.

High above was the ruin's rim, The Throat entrance. Sea spray drifted over the edge, froze, and drifted down as snow. It piled up behind him in a huge drift against the building.

Haunting cries caught Josh's attention. In the distance, a swarm of gargoyles winged toward him.

Josh backed from the edge. Something grabbed him from behind. He yelled and spun. Pete! Dandelion!

Josh grabbed them both in a hug. "I thought maybe you guys went over the edge."

"I think pretty much everyone landed in the snowdrift." Pete gestured behind with his chin. Other survivors moved through the blizzard as dark shadows.

Trying to keep his teeth from clacking, Josh worked snow from an ear with his little finger. "D-did we survive or are we in Hell?"

Dandelion pointed below. "That's Hell. Right now we're in the ruins of Ghaolan, the Modus fortress. Welcome to The Throat."

"Are the bones in *there*?" A thrill spun in Josh's stomach. They could still destroy Kharaq.

Dandelion nodded.

As Josh looked up at the dark doorways, the thrill faded; steam billowed between icicles that grinned like sharpened teeth. He and his friends had no team of warriors, and no ship to get home, even if they were able to get the bones.

Josh's mind reached for Vastroh. Was he supposed to believe everything's going to be OK in a place like this? There was no way to know how things would turn out, and if fear was a choice, so was hope. He might as well focus on good possibilities.

Josh didn't hear anything or feel anything from Vastroh, but he was alive against the odds. Was that his answer?

He imagined Vastroh waiting inside. In his mind, they grabbed the bones and flew back on his flaming dragon. Josh mastered the fire spell and blasted Kharaq's bones. Crowds of families and freed slaves filled the streets and countryside, cheering.

"What are you grinning about?" Dandelion gave Josh a strange look.

Josh looked at his hands. They didn't look like zombie hands anymore. His grin just got bigger. He gestured toward the dark doorways and started the climb. "Let's go get those bones."

Pete gave his friends a haggard glance.

"Campitius?" Dandelion glanced at his face.

Pete nodded. "Campitius is showing me all the ways we'll probably die in there."

Dandelion took one of the brothers' hands in each of hers. "At least we're together."

Josh wasn't sure anything had ever felt so good.

Inside the ruin, it took a moment for Josh's eyes to adjust. A wide road bent away to his left and right. Dozens of graceful, arched passageways branched away from the road. There were no corners, everything flowed in soft curves.

Dandelion blew out a low whistle. "I read the Modus shaped this fortress from the lava."

Josh wiped his forehead. It was hot in here. Stone gargoyles crouched at each intersection. At one time, lava had poured from their open mouths into basins. Only a few still worked. Most were oozing red and black globs with wings and eyes.

Carved into the wall directly in front of him was a large map. Miniature stone people bustled in and out of tiny doorways. Vamirrion pressed a finger on a gaudy gateway, then pointed down the road to their left. "The temple is at the bottom of the western spire. That way."

Barking echoed outside the doorway.

"Move." Laevie spun and ran in the direction Vamirrion had pointed.

Everyone followed. With Josh's boots from the Fathomless, he shot ahead of the group. He'd barely rounded the corner before he ran into Laevie. Pete and Dandelion piled into him, and the other group members into them.

"Stop, stop." Laevie screeched, scrambling backward.

The end of the road jutted into space. Half the fortress was missing.

Vamirrion tugged on his beard, watery eyes staring across the chasm to the ragged rooms and halls on the other side.

"The temple is on the other side, right?" Josh looked up at the old man.

The old wizard slowly shook his head.

"Oh no," Dandelion moaned.

"Fallen? Into hell?" The merchant squawked, rubbing his face as if it would wash away the scene.

"Why don't you jump in after it?" Laevie nudged him toward the edge.

"Hey!" the merchant shrieked. "That's not funny."

Dandelion's face was tight. She pointed across the opening. Sections of the wreckage near the top bled like a giant wound. Great red globs of lava rolled from doorways and plummeted into the night below. "It was the volcano, wasn't it?"

Josh's breaths were quick and shallow. He ran fingers through his hair. No wonder Kharaq's generals had never returned. Now, neither would he and his friends. The bones were gone. The princess was dead. Soon Kharaq would kill the oracle, the Nandu, the trees, and every other good thing in this world. And Dad would be stone forever.

Would they? There was the tiniest nudge in the back of his mind.

No. Josh clenched his fists. That hopelessness, that was the occot's voice, wasn't it? Hopelessness was a lie. Have faith; faith isn't looking ahead, it's looking back. Being frozen in a block of ice felt like the end. It wasn't. Getting swallowed by the desert or attacked by Kharaq's monster had felt like the end too. Look how those turned out. How was this any different? He pictured the slave square turning gold and the chains melting. *That* was the truth.

"Kid." Laevie grabbed Dandelion's shoulder. "Just run faster than him, OK?" With a nod toward the merchant, she flicked her eyes to the sky below and pushed through the group, back the way they came.

Dandelion followed Laevie's glance and gasped. "Gargoyles!"

Swarms of the ruddy creatures winged toward the opening, howling and snapping at each other.

"Out of my way!" The merchant shoved his way after Laevie.

The group turned and ran back down the way they'd come. Josh stumbled after them. Laevie angled down a passage lined with doorways. Howls echoed after them.

"Try the doors." Josh shouted, shakier than he'd have liked.

The group spread out, trying door after door while they hurried down the hall. All were locked.

Every moment, the baying grew closer.

As Josh reached for a wrought-iron gate, thunder boomed. The walls shivered. Dust drifted from the ceiling.

"V ... volcano?" Josh staggered into the center of the passage.

The group froze and stared at each other wide eyed.

"We're going to die," the merchant wailed.

"I found one!" Dandelion was breathless. Studded iron bands crisscrossed a heavy oak door.

"How do we know it's safe in there?" The merchant wrung his hands.

Howls and the whoosh of wings raced around the corner.

Dandelion pulled two daggers free and kicked the door open. Laevie held her dagger out in front. Pete gripped his sword with both hands; scarlet letters danced on the blade.

"Quickly now." The old wizard lifted hsi hands, ready to cast a spell.

And they stepped through.

Once inside, the warriors, Royce and Reilly, slammed their muscled shoulders against the door. Outside, bodies thumped against it.

"Lock it," Laevie hissed. "Or give me your picks."

"I can't see." Dandelion fumbled noisily with the door.

"Lucem Papilo." A dozen candle-bright butterflies fluttered to the ceiling from the old wizard's hands.

"Better?" He smiled.

Josh's shoulder was against the door. Claws scraped the stone outside. The oak boards shuddered every time a beast slammed against it.

Josh's heart thundered in his chest. How did the wizard always stay so calm?

"It won't lock without a key." Dandelion knelt by the keyhole, voice strained.

The merchant pushed the wizard toward the door. "Hey gramps, how about some magic on that before we get eaten?"

Vamirrion shrugged the merchant's hands away and pressed two fingers against the lock. With a squeak, it clunked into place.

"Do you have to be such a toad?" Laevie scowled at the merchant.

"It *was* a good idea." The old wizard smiled toward her. He turned toward the merchant. Kindly eyes glinted like steel. "However, there is no need to be rude."

"Yeah. Be polite. Like this." Laevie rolled her eyes toward the wizard. "Please sir, would you turn him into a toad? A quiet one?"

The merchant scowled.

Hair stood on the back of Josh's neck. His back was to the room. They'd all been so focused on the door, no one had looked to see what was behind them. The thought seemed to occur to everyone at once. They all turned.

Rows of beds and iron lockers lined the room. Weapons and armor piled on the beds and leaned against walls.

"It looks like barracks." Pete stepped into the room, sword first. "Let's make sure nothing's hiding in here."

Laevie snatched a dagger from a locker and walked into the room with Pete.

Royce and Reilly went from locker to locker pulling out weapons and armor until they were covered with steel.

Heat radiated from cracks across the floor and ceiling. Sweat beaded on Josh's forehead.

"That looks like an echo-pack." The wizard touched Dandelion's shoulder.

"Yeah, anything good in there?" The merchant grabbed a strap.

Dandelion spun and pressed two daggers to his throat.

"Oh, hey kid. Just asking." The merchant raised his hands and stepped back.

"Atta girl." Laevie glanced over her shoulder and chuckled.

Dandelion pushed him back with the dagger points until he bumped up against a bed and abruptly sat.

"Stay there." She glared down at him, waiting until he gulped and nodded before she walked back to the wizard.

She huffed and scowled, pulling items out of the pack. "Do you think you'll know what some of these are? I had them separated, but now they're mixed up again. And I lost my library on the ship so I can't look them up."

Rumbling shook the room. Dust drifted from the cracks along the ceiling. Everyone looked at each other.

Pete buckled a spare sword around his waist. He barely closed the clasp before belt and sword clattered to the floor. "What do you mean, 'garbage'?" Pete muttered to his armor, picking the belt back up. "It's a spare. Shut up."

Laevie slid several daggers into the empty loops on her vest. "How were you kids planning on getting us out of this hole?"

Josh gestured toward Dandelion. "She has a flying vine that ..." He froze, face white.

"What.?" Laevie crossed her arms.

"We, um. It died." Josh licked his lips and knelt by Dandelion. "Please tell me Remy gave you a magic rope or something?"

"No she doesn't." Pete glared at his armor. "You didn't think of it either."

Dandelion dug through the pile with a haunted look. "Maybe there are stairs out there."

Josh took a ragged breath and rubbed his temples. "There must be a way out. How did the original population get in and out? We also need to get past those creatures outside the door."

"That's easy." Laevie flashed the merchant a disarming smile. "Toady there creates a distraction: he gets eaten while we all get away."

"It wouldn't work." Dandelion grinned. "Monsters can taste."

He sneered back.

"Hey. Sit!" Laevie pointed a dagger at the merchant.

While they talked, he had taken a tentative step toward the pile. He plopped back on the bed and glowered.

Laevie raised her eyebrows at Josh. "Well, fearless leader?"

Josh looked up at the old wizard. "What would you do?"

Vamirrion smiled. "When I don't know what to do, I simply take the next right step." His gaze paused on a silver feather pendant. Gem dust glittered in tiny engravings along the shaft. "May I look at that?"

Dandelion handed it to him.

He held the feather close to his face, lips moving while his fingers followed the lettering. Finally, he looked up. "It's for some kind of flight, but I can't tell the details." He turned to Josh. "It must be claimed to know for certain."

"No!" Laevie grabbed the wizard's hand. "Never claim something you don't know. It could be a horrible curse or scourge. Or kill us all."

"Like a Black Doorway," Josh mumbled.

Pete and Dandelion glanced at each other.

The old wizard smiled and patted Laevie's hand. "I know, child. I've been a wizard for a *very* long time."

"Plus, Remy wouldn't have given us something bad. Right?" Dandelion's brows arched up.

Pete held up the truth-seeing ring Remrald had given him. "It looks safe to me."

Vamirrion shrugged. "I don't see we have much choice."

Bushy eyebrows rose toward Josh. "I have more experience with these things and if it's evil, I have defenses. However, these items are very valuable, and this one is yours."

Josh picked up the feather. His voice was quiet. "I'll claim it. I'm not afraid."

Something had changed. He *really* wasn't afraid. Could things get any more hopeless than what they'd already survived? They weren't alone in this. He visualized the warrior on his fiery dragon — a warrior bigger than failure.

"It's mi ..." Josh began.

Before Josh could claim the feather, the merchant snatched it from his hand and ran to the other end of the room. He jabbed a chubby fist at the group. "I'm claiming this. You deserve to be here. I don't."

A shuddering boom drowned his voice. The cracks across the walls and ceiling gaped. With a jolt, his end of the room sagged downward.

The merchant squealed and scrambled up the sloping floor. The building convulsed again, and the room lurched further. He slid backward in an avalanche of beds and weaponry. Dust filled the air.

"It's mine. It's mine." He punched the air with the pendant.

Nothing happened.

The merchant scrambled over the beds, squealing in fright. All josh could think of was pet day, when someone accidentally stepped on Jenny's pot belly pig. They should rescue him. Josh wished his only reason was common decency, but he wanted that pendant.

"Help me make a rope—" Josh was grabbing blankets from a nearby bed when the walls exploded.

Dandelion screamed. Stinging bits of rock spattered the group. They watched, aghast, as the merchant's half of the room ripped free, and fell, spinning out of sight. Josh could still hear his scream long after the merchant had faded into the distance.

Icy clouds of dust and sulfur swirled in. Overhead, molten stone spewed into the somber sky. Wind whipped the deluge into a glowing scarlet rainstorm, drifting over the opening.

Dust settled on the group's dazed faces. No one liked the guy, but no one *really* wanted something like that to happen either.

And the merchant had stolen their way out. Josh couldn't believe he was *actually* going to leave all of them behind. They wouldn't have left *him* behind. Josh swallowed hard. Now no one was getting out.

Howls and beating wings pulled Josh's attention to the sky. Just beyond the lava rain, gargoyles swarmed toward them.

Laevie shrieked and spun for the door. "Unlock it."

Great cracks now laced the door frame. Stone sagged into wood. Vamirrion used his spell, but the door wouldn't budge.

Royce grabbed a sword and pried at the stubborn oak. Reilly joined him.

Behind them, Gargoyles flapped just outside the spray. They dodged in and out, trying for a way through. One made it. Then another. In moments, a stream of fangs and claws swarmed in.

Pete stood at the broken edge of the room, sword poised. Crimson letters rippled along his blade. His armor, Campitius, gleamed red, flowing over his head and legs until he was covered in shining crimson plate. Barbs moved in waves across his chest and back.

Dandelion scooped magic items back into her pack. Josh was frozen. Should he start grabbing magic items and claiming them, hoping for something to help them fight? What if they were just for protection or knowledge? The whole group would be dead if he used even one incorrectly. Instead he grabbed a sword from a nearby bed. He didn't really know how to use it, but he didn't know how to use the magic stuff either.

Vamirrion's hands wove. Wind shifted through molten spray, splattering lava on the oncoming beasts. Bursting into flames, they turned back into the flow, squalling and biting. Dead gargoyles plummeted with smoky trails.

The howling mass of creatures changed direction and headed toward him.

"Rapina." The old wizard made a throwing motion. A crackling ball of electricity spun toward the gargoyles.

As the sphere hit the creatures, a web of energy sizzled across the horde, leaping from creature to creature. Gargoyles yelped and crashed into each other, legs and wings spasming as they tumbled away into the darkness.

The rest circled outside the lava, yowling. A few darted in and out, but none came in.

"Nice one!" Laevie kicked a convulsing gargoyle off the ledge.

"Fetter-web." Vamirrion smiled. He turned to Josh. "I'll teach it to you if we ever get out of here."

Josh nodded, refusing to take his eyes off the gargoyles.

"Here they come again." Dandelion shot a lightning arrow into the circling swarm. The arrow zigzagged back and forth, piercing gargoyle after gargoyle, until it finally exploded in a ball of fire.

One of the creatures dodged through the opening. In seconds it was followed by a river of them. Vamirrion clawed his hands. Firebolts raced toward the beasts. Burning gargoyles tumbled away, but it didn't seem to make a difference. For each one that died, five more came through.

Pete was next to Josh. Gleaming letters on Pete's sword carved bloody arcs in the dull red tide. Any beasts that escaped the blade met spikes from Pete's armor.

Josh wasn't doing so well. Two beasts harried him. He'd turn to stab at one, and the other would lunge.

The larger one ducked past his sword and sank teeth into Josh's boot. Despite the leather and steel, its fangs burned, red-hot. Josh yelped, slashing at the beast with this sword.

With a grunt, the gargoyle yanked Josh from his feet. The sword clattered to the floor. Josh kicked at the creature. Wrenching and tugging, it dragged Josh toward the edge.

"Josh!" Dandelion dove toward him, grabbing an arm.

A second beast snatched Josh's other leg. The gargoyles flapped and pulled, tugging Josh over the edge. Dandelion strained in the other direction.

Pete's sword flashed out. One of Josh's beasts dropped away, but before Dandelion heaved Josh back, another gargoyle had him by the foot.

The two beasts flapped and grunted. Sinewy muscles bulging, they pulled Josh out over the abyss. Dandelion screamed back. Her heels sprayed dust and bits of stone.

Pete slashed out again, but dozens more gargoyles poured through the gap. He disappeared in a frenzy of claws and beating wings.

Josh had never seen him move so fast. A blur of silver and crimson, cutting, stabbing, and spinning.

"Josh!" Pete's shouts rang above the howls.

Pete was too near the edge. The weight of their attack pushed him closer and closer. Dead beasts heaped in piles behind him. There was no room to step back.

Pete turned to scramble over the bodies, and a huge gargoyle swooped in, knocking him off balance. Pete spun, windmilled, hung for a moment, and hurtled into space.

It began and ended between breaths.

As Pete tipped over the edge, he leapt toward the beasts holding Josh. Pete caught a leg on each creature. Wings and horned faces collided.

The gargoyles shrieked and let go of Josh. The shift in weight yanked Dandelion off the ledge. Josh grabbed his brother. Dandelion grabbed Josh. Beasts and teenagers plummeted into the dusk.

Their gargoyles snarled and wailed. Their frantic wings beat against the descent. Two creatures could easily carry one teenager, not three.

Ruins of the hanging city rushed past. Windows and verandas speckled giant stalactites of hardened lava.

Most of the lower city had fallen. Wind whipped glowing flurries of lava around the stump. Black clouds boiled around the base.

The teenagers fell and fell. Their gargoyles clawed and bit at each other with terrified squeals. They tore at Pete's hands, but teeth and claws were no match for his gauntlet steel.

Pete looked like a ghost. Dandelion panted in desperate gasps.

Wind whistled in Josh's ears and stabbed icy fingers through every chink in his armor. His hands and arms were numb. With Dandelion's weight, he wasn't sure how long he could hold on.

Terror — there it was again; giant fists squeezing his throat and chest. Josh searched the sky for the burning star. Don't be afraid? How? Being afraid isn't a choice.

Is it?

The darkness had a golden tint. "I am the other choice," the voiceless voice rumbled in the back of his mind.

Josh saw it above him, the burning star, an eye of fire in a sea of black hopelessness.

"But everything's gone wrong. I mean, what am I supposed to do?" Josh whispered into the darkness.

As soon as Josh asked, he already knew the answer. "What" wasn't the point. The point was "who" — that he and the fiery warrior did it together.

Josh had failed no matter what he tried. Yet he'd survived no matter how badly he failed. Anxiety was all about trying to control how things worked out. For the first time, it made sense; if they did it together, it would work out even when it didn't work out. Let the chips fall.

"OK. But what if I die?"

Josh felt him smile. "We'll do *that* together too."

Nothing changed. They still plummeted into the world of the dead. There was no way back up. There was no way to defeat Kharaq and save Dad.

And yet.

Everything changed. In the midnight of his choking terror, the tiniest pinhole of light twinkled. Hope.

The further the teenagers fell, the more frantic the two gargoyles became.

A piranha-sized tongue of fire burst to life in front of Josh. It swam around them for a while before another appeared, and then another. The number grew until hundreds swirled in a fiery whirlwind. It was fascinating, even beautiful, until the first bite.

One flame darted in, then two, then they swarmed, a hundred at a time, biting out little smoldering divots. The gargoyles howled with each attack.

The bites had no effect on the boys' armor, but it wasn't long before the creatures found their faces. Pete's armor formed a visor. Josh buried his face in his arm while the flames attacked his neck and ears. Dandelion screamed and screamed, whipping her head back and forth.

"Get away from us," Josh screamed.

What if she let go? She'd die. Maybe it didn't matter. Was falling worse than being eaten? With every squirm, his fingers loosened. In a second, they'd all find out.

With a howl, the gargoyles tucked their wings and fell. Smoke from the bites trailed behind. The flames followed for a while and finally gave up.

A rush of color blurred past Josh's vision. The gargoyles squawked and started flapping again. The teenagers fell through a sea of rainbow threads, tendrils of smoke hanging hundreds of feet long.

Nearby, the skeleton of a dragon twitched. Tattered skin covered mottled brown-gray bone. Raising its head, the creature coughed a mournful howl and then hung limp.

The gaunt remains of creatures hung here and there throughout tangles.

The gargoyles jolted left and right to avoid the threads. Each move sent red hot spikes through Josh's wrists and shoulders. He gritted his teeth. Don't let go. Don't let go. His breathing came in gasps and grunts.

Somehow, they made it through the threads. Below them, spread the scorched countryside: rugged mountains, charred clutching trees, jagged black rivers.

Pete moaned, his eyes squeezed shut and lips pressed tight. Josh had no idea how his brother had managed to hold on this long.

"Hang on," Josh murmured.

The gargoyles gasped for breath, flapping more slowly. Were they falling slowly enough to survive a landing? And a landing on what — or in what?

Directly beneath them yawned a volcanic crater. Waves of ambers, browns, and blacks crept across a sludgy lake. A skyscraper-sized piece of the fallen city lay broken over the crater's rim, half submerged in the basin.

Foghorns bellowed. Dull gray eels the size of freight trains wormed toward them. Josh's stomach clenched. One bite would fit all three friends *and* the gargoyles.

Above him, the gargoyles howled and tore at Pete's hands.

Movement behind the eels caught Josh's' eye. Millions of tiny pieces of utter blackness gathered from the surrounding night, a cloud of swirling hornets. He wasn't sure he could actually see them as much as seeing the void where the night wasn't. What was happening?

The swarm grew until it filled the sky, forming horns and jaws and snarling lips.

Dandelion's yelling rose a notch, "a Devourer?"

The gargoyles squealed, wing-beats rising to a frenzy. The gallop of Josh's heartbeat followed.

Bellowing, the eels fled with terrified twists in opposite directions.

The Devourer's jaws opened. A dozen glistening tongues streaked like bullets of darkness toward the nearest eel, exploding around the creature in a thousand points of blackness.

A faint, eel-shaped mist floated from the beast, and the carcass fell, tumbling end over end until it splashed into the lake. But it didn't sink, it melted.

Above, the devourer gobbled the luminous eel spirit and turned its multifaceted eyes toward the friends.

Josh choked, his gaze flipping between the devourer and the lake. They were going to have their souls eaten or die screaming in a lake of acid? Any courage Josh had dissolved. Help! Please help!

"My eyes." Dandelion buried her face in her arm.

The nearer they got to the lake, the harder it was to breathe. Tears rolled down Josh's face. His nose and throat were on fire. He coughed and almost lost his grip.

Pete gasped for breath. Josh could feel him shake.

"Hold on," Josh whispered.

The devourer's mouth opened. The gargoyles screamed. Swarming flecks of blackness shot toward the teenagers. Pete's eyes bulged.

And he let go.

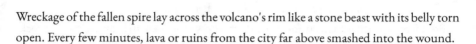

Wreckage of the fallen spire lay across the volcano's rim like a stone beast with its belly torn open. Every few minutes, lava or ruins from the city far above smashed into the wound.

The teenagers bounced down the jagged slope of broken stone and landed in the rubble at the bottom.

Josh lay on his back and tried to catch his breath. His armor had turned to stone when he fell, but it still felt like every rib was broken.

Pete lay nearby, covered head to toe with his armor. Moaning, he slowly he wrapped his arms around his chest.

Dandelion had no armor! Josh jolted upright and gasped in pain. He wrenched himself free from tiny, decaying roots that circled his arms and legs. More reached up toward him from the cracks as he stood.

Cries rang overhead. Muck brown creatures circled like vultures. Long necks with bright red heads craned from bodies that spread as if poured. They gnashed needle-like teeth and focused on an area higher up the slope.

Please don't be Dandelion. Josh clenched his teeth against the gnawing ache in his gut.

He climbed the broken pieces of walls and doorways. Atop a large section of road was a pile of something. The closer he got, the harder it was to breathe. A boot. A bow and quiver full of crackling arrows. A hood with a tangle of autumn hair.

"Pete, get up here!" Josh wailed, and broke into a run.

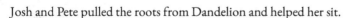

Josh and Pete pulled the roots from Dandelion and helped her sit.

Dandelion gasped short, shallow breaths. Blood welled from cuts on her face. She groaned and lifted one side of her vest. Swashes of purple bruising spread across her stomach.

"That looks really bad." Pete's brows knit.

"I'm fine." Her voice was hoarse. She cradled one of her arms against her body. "Figure out what we're going to do about *those* instead."

Josh followed her gaze. All around them, rat-sized crab creatures crept from the acid. Gray moss draped around a dozen jointed legs. Clumps of dark green antennae waved from their heads and backs. They scuttled sideways toward the teenagers in short dashes, shadow to crack to shadow.

"Watch out!" Dandelion screamed and ducked her head.

Boulders smashed into the ruins above them, showering them in broken shards of rock. Boulders tumbled down the slope. The friends crouched until the dust settled.

That was too close. They needed shelter. "There." Josh pointed up the debris slope to a large opening in the side of the ruin.

Dandelion tried to stand and cried out, gripping her ankle with both hands. "I think it's broken." She wheezed in shallow gulps.

Pete stepped in and put his arms around her.

She yelped, batting him away. "What are you doing?"

"I ... I was going to carry you." Pete's face shone crimson.

"No you're not!" Dandelion grabbed Pete's shoulder and leveraged herself to her feet. "I told you, I'm fine."

Josh took her other side and, together, they moved over the rocks toward the opening. Every step, she gasped and bit her lip. Beads of sweat shone on her forehead.

No one said anything. What was there to say? Dandelion was gaunt and pale, and looked worse every minute. That bruise was probably internal bleeding. She needed a doctor.

Josh shook his head. A doctor? They were in *hell*. What were they going to find down *here*? Maybe a math teacher.

The opening turned out to be a massive hall. Everything was sideways, so they sat on the wall, back to back, to keep a lookout in every direction.

How long would it take for the roots to get this high? How long for the slimy crab-things to reach them? Vulture-cries closed in from overhead.

Dandelion slumped into Josh. Her every breath had a sickly rasp. How long did *she* have?

Josh wiped his eyes and sniffed. The acid-air was cold, yet it burned. With it, a gnawing hopelessness cut straight through Josh's resolve, the way icy wind bites through a t-shirt.

"I can't believe we're dead." A tiny sob escaped Dandelion.

"This is worse than death." Pete's eyes were vacant.

Look at my tarnish! This air is worse than death. Josh's back touched Pete, and Campitius rang in Josh's mind.

Dandelion wrapped arms around herself. "There's no way back up. There's no way to kill Kharaq. I'll never save my brother. I'll never be part of a family. Everything good is cursed. Forever."

Teeth chattering, Josh looked up through the opening. In the distant sky burned Vastroh's star. Help.

Outside, giant blobs of lava smashed onto the ruins, splashing red and gold across the rubble. Fireballs roared overhead. Their reflection scattered multicolored lights across the lake's surface. It was beautiful.

Beauty? In the middle of hell? Josh scratched the mark on his hand. This place dragged at his mind just like the occot. He already knew how to win *that* fight. *Do something about it.*

"We *can't* fail. Vastroh watches over our destiny. See?" Josh pointed at the burning star. He tried to sound confident.

Pete scoffed, "We *have* failed."

Dandelion put her face in her hands. "The Cambium Dreams are a joke. Destiny is a lie."

"What's in your backpack?" Josh put a hand on Dandelion's shoulder.

"Ouch." She twisted away and put her face back in her hands. "What difference does is make?"

"Just dump it out and let's see." Josh bit his lip. He didn't know what else to do, he just knew real freedom happened when you worked toward it.

He glanced at roots crab-creatures creeping through the doorway. His mouth was dry. Please let there be something in that backpack.

Dandelion piled trinkets, rings, and pieces of armor on the floor.

"What's this?" Josh picked up a worn leather-bound book. Several pages were missing. Only their charred stubs peeked from the crease.

"How should I know? A spell book?" Dandelion fingered an odd brown sac. It had no opening. She shrugged and set it back down.

"Oh!" Josh squawked and dropped the book. Smoke rose from the binding. The page he'd just read floated away as ash.

Pete and Dandelion looked up.

The wizard has found the Opneust. Rise warrior, lest your steel be outdone by his magic.

"Woah." Josh slowly raised his eyes, bright with excitement. "It *is* a spell book. I ... I just learned a spell. All I did was read it."

Josh jumped to his feet. He glanced around the room. His eyes settled on a slimy acid crab.

"Quatio." He gripped the air pulled his hand toward him. Colors glowed through his armor and raced up his arms.

The creature slid toward them even as its tiny, jointed legs scrambled to get away.

"Ugh!" Dandelion grimaced.

Josh opened his hand, and the acid crab fled the hall. He laughed out loud. "It's a grapple spell. It pushes and pulls. Watch this." He swatted in the direction of another creature. With a squeak, the crab spun through the air.

Pete and Dandelion stared.

Josh flipped to the middle of the book. It was blank. All the pages were blank but the first, so he read that. With a flash, it disappeared. As it burned, colorful script appeared on the next page.

"I can only read it in order." He grinned at the other two and began to read as fast as he could. One page flashed. Then another, and another. Ashes floated around him. His skin blazed like fireworks under his armor. He grunted with effort. Sweat dripped from his forehead.

"Stop it!" Dandelion snatched the book. "I knew a kid who came home from magic school and the whole right side of his body didn't work. He fried his brain with a spell that was too hard."

His mind will burn like those pages. Cut the book with your sword.

Josh glanced at Pete and grinned. The more he thought, the bigger the smile grew. "I'm remembering. Look." Josh pulled his shirt down an inch at the neckline. Brilliant white specks of light danced in a sunburst at his throat.

"A blood rune?" Dandelion breathed an awestruck whisper.

"I have lots of runes. They show up as I remember." He pulled up a sleeve to show a glowing dragon tattoo in fiery reds and golds around his forearm. "I was always jealous of Pete. He's had special training his whole life. I just realized, I have too — during the years I can't remember *and* the ones I can. Everything Mom taught me, all the lessons, training and mind exercises, were for magic."

Josh gently pried the book from Dandelion's fingers. "I was born for this."

His eyes played over her face. "Are you feeling better?" The pasty sheen was gone from her skin. Sparks were back in her eyes.

"I'm fine. I told you," Dandelion huffed. "What we need is that floating pendant the muckman grabbed. Then we could fly back up."

"I suppose you mean this." A gaunt wizard stepped from the shadows behind them. Light glinted from a silver feather in his hand.

CHAPTER FOURTEEN

TEN THOUSAND SPIDERS

Josh's mind short-circuited. There were other people down here? How did that guy get the pendant?

Pete scrambled to his feet.

"Sisto." The wizard held up a hand.

All three teenagers froze. Josh's gasp caught in his throat. A page stood half opened. Pete's sword was half drawn. Dandelion's hands reached for dagger handles. All perfectly still.

"It is mine." The wizard slowly let out his breath. "I saw it fall with your friend. Your talk of it confirmed it was safe to claim." A gold chain hung around his neck. He fastened the feather next to a white drawstring bag the size of a golf ball.

"Now finish what you were saying about the emperor." He limped into the room, waving a hand toward Dandelion.

For a moment, the air in front of Dandelion's face turned opaque. A tendril of hair tumbled over her cheek. She gasped for air.

"Go on. Don't be shy." He tucked the pendant under his robe.

"I ... can't breathe," Dandelion's voice labored.

"So overrated. No one cares if you're dead around here. Now, tell me about Kharaq."
He blinked at them, an arrogant smile playing on his lips.

"I know who you are," Dandelion growled. "You're Malum, commander of the dark armies. You disappeared while trying to hide Kharaq's bones."

The gaunt wizard bowed slightly. "At your service. And how would you know of my *secret* quest? Such a bright little thing to have found me." He rubbed his chin and looked intently at Dandelion. "You spoke of killing Kharaq, so I must surmise that you wish to destroy the bones. And he hunts you now?"

"He'll never catch us." Dandelion struggled within the binding spell.

"So right you are. Although I imagine this is where he'd want you to end up anyway." The wizard laughed. "Oh, and thank you for confirming his return. I'm quite sure he'll want his body back." He fingered the glittering white bag at his neck.

Dandelion's face burned red. "I didn't tell you anything."

The wizard pursed his lips and raised eyebrows.

Dandelion squirmed.

He raised his chin. "Where better to hide the bones than in death? 'The only safe place in the world is out of it.' Brilliant, if I do say so myself."

"You have a lot of gall quoting a cambium poet." Dandelion's expression darkened.

Booms echoed around them. The walls and floor shuddered as massive stone slabs crashed down outside.

"Yes. Safe. Except when my piece of the city fell." The wizard floated toward the door. "Well, it was awfully nice chatting. It's been so very long since I've had company."

That white bag! Everything they'd been fighting for was twenty feet away. If Josh could have moved, he could have grabbed it. Victory was in their hands, and all they could do was watch it float away. Josh wanted to scream.

Jointed legs and green antennae crept toward the teenagers.

"A word of advice," the wizard called down to them. "Don't stay in one place for long. Being eaten by a swarm of those is"—he shuddered—"gruesome."

Dandelion eyes toward the slimy creatures. "We, ah, can't move."

"Such a bright little thing." He barked a wicked laugh and disappeared into the dark sky.

The shadows came alive with squirming legs and antennae. The clicking of tiny feet filled the room.

"Quatio," Josh shouted toward the creatures in his mind. But he couldn't breathe, let alone speak.

"J ... Josh, can't you do your spell to make them leave?" Dandelion's eyes darted back and forth.

Mentally he pushed as hard as he could. Nothing happened.

"Yah! Get away!" Dandelion yelled. A few acid crabs scuttled away, but in moments the floor was a wriggling carpet.

Josh shuddered, remembering his first meeting in the cave with Kharaq. Pete had broken him out last time. There must be a way out now. He racked his brain and sorted through the spells he'd just learned. None of it was any help.

Dandelion shrieked. Tiny pincers nipped at her leg. Josh could see her muscles tense and spasm.

More acid crabs climbed on the brothers. Slimy antennae tickled and touched. Pointed claws pricked. Acid burned with each touch.

Then they began to eat.

Josh tried to scream. He kicked and fought against the binding spell. Bile rose in his throat; not even a finger moved.

Pete's eyes were wide, his face white.

Josh's mind floundered. If only he could remember all his training. He tried to calm his thoughts. But with each nip of the acid crabs, electric needles stabbed his legs and wrists. His muscles spasmed uncontrollably. Any shred of concentration shattered.

Help.

The air thickened. Josh *felt* the boom outside before he heard it. The force of the impact hammered his elbows and knees. The stone floor buckled. Josh and the others were flung from their feet.

The ruins outside exploded in debris. From far above, the rest of the hanging city had broken free and smashed into the fallen ruins.

Slabs of ceiling collapsed into the room. Boulders tumbled over the opening. Along with the roar, Josh heard breaking glass. As he hit the floor, tiny gleaming shards tumbled from his body and dissolved into mist.

He could move! He scrambled to his feet and brushed furiously at the acid crabs.

Pete and Dandelion were already on their feet. Dandelion swatted at her face and body.

Josh spun toward the entrance. It was completely blocked, yet acid crabs still poured through tiny spaces between the rocks. There had to be another way out. Light streamed in from ragged gaps in the ceiling, but the nearest opening was easily two stories overhead.

The three kicked and stomped, but the crabs swarmed up from the floor and leapt from the walls. When Dandelion swiped them off her chest, dozens more streamed up her back. They caught in her hair and climbed down on her face.

Tiny green dots peppered her skin, splaying outward from each place the crabs pinched. Josh gasped and looked at the same dots on *his* wrists.

Pete was the only one who could stay ahead of the deluge. Waves of spikes rolled across his back and arms. Campitius killed the creatures as fast as they climbed on.

"Stand together," Josh yelled to Dandelion.

They stood back to back, swiping as fast as they could. It didn't really help. Josh's arms were aching. Beads of sweat ran down Dandelion's face.

"Stop. Stop!" Josh shouted between heaving breaths, flinging a handful of crabs at the flow.

Every leg and antennae froze. For a moment everything was still, then acid crabs shot away in a thousand directions. With squeaks and clicks, they fought each other for the openings. As fast as they had streamed in, they were gone.

Dandelion sank to the floor and stared at the ceiling.

"What did you do?" Pete turned to Josh wide eyed.

"I ... I ... it wasn't me." Josh scratched at a green spot and looked around.

Moans shuddered through the stone. Reek wafted up the hallway. Acid! The ground shifted, tilting slowly down.

Josh windmilled, trying to stay upright. His stomach lurched.

Dandelion was on her feet. "The city is sinking!"

The teenagers gaped at each other. Cracking sounds rang like gunfire. Hairline fractures raced along the walls. Dust drifted from the passageways.

"Maybe there's a way out down here." Pete disappeared down the hallway.

Behind Dandelion, a giant slab crashed to the floor. She snatched up Josh's spell book and slapped it into his hands. "Look for a floating spell or magic wings or something."

She spun and leapt for the magic items, frantic fingers digging through the pile.

Pete reappeared, running toward them, hand over his nose and mouth. Burning fumes wafted behind. Eyes watery and bloodshot, he stopped beside Josh and sucked huge breaths. "That hall only goes down into the acid. We're sinking fast."

Dandelion screamed. Waves of orange and purple bubbled up around her. She rolled on the floor, convulsions racking her body. Pulling at her hair and face, she screamed again, and disappeared in the flow.

⊷◈⊶

Josh stared at what flowed over Dandelion. It wasn't acid. It was thousands of tiny legs and bodies.

Spiders!

Dandelion's face was opaque with tiny strands of web. Josh and Pete tore at the threads. But instead of freeing her, sticky web covered *their* hands and arms.

The harder they fought, the faster the silken cocoon encased the boys. The spiders poured from the little brown sac in Dandelion's pile of magic items.

"Crush it. Kill the spiders." Pete was almost completely covered.

"No!" Dandelion grabbed Josh's hand. "Pete, tell your armor to stop cutting. Look."

Web shifted around them in a spherical cocoon. It wasn't sticky on the inside. It felt a lot like a camping tent.

Dandelion laughed. "Look at the spiders. Recognize the colors? Remember when we escaped the sand king in the fathomless? They have to be babies from the magic spider Remy used to repair the carpet. Which means ..."

"Their web floats." Josh looked down. Their cocoon was already halfway to the ceiling. Acid bubbled across the floor below.

Josh wasn't sure if he would laugh or cry. He sneezed. Pete chuckled. Dandelion snickered. In a moment, they all laughed until tears rolled down their faces.

"Can you use that grapple spell to direct us out that hole?" Pete wiped his eyes and pointed overhead.

"Quatio." Josh opened his hand outward. They drifted toward the hole.

Tiny spiders scurried over the cocoon, weaving their shimmering strands. The thicker the cocoon wall, the faster the teenagers rose.

Soon the acid lake shrank far below them. Using his spell, Josh whacked any vulture things curious enough to come close. Dandelion searched the dark skies for a Devourer, but none showed.

Lava from the city overhead whistled past in globs and clumps. Josh was careful to stay out of the flow.

Between grapple spells, Josh gobbled the spell book. Page after page dissolved to ashes. Face haggard, he leaned heavily over the book.

Some spells were useful, like a shrapnel spell that exploded a boulder into sharp pieces toward an enemy. But most were trivial, like how to soothe an itch or unlock a door.

"Why do you have the look on your face?" Dandelion scratched at several green spots from the acid crabs.

"Scabitu. " Josh waved a tired hand toward her and grinned. The toxic green bumps faded to a soft mint.

"Oh. Thanks. That's a lot better." She traced fingertips over the spots.

"Want me to soothe yours?" Josh turned toward his brother.

Pete's chin lifted. "Nah. I can handle it."

Only because I protected you. Now find something to slay, Campitius huffed.

Josh glanced where his shoulder touched Pete's and went back to the book. "Hey look, fetter-web!" Josh grinned and pointed at the page.

Pete raised questioning eyebrows.

"That electric webbing Vamirrion used on the gargoyles ... never mind." Josh's eyes went back to the book. Another page went up in smoke. Then another.

Josh wiped his brow. "These are getting harder."

"Maybe you should save your energy for the lava." Dandelion looked worried.

Josh shook his head, eyes bright.

By the time the hanging city was in sight, Josh's face was buried in Dandelion's shoulder. He was fast asleep.

"Wow." Dandelion felt her ankle.

"It's better, isn't it?" Pete pursed his lips.

"Yeah." Dandelion wiggled her foot.

Pete nodded at Josh. "It's him, or, his gem. Aura said the stone healed us after we went over that waterfall. Maybe that's why Kharaq won't die."

Dandelion sighed. "How far ahead do you think Malum is?"

Pete shrugged.

Dandelion's expression darkened. "How are we going to catch him? If we catch him, how do we get the bones from him? How far will this cocoon float? Across the ocean? Back home?"

"And we still have to get past the gargo ... Aaah!" Pete yelped and lurched forward.

Globs of lava streaked by so close, a huge gash melted into sparkling embers. Burned spiders floated away. Others swarmed toward the opening, weaving the hole closed.

Cut it back open. We need an opening to kill things out there.

"What happened?" Josh glanced at Pete's armor and rubbed his eyes.

"A piece of lavaaaah ..." Dandelion leapt to the other side. "Push us away. Quick!"

Burning droplets sizzled straight through the cocoon. The reek of burned hair filled the space. More dead spiders floated away. Their tiny siblings scurried over the holes.

"Quatio." Josh gulped, pushing them out of the flow.

Dandelion pointed above them. "That's the opening to the world of the living, but how do we get to the middle?"

Even though no lava flowed in the hole's center, curtains of magma streamed down every side.

Pete glanced at Josh's spell book. "Anything in there?"

"Iron Dome," Josh squirmed.

Steel's better.

Pete flicked Campitius

Josh ran fingers through his hair. "It *should* create a shield made of magic over the top of the cocoon. I just don't know if it's strong enough, or ..."

"If *you're* strong enough," Dandelion's voice was soft.

Josh nodded. "I'll have to make the dome and hold it. Then at the same time, push us sideways through the flow. And then stop in the center."

They drifted beside the fiery rain. Josh watched the smoky trails stretching behind each glob. He'd never been so scared. After everything he'd been through, he knew the answer. Fear is normal. Do it anyway.

But knowing didn't make him feel any better. If they died completing some great quest, at least they'd die heroes. He imagined bards singing their story, or mothers whispering "thanks" for a chance to raise their kids in safety.

But Josh didn't have Kharaq's bones. Dad was still trapped. Failing now meant they died for nothing.

Failure also meant he killed his friends. They'd all been lucky enough not to die from his previous attempts. How could he risk their lives again? On a spell he'd never even tried?

Dandelion squeezed his hand. "Without *you*, we have no hope at all. I believe in you." She smiled. "Wizard."

Josh squeezed back. He tried to smile, but he didn't feel like a wizard. What did being a wizard feel like, anyway? For that matter, what did being brave feel like? He could hear Aura's croaky whisper. *Feeling is nothing, doing is everything.*

'Be' the iron, human.

Pete rolled his eyes at Campitius. "Good luck, Josh."

Luck. What was luck? Josh could just see Vastroh raising an eyebrow, *I am your luck.* Josh took a deep breath. Yeah, I guess you are.

He looked at his friends. "The book said to use my fist as a foundation for the spell. If my fist stays closed, my concentration stays steady, and the shield won't break."

Pete and Dandelion nodded.

Josh muttered the incantation. Faint colors swam in oily rainbows above the cocoon. He slowly clenched a fist in front of his face. Air shimmered around his knuckles.

Opening his other hand, he reached out with his mind and grasped a piece of the city. Deep breath.

Dandelion and Pete watched wide eyed.

"Quatio."

In an instant, magma streamed around them. Josh frantically pushed them left and right, dodging the burning globs.

He wasn't fast enough. A huge lump smashed against the shield, jolting the cocoon sideways. Josh landed on the floor on his face, fist underneath his chest. Pete and Dandelion landed on top of him.

Fear tore at Josh's concentration. They were right under the lava stream. He couldn't get up. He couldn't see where to move the cocoon. He couldn't hold the shield for long under this heat ...

Stop it! Focus. Josh squeezed his fist as hard as he could, forcing his magic out to the edges of the shield: *rigid, unyielding, impenetrable.*

Pete and Dandelion untangled from each other and sat Josh upright.

"You did it! Your spell held." Dandelion pointed above them. "And look, I can see the sky. The *real* sky."

Josh glanced up for a second. His heart skipped a beat. In the living world, The Throat's volcano erupted. Ash and magma churned into the living sky. They were almost free.

Another lump of lava knocked them sideways. Then another. Blistering stone pounded against the shield.

Josh's attention snapped back to the flow. Globs whooshed by on every side. Push. Pull. Push. The cocoon would almost reach the tranquil center and a glob would knock them sideways. Sweat ran down Josh's face and soaked his shirt. His breath came in heaves. This wasn't working.

A mass of lava hit the shield. Instead of sliding off, it sat on top. Magma ran down the sides. The shield's colors swam under the heat.

Josh sucked in ragged breaths. It felt like the molten boulder sat directly on his shoulders. His joints popped under the weight. The rusty taste of blood filled his mouth.

"Oh no," Dandelion gasped.

Josh's whole body shook. He tried to push the lava off with a spell, but only bits and pieces broke away. Smoke rose from his fist. He had to get it off the shield before ...

With a hiss, the shield gave way, and the mass fell through, landing in Josh's lap. Josh yelled and leapt to his feet. Magma slid from his stone cloak. Web sizzled and melted at his feet, and the Lava fell away in a puff of smoke.

Josh fell after it.

He didn't have time to breathe, but a million thoughts raced through his mind. *You fall, you die.* Instinct commanded his hands open to grab the edge of the hole. *Open your hand and your friends die.* Training ordered his fist closed, his mind focused on the shield above them. Either decision, everything was lost.

Above him, Pete and Dandelion grabbed for Josh. Dandelion was closest, catching Josh's hood.

Josh gagged. The force of the robe around his neck felt like a hangman's noose. It was the best thing he'd ever felt. He hadn't fallen, *and* he hadn't opened his fist. It happened so fast, he wasn't sure how he'd chosen to be brave.

More lava streaked past. Josh heard Pete and Dandelion grunting and shouting above him. How long could they hold him? What would happen when another glob hit them?

Don't look. Don't think about it. Just think about the shield. Rebuild the shield. Don't give up.

He was a wizard. He would die before he gave up.

Josh dangled below the cocoon, his eyes squeezed shut. Gripping one fist with the other, he forced power around the web.

Magma pummeled the shield, knocking them left and right. Pete and Dandelion rolled on the floor and pulled at Josh. They'd almost get him up over the lip, and a glob of lava would knock them sideways.

Josh groaned. His shield flickered and sagged. It was strong enough to keep the droplets out, but larger blobs hissed right through. Acrid smoke filled the cocoon. Clouds of dead spiders floated like campfire embers.

With so many spiders dead, it took longer and longer to fill the holes. The cocoon rose more and more slowly.

"Hang on Josh!" Dandelion shouted and pulled. Burns smoldered on her leather jerkin.

"I ... I can't," Josh could barely get the words out.

"Yes you can." Pete reached under Josh's arm. "You're the Wizard from the Cambium Dreams." Pete looked up. Color drained from his face. "Pull, pull," he shouted at Dandelion.

A glob hurtled toward them, so big, it roared as it fell. Fire streamed behind it.

Pete and Dandelion heaved. The mass smashed into the cocoon. Molten droplets burst in every direction. Josh slumped. The shield dissolved into colored fragments. They spun sideways, and the glob roared past.

Pete rubbed his eyes. Dandelion gasped. Their web chamber floated in the center of the opening. Lava fell on every side. Far above, sunlight glinted through boiling clouds.

The cocoon hung in rags. There was barely enough web to keep the teenagers from falling out. A few tiny spiders worked furiously at the holes.

Josh lay limp against the web wall. Blood trickled from his nose. His hands were blistered, his eyes bloodshot and red rimmed. He looked up. "We made it?"

"We made it." Dandelion grabbed him as hard as she could. Her face buried in his chest, she laughed and sobbed, "we made it. You were amazing."

Pete bit his lip. He wrapped arms around both of them and whispered, "and legend becomes real."

Thanks to me.

Pete scowled at Campitius. "Oh, shut up."

Living air! Josh could taste it, even through all the smoke and sulfur. He lay with his head in Dandelion's lap, his eyes closed. They drifted slowly upward amid the volcano's roar. Wind warmed by magma swirled around them, lifting them toward the entrance.

The holes in the cocoon closed *so* slowly. It was threadbare and had hardly enough web to rise.

Mountain crags quaked overhead. Pieces of the city crumbled and fell with the lava.

Josh hardly dared think about it. They had survived. Freedom was just on the other side. How would they get the bones? How would they save Dad? He had no idea. But once they were free, they had options. *And he was a wizard.*

Dandelion pulled out a handkerchief and dabbed Josh's forehead, then wiped the blood from his nose.

Pete gasped and gripped Josh's arm. Pete's eyes bulged. "Do you think you have enough energy to pull us up?"

Josh shifted so he could see. Outside the hole, magma geysered into an ash gray sky. Rivers of lava piled against the remains of the fortress. The ragged walls slowly leaned toward the opening.

"The fortress!" Josh hissed. If it fell, it would cover the hole like a giant lid. They weren't rising fast enough.

Dandelion twisted her hands.

Josh could barely sit up. How could he cast a spell? Images of sitting on a horse flooded into his mind. Josh's knees and elbows were covered with mud and his nose bled. Dad held the reins out to Josh. "Can't or won't? I've stood beside the beds of healthy men sick to death with bitterness. I've also *fought* beside men so full of arrows they could hardly stand, fighters who refused to die, and won their war. Your will rules your reality."

Josh slowly let his breath out. Focus. Sickening cracking sounds snapped his eyes to the tottering fortress. Fooocuuus. Josh gritted his teeth. His mind reached for the edge. Just as he pulled, the fortress fell.

Dandelion screamed. Pete shouted. A thousand dagger blades plunged into Josh's soul. He was too late.

The opening disappeared in an explosion of debris. Dust rolled in clouds across an unforgiving ceiling of granite. Spears of gray daylight shone through doorways and windows.

A flood of ash and lava flowed over the top, clogging the openings one by one. The flat taste of stone clogged Josh's throat. His heart was a stone. He couldn't think, couldn't feel, couldn't breathe.

They were stuck in hell.

CHAPTER FIFTEEN

QUEEN OF THE DEEP

The three friends huddled together in the ragged remains of the web cocoon. Most of the floor was missing. Sides gaped and sagged. Here and there, a few tiny spiders still scurried.

Gradually, the cocoon floated to the stone roof. So what? There was no way out. Josh watched the underworld sky billow toward them. Pretty soon, any trace there had ever been an opening would be gone.

One of Dandelion's hands covered her face. The other gripped his. Her shoulders silently shook. Pete's lips were tight, his eyes fastened on Josh.

Was it colder now? Hopelessness. Desperation. The air was thick with it. Hell's air. It soaked straight into his heart. Bile rose in his throat.

Have faith. Every bad thing can be rewoven into glittering destiny. Right?

Josh squeezed his eyes shut. Help. His head thundered. He tried to believe. He just didn't. There was no way out. "We'll look for cracks. Maybe there's still an opening." Was that his voice? It was so weak and shaky.

Pete nodded. Dandelion didn't look up.

"Quatio." Josh pushed.

The cocoon slowly drifted across the crater. Pieces of the building jutted downward. Josh saw windows and docking bays. All were filled with lumpy, gray lava; lifeless, hopeless gray.

"Oh no," Dandelion gasped.

Dull red wings beat toward them. Gargoyles!

"Can you do a, uh, shield spell again?" Pete swallowed loudly.

Josh wiped his nose with the back of his hand. Blood smeared across his glove. He looked at Pete and shook his head.

This was it then. Pete had a sword and Dandelion had daggers, but so what? Three blades against a hundred teeth and claws?

Dandelion grabbed both boys in a hug. Heads pressed together. Josh could feel her breath on his face. "Close your eyes. Don't watch me die."

Hollow howls echoed around them.

She took a deep breath and whispered, "goodbye."

Teeth and claws jabbed like shards of exploding stone. Howls mixed with screams. So, this is what death felt like: a giant fist. Sound, light, and life dripped out between monstrous, dark fingers.

It didn't hurt like Josh thought. It felt more like a tomb. There was vertigo too. Their spirits whisked away — to the Land of Light? Josh squeezed his eyes shut.

"Ow." Josh's head clacked against Dandelion's. She was still here? And Pete? Josh heard his brother's breathing.

Josh opened his eyes. Light? Dandelion's eyes were open, bulging.

The teenagers were encased in stone. Light filtered in through long, narrow cracks. Josh could smell sulfur and salt.

The stone walls moved, and bright light blazed around them. Dandelion yelped. Wind whipped her hair into Josh's face. He squinted, partly covering his eyes.

They sat in a space the size of a small room. Green stone pillars rose in a circle around them. Daylight streamed between the columns.

Dandelion screamed. She was on her feet, diving, wrapping arms around the nearest pillar.

Josh blinked and rubbed his eyes and gasped. They were in the palm of a giant hand. Webbed claws rose around them. Waves from The Throat tempest surged below. Huge green eyes peered over the fingers. Dozens of eels writhed around a fanged face.

"The princess!" Dandelion hugged the giant finger.

The princess's monster form towered twice the size it was before. She stood thigh deep, just outside The Throat-island crater.

Beside her, several people stood on a tiny sand island. Josh recognized Vamirrion, Laevie, and the man whose daughter he'd tried to save. The scaly warriors, Royce and Reilly, stood beside a pillar of tangled seaweed.

The princess set teenagers on the sand. Her monster collapsed, becoming a shimmering green woman.

All three teenagers leapt on her, hugging, crying, and laughing. She laughed and hugged back, emerald eyes glistening.

The other adults watched. Laevie wiped her eyes.

"I can't believe I found all of you." The princess stepped back and ruffled Josh's hair.

"H ... how *did* you find us? How did you get us out? How did you survive the shipwreck?" Dandelion buried her face in her emerald robes.

"That's a lot of questions." The princess laughed and squeezed. "Before I tell you the story, look at what I found." She gestured to the seaweed-pillar. Around the top, leaves unwound until a face was visible.

"Malum!" Dandelion hissed.

Tendrils of greens still wound around the wizard's mouth. He grunted and squirmed.

"What? How?" Josh gaped.

The princess smiled. "I'll tell you, but first, I think he might have something you want."

Josh raised his eyes to her. "He has Kharaq's bones."

Vamirrion's eyebrows shot up. "Is that what he carries? I sensed the god spell and wondered."

Josh turned to Vamirrion. "How do we get it from him?"

The old wizard frowned. "I know not. You risk losing the chain's cargo completely."

Malum's face settled into smug arrogance.

Josh bit his lip. He and his friends couldn't have made it this far, only to get stuck on something so small. Think.

"Campitius says we should just burn him on the altar, bones and all." Pete mirrored Malum's smug look back at him.

Dandelion shot Pete a disgusted look and scratched at one of the fading green spots on her neck. "Too bad we don't have a few thousand acid crabs to help him *choose* to give it up."

The green spots! Of course. Josh's eyes flicked between Dandelion and Pete. Her's were almost gone. Pete's were still dark.

Josh laughed out loud. Of all the worthless spells he'd learned in the last couple hours, the most worthless might be the answer. He walked up to the wizard. "I'd like the floating pendant back, please. And Kharaq's bones."

Malum rolled his eyes.

"Scabitu." Josh thrust both hands toward the dark mage. If the grapple spell could push *and* pull, couldn't the soothing spell also itch?

Bright red bumps appeared beneath Maulum's necklace. "Mmmmm!" The wizard's eyes popped wide.

"It seems you've developed an allergy to metal." Josh watched the wizard.

Malum's eyes snapped back and forth between Josh and the other group members. He squirmed and fought against the seaweed. "Mmmmm!" Beads of sweat broke out on his forehead.

Vamirrion nodded to Josh. "Very inventive."

The red bumps on Malum's neck spread up over his face and down across his hands. "MMMM. MMMM." He writhed and squealed.

"How long do we have to wait?" Dandelion winced at the wizard.

Josh held out his hand. "May I have the floating pendant and Kharaq's bones?"

"MMMM!" Malum nodded his entire body.

With a quick tug, Josh broke the necklace from the wizard's neck.

Sand exploded around their little island. The princess's monster towered above them. Without a word, she snatched up the wizard in one hand and the teenagers in the other. She strode toward The Throat and lifted the adventurers over the surging crater where they could see.

"*He* is the one who chose this as a destination; it's where he should stay." The fist holding Malum punched through the lid to hell and let go. Josh watched him tumble into the darkness until lava covered over the hole.

The princess set them back on the sand island and shrank to her normal self. The silver feather and white drawstring bag hung from Josh's fist. The world had just stopped.

Dandelion burst out laughing. She cried at the same time. "We're going to win! I thought we'd completely failed. I thought we were going to die. Now we're going to win?" She grabbed the boy's faces one at a time and kissed them. "I love you guys."

Pete turned bright red.

Josh gaped. How had they gone from being trapped in hell with no hope of escape to having everything they needed to complete the quest?

And he was a wizard!

His heart exploded like fireworks. If he jumped into the air, he'd rocket across the sky, splash into the sun, and swim around.

And he was free; he wasn't afraid anymore. Now he understood what Vastroh had told him in the slaver's square — being free was something that had to happen on the inside before it could truly happen on the outside. He could see Dad's face, a man is *who* you are, not *how old* you are. Josh's *hell* had forged a man.

In his mind, he reached toward Vastroh. Somehow everything ended up exactly where it should — no matter how Josh or anyone or anything had messed it up.

"How do we get back to the oracle and the altar to destroy these?" Josh held up the bone-bag by its chain.

Vamirrion's voice was soft. "Our world stands at the cusp of the glittering age of the Cambium Dreams, and three children lead the way." He stroked his beard and grinned. "No. A woman and two young men."

"The Wizard and the Warrior," Dandelion murmured.

"And the Weaver." Youthful fire burned beneath Vamirrion's bristling white eyebrows. His wrinkled hands rested on Dandelion's shoulders. "You're in the prophecy too."

"Me?" Dandelion's eyes got big.

"You're part dryad, yes? Have you never heard the Cambium Dreams?"

"Yeah, but—"

Vamirrion didn't stop talking. "Child of earth, you are the ground under their feet, the wind lifting their wings, their spark rekindled. You are the thread that *weaves* it all together. Without you, there *is* no prophecy."

Tears rolled down Dandelion's face.

Josh's eyes welled up too. A week ago, he should have been embarrassed. Now, he didn't care. Josh took her hand. "Of course you are. Deep down, I guess Pete and I always knew it. And whatever happens, you have *two* brothers now."

Dandelion grabbed them both in a hug. She turned to the princess. "You should have seen Josh. He's amazing. He saved us with his magic."

She grabbed Pete's hand. "Pete was incredible too. He defended all of us. Fought dozens of the creatures at once."

The tiniest smile twitched at the corners of Pete's mouth. "I lost my magic sword though."

Josh grinned at Dandelion. "Dandelion can talk to anything. We'd have dissolved in acid if she didn't get magic spiders to float us out."

The princess beamed at the teenagers. "I'm so very proud of all of you."

Vamirrion gestured to the sky. "Kharaq will have spies, so we haven't much time. I can create a portal to the altar in the city of Ersha, but not this close to The Throat." He turned to the princess, gesturing out into the ocean. "Can you create an island like this one out *there*?"

"Save your magic." The princess smiled at Vamirrion and waved her arm in a circle.

Clouds rolled overhead. Dark waves circled the island, slowly at first, then faster and faster.

Laevie sidled up to Dandelion. "You're in the Cambium Dreams? Who *are* you kids?" The rogue glanced toward the princess. "And who is *she*?"

Her questions drowned in thundering seas.

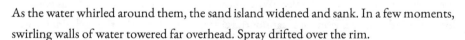

As the water whirled around them, the sand island widened and sank. In a few moments, swirling walls of water towered far overhead. Spray drifted over the rim.

Sand lurched beneath their feet. Everyone but the princess grabbed at someone for balance. Whirlpool and island raced along the bottom of the ocean toward the city of Ersha.

Josh watched the seawater whirl around them in a gray, blue, and green kaleidoscope. Up near the top, flecks of gold sparkled in the sunlight. In the darkness down near the island, chemiluminescent creatures sparkled like the starry night.

Down this far it was darker, and freezing. The princess had them all sit. They huddled close to stay warm and not have to shout to be heard.

She gestured toward the whirling water. "In many places, the ocean is too deep to make an island, so it's easier to move the water."

"How?" Dandelion stared open-mouthed.

"I am no longer the princess." Her eyes twinkled. "I am Queen of the Deep. My father ..." Edges of her smile faded. Her eyes glistened. " ... has become one with the sea. I didn't have the chance to say goodbye."

Josh slipped his hand into hers. The princess squeezed back.

"I'm sorry about your dad." Dandelion took her other hand.

The queen nodded, lips pinched.

Dandelion's hand flew to her mouth. "You're more than the Queen of the Deep. The Ilmenite King is dead too. You rule all Alaetian sand. You're an empress."

Laevie and Vamirrion gasped.

With a shy smile, the Queen glanced at the teenagers. "I suppose you're right. Now, I want to hear *your* story."

Dandelion told most of the story. Josh and Pete jumped in when they could. The others in the group were riveted.

"And then you grabbed us." Dandelion's eyes were bright. "What about you? When we saw the ship sink, we thought you were dead."

The Queen pulled a strand of web from Dandelion's hair. "I'm *from* the sea, remember? Being in the water makes me even stronger. When I saw you fall into The Throat, I reached as far in as I could. I found Laevie and the others, but they said you'd fallen all the way into the underworld.

"When the volcano erupted, and the hole began to fill with lava, I didn't know what to do. It felt like the time I lost my little ..." The queen's voice cracked. She stopped talking for a minute and looked at the sky. "When I thought I lost you, I thought I was going to lose my mind. You see, sand souls cannot travel to your underworld; the sea holds its own dead."

She took a breath and composed herself. "As the volcano erupted, the wizard floated out. Vamirrion recognized him, so I snatched him from the air. But no matter how I questioned him about you, he would only clutch at his necklace."

The queen broke into a smile. "The throat had closed, so I punched through to throw him back into hell. That's when I saw your web cocoon and realized what he might be hiding — considering who he is." After telling the story, she grabbed the teenagers in another hug.

"Shut up or I'll throw you in there." Pete glanced at the swirling water.

The Queen's eyebrows rose.

"Oh, sorry. Not you. Campitius is like a gnat. I think salt water is the only thing he's afraid of."

Dandelion laughed.

The queen smiled. "Don't worry, you're all safe with me."

As they talked, the walls of water shrank until their platform rose above the surface, a giant teardrop of sand.

Sun! Blazing hot, living sunshine. Josh turned his face upward and closed his eyes. Warmth seeped in until his fingertips tingled. Brisk fresh wind ruffled his hair, and salty spray nipped at his skin. In one day, he'd gone from the depths of hell straight to heaven.

His heart erupted in gold, crimson, and emerald fireworks. It filled his chest until he couldn't breathe. What was this? Joy? Gratitude? This was the power of The Nine, wasn't it? This was the best feeling in the world.

Josh rubbed the tattoo on the back of his hand. The occot shrank before the wonder and elation. The whole thing was impossible, but had worked out anyway. Was walking with Vastroh always like that? He cracked his eyes open and looked for the burning star.

"Thank you, thank you, thank you," he whispered. He wiped his eyes and laughed out loud.

"The cliffs." Dandelion stared at the horizon. One hand pointed, and the other shaded her face.

Josh watched the black and brown granite heave itself over the horizon until it rose hundreds of feet above the waves and stretched as far as he could see in either direction.

Directly ahead, a giant finger of rock stood out from the cliff. Sunlight sparkled from the spires and parapets of a palace perched on its tip.

Josh's stomach flip-flopped. He knew this place. Just like the forest when they first arrived. Just like Kharaq's dark wolves. "This is the city of Ersha.?"

Dandelion nodded. "That's the Sunset Palace on the rock-pillar."

The queen's island shot toward a tiny dock at the base of the column. Josh's memories were such a fuzzy tangle. He knew that behind the rock spire was a narrow ravine and a twisting stairway that lead up to the city. But he did not know *how* he knew.

As the island reached the dock, the Queen gathered the teenagers to her. "I cannot go to the city this way, but I will come with help as quickly as I can."

She sent them on to the quay where they watched the waves pound her island to nothing. She waved as she disappeared in the spray.

Without the queen, Josh's anticipation of destroying Kharaq's bones had faded to gnawing disquiet. With her, everything felt like it would just fall into place. Now, an awful premonition clutched at Josh's heart.

"I wonder who those two were?" Laevie gestured to neatly stacked piles of stones standing nearby. Wind voices whispered and moaned. She shuddered. "They say everyone in the city is like that. It's haunted."

Dandelion scowled. "Don't touch them."

"Don't worry," Laevie snorted and skirted the stones with as wide a berth as possible.

"They'll be freed when Kharaq dies, right? My Dad is trapped like that." Josh threw a hopeful look toward Vamirrion.

The aged wizard returned a sad smile. "I'm sorry, I don't know. Things don't usually work that way." He put a hand on Josh's shoulder. "Perhaps your destiny is to free everyone *else* in this world from an age of suffering and cruelty."

Josh swallowed. The oracle had said killing Kharaq would set Dad free, hadn't he? Josh thought back and groaned inwardly. The oracle had said, "Defeat Kharaq and we *have a chance* to save your father."

A chance? Josh wanted to kick himself. If he couldn't free Dad, everything they'd been through was for nothing.

The occot squirmed in Josh's tattoo. Waves of despair doused all of his joy.

With stumbling steps, Josh followed the group up the ravine.

◄●►

Water gurgled cheerfully beside the uneven stairway. Ravine walls stretched up to a cloudless sky. Here at the bottom, a big man could have touched both sides.

Josh lagged behind. Memories swept through his mind, flurries of images and smells and sensations he couldn't quite piece together. Bright yellow daisies peeked from among the stones. Dad and Mom and Josh would walk down these stairs to watch waves. Sunlight poured rivulets of crimson fire through Mom's hair. She'd pick a flower and let Josh put it behind her ear, the yellow, so vivid against her red. Dad just stared at her, and finally put a hand on his heart and shook his head.

Josh swallowed. What was he going to do about Dad? Less than an hour ago Josh was superman. Now he could barely lift his feet.

"What's on your mind, son?" Vamirrion moved as slowly as Josh. Wrinkled hands pressed aged knees for each step.

"My dad. You said killing Kharaq might not free the people trapped in stone." Josh scratched some dirt off his robe.

"Ah." Vamirrion nodded.

"What happens to the people Kharaq turns to stone?"

The old wizard frowned. "It is an especially cruel spell. People are trapped on the paths between the worlds. They're conscious but unconscious. Like a very long, very bad dream."

"The Seams." Josh tried to imagine what it must be like for his dad.

"I have two grandchildren who were in the city." Vamirrion focused on the stairs.

Josh kicked a rock into the stream. "Do you think we'll be able to free your grandkids ... and my dad?"

Vamirrion sighed. "If there's a way, we'll find it."

"How come you're never upset?"

"Oh." The old wizard looked up with watery eyes. "I wish that were true. But I've found that most of the things I worried about never happened, while things I never worried about, did. I'm a lot happier when I'm not catching raindrops."

Josh gave him a quizzical look.

"It's an old saying, to let the rain fall where it will. To me, it means trusting that Vastroh will make sure everything works out for the best."

Josh searched the sky for the burning star. Really trusting meant being satisfied even if Dad was trapped forever. Josh didn't think he could.

The old wizard glanced at Josh's frown. "Sometimes it helps to think of other things. Let's start with destroying Kharaq."

Josh imagined Kharaq falling into hell. Gargoyles, giant eels, and vulture things, all taking bites out of him on the way down. At the bottom, he dissolved in the acid lake. Josh grinned. It *did* help.

"To destroy the bones we must ignite them with Holy Fire. It's difficult to light, and usually takes three wizards, but perhaps we can do it with two. Do you know the spells for holy fire?" Vamirrion paused and leaned against the cliff wall, breathing heavily.

Josh shook his head.

"Maybe it's in the book." Dandelion walked back down a few steps, digging around in her pack until she found it.

"May I?" Vamirrion held out his hand.

Josh watched him. "The spell on the first page is the only one visible. You have to learn it to see the others."

The old wizard leafed through the book, holding a palm over each page. For a moment, ink filled the parchment then disappeared.

Josh leaned over the wizard's shoulder. "How did you do that?"

"An old wizard trick." Vamirrion winked at Josh and handed him the book. "How many of these did you read?"

Josh shrugged.

"That's a very valuable book. We used to dream of learning spells that way. Be very careful. There are no shortcuts. Not really. You'll always end up paying full price in the end."

"Were the Holy Fire spells in there?" Josh tucked the book under his arm.

Vamirrion shook his head. "I shall have to teach them to you on the way up." With a grunt, he stood and began the slow climb.

Josh stepped up beside the old wizard. With a smile, he placed Vamirrion's wrinkled hand on his shoulder. "Lean on me. I guess we all need help in one way or another."

Vamirrion smiled back.

The sun stood directly over the ravine. Golden warmth mingled with cool gusts off the water. Josh took a deep breath. Don't try to catch the rain, let it fall — along with all the worry and stress. He half closed his eyes and reached for Vastroh.

Kharaq stood in the center of a clearing, eyes gleaming red within the shadow of his cowl. His black satin robe shone in the afternoon sun. Gold leaf patterns studded with gems curled along the seams and across a wide, red-leather belt.

He cracked his knuckles and looked around. Trunks and branches clustered too closely to see the crystal spires of Ersha. But he knew it was just beyond the river.

The forest shifted and whispered.

A dozen dark-robed wizards stood around Kharaq, hands lifted. One by one, fist-sized blotches appeared in the air between trees. Sickly gray-green veins oozed outward from the stains, each billowing like smoke, growing until they reached the size of barn doors.

The centers bulged. Spear heads pushed through followed by studded nightwood shields. Three abreast, ranks of hunched goblins stepped through.

"Your birds did well reporting their arrival." Kharaq looked down at the giant burned wolf beside him.

Raucous cries turned Kharaq's face upward. With a rush of dark wings, a large crow landed on his shoulder. It leaned forward and croaked in his ear.

"Ah! They have the bones," Kharaq snorted. "And who says fate has no favorites?"

"My liege." A goblin general stood at attention. "The longbows are ready."

Kharaq turned toward the general. "No. The boy put my bones with the shard. He must willingly remove them. Leave that to me. Begin your march to the Sanctulum altar."

Kharaq tossed the crow into the air. "Watch their progress." He turned to the two closest wizards. "Keep stirring the ill-wind until I return with the gem." He looked up at trees. "We don't want our leafy friends to ruin our surprise."

CHAPTER SIXTEEN

HELL'S BLOOD

J osh's sweat dripped onto the oval, stone altar of the Sanctulum. "I need a rest." He
sank into the grass at the feet of a massive stone angel.

The other angels and demons towering around the altar seemed to glare at him with
stony disapproval. Red and gold autumn leaves tumbled across the large clearing. Dandelion and the others sat in the shade, tired of waiting for Josh to master Holy Fire.

The oracle leaned on his staff nearby. He muttered, brows furrowed. "An ill silence
mars the wind."

A breeze would have been nice. The forest branches moved in a wind, but the air was
still and hot and silent.

Josh glanced at Drompa. His robe was punctuated with even more angles than last time. Was that bark growing on his neck?

"You've almost got it. Look. The stones are glowing. Try once more." Vamirrion leaned over the altar.

No matter what Josh tried, the spell wasn't working. Crows circled overhead. Josh kept imagining Kharaq stepping through the trees. His stomach was in knots, It was impossible to concentrate.

"Can't he help?" Josh gestured toward the oracle.

Drompa turned sad eyes back. "Would that I had the power. But you're doing well. Keep trying."

Pete glanced up but didn't say anything. Using handfuls of sand, he rubbed the rust off a sword he'd found in the city.

Pete didn't have to say anything. Dozens of stone piles dotted the clearing. It was the same in the city. Laevie was right about it being creepy. From here, the trees were too tall to see to any of the buildings, but it gave Josh chills thinking of the thousands upon thousands of stone piles haunting the streets. Their only hope was Josh.

With a groan, he pushed himself to his feet. With any luck, this time Kharaq would be in hell instead of all those people.

A scraping sound turned Josh toward Vamirrion. In his place stood a neat stack of stones. Black vapor drifted away in the wind.

"Trouble lighting the fire?" A grinding whisper drifted from the trees.

Dandelion yelped. Hundreds of goblins in beaten armor stepped from the trees. Black spear points pressed to her throat. The clearing was surrounded.

Pete leapt up, sword sweeping out in front.

Kharaq's gaze turned toward Pete and lifted a claw to his chest. "Please don't hurt me." He laughed, and with a downward swipe of Kharaq's claw, Pete's sword slammed back into its sheath. "Stay where you are. You're only alive because I want something."

Pete struggled with his sword, muttering to his armor, "Shut up, I can't move it."

Kharaq laughed, "No you can't"

Fists balled, Pete stepped toward the wizard.

"One more step, and you and your armor end up like your wizard friend." Kharaq strode toward them. He stopped beside a cairn. With a meaningful look toward Pete, he pushed it over.

Dandelion drew in a sharp breath.

"You're too late, Kharaq. We've already lit the fire. Quickly son, throw in the bones." The oracle's voice sounded frail.

"Old fool, I'm undead, not blind," Kharaq snorted and turned to Josh. His demeanor softened. "Give me the bones, and you and your friends go free."

"He's lying. He wants the stone." The oracle glared beneath thick brows.

"Stay out of this, old man. See the axemen? Your next conversation will be with them." As Kharaq spoke, several goblins hefted large war axes.

The dark wizard turned back to Josh. "Give me the bones and I will create a portal back to your world for you and your brother. Keep the shard. It means nothing to me. There is no magic in your world, so you cannot use it against me."

He was lying, wasn't he? Josh clenched his fists. If only he could have lit the fire, it would never have come to this.

"I'll even set your father free." Kharaq flexed his claws. The knuckles popped.

Josh's throat tied itself in knots. His own wheezing echoed in his ears. If Josh burned the bones, there were no guarantees for Dad. But if Kharaq reversed the spell ...

"He lies. Once he has the bones, you're all dead," the oracle hissed, eye toward the axemen. "And he does not have a key to your world."

"Fool, the boy *is* a key." Kharaq's white fangs flashed. He stepped toward Josh. "I'll make the bargain even better. This is your last chance."

Kharaq waved at the trees. Several giant ogrei stepped from the forest. Each held a chest big enough to fit Josh and his friends inside. Sunlight glinted in blinding stipples from jewels and gold in each.

"These are yours. Build castles, empires. Take the dryad with you." Kharaq's eyes shone.

A flicker caught the corner of Josh's eye. The holy fire! Tiny flames guttered around the glowing red stones. He tried not to look. Did Kharaq notice?

Josh's breath came in shallow gulps. How long would it take the bones to burn? If he could get them in the fire quickly enough, would Kharaq be destroyed before he could tell the goblins to kill them?

"No." The dark wizard seemed to read Josh's mind. "The fire is not big enough. And you would *all* be dead before your fingers even let go of that bag. Then, I just pluck the bones from the altar."

"He's lying ..." The oracle choked.

Kharaq waved axemen toward the oracle. They lifted their weapons and shambled toward the old man. Their gibbering sounded like insane laughter. Chills raced from Josh's scalp to his feet.

A yelp from Dandelion snapped Josh's eyes to her. Another Ogrei stepped from the trees holding a cauldron of rough-hewn quartz.

Smoke poured from the pot; tar bubbled and writhed. Josh would never forget that black sludge. He gasped and grabbed the tattoo on his hand.

"Yes," the dark voice murmured. "Remember how much that hurt? You have *only* two choices. Your deepest desires or painful death. You can be rich beyond your dreams. Imagine the crowds cheering. Everyone will love you." Kharaq leaned in. "Or everyone suffers, and your name will be a curse."

Josh's heart thundered. His eyes flicked from Kharaq to the oracle. Axemen had almost reached the old man. Josh's bones melted. His knees slowly sagged. His mouth was so dry he couldn't speak.

Kharaq turned toward the goblins that held Dandelion. "Throw her in."

Dandelion screamed. They dragged her, kicking and struggling, toward the tar. Bits of grass and dirt flew in every direction.

"After her, the brother." Kharaq gestured toward Pete.

The goblins reached the pot and lifted Dandelion. Josh could hear her nails scrape as she clutched at their armor. Her shrieks rang from the trees, autumn hair whipping around her.

"Stop," Josh groaned. "Stop."

The goblins froze, fanged faces looking at their master. Kharaq turned smug eyes toward Josh.

Dandelion sobbed, hair stuck to her face. Her skin was ghostly pale. Her eyes seemed all whites. Tears as blue as the sky poured straight into Josh's soul.

Josh remembered her in the slave train, bursting from the dust to save them; flying them away from the slave market on her magic vine; racing all night against the inquisitor. She'd been unsinkable — always with a smile or laugh or wisecrack. She'd been their daylight on this dark journey. The thought of her sinking in the squirmy hell's blood was too much.

Something collapsed in his chest. Josh reached behind his neck for the clasp.

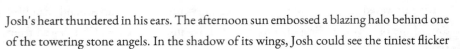

Josh's heart thundered in his ears. The afternoon sun embossed a blazing halo behind one of the towering stone angels. In the shadow of its wings, Josh could see the tiniest flicker of Holy Fire.

Across the clearing, Dandelion watched with wide eyes and trembling lips. Josh wished he knew what she was thinking. Maybe she'd have an idea about what to do. *His* only plan wasn't that good, and Kharaq always seemed to read his mind.

Reaching behind his neck, Josh gauged the distance to the altar. His hands shook so badly, he wasn't sure he could even undo the clasp. One swift motion and the bones would be in the fire. As soon as the bones left his hands, he'd cast a push spell on Dandelion. That should be enough to make her miss the pot.

Kharaq walked toward him from halfway across the clearing. A fetter-web spell would have him twitching on the ground. Plenty of time for the bones time to burn.

Sweat trickled down Josh's back.

With a click, the chain was loose. Josh kept his eyes on the wizard. Pretend you're handing it to him. Josh rehearsed Fetter-web in his mind. He pulled the chain free and held it out, then whipped it toward the fire.

With a pop, shadows of oily black flicked between him and the sun. The smell of smoke and rot filled Josh's nostrils; with it rang rasp of dark laughter.

"Thank you." Kharaq stood between Josh and the altar, gem and bones in his claw. "You must learn Quickstep," he laughed and lifted the chain-clasps behind his neck.

Nooo. Josh opened his palms toward Kharaq. "Rapina." He poured everything into a fetter-web spell.

With lazy disdain, Kharaq swiped a claw toward Dandelion. Josh's lightning ball whistled past the wizard, striking Dandelion in the chest.

Energy crackled around her. She screamed, her back arching, legs and arms jerking in spasms.

Tendrils of power leapt from her to the goblins. They yelped and tossed her away, toward the boiling cauldron.

"Nice shot," Kharaq laughed toward Josh.

Dandelion! Josh staggered toward her, hands outstretched. "Quatio."

Nothing happened.

Realization hit him like a city bus; between Holy Fire and Fetter-web, he'd just used all the magic power he had.

Movement in the corner of Josh's eye spun him around. Sword raised, Pete charged the dark wizard. Noo! Pete was too far away. Kharaq could still cast any number of spells.

The dark cowl turned toward Pete. "Join your *friend*." A claw lifted, "Ston ..."

Thought moves faster than time. Love moves faster than thought. Josh was already in the air, diving toward Kharaq's talon, toward the spell. Kharaq might win, but not like this. Not stone. Not his brother.

Josh's hands closed on Kharaq's claw, pulling it toward himself as the wizard finished his spell.

"... stone."

Power slammed into Josh. Holes peppered the cloudless afternoon sky. Black tar bled in, filling the world until there was ... nothing.

Pete poured every ounce of strength into his legs, sword point aimed for the wizard's black heart. Run! For just a moment, Kharaq was distracted. A moment was all Pete needed.

But the wizard turned too soon. The talon came up, bone bag and shard twisted in the claws. Josh dove at the hand — and was gone. A small pile of stones tottered in front of Kharaq. Pete heard his own voice roar.

He heard the wizard gasp. One of Kharaq's claws was encased in Josh's stone. Rough gray-black granite raced up Kharaq's arm.

"Impedius." The wizard gripped his arm above the spread.

The flow stopped at his hand. Kharaq raised triumphant eyes toward Pete.

A crackling sound shattered the wizard's sneer. Stone continued its flow up Kharaq's arm.

"Impedius," he hissed, gripping further above the change.

The flow of stone did not stop.

"Impedius. Impedius sacris confoundum," he shouted, changing his grip higher and higher. Granite just soaked into the gripping fingers, washing up both arms.

Kharaq's eyes bugged. He howled spell after spell. Froth flew from his gnashing fangs. Dark gray ran down his cloak in rivulets.

The wizard's voice rose to a scream. He tried to tug himself free, but his torso was encased. Sinews roped on his neck.

"Noooo!" His red eyes blazed toward Pete.

With a popping sound, Kharaq was gone. A cairn of gray-black stones stood beside Josh's rust colored ones. Kharaq's bone bag tumbled to the grass.

It happened so fast. Pete tried to turn. He flung himself sideways. But it was too late. Pete slammed into the piles.

One moment, his sword point was aimed at Kharaq's chest. The next, Pete was sprawled on hands and knees with stones scattered every direction.

Josh! Pete's breath came in gulps. He grabbed at stones and tried to re-stack them. His hands shook so badly no stones stayed.

Which one went on top of which?

Once they are knocked over, they cannot be restored, Campitius brooded.

"Shut up!" Pete screamed, snatching and stacking until his fingertips were raw. "Tell me how to fix this. Help me!"

His armor was sorrowfully silent.

Confused mutters raced through the goblin troops. Laevie ducked under the spears and ran to Pete. Her captors just watched her run.

For a moment, she knelt by Pete, one hand on his shoulder. "Really sorry, kid."

With her other hand, she reached for Kharaq's bone bag and tossed them into the flames.

Nothing happened.

Shouts rang from the goblin general. Soldiers charged the altar.

Laevie spun toward the Oracle. "Will it light?"

His face was slack, shoulders drooped. "There is not enough fire."

The goblins were almost at the altar. Laevie pulled out her daggers. "Pete! Get up."

Pete didn't move. Why should he? They were outnumbered a hundred to one. And Josh was gone. It was *his* fault.

Behind Pete, a fireball streaked from the sky, exploding onto the altar.

After it trailed a tiny spark. "Buwn. Buwn."

In an instant, the top of the altar was awash in flames. Perched in the center was Aura, blazing like the sun. "Burn," he squawked and pecked at the bones.

The bag burst into flames. Black, acrid clouds poured from the altar, rolling across the clearing. Soldiers coughed and stumbled. Laevie covered her face.

Pete gagged but didn't get up. His eyes burned as if he'd rubbed acid in them. He couldn't breathe. He didn't care.

The ground shook. With a dull boom, giant ripples of power exploded from the altar in rings of gold, fuchsia, and blue.

Trees swayed in the wind. Thunder echoed across the city. One of the angel statues toppled.

One by one, the stone piles littering the clearing crumbled. Wind whirled the powder in tiny dust devils. In the center of each, frozen people appeared; a mouth open in conversation, a hand reaching for something. They looked around with bewildered faces.

As the boom faded, goblin cries drowned in the roar of human voices, thousands upon thousands of human voices. The city was awake.

The goblin soldiers froze. The city around them was filled with people who hated goblins. Now it was the goblins who were outnumbered a hundred to one.

Wind roared through the forest. A giant oak branch swung downward, smacking the goblin genera cartwheeling into the clearing.

Branches from other trees hissed downward, batting the soldiers across the hillside. With squeals and grunts, Kharaq's army crawled under the branches into the woods.

Pete watched the other stone piles change to people. But Josh's hadn't changed. Come back too! Pete grabbed a stone, but it crumbled to dust and disappeared into the grass. No! He ripped at the dirt where it fell.

Pete lurched to his feet and staggered backward. He wiped dirty hands on his pants. He wiped them again and again, as if Kharaq's spell would just wipe away.

He couldn't drag his eyes from the pile that had been his brother who had chosen a death by stone rather than letting it go to Pete, where it belonged. Pete gasped for breath.

Dandelion lay motionless in the grass where she'd fallen after hitting the edge of the cauldron. The oracle leaned over her, wrinkled hands settling on her temples. Soft light flowed from his touch. She stirred, coughed, and opened her eyes.

The Oracle helped her to her feet. She clung to his robe.

"Wha ... what happened?" She rubbed her eyes and looked around.

The goblins and ogrei were gone, treasure and crystal cauldrons dumped in the grass. The clearing was full of people. Dandelion's jaw dropped. Her eyes flicked from the oracle to the place he usually stood rooted by the altar. She pointed at and bottom of his robe.

"You have feet," she laughed, then shouted. "You have feet! We won? We won!" She grabbed his hands and danced him around in a circle.

The oracle grinned.

Dandelion saw Pete and sprinted to him. "You did it. We won. Wizard, Warrior, Wea ..." Her steps slowed as she neared him. Her brows crinkled. "Where's Josh?"

Her eyes followed his to the tumbled stones. While she watched, another collapsed to dust.

"Oh Pete, no!" Dandelion's green eyes welled. Her lower lip trembled. "Drompa." She spun to the oracle. He had almost reached her. "You can fix this. Right?" She grabbed his sleeve. Her nostrils flared. "Please. Kharaq is dead. You can ..."

He pinched his lips and slowly shook his head.

Dandelion stumbled to the pile and sank to her knees. She grabbed a stone and tried to stack it. Pieces broke free. She snatched them up, only to have them crumble as she touched them.

Pete stared at the Oracle's feet. Slowly Pete's bloodshot eyes lifted to the old man's face. "This isn't real." Pete's voice was barely a whisper. "Josh isn't dead. The whole thing is a stupid daymare."

Pete looked around. People walked toward them. They pointed. Talked with eager voices.

He looked at the rock pile. Dandelion knelt with her hands in the dirt. Her hair hung in tangled strands around her face. Her shoulders shook. More stones sloughed to dust.

"None of this. None of you are real!" He shouted at the people in the clearing and threw the sword at the altar. He ripped his magic armor off in handfuls. Pete's voice rose until it was almost a scream. "Get off me!"

The oracle's face sank in deep lines and creases. He reached for Pete.

"You're ... not ... real," Pete gulped between words.

The oracle pulled Pete to him. Pete buried his face in the old man's robes.

Muffled sobs racked the teenager's body. "Nooo. Josh."

Dandelion stood behind Pete. Dirt ran in streaks down her face. She grabbed Pete and hugged him into the oracle, her face at Pete's ear. Her hot tears ran down his neck. "I'm sorry. I'm so sorry."

The oracle put both his arms around the teenagers and squeezed as the last of the stones crumbled into the grass.

<h1>CHAPTER SEVENTEEN</h1>

A Million Voices

In the dusk, Kharaq stood over Josh, fangs frozen mid-snarl. Josh's hands still gripped the gaunt claws. Mist curled around Josh's knees.

Josh knelt on a dark road that stretched as far as he could see in either direction. Vapor threaded upwards at the edges forming a ghostly chasm.

Frozen people dotted the roadway. Fear wrenched their faces. Josh lurched to his feet, away from the wizard. Kharaq didn't move.

They were in the Seams! Josh choked. Kharaq's stone spell them imprisoned between the worlds. Josh's bones turned to butter.

His gaze moved to the wall of vapor. Through it, he watched the world he'd just left. Pete ran toward the stone piles. Pete's face twisted as he tried to stop. Stones flew in every direction.

Josh staggered backward. "Oh no." His stone pile had been knocked over. Now he was stuck here forever.

Josh bumped into a woman, hands frozen brushing her hair. Why wasn't he frozen? Instead, he was stranded with these ghostly statues for eternity. He fell to his knees, retching.

Movement caught his eye. In the scene behind the mist, Laevie picked up the bone bag and threw it into the fire. Nothing happened.

"Noooo!" Josh leapt at the mist-wall. It might as well have been stone. He landed on his back, ears ringing.

On the other side of the mist-wall, Pete tried to stack the fallen rocks. Dandelion was a crumpled lump on the grass.

Josh threw himself against the wall again and again. He screamed until his voice was raw.

Finally he collapsed to his hands and knees and hung his head. His tears dripped into the mist. How could everything have gone so wrong? He had given everything, only to fail. His sobs faded into the drifting nothingness.

Weathered stone buildings rose on every side. Pete, Dandelion, and the Oracle walked along the cobbles toward the city center. People poured into streets and alleys. They hugged and wept and bubbled with excited chatter about Kharaq's defeat.

Pete stumbled behind the others. His mind spun. This wasn't how he was supposed to win. He'd screwed things up badly enough to ruin every win he'd ever achieved. "Josh is dead."

The Oracle put a hand on Pete's shoulder. "Look around you. These people were all but dead. Josh didn't lose his life, he spent it. His one life bought millions of theirs."

Pete didn't care about all these people. His brother was a better person than any of them. How could he not have seen that? No matter how mean Pete had been, Josh always had his back. And Pete had killed him.

"Dandelion?" A boy about Josh's age pushed through the crowd.

Dandelion screamed and burst into tearful laughter. "Slate!" She leapt on him and smothered his face with kisses. She finally let go and dragged him to Pete and the Oracle. "This is my brother, Slate."

Slate stared at Pete with huge eyes. "Is this him?"

Dandelion nodded.

Slate fell to a knee. Lips trembling, he pressed Pete's hand to his forehead. "Thank you," His voice was thick. "Thank you, thank you, thank you."

Pete pinched his lips tight. He couldn't look at Slate. Any words would have burst out in sobs.

Crowds pressed in around the teenagers. Murmurs raced like wildfire. *The age of The Dreams has begun.*

"It's them." People reached from the crowd. "He's so brave. She's so beautiful."

Murmurs grew to thunder. Hundreds of hands lifted Dandelion and Pete until they rode above the crowd on a wave of cheers and whistles. Fathers hefted their children to get a glimpse of the heroes. People leaned from windows, throwing confetti.

Pete fought for air. It was like being caught in rapids. He wanted to laugh and shout with the people. He wanted to run away, curl up in a dark corner, and weep. He was drowning. A tattered hole gaped where his heart should have been. Nothing had ever hurt like this.

Tears rolled down Pete's face. The crowds cheered for Josh. Pete could almost hear Josh laughing, see him grabbing the grateful hands thrust up to them. This is what Josh always dreamed of. "If only Josh could see this."

"He can." Dandelion squeezed Pete's hand. "He can." The same mixture of joy and agony rolled down her cheeks.

Crowds carried them to the city center, where roads circled a giant pedestal.

"Hi Dundi," a booming voice drowned the crowd. Twin blue moons squinted in the sunlight from a face as tall as the city's highest tower.

"Grandak?" Dandelion covered her mouth and giggled.

"Ya beat sandy king." The giant face beamed at them. "I been home already. I brought you sometin."

The mountain soul stood in one of the ravines that split the city into its star-like shape. He leaned over the buildings and gingerly placed a house-sized crystalline boulder on the pedestal.

The giant hands moved across the crystal's surface. Stone flowed until three figures emerged: A girl and two boys.

"Oh, oh." Next to Grandak's ear floated a carpet with Remrald perched on it. He smacked a palm against his forehead. "What did you do? Her nose is as big as yours."

"Remy!" Dandelion shrieked. "You came! I thought you couldn't leave the cave."

"Only for a minute." The curator waved back, beaming. "I couldn't let stone-brains, here, ruin your face."

"You did it! You did it. I knew you would." A pretty, blonde girl wearing a dainty dress leapt up and down from a group of kids in the crowd.

Dandelion jolted. "Jili?" Cleaned up, she looked like a different person. Dandelion waved both hands as the crowd swept her onward.

"Dandi!" a nasally voice yelled from a nearby bridge, where a crowd of Nandus swarmed up from the river below. Jraena and her sisters were in front, jumping up and down.

"Wizard. Warrior," shouted their dad, the chief.

"Weaver," whooped Jraena.

Fireworks exploded from the tops of the towers; crimson, gold, and emerald glittering against the cloudless afternoon blue. The thunder of a million voices cascaded around Pete and Dandelion, "Wizard. Warrior. Weaver."

The mist stirred around Josh. Knees sank beside his. Thick arms wrapped around him, lifting.

"I'm proud of you," a whisper. Cool woody cologne. Unshaven bristle scratched Josh's ear. "So proud."

Josh turned within the arms. He looked up into brimming blue eyes that shone with delight.

"Dad?"

Josh grabbed his dad. Memories rushed back: Dad's hands moving a rook toward Josh's queen; Dad was the one who taught him chess. Or their orchard in the autumn. Red and gold leaves raked into giant piles. Josh was laughing so hard he could hardly breathe as Dad picked him up and threw him into the biggest pile.

Memories mixed with the ache of the years Dad hadn't been there: winning the chess tournament with no one cheering; sitting next to an empty chair on Father's Day at school; finding Mom on the living room floor with her face in her hands, silently sobbing.

"Dad!" It was all Josh could say before the flood of tears. Josh was supposed to destroy Kharaq. He'd failed. He was supposed to save Dad. He'd failed there too.

Josh buried his face in his father's chest. "I tried. I tried so hard. I couldn't do it."

Dad just held his son while Josh wept.

"Son." Dad's hands unclasped Josh and stepped him back, turning him toward the scene in the walls. "Look."

Through the mist, Josh saw Aura streak from the sky and set the bones ablaze.

"Josh, you didn't fail. You won."

Popping sounds spun Josh back to the seams. Frozen people on the misty road burst into clouds of vapor. At the same time, they reappeared back in the living world.

Beside Josh, Kharaq's form dissolved. A ghostly scream wafted away with the smoke.

Josh swallowed. "He gets out of here too?"

Dad glanced at the tiny flames flickering where Kharaq had stood. "Yes, but not into the world of the living. He goes back to Hell where he belongs. This time he *stays* there."

"What about us? Are *we* stuck here? Was your pile knocked over too?" Josh's chest was suddenly tight, eyes pleading up at his dad.

His dad's eyebrows bunched. "No. I'm going back to the living world."

"What?" Josh grabbed at his dad.

Dad pulled Josh close. "This place is outside of time. *Someone* knew you needed encouragement. So I was given a few minutes."

Josh clutched his dad as tightly as he could. "I'm going to be here alone? You can't leave me."

Dad gripped Josh's shoulders. "You're never alone." His eyes moved to something behind Josh.

A river of fire filled the chasm, roaring down the road toward them.

Turning to run, Josh looked at his dad, unmoving and calm. Just as the inferno reached them, it dissolved, and a warrior in dented plate stepped up to them. Scars crisscrossed his face. His skin shone like polished bronze.

Vastroh! A thrill raced through Josh. If anyone knew a way out of here, it was *him*.

"My king." Dad sank to one knee.

"Rise faithful servant." Vastroh lifted Josh's dad to his feet. "Your time in this place is done. My world needs you again — the dregs of the wicked still need to be washed from it. And it needs a ruler."

Dad straightened. "But I have no right to rule, for I have no magic, and the people fear Alaelle."

"You will prepare the throne for the rightful king." A smile crinkled Vastroh's fierce face, his eyes settling on Josh for a moment. Vastroh turned toward the scene in the mist. "There are people waiting to see you."

Pete and Dandelion floated on the hands of a cheering crowd.

"Is that Pete?" Dad clutched at Josh.

The scene shifted to Mom pushing through the crowd. Red hair flickered like wildfire.

"Alice." Dad took an involuntary step toward the scene.

"Mom? She's *here*?" Josh's eyebrows leapt.

Dad turned to Vastroh. "What about my son? I can't leave him here alone."

"How well do you know me?" Vastroh's baritone rumble filled the darkness.

"I ... I trust you," Dad whispered. His eyes pleaded everything his words didn't say. He turned to Josh and gripped his shoulders. "Listen to the crowds cheer. You didn't give up. You've become the hero I've always known you were."

The thought of being stuck here alone clawed at Josh's guts. But as he looked up at Vastroh's face, he *remembered* all the crazy things that had happened since he got to Alaetia. Even crazier, was the way they'd all worked out OK. Impossible as it seemed, if Vastroh failed him now, it would be the first time.

Josh's terror bled out. This wasn't about knowing the future, it was about knowing who walked beside him through it.

He was terrified, but at the same time, felt like laughing. It was so confusing. His fear and pain drifted like leaves on the surface of a lake of unruffled peace.

Josh hugged his dad, squeezing a lifetime's mixture of desperation and hope. "Go, Dad. Mom needs you. Tell her I'm OK. I'll see you ... later."

With a popping sound, Dad was gone.

CHAPTER EIGHTEEN

THE TWILIGHT THRONE

E yes wide, Pete grabbed Dandelion and pointed. Sand geysered up from the ravine, cascading in a river of glittering silt toward the city center. People leapt back in surprise.

The sand boiled as it flowed. Bubbles swelled to mounds that grew until dancers made of sand burst free onto the roadway.

Dandelion covered her mouth with both hands. "She came." Tears ran down her face.

Music filled the air, fast moving and syncopated with a rolling base. The sand-dancers jumped and spun, pulling men and women from the crowd. All around them, people danced, clapping their hands and waving happy arms in the air. Skin and sand spun and laughed and sang.

As the dancing flowed to the city center, the music slowed. The roar of the crowd changed pitch. Another shout resounded from the buildings and down the streets. "Lord Commander."

"Oh Pete." Dandelion reached for Pete. "Is that who I think it is?"

The sand flow split, and a stream of ruddy sediment shot down the boulevard and over the bridge to the palace. A small crowd walked on the newly formed "red carpet" to the city.

"Dad!" Pete grabbed Dandelion's hand and dove into the crowd.

Up ahead a scream rang from the crowd. A running figure lunged across the open space and leapt headlong into Dad. He caught her easily, spinning her around in a torrent of ember-red hair.

"Mom!" Pete fought for air. Excitement and terror churned in his chest. Dad was alive. Mom had made it back here somehow. They were a family again.

Almost.

Pete slowed his pace, hungry to see his dad again, petrified about what the news he'd have to tell.

Dad lifted Mom off the ground. They laughed and cried and whooped. She grabbed his face and kissed it hard. People shouted from the buildings. Wildflower petals floated from the windows.

The city roared around them. "The Commander! The Flame! The age of the Dreams."

"Dad." Pete pushed into the circle of people around his parents.

"Pete!" Dad roared, pulling his son into the middle of the hug with Mom. "Look at you. You're a man."

Pete grabbed and squeezed as hard as he could.

Mom wrapped her arms around them both.

Dandelion stood at the edge of the crowd. Tear-streaked dirt colored her face. She watched them laugh and hug.

Pete stepped toward Dandelion, yanking her into the circle. "This is Dandelion. She's our friend. The Weaver. She saved our lives so many times," Pete stumbled over the words. "She doesn't have a mom or dad."

Mom and Dad pulled Dandelion into the hug. "She does now." Mom caught both teenager's faces in her hands, looked at them for a second and kissed them all over.

Dandelion grinned. Pete squirmed.

Murmur's swept through the crowd. The mass of celebrating people and sand souls parted. A woman in robes the color of emeralds and jades glided toward them. Full lips of deep green settled in a gentle smile.

Dad and Mom straightened.

Pete stepped forward and raised a hand toward the queen. "It is my honor to present, the Queen of the deep, Empress of all Alaetian sand." He lifted a hand toward Dad and Mom. "I present the Lord Commander of the royal house Ersha and Necrus; and the Flame, last of Modus order."

Mom and the princess curtsied. Dad bowed. "The honor is ours."

Dandelion leapt toward the queen, wrapping her arms around her and squeezing.

The whoosh of giant wings spun Pete around. Shouts rang from the crowd as a massive chazrack landed beside the group, towering over Dad. One of its horns was broken off and a giant ruby set in gold capped the stump. Heavy gold chains hung around the beast's neck and golden rings adorned its nose.

"Lord commander." The great beast sank to one knee, voice rumbling like distant thunder. "The shields of the realm pledge their service."

"Braxal, chief of the chazrack." Dandelion hissed in Pete's ear.

"I know," Pete whispered back. "It's the first time Campitius doesn't want to fight."

For a moment, Dad stared in wonder, then pulled an ornate dagger from his belt and held it handle first to the great beast. "What realm would be fool enough to refuse an honor so great?"

Smile creases wrinkled the huge chazrack's eyes, although his expression didn't change. As he stood, he pulled his own dagger from a bandoleer of woven gold and exchanged with Dad. In Dad's hands, it was the size of a small sword.

Two more chazrack landed behind their leader. One held a goblin in each hand by the scruff of the neck. The other held a half-burned wolf, one enormous fist gripping the wolf's muzzle.

"Viscero!" Dad's face darkened.

With his one good eye, Viscero glared from the chazrack's arms.

"Lord Commander." The Chief of the Chazrack gestured toward the wolf. "Give us the honor of cleansing the woods."

"What do you intend to do with the vermin?" Dad's voice was low.

The Chief of the chazrack slid Dad's dagger into a loop on his chest. "The blood moon festival begins in one week. You are all invited. There will be plenty of food." He grinned, flashing giant fangs.

"They're going to eat them," Dandelion whispered toward Pete.

Viscero's eye bugged wide. The two goblins squealed and squirmed. The other two chazrack broke into large smiles.

The twinkle was back in Dad's eyes. He bowed his head to the creatures. "The land owes you a great debt."

The giant chazrack nodded. Wind gusted around the group as the three beasts leapt into the air.

"Justice appears in the strangest ways." The Queen of the deep watched the muscled creatures disappear into the sky.

Pete grinned and stepped toward her. "It's good to see you."

The queen wrapped arms around him and Dandelion, burying her face in Dandelion's hair.

Music and laughter washed from the crowds.

The queen took a deep breath and held the teenagers at arm's length. "You did it." She looked up at Mom and Dad. "The Cambium Dreams are brought to pass by your children. I am honored to know them."

Dad and Mom beamed. Mom turned to Pete. "Where's Josh?"

Dandelion eyes filled with tears. Pete choked and stumbled backwards.

"Wizard," the crowd boomed.

"Pete?" Mom covered her mouth, eyes wide.

Blood drained from Pete's face.

"Honey ..." Dad pulled Mom toward him.

Pete turned and ran into the crowd.

——◄O►——

Pete ducked through the crowd. His knees wobbled, his breaths rasped in gulps and sobs.

Loser rang in his head. How many times had he said that to Josh? Its thunder drowned the voices in the city below. All the cruel jokes. All the heartless words. A thunderstorm of knives flayed his soul. He deserved every one.

Now that Josh wasn't here, Pete suddenly saw the truth; he was bitter. Pete had lost everything important to him when Mom moved them to Cavaris — his friends, his dreams, the coolest room ever. They had to live in exile because of Josh. Dad paid more attention to Josh because he had magic and could rule.

Mom always said resentment and bitterness are choices. Pete had chosen them and continued to choose them until they filled him with poison. He was like a brimming cup;

anyone who jostled it got a good dose. Sometimes it didn't need to be bumped, it just spilled over.

Josh was always there, so Josh always got spilled on. Instead of giving it back, Josh had given his life. Josh was the good, kind one. It should have been Pete who died.

Pete ran through the city and through the forest in its center. He stumbled to a stop by the altar where his brother had fallen. Dust was all that was left of Josh. The sky collapsed on Pete. Black mountains of shame crushed him to his knees.

"I'm ... sorry," Pete gasped between sobs. He gripped handfuls of grass and buried his face in the dust. "Josh, please ... I'm sorry."

Afternoon sun reached through the treetops with fingers of glory. His tears shone like fire in the grass.

Pete looked up in a haze of tears and sunlight. Was someone there?

"Can ... you help me ... my brother?"

A golden hand reached for Pete's forehead? Pete wiped his eyes. But there was nothing. A trick of the light.

Pete lowered his head and wept.

"Pete." A hand gripped his shoulder.

Pete didn't look up. He couldn't let Dandelion see him like this.

"Pete." The hand shook him again.

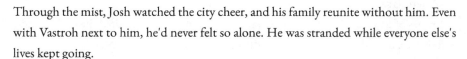

Through the mist, Josh watched the city cheer, and his family reunite without him. Even with Vastroh next to him, he'd never felt so alone. He was stranded while everyone else's lives kept going.

"Am I going to be stuck here?" Josh glanced at Vastroh, terrified of the answer. What if his being marooned here was simply the price to be paid for everyone else's freedom?

A smile crinkled at the corner of the warrior's mouth.

"I ... I think I understand." Josh rubbed his eyes. Suddenly, everything just made sense. The occot in his hand was a beast from the Seams. While everyone else had been frozen here, Josh moved freely because the occot's poison flowed in his body. Suffering buys freedom.

Josh scooped up the shard of Zothoran. Compared to Vastroh, the gem was dull and colorless. "Why is *this* here?"

The warrior pursed his lips. "The gem is still yours."

Josh glanced at the place Kharaq stood moments earlier and gulped. Kharaq hadn't had time to claim it? The power of the shard still belonged to Josh. "Without the gem and his bones, he can't come back, can he?"

Vastroh shook his head. "Well done, child. Kharaq destroyed himself. Your act of your love for your brother trapped Kharaq in his own evil. The strongest evil is no match for love.

"Today the sun rises gold. It bathes the world of Alaetia in a new age. One of peace and justice. Now, let me show you something." The warrior put a hand on Josh's shoulder.

Lava raced through his fingers into Josh's veins. For a moment, he saw reality through Vastroh's eyes. Josh was made of stars and fire. He stood colossal in the vastness of space, feet planted on galaxies. He was engulfed in a euphoria so wild and intense, he felt like his mind would explode.

Gradually, the moment passed. The misty walls of the Seams washed back in. Josh trembled so badly he wasn't sure he could even walk. He looked at his hands, half expecting them to still be on fire. "Wow! What was that? Can we do that again?"

The warrior's eyes twinkled down at him. "You can *live* like that. And someday you *will* be made of stars and fire. But now, look at the worlds." He gestured toward the misty walls.

Josh watched rivers of people cascade down the city streets. All across Alaetia, people cheered and danced. Kharaq's vermin were marched into the desert and swallowed by living sand.

"Alaetia is saved. Yet, Cavaris does not fare so well."

Images of Mom's office drifted in the misty walls. Workmen repaired the broken walls and shelves, but oily smoke still seeped through the hole Kharaq had made.

"Kharaq tore the veil between your world and the world of the dead. Many things that should not, now swim across in the moonlight. Nadris, ruler of the Necrus in that world, summons them to help her cause."

Josh gulped, "That's *my* fault? Oh no. It is. I had to play with the gem. Can … you close it?"

"That is something *you* will have to do." Vastroh's fierce blue eyes twinkled.

"Wha … uh. I don't know how."

"Nor are you powerful enough"—hints of a smile edged across the warrior's face—"on your own."

Josh's heart raced. What was Vastroh saying? Could Vastroh get him back into his own world? And his bother? "But my stone pile was knocked down. I thought bringing me back was impossible."

"It *is* impossible," the deep voice rumbled. "For you."

Josh's eyes locked on the scarred face. "But ... not for you."

Vastroh's smile grew.

"And you'll help me?" Even as he asked, Josh knew the answer.

"Always."

Vastroh gestured down the road and they began to walk. "Imagine you and I lifting a heavy stone together. For you, it is so difficult, you wonder if I am doing anything at all. But if I lift all the weight, how can you grow stronger? If I help just enough, you can accomplish things you could have never done alone, and at the same time, grow stronger into the destiny you were born to."

"You're always there, lifting?" Josh whispered. He already knew what the warrior would say.

"Always."

"It doesn't feel like it. Especially when things are really bad." Josh kicked at a rock beneath the mist.

Vastroh waved toward scenes off the road. They showed the worst of Josh's experiences, the way everything worked out even though it shouldn't have. "Look back in the shadows of your past. Then you'll see I was always there. Coincidence has a name ..."

"Vastroh!" Josh finished the sentence with a grin.

They walked together down the road. Scene after scene roiled in the mist. Josh peppered Vastroh with questions. The two laughed and talked like old friends.

Josh touched the scars on his throat and glanced at the matching scars on Vastroh's neck. "Why do you have the same scar I do?"

Vastroh put an arm around Josh. "I was holding you when you got yours."

More scenes churned in the mist. Mom and the boys stood in the tree-henge clearing where Kharaq had first chased the brothers through the back door.

This time, there was no door suspended in the clearing. Dressed in royal finery, Mom and the boys were surrounded by soldiers. He and Pete were a lot younger. Some servants carried chests, others supported cauldrons of boiling gold.

Josh glanced up at Vastroh, wide eyed. "I ... I remember. We were going to Cavaris because Kharaq had kidnapped us. You helped us escape, didn't you?"

Vastroh nodded.

Memories of the kidnapping and escape churned through Josh's mind. How could he ever forget the way Mom screamed and wept and hugged them? She started sleeping in a chair in their room at night. Finally, she couldn't take the worry and brought them to Cavaris to live with Grandpa until Kharaq was defeated.

Josh gasped and pointed at the tree-henge scene in the misty walls. As the portal opened for their journey, shadow wolves poured from the trees. Mom's soldiers disappeared in the snarling flood. Kharaq stood at the wood's edge, pointing. The largest wolf had Josh by the throat.

"That's Viscero." Josh clutched at Vastroh's arm. "I don't remember this part."

Mom screamed, hands clawed outward. The giant wolf exploded in a ball of fire. One of Alice's servants grabbed both boys and dove into her, pushing them all through the portal.

"You don't remember because you were unconscious."

The scene shifted to the other side of the portal. Josh lay in a pool of blood. Alice used the last of her magic to keep him alive. But there is no magic in Cavaris; it was too little and too late.

Josh put his hands on his neck. "Why am I alive?"

Vastroh lifted his hands to the scars on his own neck. "You can't see me there, but I took *your* death and gave you *my* life. Your mother never knew how you survived that wound."

Thank you. Josh tried to speak, but the lump in his throat wouldn't let him. He looked up into those impossibly kind eyes. Vastroh understood everything Josh couldn't say.

"Always," the warrior smiled.

Images of a boy at school making fun of Josh glowed in the mist. "You are embarrassed of the scar? There is magic that will hide it."

How many times had Josh wished the scar was gone? But now all his scars meant something. Now they were records of his journey toward destiny. Vastroh wasn't embarrassed of his scars; they made him look fierce. He wore them like badges of honor. Josh grinned. "I think I'll keep mine."

Vastroh grinned back.

"What about this one?" As Josh held up his black tattoo, he looked at Vastroh's hand and gasped. The soulless black of a hell's blood rune shone against that glowing skin. It was the same as Josh's.

"You were with me when I got *that* too," Josh could only whisper.

"I held you through every awful moment. When you understand I am there, suffering can never break you, only grow you into the hero you were meant to be."

In Josh's mind, he saw the collapsing cathedral and the giant image of Vastroh in the stained-glass windows. All those scars. The tear in his eye. "You feel *everything* we do?"

The warrior nodded.

"How do you bear it — all the horrible things people do to each other?"

A great smile dawned on the scarred face. "Because the world is also full of beauty, kindness, and love. Like you, a star blazing in darkness."

"Really?" Josh grinned, then crinkled his brow. "Doesn't everyone shine, at least a little?"

"Inside each person is a flame. Evil cannot touch it, but their own choices can build it up or snuff it out."

"Build it up?" Josh scratched his head. "You mean, if I do *great* things? Like the burn spell in the slaver's square?"

Vastroh waved at a scene beside them on the road. The three teenagers careened on the flying vine away from the slaver's square. Arrows fell like rain.

Josh pointed. "I tried the burn spell again, but it didn't work. How am I supposed to do *great* things if you don't help me?"

Vastroh chuckled. "I sent you Aura instead." As he spoke, the scenes changed again and again. "It was I who made sure the slaver found you before the wolves. In the caves, I sent you the princess. In The Throat, Vamirrion and Laevie. Remember how disappointed you were when the princess and the ship sank? If they hadn't, you wouldn't have found the bones. And when Malum escaped with the bones, I made sure the princess was waiting. When the altar needed sacred fire, I sent Aura. I was part of everything."

Josh pursed his lips. "I messed up a lot of times."

Vastroh's giant hand rested on Josh's shoulder. "And you succeeded in many more. But I'm beyond failure just as much as I am beyond success. It isn't about you doing *great things*. It's about you and I doing them together."

The scene changed again. In it, Josh stood in the center of the Necrus City slave market. Chains and manacles melted like butter. Slaves cheered and raised their hands, freed. Josh remembered the way the world turned gold. It had been effortless. The power was unlimited.

"Do you still want to know how you set an army on fire?" The eternal, blue eyes sparkled down toward Josh.

Josh nodded.

"In that slaver's square, you saw the world the way I see it. The cruelty broke your heart. That's when my magic could flow through the cracks into the world around you."

Josh swallowed. "My magic's not enough to *really* help people."

Vastroh smiled. "No."

"How do we fix what I started in Cavaris? There's no magic there."

"No magic?" The deep voice boomed. "Magic is not *a thing* any more than destiny is. I *am* magic. I just need to be invited."

"I'll invite you." Josh looked up at him.

Vastroh's eyes beamed with pride.

The scenes in the mist shifted back to the Ersha city square. Sand dancers whirled and sang. Grandak formed bridges and promenades with molten stone. Crowds lay wildflowers at the heroes' feet. Wizards conjured feasts for the crowd.

Vastroh turned Josh toward him. "You are a key. You were born in Alaetia, but you were conceived in Cavaris on a diplomatic journey. In time, you will learn to travel between the worlds at will. For now, you must choose. Two worlds beckon you. This one calls your heart. The other, your duty. To which will you return?"

Josh didn't hesitate. "Wherever you're going to be."

CHAPTER NINETEEN

DAYMARE

"Pete." Josh shook his brother.

"Dandelion I ..." Pete looked up. His bloodshot eyes grew until they looked like they'd pop. "JOSH!"

"Who's Dandelion, hotshot?" Zach laughed from the other end of the couch. He switched to a high voice and placed a hand over his heart. "Oh Dandelion, I love you."

Josh couldn't help but smile.

Pete gawked at the room, the unbroken windows, unburned walls, and gleaming kitchen table.

Zach gasped, mimicking Pete. "Oh wow, look, a door! And a window. Amazing." He crumpled in laughter.

"I ... I had a terrible dream." Pete's eyes settled on Josh.

"Daymare?" Josh smirked a little.

Zach sobered. "Yeah, me too."

"Daymare. It's not real," Pete mumbled. Distant.

Zach turned toward Josh, his face turning ugly. "Hey chicken-boy, beat it. Get more sodas and chips first."

Josh didn't move.

Zach lunged toward Josh. "Move it!"

Josh didn't flinch. For the first time, he *really* saw Zach. A lonely boy who acted tough so no one would see how scared he was — scared he was nothing but a loser. Josh sighed. He knew how Zach felt.

Pete seized Josh from behind and spun him around.

Zach laughed. "Yeah, the closet again."

Pete hugged Josh and wouldn't let go. He hugged so long, Josh blushed. Pete buried his face in Josh's ear. Pete's whisper was barely loud enough to hear. His voice cracked. "I love you, bro."

Pete stepped back and turned toward Zach. "He's my brother. If you don't want him here, *you* leave."

Zach shrugged. "Fine. Whatever."

Josh grinned, turning toward Zach. "I'll play *you*."

Zach handed him the remote. As Josh reached for it, Zach grasped his wrist. "Ooh, sick! Is that real? Your mom let you get a tattoo?"

Josh snatched his hand back.

Pete was on his feet, face white. He grabbed Josh's wrist and stared at the hell's blood rune branded in black, dripping letters. His wide eyes slowly rose to Josh's face.

Josh turned his back to Zach, facing Pete. Josh put a finger to his lips. The tiniest smile played across his face.

Memories raced across Pete's face — wolves, slave cages, treasure caves, falling into hell, a million voices shouting their names.

Pete swallowed loudly and faked a shrug toward Zach. "Yeah. Cool tattoo, huh? Mom doesn't know about it."

Josh turned to Zach. "Why don't you run over to your house and grab us some sodas and snacks."

Pete's eyebrows shot up.

"My house?" Zach scrunched his face in irritation.

"Bruh, you live, like, across the street." Josh jabbed a thumb toward the front door. "Mom's cleaning out our fridge. It's empty."

"Fine." Zach huffed and stumped out of the house.

Pete waited until the door had closed. His voice was breathless. "It was *real*? You're OK. How are you OK? I knocked over your stone pile."

Josh couldn't help the enormous grin. "I'm better than OK." Tendrils of lightning crackled across his fingertips.

"Thanks for getting your friend out-a-here so Ryan and I can get out-a-here," a gravelly voice behind Pete spun him around. Two workmen in coveralls stepped from the hall.

"You're done? With everything? Her entire office?" Josh stared at the men. There wasn't a speck of dust on them.

The one with the ladder shrugged and grinned. "Just like new."

"Uh, nice job guys." Josh watched them leave. The faint scent of paint and sawdust wafted after them.

Pete picked up a pillow and sniffed. Brows bunched, he looked around the room. "I knew something was wrong. I just couldn't place it. The house looks ..."

"Like a construction model?" Josh nodded. "That's because it is. When Kharaq chased us out the back, ET was just coming in the front door. ET called Mom and told her what happened."

Pete winced. "Meltdown?"

Josh nodded. "Then, she called her cleanup team to fix up the place; it's not safe anymore, so Mom's selling it."

"Selling it? We're going back?" Pete brightened.

Josh laughed. "I'm getting there. So, Zach and Grandpa's stone piles got taken to a magic-shielded warehouse."

"Obsidian?"

Josh nodded. "They were getting crated up when they turned back into themselves. Grandpa took it all in stride, but Zach blew a fuse and they had to sedate him. Mom put a blinder on him and brought him back here to wake up.

"They were just writing him a note with some ridiculous story, when I showed up with Vastroh."

"Vastroh? Came here?" Pete swallowed hard. "I was never really sure if he was real."

Josh chuckled. "Well, the cleanup crew will never wonder again. There was so much fire, I thought the house was going to burn down. Anyway, Grandpa's got someone on the way to pick us up. It's only a matter of time before the Necrus magic hunters sniff their way here."

"How did *I* get here?" Pete rubbed his eyes.

"Remember how the oracle taught me ice by doing it with me? Well, Vastroh showed me a few things. Talk about powerful! I have a lot of practicing to do."

"Are Mom and Dad here?" Pete swallowed.

Josh shook his head. "They have work to do there. Before Vastroh brought me here, he took me to the city of Ersha right as you ran away. I got to see Dad and Mom and the princess, even Grandak and Remrald. His coming up was a real honor. The princess, I mean queen, said that curators don't *ever* leave their treasures. Anyway, he and Gabba flew us over the crowd. I got to shake about a million hands."

Pete looked at the floor. "Yeah, me too. It was awesome — except I thought you were dead."

"I was, sort of." Josh gave Pete a wry smile. "The shard kept me alive. That's why Kharaq didn't completely die when the oracle and the trees killed him."

"He's dead now?"

Josh nodded. "Oh, yeah. I got the gem, and he got a one-way ticket to hell. Anyway, I thought I was stuck in the Seams, and then Vastroh showed up." Josh sighed deeply. "You know, he let me choose whether to come here or go back to see you guys in Alaetia. Instead of either, I chose him. And he gave me both."

Shuffling his feet, Pete stared at the floor. "You shouldn't have had to choose. You shouldn't have died either. In fact, you shouldn't have had put up with half the stuff you did, especially from me. I'm sorry."

Josh's eyes glistened. "No, I'm sorry. I was the one who got us into this."

"It seems like a lifetime ago." Pete shook his head.

"Yeah, it does." Josh nodded. "So does that time we tried cutting my hair with Dad's sword."

Pete's face lit up. "You remember that? You looked like a tumbleweed."

Laughing, Josh swiped his hair out of his eyes. "I remember everything. Mom and I talked for a long time. I made her promise to tell us the story of when she ruled the underworld and how she escaped. I told her she owes me."

"When are we going back to see her?"

"Well." Josh scratched at his temple. "We're not ... yet. We're going to South America first. To an archaeological dig with Grandpa."

"A what?" Pete's mouth dropped opened.

Josh nodded. "There's a secret war here, just like in Alaetia. I need Grandpa's help to clean up a mess I made. They need a wizard and a warrior."

Pete rubbed hands on his pants. "And a weaver?"

Josh's smile faded. "I hope so."

Pete looked down. His fingernails were caked with dirt. Both pant-knees were dark with soil and grass stains. His voice was a whisper. "Everything's all alright, isn't it?"

"It's better than alright. We won!"

Pete burst out laughing, then shouted, punching his fist in the air. "The wizard!"

"The warrior!" Josh shouted back.

"Geeze guys." Zach pushed the front door open and walked an armload of food over to the table.

"Do we have time for a game?" Pete picked up the remote.

"I guess." Josh shrugged.

All three plopped on the couch.

"Who's playing?" Zach reset the game.

"You play." Pete handed the controller to Josh. He sank into the cushions with a deep sigh.

"One more thing." Josh reached to the floor between him and Pete.

A small backpack hunched against the couch. Josh pulled the tooled leather straps open. Inside was a mound of magical jewelry, gemmed cloaks, and glittering weapons. The pile could have covered the kitchen table — way too much to fit in a pack that size. Silver armor gleamed from the top of the pile. As Pete looked in, the armor flowed, reaching for him.

The end.

EPILOGUE

E T slowed as he approached the boys' house. Chills ran down his back. A line of black SUVs idled by the curb. While he watched, a silent, black semi-truck and trailer ghosted to a stop beside them, filling the street. None of the vehicles had license plates or markings.

With a hiss, the trailer door lowered. Vapor bled into the street. Shadows detached from the SUV's. Men in black fatigues and bullet-proof vests darted to the house.

They gathered on the porch for a moment, pulling down ski masks and readying assault rifles. Then they burst inside.

Oh no! ET clutched at the steering wheel. He was too late.

While ET watched, a man slowly exited the last SUV and strode toward the house. Shadows clung to a close shaved beard and pockmarked face. Twisting symbols embossed a calf length leather coat.

ET cursed under his breath and slid down in his seat. Serpol, head of the Necrus secret police. Nadris had found them.

ACKNOWLEDGMENTS

Where do I even begin to say thank you to everyone who has been a part of this?

Stephen Baker, who needed a story about two boys. Ed Mcshane, who threw the first match on the pile of tinder that was my dried-out passion for writing. Dan Brueckner, who said the trees should be knot heads. W.M. Paul Young, who said, "Coincidence has a name ..." My beta team—your names are already in the book. Mom, when you said the pace made you nervous, I knew I had it right. Dad, it's finally done; bragging can officially start. Taras, when you started running through the house shouting, "inferneus," I knew other kids would love the story too. Erin Healy, your edits brought this to life. Betsy St. Amant, your marketing advice was amazing.

This book has a circle around it. 978-0-310-33302-9

Note From The Author

I had a visual of a soapbox derby with the cars lined up from worst to best. The worst was made of cardboard with garbage can lids for wheels. The best was polished mahogany, with chrome wheels and velvet seat covers. Can you see the kids' faces? One brushes old coffee grounds off his hood. He can't face the crowd. Another polishes a gleaming fender and waves to his fans. I realized the difference between these cars isn't the kids ... it's the time they spent with Dad.

I'm fraught with blind spots, bad habits, and shortcomings. I wanted something bigger than me. So I asked God to make this book a father/son project. Characters like Grandak, Remrald, and the princess just stepped onto the page out of nowhere. I asked for ideas and got Aura, the spider, the inquisitor, Mom's backstory, and so many more. I hope you enjoyed reading about them as much as I did writing about them. Now you know where they came from.

Although I've dreamt of writing this story for decades, I had to be destroyed before I could honestly portray Josh's journey. The truths about facing fear, about God making everything OK even when there is no way it can ever be, about suicide, and depression, as well as hope, and finding your destiny, they're all written from my journey through the depths of an utterly shattered heart to a life so good it feels like a fantasy novel. Whatever you might be going through, I hope the story encourages as well as entertains you. You might even meet Magic for yourself.

Your friend,

Daniel Tweddell
danieltweddell.com

About the Author

Hi, I'm Daniel Tweddell. I grew up in the Bornean and Philippine jungle as a missionary's kid. My neighbors had monkeys for pets. Just behind the tree line, "ex"-head-hunters slipped through the shadows with spears and six-foot blow guns. It was the perfect incubator for a kid's imagination. As an adult, I did a lot of things from writing high-octane video games with my friends to having my own companies. But I always loved castles, wizards, and monsters the best. So now I write white-knuckle stories about magic woven with truths from my life's journey. I live in San Diego with my wife and 3 kids.

CPSIA information can be obtained
at www.ICGtesting.com
Printed in the USA
JSHW012251290523
42378JS00006B/23